IF YOU GIVE A SMUGGLER A SECRET & IF YOU GIVE A RAKE A REASON

Pirates & Petticoats Special Edition Books 1 & 2

CHLOE FLOWERS

Created with Vellum

DEDICATION

For Tess Elizabeth

AUTHOR'S NOTE

My son was born prematurely; he weighed 3 pounds 12 ounces. And at 18 inches long, he looked like a string bean. I spent many weeks with him in the hospital, which is where I began writing this book.

I needed a hero. And I needed to be strong for him, so I created a strong heroine.

Writing about Keelan and Landon took me away from the sterile, white, beeping reality of the hospital and put me into the sultry South, with its sweet-smelling magnolia's, warm nights and delectable, mouth-watering food.

I enjoyed the escape. I hope you do too.

Chloe

IF YOU GIVE A SMUGGLER A SECRET

HE'LL DEMAND A KISS TO KEEP IT...

PIRATES & PETTICOATS SERIES BOOK ONE

CHAPTER ONE
A CLASH OF SWORDS

I left a gift for you at the end of the book. You'll love the recipes!

Chloe

Charleston, South Carolina
May 1811

Two figures circled, each with a sword in one hand and a dagger in the other. The first stood tall and lithe, his blade flashing, just visible in the early morning light. His opponent, smaller in both build and height, quickly blocked the slice.

Merchant ship captain, Landon Hart and his best friend and business associate, Captain Conal O'Brien, crept to the edge of the clearing for a better view of the duel.

"We'll skirt the meadow and keep behind the cover of the trees," Landon murmured. As an orphaned youth, he'd been in his fair share of unbalanced skirmishes. In more familiar surroundings, rather than among the vast plantation estates outside the city of Charleston, he would have already intervened. He and Conal had just turned down the lane to Twin Pines when they heard the collision of swords nearby.

A dense layer of dead pine needles on the forest floor muffled their steps. Soon, they were close enough to discern the whisper and hiss of the blades, followed by the strident metallic clash and *ching* as sword met sword.

Although the larger dueler had tinges of gray at his temples, he moved with a seasoned grace and nimble ease. Fluid arcs chased fleeting thrusts in seamless sequence. His sleeves were rolled to the elbows, shirt neatly tucked.

The boy's breeches were thin at the knees and stuffed into a pair of boots several sizes too large. A faded blue length of cloth wrapped around his head, tied at the base of his neck where the tail hung halfway down his back. Even in the over-sized boots that threatened to trip him up with every thrust, the surprisingly agile and light-footed waif held his own.

The two duelers seemed to be alone. No mounts or wagons lingered nearby, so this didn't appear to be an ambush or an attempt at a robbery. No seconds to serve as witnesses, nor a physician standing ready, so perhaps not a planned duel. But then, what was it?

Conal leaned closer, his voice soft. "Doesn't seem a fair fight. I'm going to put a stop to it." His eyebrows shot up as the boy's dagger flashed in an arc and caught the upper shaft of his opponent's sword. The youth beat the tip away and began his own attack with his long blade.

"Wait." Landon placed a hand on Conal's arm. His friend had a knack for acting first and thinking second when it came to physical confrontations. "I don't think it's an earnest fight," Landon murmured, as he studied the movements of the duelers. "It seems to me that it's a training session of some sort. Let's see how the young one fares. I find it peculiar a grubby whelp wields such a fine weapon yet wears those poorly fitted boots."

Conal watched another moment and nodded. He leaned a shoulder against a tree trunk.

"Step away, Keelan," the older man said in a clipped British accent. He swung his weapon in a swift upward flash toward the youngster's chest. "You are offering too short a path to your middle. It leaves you vulnerable to my long blade."

Keelan. An Irish name. Many families from Great Britain, his included, took the crossing to America, hoping to start a better life. Interesting that an Englishman took the time to tutor an Irish lad.

In answer, Keelan slashed his blade diagonally down across his opponent's exposed stomach, deftly cutting a ten-inch swath in the older man's linen shirt.

"You mean like that, Daniel?" he retorted with a smirk. He also had a British accent on his tongue. A Brit with an Irish name, curious.

"He's but a lad, hardly weaned," Conal whispered. "His voice still has the high pitch of a child."

The two combatants paused. Daniel scowled at the tear in his shirt before lunging forward, swinging his weapon in a rapid combination while the boy tried valiantly to block the attack. The blows thundered harder, the blade hissing like an angry snake. However, it wasn't the man's skill that brought the boy down.

It was the boots.

The coarse grass snagged his heel and foiled his hasty retreat. With a loud "Oof!" Keelan went down hard on his backside, the jolt knocking the sword from his grasp.

"You are finished," Daniel said. He pointed the tip of his weapon to the boy's chest.

"Hold!" Landon shouted, stepping from the shelter of the trees. If he was wrong about the training, another moment's delay could mean the child's life. He wouldn't stand idly by and allow the outmatched lad to be harmed.

Daniel's head jerked up. When the shout distracted the man, Keelan reacted. He kicked his legs up and somersaulted backward, losing both boots in the process. The maneuver put him in a crouched position, ready to fight again. Then the lad did the strangest thing.

He threw his dagger directly at them.

Landon and Conal yelped and dove to the ground as the weapon whizzed over their heads and landed in the dirt somewhere behind them.

The lad smacked the earth in frustration.

Daniel shook his head. "Your throw was not balanced." With his hand on his hip, he jabbed the air with his sword. "Your chest must point to your target before you release."

"What matters is I threw first, which yields me five points!" The boy flexed his hand and licked the inside of his thumb. "It beats the three you get for disarming me, aye, Daniel? I win today."

Daniel glanced at his wounded shirt, then over at the trees where Keelan had thrown the dagger, before he shrugged in agreement.

"An interesting game," Landon said, brushing his breeches as he got back to his feet.

Daniel turned toward them, pointing his sword at Landon's chest before stepping in front of the boy. "What is your business at Twin Pines?"

Conal stepped forward, drawing the movement of Daniel's weapon with him. "My uncle, Fynn Ahern, scheduled a meeting with Commodore Grey for this morning. I have a letter from the commodore confirming it."

Daniel lowered his sword. "The commodore does indeed have an appointment with a Mr. Ahern today. Where is he?"

Conal shifted. "He's dead. I'm Captain Conal O'Brien of the *Seeker*. This is my business partner, Landon Hart, captain of the *Desire*. We were Mr. Ahern's associates." Conal reached out to grasp Daniel's hand.

"I'm sorry to hear of his passing," Daniel said

"Thank you. It was unexpected," Conal replied.

Daniel returned his attention to Keelan. "Your skills have developed well. I'm proud of your progress." He deftly threw his dirk. The knife hit the same tree where, moments before, Conal had stood. It struck with a solid thunk, and the bottom half of a feather, wedged into the bark, fluttered lazily to the ground. "Your impatience and lack of concentration denied you the ten points you would have earned had you actually hit the target. Instead, you're left with a meager five points and a nasty little cut." He reached down and helped the lad to his feet. "Is it deep?"

Keelan studied it. "No. Slaney will rub marigold tincture on it and it'll be fine." He warily eyed the two strangers as he retrieved his stray boots.

Daniel put a hand to his chest and gave a slight bow. "I'm Daniel Hunter, valet to Commodore George Grey, the newest owner of Twin Pines Plantation." He sheathed his sword and wiped his brow with his sleeve. Although only a couple of hours after sunrise, the air was thick and still, his shirt clingy with sweat.

Landon assessed the boy. His shoulders, though slight, were straight and haughty. Not much muscle to his arms. His wrists were thin, almost feminine, making Landon even more impressed with Keelan's dexterity. Recalling the trials of his own youth, before Conal's Uncle Fynn had taken him under his wing, he knew well the importance of besting this particular skill.

"You do well for one so young," Landon observed.

The boy shot an uneasy glance toward Daniel, grabbed a boot and shoved his foot inside.

"Well, yes, er..." Daniel sent a sideways glance at the ragged figure busy snatching the second rebellious boot from the grass. The valet shrugged. "The lessons are for the child's protection. Several family members recently died under rather suspicious circumstances, so Keelan's father has decided the training should become more intense."

"Your hand with a sword is impressive, Keelan." Landon gestured toward Daniel. "It's clear you are being given excellent instruction."

Daniel smiled and inclined his head, accepting the compliment. The boy remained mute.

Landon tried again. "My crew and I must be keen with sword, pistol and dirk, if we're to survive encounters with privateers and pirates. We all do our part to defend the ship. May I voice an observation?" he asked.

"Please do," said Daniel. He relaxed only slightly, keeping his sword in his grasp.

Landon gestured to Keelan's dagger. "Work on the short blade further. 'Tis a more valuable skill to have." The tension in the lad's shoulders tightened. There was something strange about the boy that seemed a bit...off.

The youth slammed his booted foot on the ground and straightened, his face flushed. "I don't normally miss so badly," he muttered. "I suppose a sailor can do better?"

Daniel's eyes narrowed in apparent warning, and the boy dropped his gaze and busied himself by brushing the meadow grass from his sleeves before straightening the rag covering his head.

"I didn't mean to offend." Amused by his pluck, Landon added, "But in answer to your question, aye, any of my crew can do better, else they'd be dead. Now, if you'll adjust your grip like so..." Pulling out his own dagger, he placed it in Keelan's hand, careful to avoid the wound. He moved behind and reached around to set right his hold. "Mr. Hunter is correct about facing your chest to the target. But you must also cock the hand back, but keep the wrist firm, like this." He gripped the lad's wrist and made the adjustment. "Try it."

Keelan stood still, taut as a fiddle string, his other fist clenched at his side. Daniel took a step then stopped, as if someone else's legs were attached to his body and he wasn't sure how to move them.

"Widen your stance a bit and bring this foot forward." Landon placed his leg against the boy's thigh and kicked his boot away and forward, then squeezed his shoulders and gave them a rough shake. "Relax."

Oddly, Keelan remained motionless. Angry for the tutelage, or embarrassed? Keelan seemed to struggle to remain composed. Landon frowned, irritated the runt acted so ungratefully. At that age, he would have lapped up this lesson like a thirsty pup. He'd been on his own since very young, and he grew up fast. He learned many harsh lessons. Not the least had been how to defend himself against a bigger opponent.

Landon stepped back. He half expected the child to fling the knife into the pines as hard as he could and stomp away. Pride seemed to outweigh Keelan's anger, and he finally relaxed his shoulders. He balanced the blade in his hand, drew back, set his wrist, and threw. It hit, pinning the top half of the feather. The boy pursed his lips; whether it was in grim satisfaction or acute aggravation that the instruction had corrected his flaw, it was hard to tell.

"There, you see?" He clapped Keelan on the back. "You're a fast learner. We'd gladly welcome you as a ship's hand aboard the *Desire*."

"Thank you, captain," Keelan said. The corners of his mouth lifted a little.

Daniel cleared his throat. "You'd best get along now and tell Slaney to inform the commodore and Mr. Grey visitors have arrived and will be at the house shortly." He grasped the lad's elbow and steered him in the direction of the house.

Keelan gave a curt nod and scuffed away. Daniel bent to retrieve the boy's fallen sword, walked to the tree and wrenched the captain's weapon from the trunk.

Landon's bemused gaze followed the child's awkward gait to the end of the meadow, where the youth halted and turned to face them. Slowly and deliberately, he reached up to his head and threw them a jaunty salute. Before they could raise a hand to respond, the boy pulled the long blue scarf from his head.

Landon froze.

Conal's jaw unhinged.

Long auburn hair cascaded over the waif's shoulders and down to her elbows. Not a boy, but a young woman.

She flashed a triumphant smile, obviously satisfied she had sufficiently astonished them. There was a toss of her head and a flash of blue, then she disappeared. Her laughter hung on the breeze for a moment, then it too drifted away, leaving behind a stunned silence.

Landon replayed the last few moments in his mind. His arm across her chest adjusting the blade... his knee nudging the inside of her thigh to widen her stance... It's a wonder she didn't clobber him over the head with her sword.

Keelan's face hadn't been flushed with anger and restraint, but instead, in acute embarrassment. Landon caught sight of the valet's scarcely extinguished frown.

"My apologies," he said, fighting to smother a grin.

Daniel nodded. He fidgeted with his belt a moment before he spoke. "It's best forgotten, if you will." He handed the dirk to the captain. "Come, let's retrieve your horses and get them to the stables. Commodore Grey and his brother are most curious as to the nature of this meeting you have requested."

CHAPTER TWO
A TERRIBLE MISTAKE

She'd made a terrible mistake.

A stupid mistake.

Keelan trotted through the pines. She yanked Daniel's dirk from the trunk and her own poorly thrown dagger, which she jammed into the sheath.

"Too bad your short blade is weak. My men can do better," she mimicked. "We fight privateers and pirates. Gah!" She placed Daniel's dagger into the back of her waistband. "I've been training with Daniel for over ten years. I can throw a bloody dirk as effectively as any gritty sailor," she muttered, then sighed. "And now I'm talking to trees."

The heady aroma of pine surrounded her. She tore some needles from a drooping branch and rubbed them between her fingers to further release the refreshing scent, hoping to calm her nerves a bit.

She couldn't resist the impulse to prove her worth to the men in the meadow. Why did she need to shock Captain Hart as he had shocked her? Her panic had expanded while he adjusted her grip on the dagger. However, what happened next almost sent her to flight like a quail from the brush.

Captain Landon Hart touched her in a place no man had ever dared. When he nudged his knee against the inside of her thigh, the outline of his leg left a lingering heat, even after he stepped away. Even more annoying, the desire to breathe momentarily abandoned her. She almost failed to repress the overwhelming urge to kick him.

Her brain only focused on the fact that he was touching her.

Not the dirk.

Not her grip.

Not the target.

She studied her wrist. The warm impression where his fingers touched still tingled. Keelan frowned. In the past, enough suitors pushed their presence upon her: an arm casually brushed against her breast while fastening her cloak, a thigh pressed against hers while seated on a settee. While such errors certainly earned them her instant retreat from the room, a short route to the door, or occasionally a stinging slap, no man had ever jumbled her thoughts the way Hart had done so nonchalantly.

Then the captain had reached around her chest to adjust her hold on the dagger; his arm almost skimmed her breasts. She fought to restrain her outrage, because of *course* it was outrage. Doxies played loose with favors, not a commodore's daughter. She'd almost slapped his hands from hers and bolted away.

It had been terrifying.

Perhaps the word "terrifying" was a little dramatic. Still, it wasn't proper behavior between an unmarried lady and a gentleman, and Keelan was conditioned to react accordingly. Since he had been unaware of her true identity, it was hard to cast the blame solely upon his shoulders.

A greater problem existed now. Hart discovered she was a female. If he told her uncle— the consequences were dire enough to make her shiver in the dense humidity of the southern spring dawn.

Normally, she wouldn't care if he uncovered her fairer gender. However, circumstances being what they were at the moment, it was best to keep activities such as this secret.

Now, that point appeared to be mute.

The entire episode showed her with no rational sense. She'd acted as if no discourse existed at all, just another day of forbidden training in a hidden field.

Pent up frustration and anger at her own stupidity made her want to scream. Instead, she kicked a pinecone, sending it flying into the dusky underbrush. Embarrassment and humiliation had distracted her from exercising good judgment. And she *always* exercised good judgement.

Now all involved were in jeopardy because of her, Daniel, especially.

Acidic penalties churned in her stomach. She'd never forgive herself if Daniel was punished or released from service because of her reckless behavior.

Stupid, stupid, stupid!

After witnessing a drilling session between Keelan and Daniel, her Aunt Sarah nearly fainted from shock. Uncle Jared talked with her father and demanded that the exercises cease. For added insurance toward her compliance, he confiscated her boots.

Out of respect for his sister-in-law, her father acquiesced publicly, but privately encouraged Daniel to continue schooling her.

With good reason.

An assassin killed her mother, her other aunt and cousin all within a few weeks of each other, forcing her and Papa to escape to the Carolinas, fearing for their lives. Uncle Jared should be more understanding, but he coddled his wife, rather than put safe guards into place to protect her.

Keelan groaned. If the captain mentioned what he'd seen, then her uncle would flog Daniel for disobedience, and her father would use the occasion to bring up marriage. He believed he could secure her future by wedding her to ancient Mr. Pratt. For some reason, hebelieved that if she married and took another name, the killer wouldn't be able to find her, which was a ridiculous assumption.

The more pressing objective at the moment was silencing Hart. It was crucial she meet with him alone and persuade him to remain quiet about the scene he'd witnessed. Would he agree to keep her secret?

What kind of man was he?

Respectable? He was a ship's captain; that had to count toward an honorable reputation, did it not? A man with influence and responsibilities? A leader of men? Surely a crew wouldn't stay with a commander they didn't trust.

Distinguished by their dress, both were men of significant means. With his sun-bronzed skin, and hair dark as pitch and hanging about his shoulders like a wild mane, it was easier to picture Captain Hart as a Persian or better yet, a pirate.

Maybe a Persian pirate.

He displayed the cocky arrogance of a man accustomed to taking what he pleased. His strong self-assurance was unnerving. Even the air about him vibrated with intense power and confident composure.

His russet-haired business partner O'Brien, with his neatly trimmed mustache and beard, seemed amiable. Quite the contrast to the smug, bold and terribly conceited Captain Hart.

The path broke through the trees near the stables, and she crept inside to return the boots she'd borrowed earlier from one of the slumbering grooms.

Keelan headed toward Slaney, her maid, who stood amid a flock of at least two hundred chickens and geese. The petite woman with boisterous pepper-and-salt curls and twinkling gray eyes had been with her family for as long as she could remember. Back home in Chatham, England, Mother was content to let the maid care for her and raise her.

Mother acted as if she resented Keelan's intrusion into her life and spent most days in her shop. Time with Slaney had been much more enjoyable than with her melancholy mother, who never spoke unless to criticize.

That life was gone now.

The scandal surrounding Papa's court-martial, followed by the strange deaths of her mother and aunt, disrupted the orientation of her plans like a stream of water redirected by a jagged rut carved into the earth.

Slaney, quite the opposite from Mother, teased and laughed and told exhilarating stories about pirates and giants and magic faeries. Slaney, dried Keelan's tears, wrapped her scrapes, and taught her how to draw and mix healing herbs.

Daniel taught her the significance of strength and speed in defending herself. She chewed at her lip.

And now, she had just endangered his well-being and employment.

"This squawking and honking is enough ter wake the dead," Slaney grumbled. She scattered another handful of grain over the dirt yard and shrieked when a bold rooster pecked at a stray kernel from the top of her shoe.

"These are the only shoes I have, ye wicked cock! Be off with ye!"

With an insulted squawk, he flapped away to dodge Slaney's swinging foot. The sea of poultry parted briefly with his departure, but soon clucked its way back into a mass of scratching and pecking fowl.

"Good morning, Slaney."

"A fair morning to ye, Mistress," the maid replied with a frown. Slaney clucked her tongue with disapproval, sounding much like the chickens still milling at her feet. "Yer a sight! The entire house will soon be awake. Should Himself see ye, there will be hell to pay, for sure. Best ye go inside and clean up, lass."

"Is Uncle Jared about yet, then?" Keelan asked, ignoring the maid's mild tirade. "There are two merchant ship captains here to meet with him and Papa."

"I'll tell him. 'Tis already almost seven o'clock, and ye know break-fast is served at half-past eight."

"I'll be on time, Slaney, don't worry." A movement caught her eye, and she glanced up. Daniel and their visitors led two horses down the lane toward the stable. There was still time to have a word with Hart.

Slaney lowered her brows in an unconvincing scowl. "Well, don't get distracted this morn. Your father will want to speak to ye, and I'll not have him see ye lookin' like a common street rat."

"How is Papa?" Hopefully his color and appetite had returned with a sound night's rest.

Slaney's expression softened. "Weary. He's up and sittin' in the chair by his window. Perhaps if you sit with him, he'll eat something."

She nodded. "I will." Slaney appeared happy here in America. It was a magnificent country, to be sure, but life on a plantation differed vastly from living in England.

"I miss home," Keelan murmured.

"Ye are the daughter of a Commodore and a shopkeeper. Ye have known only the bustling world of Chatham, buying wares at the docks from ships loaded with items from exotic places." Slaney rested a hand on her arm. "It'll take time to get used to the slower pace of country life."

"I suppose you're right." Keelan stared at the pecking birds. "He'll wish to talk about how an alliance with Mr. Pratt would merge the two plantations into the largest in the Lowcountry."

Slaney could only give her a sympathetic look.

"I don't want to get married."

Not yet.

And wedlock to Pratt? Not *ever*.

Marriage.

The word tasted bitter, like rancid oil, and unripened nuts.

"'Tis Pratt ye be rejecting, not marriage," Slaney said, voicing her concerns exactly.

"After seeing how those bonds affected my parents, why would I be in a hurry to wed?" As a commodore in His Majesty's Navy, her father was away for months at a time, leaving her mother alone and unhappy. During the short time he spent in port, Mother commanded most of it, becoming jealous of the small intervals he gifted to Keelan.

Slaney sighed. "Not all marriages play out like yer parents', lass."

Still... plenty were. Keelan withdrew a handful of corn from Slaney's bucket, then tossed it across the ground. "Why are you feeding the chickens? Isn't little Joseph supposed to do this?"

Slaney blew a wayward wisp of silver hair from her face. "You needn't concern yerself about such matters. But if you must know, he's tending the smokehouse because they just put up a hog."

Keelan couldn't help but smile. Although she tried to hide it, Slaney had a soft spot for chickens.

The maid flung the remaining grain with the breeze and waded through the mass of birds. "I'll warm the water for yer bath. Don't tarry long, child."

Shaking away the dark musings of marriage and her ill father, Keelan turned and ran to the rear of the house, enjoying the bracing coolness of the dew-laced grass on her bare feet. She'd never had such liberties in Chatham. One thing about residing in the Americas, the broad stroke of "Freedom" stretched well past British social conventions.

Most mornings, she sneaked in the back servants' door, to avoid any encounters with members of her extended family. While she was grateful Uncle Jared agreed to run the plantation until her father's stable health returned, she must now interact more with her spoiled cousin, Doreen. Thankfully, the girl slept most mornings until midday.

She paused. Would it be better to wait by the barn and hope to catch Captain Hart before he went into the house, or should she change first?

What if they saw her dressed in boys' breeches? She should change.

Keelan grabbed the latch and sucked in her breath at the sting that shot across her injured thumb. Fresh blood streamed along her palm and dripped off the heel of her hand. It wouldn't do to track it inside. She needed the marigold tincture Slaney used for cuts and bruises, so she darted for the kitchen house to find the maid's herb box. It shouldn't take long to dress the cut and dash back to her room.

CHAPTER THREE
A SCONE THIEF

D *rat.*

The kitchen was empty.

A teakettle hung from a metal arm beside the hearth, steam still puffing from the spout. In front, and keeping warm, a platter of rice scones perched in the middle of the bench. Corn mush fried and crackled in an iron skillet, the aroma permeating the air. Keelan's mouth watered and her stomach rumbled, driving all other immediate issues from her mind.

An hour and a half was a long time to wait for breakfast.

Sneaking a furtive glance around, she liberated a hot, flakey scone. Too hungry to bother with butter or jam, she took a bite and closed her eyes as it almost melted on her tongue.

"Well, it's 'bout time ya come visit me, Miss Keelan," Ruth said, as she emerged from the pantry.

Keelan jumped, and the scone flew from her grasp. It bobbled in between her hands until she regained possession. "Ruth, you gave me a start!" She grinned at the short, plump cook and gestured guiltily at the pastry, crumbling against her chest. "I hope you don't mind. I'm famished."

The slave gave her an odd look, but recovered rapidly. "Goodness gracious, dis here's your home. You can git somethin' to eat anytime."

Her *home*. Even after several months, she still felt like an intruder. This culture was just so *different*.

The kitchen door opened and Slaney whisked inside. Kicking it shut behind her, she settled a garden basket on the table. "Wouldn't hurt ter put some meat on her bones. The lass will flutter away like a milkweed thistle in the breeze one day and we'll never see her again." The basketful of herbs wafted through the room in direct combat with the frying mush.

"All she need is a few more months of my cookin' and she'll fill right out," Ruth said with a chuckle.

Slaney gave Keelan a stern glare. "What she needs to do is get herself up to the main house and dress for breakfast," she chided, pulling a handful of herbs from her basket.

"Oh, Miss Keelan," Ruth stared at her wound. "How did you cut yo' hand?"

Keelan and Slaney exchanged glances. The household slaves likely gossiped as much as any other servants. It wasn't as if she could obscure the fact she was wearing boy's attire.

"I mishandled a dagger. Daniel is instructing me how to defend myself in case those who murdered most of my father's family in England follow us here."

The slave paused, then shook her head. "I was sorry to hear 'bout dat, Miss Keelan. But dey didn't kill 'em all did dey?"

Was it only a matter of time before they achieved that goal? "No, so far my father's elder brother has eluded them, although they been made several attempts."

Slaney inspected Keelan's hand. The woman tsked as she examined the cut, then pulled out a wooden box from the cupboard. She selected two small bottles and a clove of garlic.

"Let me see, lass." She held out a hand expectantly. Keelan eyed the bottle before she did as she was told. Slaney was a skilled healer, but there always seemed to be additional pain involved when it came to treating cuts and ailments. Slaney poured a few drops on the laceration.

Her suspicions were valid. Keelan sucked in her breath at the sting. "Ouch! What is that?" She snatched her hand away and shook it. "That burns like the devil!"

Slaney grabbed her hand. "Such language from a gentle lady. Yer mum, God rest her soul, would be horrified at the way ye go on. Now sit ye still. 'Tis vinegar. That or whiskey must be applied to properly cleanse a wound." Her mouth flattened. "Ye should know that, as often as I've mended ye."

Duly chastised, Keelan sat and put another chunk of the stolen scone in her mouth while Slaney splashed more vinegar on the cut. The sting made her eyes water, but she didn't dare let out a peep.

Next, the maid reached for the garlic, pulled off a clove, sliced it in half, and rubbed it on the cut, eliciting another wince from Keelan. Why did everything have to *sting*?

"This will prevent infection," Slaney said. Lastly, she splashed the marigold tincture over the injury and bound it in a narrow, damp, linen cloth.

"Keep it covered," she said. "'Twill guard against the pus."

"Thank you." Even though Slaney put her through mild torture with every cut and bruise, the woman meant well.

Keelan pointed to the last bit of scone. "Ruth, I would love to learn how you make these." She popped the rest into her mouth and munched happily. It was something her mother might have sold in her shop, partnered with jellies, jams and sweet biscuits.

The cook's soft, brown face broke into a pleased smile. "Come in the mornin' 'fore sunrise, an' I'll show ya in no time." She shifted and pulled a plate from the shelf. "Now sit yo' self down, child. I can't stand to see ya starve to death right here in the kitchen house."

To Keelan's dismay and delight, Ruth served her fried corn mush doused in cane syrup, a cup of tea, and another scone slathered with fresh butter and dripping with sweet, amber honey.

Mentally calculating the time it would take Daniel and the two other men to reach the stable, remove their tack, settle their horses, Keelan estimated that she had a couple of precious minutes. There would be no time to change first. She shoveled a large forkful of mush into her mouth, trying to conjure the appropriate words to persuade the men to keep her clandestine activities to themselves.

Slaney glanced out the window. "Daniel and our visitors are near. I'd best get along and tell Mr. Grey his guests have arrived." She shot Keelan a sharp glare. "And you mistress, should go before you're caught in those...clothes."

She probably would have said 'rags'. The maid had been privy to Daniel's training for the past several months, and often huffed at the impropriety, prompting him to just as often remind her that many things were accepted in American society that weren't at home.

Keelan's fork clattered on her plate and she practically flew out of the door. If Uncle Jared saw her before she had a chance to speak with Hart...

❧ 4 ❧
CHAPTER FOUR
A CAPTURED EAVESDROPPER

H*urry!*
Slaney's warning echoed in her head. Keelan took a shortcut through the garden. With the exception of her cousin Doreen, the entire household was probably awake. No time to dawdle, as Ruth would say.

She ducked beneath an arbor laden with lazy, purple wisteria blossoms. Aunt Sarah's garden created a buffet for the senses. Eight neatly trimmed squares of fragrant lavender, rosemary, and thyme hedges barely accommodated the bright bursts of colorful flowers flaming up toward the blue South Carolina sky. The neat checkerboard of raised beds flowed down over several tiers and stopped near the glassy surface of a small pond.

The sound of Daniel's voice jolted her into motion as it filtered through the hedges. "Twin Pines is a 300-acre plantation. The main house sits at the end of the long lane you started down earlier. We've only been here a few months. The commodore's younger brother, Mr. Grey, has extensive knowledge of milling lumber and is an extremely effective overseer. He splits his time between his business in Charleston and the mill here."

"So, Mr. Grey owns warehouses at the docks and also works here?

That seems a heavy burden," Captain O'Brien's Irish lilt drifted through the hedge.

"Are you discussing the mill or the warehouses?" Daniel asked. "If it's the mill, Mr. Grey might wish to take you on a tour later. I should let the grooms know, so they have his gelding ready."

O'Brien fished out a handkerchief and wiped his brow. "Actually, we are more interested in speaking with his brother about my Uncle Fynn's request. Seems Fynn was eager to meet with him about something. We found several letters from Commodore Grey among his things, one confirming an appointment today."

Keelan sucked in a breath. A meeting with her father? Perhaps regarding the scandal.

Their lives changed on that stormy day when her father gave a tragic order to sink a ship he had been convinced was a French privateer trying to pass as an American merchant vessel. Her father attacked it.

Unfortunately, it had not been the privateer. All souls were lost, her father court-martialed, and their family disgraced. Thieves pilfered Mother's shop.

Thankfully, Papa's closest friend had been influential enough to keep her father from prison. The speculation that now someone was killing off the rest of the Greys in England amplified the scandal.

Papa had an older brother in Chatham and a younger one, Jared, in America. After his eldest brother's son was found dead in a stable and his wife and Keelan's mother were killed in separate but equally suspicious carriage accidents, it became obvious someone was eliminating members of the family one by one.

The murders prompted their long-time friend to smuggle Keelan and her father out of the country to protect them. He'd also financed the purchase of the plantation and bribed a ship's captain to whisk her and Papa out of Great Britain, to the southern colonies. Her breath froze.

Had the assassin finally tracked them here?

Was it one of the two captains?

Daniel would be on guard with the same suspicions, of that she was certain. Too much had already slipped by them, putting the entire family on edge. Daniel would be extra vigilant.

She crawled behind an iron bench. Daniel, Captain Hart, and Captain O'Brien walked along the outside of the hedge. Curious, she crept closer to peek through the bushes. Would Daniel ask the men to remain quiet about the scene they had witnessed in the meadow? If he did, it would prevent her from having to plead her case to Captain Hart, a task she dreaded doing on her own. Had they already talked of it? This area was very private; a secluded place to speak in confidence.

She couldn't assume the topic had already been discussed. She considered stepping out and intercepting them as they passed. That plan would only work if the men turned left rather than right toward the front door. If she drew Daniel's attention, she could indicate she wanted to speak with them. She hurried to a gap in the shrubbery to signal him.

Daniel's voice drew closer. "Behind the Grey's house sits a kitchen house, a chicken coop, smokehouse, and a few outbuildings. In addition to crops and timber, Twin Pines also produces turpentine."

She squeezed between two bushy shrubs near a cherry tree and cautiously peered through the foliage. Daniel pointed west, his back to her. Landon stood next to him. Where was the other man? Conal O'Brien?

The valet droned on. "Beyond this garden is a small spring-fed pond, which takes up most of the meadow bottom to the east. There's another much larger lake on the plantation a few miles southwest."

Captain O'Brien stepped through the arbor.

Oh no! There was no way to escape without exposing that she'd been eavesdropping. She caught her breath sharply. This wouldn't work at all. Why would they agree to do a favor to someone who'd been spying on them?

Curse her terrible luck.

Now, she'd have to wait until they left, then run to catch them before they made it to the front door.

Drat! That was impossible without being visible from her uncle's study.

She was doomed. Worse, Daniel would be punished too.

He and Captain Hart soon followed O'Brien. Keelan retreated further into the scratchy bushes behind the sweet blossoming limbs of the cherry tree. She winced as several branches poked the back of her head, legs, and arms.

"This is Mrs. Grey's pride," Daniel said, only a few yards away.

Conal stated his approval, "Tis carefully tended, for sure. Pleasin' to the eye."

Landon agreed. "Mrs. Grey has reason to be proud. The cherry blossoms are especially magnificent," he added loudly, sounding closer than the others.

Her heart jarred the walls of her chest. She crouched lower into the shadows of the shrubs next to the tree. Captain Hart was dangerously close to her hiding place. She dared not take a single breath.

"Look at this," Conal said. "The detail on this bench is as fine as any I have ever seen."

He ran his large hand over the ornate ironwork. The fragrance of a rose bush apparently caught his attention, and he stepped over to sniff the flowers. He plucked a blossom, lifted it to his nose, and inhaled. Keelan's pulse pounded frantically. Although Conal stood several yards away, if he happened to glance to his left, he would discover her. She could only retreat so far into the shrubs.

Why hadn't she tried to intercept them earlier instead of just standing here pondering it?

Captain Hart coughed.

Conal jumped, then grinned. "After five months at sea, 'tis a relief to have somethin' nicer to smell than salt water and eighty unbathed seamen."

"Come," Daniel said, laughing. "I'll take you inside to meet Mr. Grey and the commodore."

The conversation droned on after the men walked from the garden, but Keelan couldn't hear it clearly.

Drat, again.

She'd missed her opportunity.

Were they gone? She waited. After a moment, she leaned forward to glance around the branches, but froze at a sharp, painful tug on her hair. Reaching behind her head, she sought the origin of the entrapment. Her wild hair was snared. She groaned in frustration. This kind of delay was not what she needed now. She tugged, but succeeded in freeing only a few meager strands.

She tucked her chin to her chest and groped for more tangled curls. This was a fine mess. If Aunt Sarah caught sight of her now, she'd drop in a dead faint.

Again.

"Damn!" It didn't help her cause, but the curse certainly conveyed her mood at the moment. It almost made her feel better.

"That's an understandable expletive for a young girl posing as a boy, however, as a young girl masquerading as foliage, it's a bit disconcerting."

Hart!

Keelan ceased her struggle, mortified. A shadow fell over the ground at her feet, followed by black riding boots, lightly dusted from the road. She raised her gaze over fine black breeches and tapered waist. She lifted her gaze higher, and it stuttered at a white linen shirt untied at the neck, before she took in the broad shoulders, strong jaw, small scar on the chin and a straight, but haughty aquiline nose.

Captain Hart stood in front of her, his crystalline blue eyes glittering with amusement.

This was going to be trouble.

A slow smile pulled a dimple into his cheek. "You can come out now. I'm afraid you've been discovered."

CHAPTER FIVE
A SMUGGLER'S TERMS

P*irate.*

   With his ebony hair wild about his shoulders, Keelan pictured Landon Hart with a brace of pistols and a scabbard, standing at the helm of a wicked pirate ship. His mouth was perfectly shaped. When his white teeth flashed, his smile was so brilliant she stopped breathing altogether.

He was beautiful.

Azure eyes took on a mischievous glint, making her wonder if he'd read her mind.

Although her mouth had gone dry, she managed to dredge up a few raspy words. "I would gladly come out, but my hair is trapped." He referred to her as a girl, which was more annoying than being caught in a bush. "I am not a *mere girl*. I'll have you know, I'm nineteen." She clenched her jaw and struggled harder to yank her hair loose. *Ugh*. She had the most abominable luck.

He strode closer, bringing an aura of delicious power with him. Broad shoulders blocked out the sun. "Perhaps I can be of some assistance and liberate you from your bushy captor." He threw her a lazy grin followed by a long, unsettling appraisal from top to toe and back. His molten gaze faltered at her lips and he stilled.

Hart's nearness had a troublesome effect on her lungs, and she found it difficult to draw a breath. There was a rakish quality in this man, to be sure. She'd learned early to be watchful of those characteristics.

As if he noticed his proximity flustered her, he stepped nearer. Heat rolled off him in waves, along with the scent of leather and sandalwood shaving soap. He probably also knew he was ridiculously handsome. She wouldn't be the least bit surprised if he was terribly conceited and prone to more than a little deceit, as well.

Once again the word "pirate" came to mind.

She forced an even tone, despite a thudding heart, then pulled anew. "No, thank you. I'm sure I don't need your help." A sharper pain shot across the back of her skull. "I can do it, really, Captain Hart." That was probably a lie. Why didn't he just leave her alone? Or just leave?

Either or would be fine.

She couldn't *think*.

"Nonsense." He gently clasped her wrists and drew them away. His fingers were very warm. Well, it was also a warm morning. Sunny. Humid. Very, *very* warm.

And he was too *close*.

The scent of him mingled with leather and fresh spring air, which combined for a heady mix of male and danger and unsettled calm.

Her pulse jumped wildly under his touch, and the prospect he might feel it too terrified her. Tiny prickles of fire zipped under her skin where his fingers brushed.

"Hmmm." He leaned over her shoulder and studied the tangled web of curls. "It would seem you have a dilemma, my sweet. There is an extensive amount of curls and several twigs involved." He reached for his dagger. "I can cut you free—"

"Wait!" she squeaked. "Can't you cut the branches instead?" She choked in a scant breath, as that was all that could fit at the moment. Why was it so difficult to breathe?

The desperate desire to save her scalp and the powerful urge to flee warred with each other in her mind. The savage aura surrounding Landon Hart sent her nerves into a frenzied dance, and she hated she couldn't keep calm and act nonchalant. Unaffected. Bored.

Would he leave her if she demanded it?

Doubtful.

Humor warmed his eyes to a velvet blue; he was having too much fun at her expense to withdraw now.

He gave her a mock frown. "It'll require a great deal of effort to both disengage and keep these silken strands of copper and gold intact."

His voice dripped words like honey over scones. Thick and sugary. Her gaze drifted back to his lips. It took a moment to remember what he'd actually said. Another before she could form an entire sentence.

"I'm confident in your skills." Hopefully she conjured enough sarcasm to mask her unease. At least she didn't stutter.

It nipped at her pride no small amount, but obviously she needed his aid. A chunk removed from her hair and a sliced finger would be impossible to hide.

Uncle Jared was already suspicious of her tendency to rise before the sun, unlike his family, who usually slept through breakfast. One more of her incidents would likely push him past the limit of his patience. Although he was a servant, Daniel was like a beloved uncle to her. She would do whatever she could to prevent him from being punished.

Still, no one liked to beg. Releasing a slow breath, she willed her tone to remain steady.

He was still much too close. And *hot*.

"Can you spare a moment to untangle them?" She nudged away her pride and added, "Please."

Landon sighed dramatically and touched his fingers to his broad chest. "How can I possibly refuse such a distressed and heartfelt plea from such a comely maiden?"

A breath of tentative satisfaction escaped. She wished to believe he could be chivalrous, but her instincts were nevertheless on alert.

"However," his casual perusal skated from her eyes to the tangles and back again. "As a tradesman, my time and labor always come at a cost."

Gentleman, ha! It had been foolish to hope. Naïve, even. The cautious sense of relief chilled. "A cost?" Her voice could have coated the garden with frost, yet he seemed entirely unaffected. "What cost would that be?" This was not going well.

His expression remained stoic while he scratched his chin. "The lowest on my books for freeing a young lady from a barbaric bush is..." His eyes darkened to a sultry blue and again dropped to her mouth. His nostrils flared. "A kiss."

A *what*? He couldn't be serious.

She opened her mouth to rebuff him. Remind him of his place. And hers. Her first kiss would not result from a...a...barter! Or blackmail, or...

He dare *not*!

No matter how she struggled, words eluded her. She swallowed. It was as if he'd uttered a spell paralyzing her mouth and limbs. Only her eyes worked at the moment, and she couldn't even get them to glare instead of widen like an astonished doe.

Hart ran the outside of his knuckles along her jaw before cupping her chin, causing every nerve ending to vibrate. He leaned forward and lightly stroked her lips, feather soft, tasting. The pressure of his mouth intensified, and she lost control of her eyes, too. They closed.

His mouth, both soft and hard, consumed her sense of time. A tiny hum escaped from her throat. When he parted her lips with a hot, slick tongue, it shocked her enough to gasp. A tingling sensation swirled deep in her belly and her body curved into his. Need surged. A low satisfied rumble vibrated in his chest and he dove his fingers into her hair and deepened the kiss. Stroking, probing. Her strength ebbed, as if some sort of magic transferred the energy from her body to his, and she numbly wondered if her legs would hold. He trailed kisses along her jaw, pausing near her ear. A sharp zing shot around her neck, causing an involuntary shiver to follow.

"You taste of sweet maple syrup," he rasped, before taking a smooth inhale. "And smell like a spring morning."

Her lids fluttered open. Warring with a mixture of bewilderment and shocked desire, she struggled again to find her tongue.

"That...that..." Her hands were gripping his forearms, and she released him as if her fingers had been scalded.

Blast it all. She'd stuttered!

"Was delicious," he finished for her. "Your lips drive a man mad longing for another taste." The side of his mouth quirked up, but his voice seemed oddly hoarse.

He mocked her, surely. And it was nothing more than maple syrup and corn mush. And she was nothing more than a flustered maid, paralyzed by something as ridiculous as her first kiss.

Stupid girl, letting a man like him get you ruffled as a spring bird.

She fought to regain her composure, which at best lay in tattered shreds at her bare, dew-drenched feet. Her body's reaction both surprised and angered her. Surprise because of the unexpected pleasure that invaded her core in a swirl of sultry satisfaction, anger stirred by that all-knowing, hooded perusal through those thick, inky lashes, and the stupid stuttering. He knew how his kiss had affected her, probably relished the sense of mastery it gave him, which only fueled her intense determination to give him some sort of dressing down.

His fingers burned through the fabric of her sleeves, and for some reason, she had the front of shirt in her fists. Her knuckles skimmed against the hard ridge of a rib. She let go and grasped his hands, in a vain attempt to peel his fingers from her waist, which was in *flames*.

"You have no sense of propriety," she sputtered. There. That sounded proper. And chastising. At least her voice worked again. For the most part.

"No," he agreed. "But then, I never claimed I did. Now—" He leaned close again.

"Don't you dare!" She narrowed her eyes, giving him her best death glare, unsure she'd be able to keep her dignity if he kissed her again. Not that she wanted him to kiss her again.

Of course she didn't.

Heaven knows she'd almost melted from the first one.

He chuckled, let go and began untangling her hair. "You've paid me well, my lady. I'm honor-bound to fulfill my duties."

She snorted, not caring how unladylike it sounded. "I doubt you understand the meaning of honor," she said, convinced he was more rake than anything else. "You deserve to be slapped soundly." He truly did. "No gentleman would take such liberties, or suggest such a bargain." Pointing out the fact he was no gentleman would undoubtedly come as no surprise to the scoundrel. In fact, it wouldn't alarm her if he was proud of it.

He paused, laughter glittering in his eyes. "Liberties? I seized no liberties, only fair payment for my services."

"It gives me cause to wonder how many other ladies you have seduced into a kiss with your silver words and roguish charm," she retorted.

If it was possible (which a moment ago she would have argued it was *not*) he leaned even closer. His breath warmed her ear, his whisper from deep in his throat. "A gentleman never tells, my dear. Suffice it to say none were unwilling and not all were ladies."

"You..." Her voice betrayed her again, and she barely choked out the rest of the sentence. "You really are a rake."

He gave her a wink, which stirred up those stupid butterflies again. "I will say, none as intoxicating as you, my love."

"I am not your—*augh*!" Her cheeks grew warmer, and she was ridiculously pleased at his compliment. Did most women fall all over themselves for a chance to enjoy his attentions? She was not like most women. *Not at all*.

If he thought to place her in the same category as those weak-willed, twittering females, he had a thing or two to learn about Keelan Grey. She absolutely didn't *twitter*.

A flippant veil of nonchalance draped over her demeanor would help. If only she could more succinctly conjure that veil. Damned if dragging her stare from the cobalt eyes of Landon Hart almost required more strength than she could muster. It didn't help that her attention locked on to his amazing lips, still curled into that *I know what you're thinking* smile.

He changed the topic, thank goodness. "What's a beautiful woman like you doing dressed as a street urchin and playing with blades?"

Beautiful? An odd fluttering rippled over the skin of her stomach. She clenched the muscles, demanding it stop. Her eyes jerked back to his, expecting to see them glittering with jest.

But only a calm interest lingered there. He lifted a brow, awaiting her answer.

She took a careful breath. He'd just presented an opportunity for her to talk with him about her problem. Her heart gave a hopeful thump. Perhaps she could still salvage the day.

She dragged her attention away from his chiseled face. "My father instructed Daniel to train me to defend myself." She fiddled with a small branch.

"It appears he's been doing it very well," he complimented, a smile in his voice. Perhaps this was a game for him, but to Daniel it was not. To *her,* it was not.

Argh! She wanted to shake him and make him understand how dire the situation had truly become. She curled her hands into fists to prevent them from going for his neck.

Take a breath. Speak calmly.

"Since it upsets my Aunt Sarah, my uncle has forbidden me to continue the training," she went on, pretending he hadn't spoken.

He chuckled. Now *that* was a dangerous sound; it made her toes tingle. "Ah, so I see. The prohibited exercises continue in *secret* now," he said.

Unnerved by how he made the word "secret" sound so deviant, she nodded and plucked at the leaves. It seemed safer than looking directly into those eyes again.

Might as well simply say it.

Taking a deep breath, she plunged ahead. What's the worse that could happen? *Ridiculous question.* "I would sincerely appreciate it if you would keep that knowledge to yourself. For *Daniel's* sake," she added.

"For *Daniel's* sake?" Doubt threaded his words together, making her want to pinch him hard.

She nodded. "He'd be disciplined severely if Uncle Jared finds out we defied his orders."

"But what about your sake?" he said, eyebrows raised.

"I can deal with any repercussions which affect only me," she hissed, anger tightening her fists. He didn't understand her plea. This wasn't about her, it was about protecting Daniel. "I don't want Daniel in trouble."

His face went carefully blank. "Are you lovers?"

"What? No, of course not!"

He glanced up and appeared to ponder her request, all male arrogance in that *"I know I'm blocking out the sun"* kind of way.

What a conceited horse's ass.

She had to bite her lower lip to prevent herself from saying it out loud. Perhaps Aunt Sarah was right when she'd questioned whether Keelan was spending too much time in the stables. *Such language.* And the captain still pondered.

After a couple more moments of torture, he smiled. "Your clandestine activity is safe with me."

Her quiet sigh of relief was short-lived, however, as he continued to beam, white teeth gleaming brighter than the midmorning sun, which he still blocked. He had another dimple on his left cheek, which was as distracting as the one on the right.

"My terms for keeping a lady's charade a secret are—"

"You wouldn't!" she whispered. Would he? Another one of his kisses would be her undoing.

Worse, what if one more kiss didn't buy his silence? What if he wanted more? A strange thrill rippled up her spine, and she fought to squelch it. She'd not jeopardize her future any more than she already had. As it was, they were lucky no one had seen them. Her family would spare no time dragging Hart before a man of the cloth at gunpoint and forcing him to take her as his bride.

The thought both elated and destroyed her. She'd be the lonely wife of a man married to the sea.

Just like Papa.

She could not let that happen.

She *would not* let that happen.

Her mother lived a miserable, lonely life while her father was at away at sea with the navy. She would not become her mother. Brittle...bitter...sad. Keelan was made of sterner stuff.

She lifted her chin. "Should a member of my family witness—"

Scorching fingers circled her wrist and stilled her tongue. He pressed his lips to her palm, then sucked lightly at its center. His wicked mouth ignited a searing sensation all the way up her arm and along the sensitive skin of her neck, leaving her too stunned to speak, too aroused to reason. The power she sensed earlier pulsed through the surrounding air, and she found herself unable to move.

Unwilling to move.

How did he *do* that?

He released her hand. "I shall collect my due another day, sweet Keelan." He gave her a mocking wink. "I promise to remain mute on the topic. In addition, I am pleased to tell you I've liberated those imprisoned locks of silk from this malicious bush. You, my dear, are free to go about your clandestine business."

Not yet trusting herself to speak, she stared at him. The raw hunger in those piercing blue eyes shook her almost as much as her reaction to it.

A smile spread across his face with the slowness of a sunrise. "It's indeed been my pleasure serving you." The mockery in his voice made her want to punch him. "As much as I wish to linger, regrettably I must go, though it takes all my strength as a man to do so." He gave her an exaggerated bow, bade her farewell, and left the garden.

Definitely arrogant. And conceited.

In a mute stupor, she watched him walk away. Numbly, she lifted a shaking hand to her throbbing lips, still swollen and hot, and uncurled her hand. It burned as if Hart had dropped a hot coal on it. The sensations both thrilled and terrified her. She inhaled and tried to steady her frayed nerves and slow her pounding heart. Even as reason had warned her to resist, her body hadn't listened. No man had never attracted her this way before. It left her horrified, bewildered, and dangerously curious.

Her mother might not have been the most nurturing parent, but she made sure to inform her daughter about the men who commit their lives to the sea. According to Mother, most were quite libertine in their way of life, and they lacked moral principle and any sense of responsibility, as did the women with whom they tarried. Keelan released a sharp breath. God forbid she turned into one of *those* women.

She'd grown up being suspicious of men like Captain Hart: wanton and promiscuous. Hart and those like him seduced maidens for sport.

Her naivete likely amused him. Her cheeks burned at her stupidity and shame of being among the women he had seduced into a kiss. Surely there were a lot of them, as he was so talented at the practice.

She wouldn't fall prey to his game again. And she most certainly would *never* seek the arms of a sailor who traveled from port to port. Why would she ever choose to live her mother's life, full of longing and bitterness?

CHAPTER SIX
A TEST OF SKILL

A shrill scream shattered Keelan's musings, snapping her attention to the yard. She raced from the garden, searching for the source of the alarmed cry. A young slave boy, of perhaps nine or ten years, burst from the smokehouse, his shrieks ringing across the grounds. He wobbled and fell.

Keelan recognized the child as Ruth's youngest, Joseph, whose chicken-feeding duty had been performed earlier by Slaney. Although crippled, he did a fine job tending the smokehouse, fueling and keeping the coals smoldering while defending the meat from the dogs.

Handling the fire poker as a brace, he now struggled to heave himself to his feet. Keelan ran to help. Had he been burned? Slaney had an ointment that would help.

Before she could close the distance between herself and the boy, a snarling wild dog limped out of the building, its short thick fur raised along its spine. The boy shrieked again, and in his panicked haste to retreat, lost his footing and tumbled back to the ground.

Behind her, the door to the kitchen house banged open. Ruth emerged and yelled for help.

Keelan's chest constricted in panic. The dog staggered toward the boy, it's gaping mouth frothing wildly. Joseph brandished the poker in the direction of the enraged creature and swung, striking its muzzle. The animal yelped, shook its head, and its yellowed eyes locked with Joseph's terrified ones. There was no time to traverse the gap between them. Her dagger! Keelan slid to a halt, snatched out her dirk and threw.

And missed.

Daniel's voice echoed in her head telling her she rushed the throw, her chest didn't point to the target. Her wrist wasn't cocked correctly (Hart's voice). She didn't hold it firm (Hart's voice, again).

The movement or perhaps sound of the wayward blade striking the packed dirt diverted the dog's attention from the boy to her. A violent jolt shot through her limbs, and for a second she was paralyzed. Joseph still sat, frozen in terror, defenseless on the ground.

The rabid dog swiveled its head back to the boy. The image of it attacking the child spurred Keelan into action. She clapped her hands and shouted, again gaining the beast's attention. It turned and took a step toward her and lowered its head. A low, insidious growl emanated from deep within its throat.

At least if it chased after her, she'd run and hopefully get to the kitchen house first. It would give the child time to scramble to his feet and lock himself in the smokehouse. It was then she remembered Daniel's dagger she'd wedged between her waistband and belt.

She gripped it and paused long enough to take careful aim, replicating the grip Captain Hart had showed her, then stiffened her arm and let it fly. The knife pierced the matted coat behind the animal's shoulder. It snarled and snapped its jaws at the hilt as it fell, twisting and writhing less than four feet from where Joseph sprawled, wide-eyed, on the ground.

⚓ ⚓ ⚓

ONE LOOK at the thrashing wild dog told Landon the animal was diseased and deadly. Even wounded, its bite could kill. If Keelan got too near... He doubted the proud young woman would heed a warning to go no closer, so he broke into a dead run. Just as she threw the second dagger, he sprinted past her, grabbed the boy, then swung him up over his shoulder, and carried him further from the creature before depositing him back on the ground.

Keelan stumbled past and knelt by the young boy's side. His shaking hands still clutched the poker; tears spilled down his face as he drew in shallow, ragged breaths. His eyes were filled with shock and fear, and he stared at Keelan as if she had sprouted three heads.

"Are you hurt, Joseph?" she asked softly, helping him to his feet. She clasped the boy's arm and gently brushed a spot of soot from his nose.

Joseph shook his head, his wary gaze locked on her flushed face. Two other slave boys crept up to Keelan's side.

"Good God, Miss Keelan, you pierced the monster's heart!"

Landon nodded in appreciation. "An impressive throw." It was. His throw would have been no less true, although he wouldn't have missed the first time.

The boys' eyes brightened in awe. "How'd you learn to do dat, Miss Keelan?"

With an impish glint in her eyes, she responded, gesturing to Landon, "Captain Hart taught me this morning." She tossed him a smug smirk.

The chit was smart. She just put him in Daniel's place. When gossip traveled about the plantation, they would associate his name with the incident.

One boy leaned forward and spoke in a scratchy whisper, "Ain't no one goin' to believe dis."

"Ain't nobody... goin' to hear... 'bout it," a stout black woman panted, stopping for breath beside Keelan. She pointed her meat mallet at the boys. "As far as anyone knows, I kilt this devil." She shuffled over to the dying creature and brought the mallet down on its skull with a sickening crack.

Keelan cringed and turned away. For all her bravado, she didn't have the strongest stomach. Would she faint at the sight of blood? Somehow he didn't expect it, but ladies were an unpredictable lot.

The woman spoke again. "Miss Keelan did a brave thing. Don't you be making trouble with her papa and uncle by blabbin' about it. Understand?"

"Yes'm," the chastised boys answered in unison.

She wrung her hands as she turned to face Landon. "Please, sir, I don't want no problems for Miss Keelan."

Landon inclined his head. "Rest assured. I won't retell this tale. It will be our secret."

He slid a knowing glance at Keelan. There would be a price, though. She narrowed her eyes, reading his expression perfectly. Landon grinned. He suspected she didn't trust he'd remain silent, which made the situation more entertaining. It would be entertaining to tease her a bit more, enough to win another of her fiery kisses. Or maybe two.

"Don't worry about me, Ruth." Keelan patted the woman's arm.

Ruth bent over and tugged the dirk free, then wiped the blade on her stained apron. "Miss Keelan, I'll git this knife back to you soon as I boil it clean again." She flung her arm at the two older boys. "Now take dis mad animal down past the creek and bury it deep." She shooed them away. "Go on, now."

The braver of the two scuffled over and nudged the mud-caked, wild dog with his toe. Satisfied it was indeed dead, the boys grasped its hind legs and hauled the carcass away.

Ruth grabbed her son with the fierceness of a mother bear and crushed him to her bosom. Joseph let out a jagged sob. Tears slid down Ruth's cheeks as she and the boy swayed together in the dirt yard.

Keelan's face softened. With what? Tenderness? Yes, but there was something else. Landon's chest clenched as he realized what he was observing.

Longing.

Her reaction stirred his curiosity. Which did she long for? A child to love or a mother to love?

Keelan shifted and caught him staring. Her face became shuttered, once again masking that raw corner of her soul.

The slamming of the front door jolted everyone into action.

"You'd better leave," he advised. "I'll take responsibility for the events here."

Keelan gave him a hesitant, but grateful nod and whirled toward the garden path. Her gaze sliced to a first-floor window, and she drew in a sharp breath. Her mouth parted briefly before snapping shut. He twisted in time to see a hand release the curtain. He'd not readily give away her secret, but if someone else had seen the commotion, his promised silence might no longer matter.

Keelan ran to the servant's door, like a forest sprite in bare feet. Landon shook his head in wonderment. She'd tweaked his interest, for sure.

He'd see her again.

CHAPTER SEVEN
A MARRIAGE DILEMMA

Keelan tiptoed up to her quarters, where Slaney had a bath waiting in the next chamber. She disrobed, hiding her waif's garments in an old trunk. A blissful sigh of contentment escaped her lips as she sank into the water. Warm, but not too hot. She sniffed. Fragrant. A bundle of herbs secured in a linen pouch floated in the water, steeping. Lavender, hyssop, and basil. A tincture of the same combination sat in a small bottle by her bed.

"Rub it on yer skin, and it'll keep ye from becoming a tasty meal for the wee buggers at night," Slaney had earlier explained.

Keelan reached for a small pat of scented soap and frowned as she pondered the secret observer in her father's study. She worked up a lather and scrubbed her head and face.

Her hands froze as a thought hit.

Of course. Her father, Captain O'Brien, and Uncle Jared might have been waiting to discuss business. She groaned. The spy could have been any one of them. Her shoulders tensed. She would find out soon enough.

Bright blue eyes interrupted her thoughts. Hart's slow, easy smile had sent her heart tripping, even though he'd claimed an advantage over her while she was in distress, the black-hearted scoundrel. He'd kissed her on the lips. Were all kisses that... *invasive?* Thrilling?

Chiseled cheekbones and an ebony mane completed the picture in her mind. She ought to berate herself for letting such meanderings carry her to a place she would never go, but any woman would be helpless to control herself from mooning over that man, at least a little.

This is nothing more than a passing infatuation.

Hart would not linger long here. Soon, his ship would take him to far off ports, where other more willing young maids would fill his arms and his desires.

Her breast tingled at the memory of his arm moving near it when he had reached around her body to set right her grip. Everything about him was memorable, from his face to the bulging muscles on his arms, flat stomach, and the strong male hardness pressed against her belly while they kissed... Keelan leaned her head against the back rim. She would now hold every future suitor against the standard Landon Hart's kiss established. She almost felt sorry for them; they'd never meet the mark.

Not that she'd ever admit that to Hart.

Slaney had always said that the sensations of lust differed vastly from those of love. She wasn't sure how to tell those two emotions apart, but Keelan recognized a rake when she met one. He was definitely not the type who would offer devotion and an honor-bound oath, which truly was the only thing that could save her from Pratt.

Hart likely did not need to give promises of love and marriage. There were many women who'd gift their bodies for his pleasure, regardless.

She straightened. Her father might argue, but her hand (as well as her virginity) was hers to keep or hers to give; she would relinquish them only for love and honor, no less. A man like Hart had no reason to provide either.

Not that she cared. Neither did Pratt for that matter, yet her father was more than willing to push her to the old man.

Still...the situation Hart controlled sent her stomach churning. Just how did he plan to "collect his due another day?" More importantly, what would he demand?

A small clock on the mantle chimed the eighth hour. Keelan expelled a lungful of air. She could change nothing by sitting in the cool water and worrying about her reckless behavior. As tempting as it was to permit the fingers of procrastination to grasp her limbs and pull her deeper into the bath, she forced herself to rise.

Slaney's light step followed her soft knock on the bedroom door. "'Tis me, myself, Mistress. Ruth made some Indian corn porridge for ye ter take to yer Da.'"

The cheerful maid popped her head into the bathing room and handed Keelan a towel. "Come, I'll help ye with yer dress and yer hair." Slaney crossed to the tallboy and began to sift through Keelan's undergarments. "Will ye wear the blue gown to the ball? 'Tis yer most flattering, ye know. I pressed the ribbons yesterday in the event ye may need them."

"I suppose the blue one will be fine." Keelan toweled her arms. Cousin Doreen's upcoming ball was the talk of the Lowcountry. Dr. Everett Garrison, of course, would attend the affair. Circling another dance floor with him would put her feet at risk of irreparable damage, she was quite certain of it.

Remembering the most recent party she'd attended with him, she mumbled, "I am not looking forward to Dr. Garrison treading upon my toes like a mule on hot coals."

At Slaney's disapproving frown, Keelan bit her lip and reached for the light chemise Slaney had retrieved from the tallboy. Dr. Garrison had wiggled quite smoothly into the good graces of most of the women in the manor. Slaney was no exception.

"Dr. Garrison is a kind man, child. Where would yer Da' be now without the medicines he provides?" Cocking a jaunty brow, she admonished, "It wouldn't hurt fer ye to show a little more gratitude toward him."

Yes, they were lucky he traveled with them to Twin Pines after Papa became ill on the journey from London to Charleston.

Slaney was right; she should act more grateful. Still, it would be difficult. Whenever she and the doctor were in the same room together, she could sense him watching her every movement. It made her neck tingle and her chest twist.

Slaney stooped and gathered the discarded towels. "We're in America now. Things are different here. Although Dr. Garrison is a wee bit clumsy and shy, he's kind. He's been a close friend to your Da' and tended to his melancholy when yer mum died." The maid reached for the vial on Keelan's bed table, poured a few drops of oil into her palm, and rubbed Keelan's arms. With any luck, those flying insects would avoid her tonight.

Dr. Garrison worked diligently to find the cause of her father's illness, spent many evenings in the study poring over his medical journals and writing letters to colleagues in London and Richmond. A tall, awkward man with gentle brown eyes and a quick smile, he had charmed his way into the hearts of all the women in the household.

Except for Keelan's (although it wasn't for a lack of trying).

"Papa, in truth, doesn't seem to care that Dr. Garrison is interested in courting me. You realize he is pressing for me to wed Mr. Pratt, instead." Just saying that name made her nauseous.

Slaney's mouth flattened, and she gestured for her to step into her gown.

Keelan cocked her head, sensing the maid's disquiet. "What's raised your ire, Slaney?" The maid's eyebrows shot up and Keelan laughed. "You've been with me since I was a babe. I can tell when you're annoyed."

Slaney flicked her hand. "I'd just like ye to find better than old man Pratt."

"A goat would be better."

Slaney giggled as she fastened the buttons. "Another reason that mayhap you should consider Dr. Garrison's attentions."

To show his gratitude, her father had serendipitously offered to provide the doctor with a portion of their much-needed funds to establish his office in Charleston. Her father had done this without her opinion on the matter. She would have advised against it, since they had precious little left from selling her mother's shop in Chatham.

Keelan couldn't precisely determine why she objected to Dr. Garrison when everyone else seemed to find him so alluring. But there was something... Some vague, indefinable thing about him, beyond his jolting movements, his manner, the way he looked at her, that made her uneasy. He was always polite and kind, yes.

Maybe that was what bothered her.

He was *too* polite, too ingratiating, and too eager to win the favor of her and her father.

Whatever it was, she was never at ease around him.

Uncle Jared had even offered Dr. Garrison a room in his townhouse on Meeting Street, to give him time to establish his practice before investing in a residence of his own. However, as her father's condition worsened, the doctor made fewer trips to his Charleston office, then stayed with the family at Twin Pines to tend his benefactor. Which seemed loyal and kind...on the outside.

She turned to face the open balcony doors and stared at the long magnolia-lined lane as Slaney quietly buttoned the back of her gown. Her room was on the upper corner of the house, giving her the luxury of a view from the north and east sides. A movement caught her attention, and she peered through the magnolia branches toward the garden.

To her surprise, Doreen and Dr. Garrison were walking across the far yard toward the kitchen house, little Joseph limping between them. When the boy stumbled, Everett stopped and hoisted him up onto his shoulder. The boy squealed while Dr. Garrison jostled him up, down and sideways, as if he would dump the child at any moment. Doreen let one of her rare smiles escape as she walked along with them.

The doctor lowered the boy to the ground as Ruth opened the door. After speaking with her for a moment, Dr. Garrison patted Joseph on the shoulder. Apparently, the child was no worse from the harrowing ordeal with the rabid dog. He offered his arm to Doreen, and the two of them headed back toward the house. It was the first time Keelan had seen her up and about before noon.

As kind-hearted as the doctor was, Keelan didn't want to marry him. Nor did she want to marry Pratt for financial reasons. She pinched the bridge of her nose, knowing she'd do her duty as a dutiful daughter, but it wouldn't prevent her from trying to find a more pleasing route to the altar. If only she could devise a way to please him without having to spend the rest of her life miserable.

She still held to the dream. Her mind drifted to Hart's kiss in the garden. Why couldn't she fall in love with a man who ignited her body on fire and whose kisses left her breathless?

She wanted a man willing to lay his heart bare, pledge to her his undying faith and devotion, and hold hers in his hands to cherish and protect until the end of his time.

But if her uncle and father had their way, she would wed a man for convenience.

If that was to be the case, she'd rather not marry at all.

Again, her mind wandered to a muscular man with wild, black hair and eyes the color of a cloudless sky. His fingers were vibrant yet tender, and the outside of his thigh hard against hers. His lips were hot and passionate, and...

Stop being foolish.

She'd witnessed the effect her father's tedious tours at sea had on her mother. The loneliness, which accompanied his absence, had turned Mother into a quiet, withdrawn shadow.

Always sad. Always waiting.

Keelan whirled from the window and sat down. Reaching for a small dish full of pins, she busied her hands. She selected one and held it as Slaney brushed her long, russet locks. The maid remained uncharacteristically silent as she reached over and plucked the pin from her fingers.

"I did not mean to sound ungrateful before," Keelan finally said. "Indeed, Dr. Garrison has been most comforting to my father. He's a very kind man and genuinely cares about us. I believe he fancies me, and I don't want to offend him. I only wish I could find a kind way to tell him I'm not interested in his attentions."

Slaney paused behind her, and Keelan envisioned the maid's stern countenance. Thinned lips. Frowning eyes.

"Then you'd best find the words and ply them to his ears soon, lass. Men can't stand women who play with them like a sated cat toys with a mouse. It makes them irritable."

She turned to Slaney. "I am not some shameless trollop who flirts with men simply for sport."

"Of course yer not!" Slaney confirmed in a protective tone then continued, softly chiding, "But ye have made no attempt to tell the man his efforts are in vain, either."

"That's not... " The denial faltered on her lips. She put the dish down and tossed the extra pins into it, a twinge of guilt twirling in her stomach. "You're right. He's trying hard to help Papa. I can't stand the thought of hurting his feelings by telling him I don't welcome his affections. Although he's a sincere and compassionate man, I can't love him."

"Oft times love comes later, lass." Slaney placed her hand on her shoulder and gave it a motherly squeeze. "Yer head is full of girlish dreams of a knight in silver armor coming to sweep ye away to his castle in the clouds. But, if ye set yer standards at that lofty height, ye might find no one capable of making the climb."

CHAPTER EIGHT
A PLEA FOR TIME

"He has the personality of a doorknob." Keelan paced to the bedroom window. "Mr. Pratt's an old sniffling, drooling beast of a man and I do not wish to marry him, Papa. Please don't ask this of me."

Her father's mouth twitched before he narrowed his right eye at her. His morning nap renewed some of his strength. He had wasted no time bringing up Pratt's marriage proposal.

"Keelan, don't be selfish. Think of what this union could do for our family. My old friend spent a fortune to purchase this property and transport the two of us here. The money from the sale of your mother's shop is nearly depleted. We can't afford much more of a delay." He clutched the bed sheets and stared at his white knuckles, leaving the rest unsaid.

If they lost Twin Pines, they would have nothing left, not even enough to invest in rent for a store. Her stomach churned. She wanted to be a dutiful daughter and do her duty, but to sacrifice her life to become a miserable aging slave owner's wife made her dismally queasy.

She turned to face the window in an attempt to hide her growing vexation at her father and bit back the accusation burning on her tongue. If he hadn't sunk that ship, she'd be running their merchant trade, instead of living in another country, arguing against a business merger requiring her to wed.

Her father's voice dropped, exposing his wounded pride. "Mr. Pratt owns land twice the size of Twin Pines, and combined, the property would become the largest in the Lowcountry."

Uncle Jared moved his family to South Carolina a couple years earlier and offered to live here and help run the plantation until she and her father became comfortable with the task. Thank goodness for that. Neither she nor her father were prepared for the differences in conducting estate business. They knew nothing of turpentine manufacturing and even less about maintaining slaves, which placed them nowhere near an area of satisfied comfort.

Although Uncle Jared did his best, Twin Pines faced the new harvest with dwindling funds and increasing uncertainty. They still didn't have a solid budget for generating future profit needed to pay their creditors.

"Papa, you are asking me to sacrifice happiness for wealth." If their places were reversed, *he* surely wouldn't want to marry Pratt.

"If you have wealth, then you will have happiness. Daughter, I am ill. I would like to have you settled before I die. Don't begrudge an old man his satisfaction on this issue."

If her father did nothing exemplary the rest of his days, one could always say that he excelled at smothering a person with guilt. She turned from the window to face him. "I can settle myself comfortably without relying on a husband."

Especially one older than my own father.

She put her fists on her hips. "I handled all the ledgers for Mother for many years. I'm confident I could run a place in town that would be as successful, maybe more so." She hid the exasperation from her voice. Losing her temper would accomplish nothing.

She moved to sit on the edge of her father's bed. "Think, Papa!" She couldn't squelch her enthusiasm. "Barrels of exotic spices and brightly colored fabrics from the southern climes, beautiful carvings... I'd sell them not only to the people of Charleston but also to merchants we know in London."

It was unconventional for a woman to own and run a business, so the shop had been in her father's name. But her *mother* made it successful. With her father away at sea for months at a time, it not only brought in a steady income but also kept her mother almost too busy to be lonely. Her father sold it, of course, after her mother was killed. Rather than using the money to open a similar one in the city, he chose to invest in land. And in Dr. Garrison.

She didn't like the situation. She couldn't put a finger on the reason why, but it was as if the plantation fit like a shoe that was two sizes too uncomfortable.

"You have a quick mind with numbers, that's for sure," her father agreed. "That is why I need you to keep the plantation ledgers in top form."

Keelan fidgeted with a loose curl near her ear. "I dislike accounting for people as one would for livestock. It doesn't sit well with me."

The sound of him shifting in his bed made her alter her attention and reach for the water pitcher and glass. Her heart lurched at the sight of his shrinking frame. His skin had melted to his bones. The sickness had attacked him on the journey here and continued to weaken him as the months passed. Even the continuous efforts of Dr. Garrison hadn't helped.

"Is the new medication from Richmond easing your pain any?" She poured a cup of water for him and pressed it into his hand.

"Nay. I hate the way it twists in my stomach, but the doctor said it takes time to work. I must trust he knows the way of this sickness." He sipped the water and gave the glass back to her. "Hold out your hand, Keelan."

Her father held a red ribbon on which a gold ring dangled. A signet ring.

"What's this?" She allowed him to drop it into her palm.

"This is yours. I want you to have it now."

She peered closer. An interesting gift for her father to buy her. Without trying it on, she could tell it was way too big. Not wanting to hurt his feelings by pointing that out, she smiled at him. "Thank you. It's beautiful."

"Yes, well, it's an important heirloom. It has a special story attached to it," he said.

"Oh? What story?" She tied the ribbon around her neck and let it fall into the crevice between her breasts.

"Well, you see...er, it once belonged..." He paused and stared up at the ceiling for a moment, then batted his hand. "Never mind. I'll tell you about it another time. You're probably hungry and eager to eat breakfast."

He'd been having trouble remembering things lately and would occasionally lose his line of thought. Not wanting to embarrass him by pressing for more information, she simply nodded. "Another time, then. I can't wait to hear the tale." She smiled and patted his hand, gaining a slight grunt of satisfaction from him.

Her father's illness also added a more urgent impetus to his decisions, thus the topic of marriage arose with increased frequency. She closed her eyes and took a deep, calming breath.

Time.

She needed to develop a valid plan to support her cause. That required careful planning, and that required *time*.

"Papa, perhaps if we delay making a decision about Mr. Pratt for a while longer, a better resolution will present itself after the ball," she asked hopefully, keeping her voice soft.

Soothing.

Her father lowered his bushy brows. "If you're thinking you'll be able to persuade your uncle to financially back an enterprise for you, I'm afraid you'll be disappointed. He agrees with me. It's time for you to settle down and start a family."

She clenched the arm of her chair. "A shop in Charleston could generate enough profit for us to live comfortably. I'd be very, very happy and you never know, perhaps I'd meet a gentleman there who will make a suitable husband."

She tilted her head and smiled as her father harrumphed yet again. "You know how much I enjoyed being in town. I've always preferred city life to the country. I enjoy the more social aspects of being closer to the throngs of populace. Please, Papa."

Her father sighed heavily and leaned his head back, closing his eyelids. "Your mother could always bend me to her will the same way as you do now. You have her eyes, you know. Sparkling emeralds of light."

His voice slurred. Was the new medication finally taking hold?

"And fiery curls that glowed like burnished copper at dusk," he whispered.

Keelan smiled, although she was perplexed. "Mother's hair was pale brown. I appear to be the only one in the family with the anomaly of auburn hair."

Her father's lids twitched as if he was making a feeble effort to open them. "Nay! In her youth, your mother had hair like yours." He heaved a long sigh. "Losing her was the cruelest punishment God could have dealt me. So many years of longing and grief have left me... broken and bitter."

The medicine was sending her father adrift from reality. Her mother had been dead less than two years. He made it sound like it had been decades.

There had never been much warmth between her parents. Their relationship had always seemed distantly formal, at best. As a child, Keelan prayed for brothers and sisters, with the hope it would create a warmer family circle. They were all three left bereft.

Although she dreaded abandoning England for a southern planta-tion in the American south, her spirits had been buoyed by the thought of living with her cousin, Doreen. She'd had hopes of the two of them becoming close, like sisters.

Doreen had been sweet enough at first, but when gentlemen callers began asking to see only Keelan, her cousin's mood had soured. Now they rarely spoke.

Perhaps it was just a dream to one day have a large loving family. But it was her dream, nonetheless. Her father's current desire to see her wed to Pratt conflicted directly with that goal, making her deter-mined to find a way to satisfy her father without throwing her life away in the process.

There was a better solution out there somewhere, and she would find it.

Papa's face relaxed in slumber. Sighing, she stood, leaned over to kiss his forehead, and tiptoed from the room. She shut the bedroom door and headed for the stair. The faint clink of china told her the morning meal had already been served. She descended to the first floor and neared the dining room entry, pausing when she came within range of the conversation.

"What brings you to our gentle city, sir?" her aunt asked.

Keelan froze as a newly familiar voice responded. "I have cargo to deliver to our other buyers. Additionally, we had a serious skirmish with pirates, leaving our ship in need of repair. It requires us to move the rest of our goods into one of your husband's warehouses for a few weeks."

"Pirates! Oh my!" Aunt Sarah exclaimed, "Captain Hart, how did you ever get away unscathed?"

A low chuckle sent a shiver across Keelan's shoulders.

"It sounds much more adventurous than it really was, Mrs. Grey."

9

CHAPTER NINE
A MYSTERY UNSOLVED

F ynn Ahern's intentions remained a mystery, leaving Landon and Conal at a loss as to the reasons for the meeting. Yet, at the mention of Fynn's name, Landon could have sworn something flickered in the commodore's eyes.

Surprise? Anger? Panic?

Although the commodore denied any knowledge of Fynn, Landon didn't believe him. The man was lying. He could tell by the set of Conal's shoulders that his friend hadn't been convinced of the commodore's sincerity, either.

There was nothing more to be said after that, so he and Conal met with Jared Grey, the commodore's younger brother, to finalize arrangements for them to rent temporary warehouse space. They would be in Charleston for a few weeks while their ships were in dry dock. Plenty of time to further explore the mystery of Uncle Fynn's interest in the commodore.

But all in all, the day hadn't been a total waste of time.

There was Keelan, the spirited young lady he'd met; her vivacity, as well as her curves, which she'd hidden so well while sparring, but revealed more intimately while kissing, were tantalizing. Alluring.

The most humorous part was that he'd earned another kiss by

agreeing to remain quiet and not tell her uncle about her activities, when he had absolutely no idea who her uncle was. Not that it mattered. He had no reason to mention her antics to anyone, anyway. Besides, he was a bit chagrined to have been so deceived himself.

He should have guessed her fairer gender, if nothing else, by the slender fingers and fine wrists. But she played her part well. He saw what she wanted him to see... a young boy yet to sprout his first whisker.

He turned his attention back to Mrs. Grey, who'd been asking him about pirates. Thankfully, Conal had been paying attention and answered for him.

"Well, to better outrun them, we had to lighten the ship, by dumping most of our fresh water and provisions. Thankfully, we were only a day's sail from port, so our needs weren't dire."

A small movement by the doorway caught Landon's attention. The edge of a skirt. An eavesdropper? Grey noticed it as well.

"Well, come in, girl!" he barked. "'Tis bad manners to hang by the keyhole. Come meet our guests."

Landon prepared to greet the girl Jared Grey called into the room and shoved his chair back to stand along with the rest of the men, expecting Grey's young daughter. Every child gets caught at least once with their eye to a keyhole, spying on the adults inside.

But it was no little girl who entered.

Breakfast had just become much more interesting.

"Good morning, Uncle. My apologies. I was surprised to hear unfamiliar voices. I didn't know we had guests for breakfast."

Mrs. Grey blushed. "Oh, Keelan, forgive me! I became so enthralled in Captain Hart's tales, I completely forgot to send Tillie up to tell you. Come, my dear, and meet two most *fascinating* gentlemen. They were just about to tell us a scandalous tale of pirates!"

Keelan bent to kiss Mrs. Grey's cheek, then straightened and gazed casually about the room.

The girl had transformed from the nervous, saucy chit in the garden to a calmly composed, graceful young lady. He'd witnessed her calm during the frightening episode with the dog, but the demeanor she displayed now went beyond that. By the tilt of her chin and the graceful curve of her neck, she could have passed as an aristocrat's daughter, a young lady of the *ton*.

The simple light green gown fit her perfectly; those curves he touched while kissing her were much more evident now. Even knowing earlier that she wasn't a boy hadn't helped his imagination to picture her dressed like a woman.

At least not *this* woman.

How long it would take to crack that chilly, regal shell of hers?

Mr. Grey broke the brief moment of silence. "Gentlemen, allow me to introduce my niece, Miss Keelan Grey. She is the daughter of former Commodore George Grey, my elder brother."

⚓ ⚓ ⚓

UGH.

Keelan wasn't sure which was worse, Dr. Garrison and his eager smile of adoration, or the hulking form of Landon Hart, who even now looked at her with a raised eyebrow and a lascivious grin. Both he and O'Brien practically filled the room with their bulk, dwarfing her uncle and making Dr. Garrison look like a willowy stork.

Wide shouldered and tall, O'Brien was thicker, all muscle and brawn. Hart was sleeker, like a panther, coiled and alert. He flashed animal white teeth in a ferocious smile when she stepped into the room. Although her composure was more fragile than a thin layer of porcelain, she'd never let the arrogant sea captain discover how his presence rattled her. She bit the inside of her cheek and willed those stupid fluttering butterflies to settle.

She should have expected Uncle Jared to invite his guests to breakfast. She pressed her lips into a thin line; she'd been too distracted by this morning's events to think ahead clearly, which was unlike her.

Uncle Jared continued, "Keelan, I present to you Captain Hart and his business partner, Captain O'Brien."

O'Brien, being the closer, reached her first and bowed grandly. "Tis a pleasure to make your acquaintance, Miss Grey." His kind, emerald eyes twinkled with her secret.

She returned Captain O'Brien's greeting with a curtsy and a small smile before she turned to Hart. Since Captain Hart's back faced the rest of the room, no one but Keelan saw his appraisal moving in slow admiration down the length of her body, making her feel as if she were standing in nothing but her shift. His eyes took on a brightness that betrayed the wayward meandering of his thoughts, which was disconcerting to say the least. The kiss in the garden was something she'd been trying very hard to forget, although unsuccessfully. Well, perhaps she didn't really try that hard, but being in the same room with the captain made the exorcism downright futile altogether.

"Miss Grey." Landon's deep voice resonated with warmth and mirth while he bowed and extended his right hand, grinning mischievously. He was intentionally baiting her.

He knew of her wound, yet awaited her to place her hand upon his. Keelan clenched the fist hidden in her skirt. She glared at him and with every fiber of her being, wished his outstretched appendage would fall off.

Along with another appendage... or two.

He raised a brow, then had the audacity to wink. *Wink*!

Of course, to refuse to offer her hand would be embarrassing and rude. If her aunt and uncle noticed her injury, how would she explain it? Seeing no other option, she complied. "Pleasure, Captain Hart." She tried to give him a tight smile, but her face felt frozen.

He placed his knuckles beneath her palm as a rest, heat radiating up her arm like a fire racing across oil-soaked fabric. He bent to brush his lips across her fingertips. "Believe me when I tell you," he murmured, his voice husky, "the pleasure is truly mine." He glanced at the wrap on her thumb and placed a gentle kiss on the injured digit.

Barely keeping herself from flinching, a blush splashed over her cheeks. She snatched her hand back and hoped the glare she gave him would give him cause to behave better. Although, given what she already knew about the man, it was probably a vain hope, indeed. She steeled herself for an onslaught of Captain Hart's ornery charm.

Dr. Garrison hopped forward and clutched her recently released fingers. "Flowers pale next to Miss Grey." He squeezed her hand, including her wounded thumb, making her flinch openly this time.

"Goodness, Miss Grey." Dr. Garrison said, looking down, "What happened to your thumb?"

She glanced down and shrugged with what she hoped was a casual air. She hated to lie. Mainly because she was awful at it.

"I was in the kitchen house this morning." That part was true. "I'm afraid I was rather clumsy in the way I handled a knife." Also true. "But Slaney has treated it and it's much better."

Still true. She released a tense breath.

"Slaney is very good with her herbs." Aunt Sarah nodded and turned her attention to her tea.

The doctor led Keelan to a seat next to him, and she fought to suppress a despondent groan.

Captain Hart sat directly across the table. Her breath stilled as his gaze traveled leisurely down the length of her neck and paused. She could only surmise he was ogling the more feminine curves her current garments exposed, compared to the loose-fitting shirt and breeches from earlier this morning. The heat of a pink flush crept down her neck and bloomed across her chest, and she fought the urge to cross her arms over it. She lowered her brows at him as his gaze returned to capture hers. Smiling, he nodded in return.

Annoying man. She wished his approval didn't please her, but it did. Accepting a cup of tea, Keelan quietly sipped as she fought for calm and tried to ignore the voice in her head reminding her that one comment from him could land her and Daniel in serious trouble faster than one of those butterflies assaulting her stomach could blink.

Everett's head swiveled from Captain Hart's direction to her and back again. His eyes narrowed slightly. In fact, if she hadn't been looking right at him, she wouldn't have noticed how his cheek twitched. Had he caught the look she and the captain exchanged?

Aunt Sarah leaned forward in her chair. "Tell me, Captain Hart. Do you often have to deal with pirates in your travels?"

Thankfully, Hart turned his attention to her aunt. "Occasionally. We have to be diligent. We keep constant watch for pirates as well as privateers. This last encounter had been with a particular group which crossed our path in the past."

The steely tone in Captain Hart's voice made Keelan pause in mid-sip. Hart and the pirates had a history, then.

"I'm ready to return and give those pirates their just due," O'Brien growled, breaking off a chunk of scone. At the perplexed looks from the rest of the table, he explained. "The cannon shot that blew away the mizzen topsail and yardarm of my uncle's ship sent splinters and shards raining down on the crew. Killed my uncle. May those pirates rot in..." Captain O'Brien's eyes suddenly widened in horror, his face reddening. "Beggin' your pardons Mrs. Grey, Miss Grey."

Hart added, "Captain O'Brien's uncle captained the third ship in our small fleet."

Dr. Garrison interrupted, his words sounding sharper than usual, "'Tis a cruel end to meet. I, too, have lost family to the sea. You have my sympathies, sir."

The doctor's comment attracted Keelan's attention. Curious, Dr. Garrison had never mentioned that before. Perhaps that's why she'd seen him staring vacantly at the wooden model of Papa's ship, which sat on the desk in the study. Maybe he'd been thinking of loved ones lost at sea.

Simon, Ruth's husband, refilled her cup and she nodded her thanks, then reached for the cream. Normally, she preferred her tea without the cream's cooling effect, but the warmer spring temperatures in South Carolina demanded she adjust her preferences. Adapting to drinking tea at a more tepid temperature hadn't taken long.

Hart continued, "Fynn took me in hand when I had nothing and taught me everything I know about the sea. His loss has weighed heavily upon us all."

"You have our sincerest condolences, gentlemen," Uncle Jared said, laying down his fork.

Captain O'Brien leaned forward. "The main reason we initially accepted cargo bound for Charleston was to give my uncle an opportunity to meet with the commodore. Uncle Fynn wouldn't say why, other than he wanted to be certain of his facts before he divulged his theories. We'd hoped Commodore Grey would be able to tell us, but he didn't recall ever meeting Fynn Ahern."

Uncle Jared's face went blank. He shook his head as if it was on a wooden post. "Fynn Ahern. I don't recognize the name either." He picked up his fork again, speared a piece of ham, and went to work cutting it into small squares, keeping his head down as he sawed through his meat.

O'Brien sent Hart a slight shrug, but watched Uncle Jared closely.

He was *lying*. Her uncle's shoulders tightened. Was he wondering if O'Brien's uncle had sought out her father because of the sinking of that merchant ship? Had it been one of his? Had Fynn Ahern lost a loved one? If so, it was likely he tracked down Commodore Grey for retribution.

"I'm sorry for your loss, Captain O'Brien," Aunt Sarah said. "I beg your forgiveness at the indelicate nature of my earlier question."

"No apology necessary, Mrs. Grey," O'Brien said. "Were it not for the skills of Captain Hart, none of us would have escaped those pirates' greedy claws at all."

Hart shook his head in humble disagreement as he reached for his napkin. "It's the speed of the *Desire* that saved our skins, Captain O'Brien. That and a crew who knows every breath she takes."

"Aye to that," O'Brien responded, slapping his thick thigh. "Would that I could find a lass who handles as well, I'd marry her and leave the sea forever!" His laughter spread, and she had to admire the way he set aside his pain to lighten the mood. His face had a familiar gentleness about it, like a well-used quilt. The same couldn't be said about his friend Hart, who didn't bother masking his deviant thoughts. There was no gentleness in Hart's face. It was all hard angles and predatory planes.

Captain Hart continued. "Conal's uncle ran the trade routes from Cartagena to Boston and back for years. Cartagenian pirates and priva-teers are thick along the southern route, especially in the gulf region. It's not unusual to encounter them."

"It's Gampo, that bloody second of Lafitte's who will see the broad side of my ship's guns one day," O'Brien said in an angry voice. "Or the sharp end of me saber." Again he apologized. "I beg your pardon again for me language. But I mean to avenge me uncle's death. 'Tis no less than the pirate deserves."

Captain Hart gave a sharp nod. The hunger in his eyes told her he would relish the opportunity to take such a plan of action. A cold quiver skittered down Keelan's spine, making her wonder exactly how dangerous Captain Landon Hart could actually be.

CHAPTER TEN
PIRATES AND PETTICOATS

Uncle Jared scooped several spoonfuls of potatoes to his plate. "Gampo. It sounds as if you have quite a history with him."

Hart let out a cool chuckle. "Because we have slipped through his fingers so many times, I think we've become as much of a crumb in his craw as he has in ours."

"Why didn't you plow a hole in her hull and sink her?" Dr. Garrison's expression was uncharacteristically harsh, bordering on bloodthirsty.

Conal O'Brien lowered his brows, his face registering surprise. "Well, that would have made us murderers, wouldn't it?"

"But it would have been justified," Dr. Garrison argued. "An eye for an eye." He reached over and stabbed a piece of ham. "He should pay for it," he muttered.

"It would have made them *pirates*," Keelan bit back a smile. Hart glanced up and caught her in a heated blue gaze. A mischievous glint in his eyes told her she wasn't far from the truth. She couldn't help wondering how Hart could deal with a pirate such as Jean Lafitte's second in command and still maintain his code of ethics. If he even *had* one.

A conundrum, to be sure.

"There are other ways to mete out justice," Hart said, as if reading her thoughts.

What other ways were there? Perhaps Hart's code of ethics merely stopped short of murder. Maybe all else was fair game.

O'Brien shifted in his seat. "Their captain is a pirate to be certain, but often times, pirates take prisoners and slaves and force them to do their bidding. You can never be certain *all* hands are willing."

Ruth bustled in, placed a fresh pot of tea on the sideboard, and removed the empty pot and meat platter, tossing Simon a quick smile.

Aunt Sarah spoke, her brow furrowed. "Ruth, how is Joseph doing? I heard he had a fright this morning."

Keelan froze. Afraid her expression would betray her unsettled nerves, she pushed around a bit of shirred egg on her plate and surreptitiously watched Ruth's reaction.

Ruth dipped her head. "He doing fine now, ma'am." She glanced at Keelan then gestured at Hart. "I'm grateful for dis kind gentleman's help."

"I'm glad I was there to assist." Hart actually spoke with a hint of modesty, prompting Keelan's brows to jump in surprise. He responded with the tiniest narrowing of his eyes, although they held a hint of humor.

O'Brien swallowed a bite of fruit and nodded. "From the study window, I saw the knife strike the creature. It was a very good throw."

Keelan almost melted with relief. *Thank goodness!* She let out a grateful sigh. It wasn't Uncle Jared, it was Captain O'Brien at the window.

Dr. Garrison cleared his throat and folded his napkin into a precise rectangle and placed it on his lap. "I examined the boy prior to breakfast, to make sure he wasn't bitten by that rabid creature. He was unharmed."

"Thank you, Dr. Garrison," Aunt Sarah gushed. "We're so lucky to have you with us today."

Simon took the hot pot and filled Keelan's cup, along with the others at the table.

Uncle Jared placed a spoonful of the fruit on his plate. "What hear you, Captain Hart, of the possibility of war between the United States and England?"

"War!" Aunt Sarah exclaimed, putting down her fork. "I thought the United States remained neutral with regard to the conflict between France and England. Has that changed?"

The United States may have remained neutral, but by the gossip at the Chatham shipyards, the British had other plans. Keelan watched the captains closely, wondering if they would confirm what she'd heard months ago.

Hart spread jam on his scone. "It appears neither France nor England is willing to trade with a country who will not declare its absolute allegiance. It is only a matter of time before we are forced to choose sides."

Jared leaned in. "Will you have to adjust your trade route?"

Hart gave a slight shrug, "Possibly. Our primary mission is to avoid the British navy and the French privateers." He glanced at Keelan, and the corner of his mouth tipped up. "And other pirates."

Other pirates? Was he teasing her or was that a subtle hint?

Sarah pressed her hand to her throat. "Are you saying the British navy will attack unprovoked?"

Captain O'Brien shook his head. "Not attack, exactly. The English still think of us as British citizens, not Americans. They continue to illegally search our ships and impress American seamen into service for the British Royal navy. Privateers are given letters of marque from the king, giving them authority to take possession of enemy merchant ships in exchange for a share of the prize. It makes for dangerous waters."

Uncle Jared grunted in agreement. "Disrupt a country's trade and you weaken the resources needed to fight," He tapped his finger on the table as he spoke. "Congress can no longer remain reticent. They will have to act soon. I believe it's only a matter of time before we're all pulled into war." Her uncle sighed and shook his head. "Though we cannot afford it, since this country is still building its forces. It doesn't yet have a strong navy to protect the coast."

Hart cocked his head and placed his elbows on the table, lacing his fingers. "The United States has several frigates on the seas. Commodore Hall, of the *USS Glory,* is a good friend of mine."

Uncle Jared looked hard at Hart. "This war will not be fought solely on the seas."

"That's certainly true, Mr. Grey," Captain Hart agreed. His gaze locked on Keelan as she bit into a scone. "We all might be asked to do our part. Why, who knows, perhaps women will have to be instructed to bear arms as well."

Aunt Sarah immediately responded to Hart. "What a silly thing to demand. There are better ways for women to help in times of war."

The twang of Keelan's nerves fraying like taunt twine was almost audible. She tried to swallow, but the scone had turned to dust, throwing her into a violent fit of coughing.

"Are you all right, Miss Keelan?" Dr. Garrison asked, patting her back.

Aunt Sarah gave her a concerned glance. "Dear me! Simon! Bring some milk at once."

Attempting to wash down the offending morsel with a gulp of tea, Keelan instantly regretted the action when the scalding liquid hit the back of her throat and threw her into a worse fit of coughing and sputtering. She did her best to ignore the two captains who attempted to hide their amused smiles behind their own cups.

Insufferable ingrates.

"War and weapons are no place for women or children," Uncle Jared stated after she had finally regained control of her breathing, oblivious to the cause of her discomfort. "It's a man's duty to protect his own and be noble enough to never engage the fairer gender in battle."

Keelan reached for the cream pitcher, and poured a liberal amount into her teacup, while staring hard at Landon Hart, wishing he were the one mute from a scalded tongue.

Dr. Garrison was watching Captain Hart intently. His gaze shifted to her, then back to Hart a second time. She needed to maintain better control of her emotions. To have Dr. Garrison watching her this closely was always worrisome. If he started asking questions, there was no guarantee she'd be able to provide an answer without lying.

And as everyone in her family knew, she was a *horrible* liar.

But Hart seemed unaware of or unconcerned with her internal battles. Probably both. He countered Uncle Jared's comment with a question. "You say it's a man's duty to be noble enough to avoid engaging the fairer gender. But what if the fairer gender fires the first shot?" Landon Hart asked, a wicked gleam in his eyes. "What then?"

Uncle Jared paused and gave the captain a puzzled frown. "To what do you refer, Captain?"

Keelan gripped her napkin tightly. Her heart ricocheted against the walls of her chest, its vibration pounding in her ears.

I'm a naïve fool.

She should have suspected he wouldn't keep his word. Regardless of his promises, and her honest payment, he was a scoundrel. A black-hearted man with no scruples or honor.

He was a seaman.

Surely, even a pirate would be less nefarious!

Afraid her expression betrayed her emotions, she stared at her clenched fists. A sickening sense of dread pulsed in her stomach. If Daniel suffered a punishment because of Landon Hart's broken promise, she would seek her own vengeance.

And although Hart seemed to harbor no moral compass when it came to keeping his word, he was about to learn that Keelan Grey *always* kept hers.

Landon chuckled, placed his elbow on the table, and rested his chin in his hand. "There are tales of a lady pirate who dressed like a man. For a while, even her husband's crew did not know her fairer gender."

A lady pirate?

Keelan let out a long, slow breath and managed to narrow her eyes at Hart. In return, she received a merry wink. *Dratted man.* Taking a smaller sip of tea, she tried to hide her agitation. So, he enjoyed watching her squirm in her chair. She wished she could turn about the conversation in a way that would make him squirm, too, but couldn't think of anything that wouldn't also put herself in the same position.

To Keelan's surprise, her very proper aunt's eyes widened before her excited intake of breath drew the captain's attention. "How scandalous! Please tell us more about her."

"Her name was Anne Bonny," he answered. "She handled a blade and pistol as well as, and sometimes better than, any man. Eventually she was captured and sentenced to hang in Jamaica."

"Oh, dear," Aunt Sarah sighed. "How very sad."

"However," Hart continued, "she was with child at the time and received several stays of execution. Until one day, she vanished from the gaol."

"Vanished! Where did she go?" Aunt Sarah leaned forward. "She escaped, didn't she! How?"

The captain shrugged massive shoulders. "It is alleged that a group of loyal friends crept ashore in the dark of the new moon to rescue her."

Unable to help herself, Keelan asked, "And what of her husband?" The story seemed incredibly romantic to her, but why would her husband not lead his men?

"Calico Jack Rackham had been captured the same time as Anne. No reason existed to stay *his* execution." Hart tilted his head, studying her.

That was a bit disappointing. She could easily envision a handsome dark-haired pirate, proudly standing at the bow of his grand ship with his legs braced wide and arms folded across his expansive chest, as he sailed into danger to rescue his love.

"Pity," Aunt Sarah murmured, apparently as disappointed as Keelan. "What of the child?"

Captain Hart's brows furrowed. "She and her son disappeared. I've heard different rumors that she changed her name, or married and started a new life in Virginia. Other tales place her in New Orleans. She was never heard of again."

To meet a woman such as Anne Bonny would be thrilling. Imagine, a lady pirate, as lethal with a sword as any man, and also keen with a pistol. Keelan was less skilled with a firearm. Tomorrow, she'd ask Daniel to teach her.

Without shifting to look, she could almost feel the doctor's gaze. Ignoring the chill slithering across the back of her neck was almost impossible.

"How long are you at port, Captain Hart?" Dr. Garrison changed the subject.

Keelan straightened in her seat, drawing another curious perusal from her aunt. Trying to appear unconcerned, she pretended to focus on rearranging her napkin over her lap. When Captain Hart didn't immediately answer, she chanced a glance in his direction.

Landon Hart sat back in his chair, as if waiting for her to look at him. "A few weeks." He shifted his gaze to Keelan. "At least."

Oh, dear.

"Well, then," Aunt Sarah said. "You must allow us to offer you the full hospitality of Twin Pines. We would love the pleasure of your company. And you too, Captain O'Brien."

No! Keelan's lungs froze. She would not be able to abide seeing Hart and his bloody, rakish grin on a daily basis.

"That is a most gracious offer, Mrs. Grey. I can only imagine the full extent of what Twin Pines has to offer." The handsome captain smiled. Dimples dimpled. Crystalline eyes glittered. Aunt Sarah had no chance against such an onslaught of charm and magnetism.

Keelan was doomed.

She fingered the handle of her cup, which prompted Simon to refill it before slipping out of the room with the empty teapot. She eyed the cup like a snake waiting to strike. No more hot tea for her this morning.

"Unfortunately," Landon continued, "my ship demands close supervision, and most of my business duties remain in Charleston. Therefore, I have already secured lodging arrangements. However, I sincerely appreciate your warm and gracious offer, Mrs. Grey."

Thank goodness she'd be spared the torture of the captain's presence in the house for days and days. But as her stomach climbed up into place, Aunt Sarah sent it spinning away yet again like a child's top on a polished floor.

"As compensation for our disappointment, you and Captain O'Brien must accept an invitation to our ball next Friday," her aunt countered.

"We'd be honored." Hart responded with a polite dip of his head.

Aunt Sarah clapped. "Wonderful!" She passed a dish of potatoes to the captain. "Do try these, Captain Hart. Mr. Grey had them shipped from Philadelphia. He absolutely loves them. Keelan dear, you've hardly eaten a bite. Are you well?"

"I'm fine, Aunt Sarah." She met Hart's amused gaze. "I seem to have lost my appetite this morning."

He remained stoic except for a mischievous twitch of his mouth.

Conal O'Brien leaned forward. "Miss Keelan, have you any kinsmen in Ireland, or perhaps Scotland?" The captain's deep forest eyes studied her intently.

It wasn't really an odd question. Not many British had hair like hers. "No. My parents' families are both quite well-recorded."

"Tis hard to believe a lass with your hair and eyes dinna have roots in Ireland or Scotland." Conal O'Brien pursed his lips as he stared at her a moment longer.

"I'm a bit of an anomaly, I suppose. I'm the only one in my immediate family gifted with auburn hair." She shrugged, an attempt to remain nonchalant. Even a fool would jump to the next question, or assumption. *Any chance your mother strayed? Took an auburn-haired lover?*

Not only was it an unusual auburn shade, it was wild and chose to curl on a whim. No matter where she went, she had to withstand the surreptitious stares. Her hair drew people's attention as if it was a character separate from her yet still connected, like an extroverted twin.

Best to depart before any more questions were broached.

"I'm going up to sit with my father for a while." She nodded to each of the other three men who had risen from their seats. "Dr. Garrison, I will speak with you later, and gentlemen, it was a pleasure to meet you both." She tilted her head. "Captain Hart, I understand Charleston has excellent shipwrights. I hope you are able to complete your business here quickly."

And continue on your way as soon as possible.

Hart returned to her a charming smile. "Why, thank you for your concern, Miss Grey. I don't anticipate delays. However, in the interim, I shall enjoy my visit. It seems the Charleston area has an abundance of wonderful sights. I might decide to extend my stay in order to take them all in."

Simon appeared at the doorway of the breakfast room. Uncle Jared motioned him inside. "What is it, Simon?"

"Mr. Pratt's in the parlor and's asked me to tell you he wishes a word."

"Perhaps Pratt would enjoy some breakfast." Uncle Jared reached for another scone. "Send him in."

With a respectful nod, Simon disappeared. Keelan couldn't stop her teeth from clenching together. Mr. Pratt wasn't simply passing through. He probably intended to talk to Papa about proposing.

Propose! Ugh.

Well, she wasn't staying to find out.

CHAPTER ELEVEN
A FLIGHT OBSTRUCTED

T*ime to go.*

Jumping to her feet, Keelan darted to the sideboard where she picked up her father's breakfast tray.

Dr. Garrison pushed away from the table. "Allow me to carry that for you, Miss Grey." He tossed his napkin down, successfully knocking over his tea. "Oh, quite sorry," he cried, horrified, as he clumsily righted it then dabbed at the spill with his napkin. When the stain simply spread, he abandoned his efforts and stood, tipping his chair over in his haste.

With an exasperated grunt, Uncle Jared extended his arm and pulled the chair upright again. Garrison gave him a quick, embarrassed smile.

Keelan briefly caught the intrigued look Captain Hart exchanged with O'Brien before he turned his attention back to her. He smiled one of those dazzling smiles that probably made every woman on the planet swoon. "It was a pleasure making your acquaintance, Miss Grey. I shall speak with you again at the ball. I would be honored if you would reserve a dance for me."

A dance with him? That would be dangerous.

And exciting.

But mostly dangerous.

Better to avoid that temptation. Keeping her expression as blank as possible, she nodded. "Of course, Captain. Until then, good day." There. She'd lied effectively, which did a lot to boost her confidence. Nothing good would come from dancing with Captain Hart. Later, she'd determine how to avoid it.

However, her attention at the moment must stay focused on the most dire objective: her mission to stay out of Pratt's sight.

Dr. Garrison followed Keelan as she attempted a hasty escape up the stairs. "Miss Keelan, *please* allow me to carry the tray." He pulled himself up by the banister rail, trying to keep within three steps of her. She was, after all, *most* determined to avoid Pratt.

"I can manage, Dr. Garrison," she said with forced cheer while continuing her climb. If only he would leave her alone and let her dash upstairs. If no one was watching, she could hike up her skirts and take the stairs two at a time, even with the tray. The porridge didn't slosh, thank goodness. With Garrison nearby, she was forced to climb the steps in a more genteel manner.

"Please, I must insist." He took the steps two at a time and placed his hands on the tray next to hers. "And I do wish you would call me Everett."

Of course he insists. Keelan sighed and allowed him to take it from her while doing her best to avoid rolling her eyes when he jostled the dishes as he took possession, spilling most of the cream. Freed from the encumbrance of the tray, she quickened her pace up the stairs.

Almost there.

"Well, good morning, Miss Grey." The reedy voice rasped over the plastered wall like dry leaves, making her breakfast churn in her stomach.

She looked longingly at the last three steps.

Turning, she managed a stiff nod. "Good morning, Mr. Pratt." He stood in the hall, one hand clasping a limp handkerchief and the other a sturdy cane, bearing his bulk.

"Would you care to join me in the breakfast room?" He dabbed his mouth and gave her a closed-lip smile.

"Thank you for the invitation." She gripped the banister. Perhaps the reason he didn't show his teeth when he smiled was because he didn't have many. Maybe he had none. "However, I have already eaten and am taking my father his meal."

Pratt's eyes hardened, but the thin line of his mouth remained slightly upturned. "Allow the kind Dr. Garrison to deliver the tray to your father, my dear. Join me. I insist."

Why must men always *insist?* A murky sensation clamped over her shoulders as she walked back down the steps, feeling much like a doomed prisoner plodding to the gallows. Pratt waited patiently and held out his arm for her. She slowly looped her hand around his elbow to rest on his forearm and did her best to fight off a nauseous shudder that threatened, although she feared nothing would be able to pull her from the foul mood in which she now found herself. And to have Hart witness this awful moment made everything worse.

Pratt strutted into the breakfast room much like a bandy rooster in the yard.

Uncle Jared jumped up and shook Pratt's hand. "Pratt! Welcome! Won't you join us for breakfast?" The pleasant smile on his face faltered a bit when he met Keelan's glare.

"I'd be honored." Pratt pulled out the chair Keelan had recently vacated. "Here, my dear." Then he lowered his bulk into the seat beside her. Once again, she had to face the amused countenance of Captain Hart, which wasn't quite as bothersome as the presence of the man seated next to her. Well, maybe it was. She was caught between a snake and a panther.

When Hart quirked a brow in silent question, she threw him a glower through her lashes that should have withered a watermelon. He rewarded her with a slight widening of his crystalline eyes, to which she could only pretend to ignore. Along with the smirk, damn him.

Introductions were soon made, and Simon placed a full plate of food in front of Mr. Pratt, who shoved a heaping spoonful of shirred eggs into his mouth before he spoke. "I have considered the proposal you and the commodore presented to me." He nudged Keelan with his shoulder and winked at her.

Small bits of egg tumbled from his mouth with the words "proposal" and "presented," The urge to gag was overpowering. The only thing keeping her from bolting from the room in hysterics was her father's earlier promise to delay any decisions until after Doreen's ball. That didn't give her a lot of time; she'd have to come up with a reliable plan. At the moment, the most appealing consisted of packing a small satchel and running away.

It was a solid option.

Certainly Landon Hart was heartily amused. She cast a fast glance at him. Instead of amusement, however, a shocked look flashed across his face before it was replaced by one of pity. As if he were thinking, *Rotten luck for her.*

She pressed her lips together. It *was* rotten luck, but she didn't need his pity. A hiding place somewhere on his ship, however, would be very helpful.

Pratt continued. "You'll be happy to know I have decided to accept it, and I shall have papers drawn up that will merge Great Oaks with Twin Pines as soon as the nuptials are completed."

Nuptials *completed?*

Uncle Jared shifted uneasily in his seat, avoiding eye contact with her. "Ahh... well, then, I shall relay that to my brother."

She stared pointedly at her uncle. "You should know that Papa has decided to postpone making any firm decisions until after Doreen's ball next Friday."

"You don't say?" Pratt perked up a bit. "He seemed most eager at the time of our prior conversation."

Don't panic. There's still time.

The gusting sound of a tornado filled Keelan's head, for a moment blocking out all other conversations. She had to devise a way to avoid all this. She hoped to marry someday, but she wanted it to be a man of her choosing.

Someone she loved.

Someone who loved her.

Her hands curled into fists. She would *not* marry Pratt. There had been a greedy gleam in his eyes when he spoke of the *merger*. It was apparent he wanted the land badly. Her father expected her to be an obedient daughter, and she'd always tried hard to be so. But she would indeed run away before she'd *ever* marry Pratt.

Or... she could find a way to use Twin Pines as leverage for what she wanted.

Keelan jumped at a sudden pressure on her thigh. Her breath caught in her throat as she realized Pratt had put his hand on her leg. She frantically searched for a fork, but none were within reach, since Simon had cleared her place when she left earlier. More rotten luck.

Hart handed the large fruit bowl across the table to Pratt, forcing the man to remove his groping hand to take it. "Mr. Pratt, won't you try the brandied fruit? It's the best I've ever tasted."

"Thank you, Captain Hart. Don't mind if I do, as long as it isn't too chewy. I lost another tooth this morning, so I have to be careful." Pratt busied himself scooping several spoonfuls of fruit on his half empty plate.

Keelan let out a relieved breath and chanced a glance at Hart, who gave her a sympathetic smirk. She choked back a snort of laughter. Captain Hart had a quick-mind, to be sure. If he wasn't such a rake, she'd actually admire his tactics. She pushed her chair back and rose.

"Please excuse me, gentlemen."

As the other men stood, she managed to spin away before Pratt could push up from the table and reach for her hand.

"Join me in the parlor later, dear," Aunt Sarah called as she whisked from the room. "I'll be working on my needlepoint and would love some company until Doreen joins me."

"I would love to, Aunt Sarah," Keelan called with as much enthusiasm as she could muster, which was minimal, considering her loathing for needlepoint. At least she would be free of Pratt's groping, and Hart's mocking but smoldering looks.

And his perfect smile, which made her stomach flutter and dip, (damn him, again).

12

CHAPTER TWELVE
A PROPOSAL

Things were not going as Everett Garrison had planned.

He walked to the window of the old man's chamber and ran a hand through his hair. The events of the day had, so far, *not* been to his liking.

Pratt's visit was unexpected.

The merchant captains' visit was also unexpected, as was the alarming interaction between Keelan and Hart. There was no mistaking it.

"What has you so agitated, Dr. Garrison, that you must pace a trench in the floorboards?" Commodore Grey paused, his spoon halfway to his mouth.

Everett clasped his hands behind his back and spun on his heel. "I'm very concerned with Mr. Pratt's pursuit of your daughter's hand."

"You don't say." The fool swallowed a bite of the Indian porridge, then dug in for another.

Now that the topic had been opened, he must move forward with care. After witnessing the subtle exchanges between Captain Hart and Miss Keelan during breakfast, he'd come to the conclusion it was time to act. It was obvious those two shared an attraction or interest. He couldn't allow it to continue.

Then there was old man Pratt. He was another massive obstacle to overcome, due to the man's wealth.

Most distressing.

Acidic anger roiled in his stomach and it was a struggle to keep his tone calm, logical and authoritative. "Sir, over the past couple of years, we've developed a strong acquaintance." He'd rehearsed this speech a dozen times in his head. It was imperative he sound practical.

The old man nodded. "Yes, I certainly agree. The tenderness you showed my injured wife was what spurred me to seek your help with my melancholy after her death."

Everett frowned. "I still regret the damage was too severe for me to save her."

The commodore lowered his spoon and sighed. "I know, young man. I'm appreciative nonetheless, which is another reason I wanted to assist you in settling here in America, knowing it was a goal of yours." He reached for his tea, a slight tremor in his hand.

The effects of the medication.

"Yes, sir, and I am eternally grateful for your financial backing. It's allowed me to secure a Charleston office and begin my medical practice with enormous success." Even as he said the words, they reeked of bitterness and pain. All the money in the world would not bring a loved one back from the dead.

"Glad to hear it, Garrison."

He fingered his watch chain. "I have also had the honor of befriending your daughter. I have grown quite fond of her and, like you, desire for her happiness. I understand a father's aspiration to make sure his only child is properly married, but my casual observation of Miss Keelan and Mr. Pratt together tends to give me pause."

Grey's eyebrows fell. "How so?"

Careful here.

"Well, sir, she almost fled from the room when Simon announced Pratt's arrival, and she seemed most distressed when he caught sight of her and insisted she join him." He tried to appear sympathetic. "I don't believe she fancies a union in the slightest."

The miserable recreant let out a beleaguered sigh. "I know. She said as much. Working in her mother's shop made her too ambitious and too independent. Living on a plantation out in the country hasn't helped." His eyes were sad and weary. "I'm dying. I can sense it. I can taste it, the rotten, bitter flavor of age and decay." His gaze travelled to the window and his voice softened. "I want to see Keelan suitably cared for before I die, Dr. Garrison. That is my wish."

Everett nodded and gave the commodore a compassionate smile. "I understand. Therefore, I propose an alternative."

Grey turned his attention back to him and raised a shaggy brow. "Go on."

"I have been building a successful practice over the past year. Word of mouth of my expertise contributed substantially to that end. Your daughter favors a civilized life in town." His palms began to sweat, and he rubbed them on his trousers. "I could give that to her." He stepped closer to the commodore's bedside and laced his voice with as much empathy as he could muster.

"Commodore Grey, I would be honored if you would grant me permission to ask for your daughter's hand. As I said earlier, I'm fond of her and would be most diligent in seeing to her happiness and care. She would be able to live comfortably and we could open a store, if she desires to do so." He watched the man closely.

The commodore wiped his mouth with a napkin then pushed away his tray. "Dr. Garrison, I will be blunt." He grasped the edge of his blanket and pulled it up. "At this stage of my life, a sense of decorum commands less power over my tongue, anyway. You must understand that Keelan's future is my primary concern. If she marries Pratt, he would see her well-cared for in the event of his death, because she would possess something tangible in the end—land. A lot of it."

Everett ground his teeth. This conversation wasn't progressing in the direction he wanted.

The commodore continued, "However, in the case of *your* death, there'd be nothing she could use to provide relevant income." He held up a hand to cut off Everett's protest. "Be assured, Garrison, I'd prefer she marry a young buck like you rather than an old stag like Pratt. But her long-term welfare is of the utmost importance to me."

Everett tilted his chin down and pursed his lips, fighting a scowl. "I understand, sir. But I would implore you to recall your daughter's intelligence and experience in trade. I have complete faith that an enter-prise run by her would soon surpass those of other merchants."

The wretched man scrutinized him for a long moment. The tension in Everett's shoulders eased a tiny bit when he broke eye contact and stared down at his gnarled fists.

"You made a sound point, Dr. Garrison. I shall consider your proposal, but Keelan must agree to it first. Only then will my younger brother and I further discuss the possibility."

13

CHAPTER THIRTEEN
A PIRATE FOR HIRE

Gampo was late.

For the tenth time, Everett scanned the dimly lit pub as he fingered the handle of his mug. It was early in the afternoon; too early for the place to be noisy with men half in their cups, but late enough for several patrons to mill about, enabling him to blend in with the back wall.

Two men, about his height, but probably forty pounds fleshier, trailed by a short, thick tar, snaked their way past the bar and headed in his direction, the one in front obviously the leader. The planes of his muscular shoulders and commanding jaw had the other customers allowing him ample berth. He and his men pulled out chairs and sat at the table next to him.

A tavern wench sauntered up and gave the men a slow, sultry smile, her eyes moving from each with a half-lidded gaze. "What'll ye be havin' fine fellows?"

The one with several fresh jagged scratches and cuts on his cheeks and arms gave her a lusty leer as he flipped her a coin, which he eyed with interest as she slipped it down her bodice. "Bring ale and a trencher of fruits, meats, and cheese, fine lass."

"And bread," the short one added.

She nodded before she swung toward the bar, tossing a quick grin over her shoulder. He gave her a jaunty wink before turning his attention to Everett. "A man shouldn't drink alone, especially since the day's still young."

Everett tipped his head in recognition of the code words the man spoke. "You'll be Gampo?"

"Keep yer voice down, man," the thick one growled.

Gampo's cool, lethal smile did not reach his eyes. He touched his hat. "'Tis I. And you'll be the one requiring my services?" A slight accent wove its way between his words.

"I am," Everett responded with what he prayed was an authoritative tone.

Gampo gestured to the two men. "Crowe and Pike, my quartermaster and bo'sun."

Everett nodded a greeting. "It's my understanding that a merchant shipping company formerly run by Mr. Ahern has been an enigma for you in the past."

Gampo quirked an aristocratically shaped eyebrow. "Formerly run?"

"Apparently, Mr. Ahern died during your last engagement." Everett watched the man closely.

Gampo sat back in his chair. "That's the true word? More's the pity." He rubbed his chin for a moment before he continued, "Sí, they caused considerable pain to the marrow over the years." He brushed a strand of ebony hair from his eyes. "What's about it?"

Everett took a shaky gulp while the server distributed three frothy ales to Gampo and his two companions. She bent a little lower while she deposited Gampo's before him, providing him a brief peek down her blouse, which from his grin, he enjoyed tremendously.

She left, and the men turned their attention back to him.

Everett grimaced. "I, too, harbor a vexation with the same company, more particularly Captain Hart. I believe we can be of equal service to each other." He folded his hands. The pirates would never turn down the low hanging fruit he was about to offer.

Gampo pulled a gleaming dagger from his belt and pierced a dried peach slice. "What's in your head about it?" He tore the fruit from the knife with his teeth and chewed slowly.

Everett shifted in his seat, eyeing Gampo's dagger. "Well...er, I possess knowledge of Hart's plans. His ships are in for repairs, he'll be moving cargo soon for safe keeping."

Gampo reclined in his chair. "And what makes you think I've a mind to care? My argument's with Ahern, not Hart."

He glanced from Gampo to the other two tars, who were eyeing him warily from behind their mugs. "I heard that they've done some damage to your vessel on several occasions. I'm thinking you'd like some compensation to use toward the costs of repairs. And such."

"And such." Gampo repeated, leaning back. His voice dropped. "By the devil's twisted tail, are you tossin' the notion of stealin' his ship's holdings? Or mayhap his ship from dry dock?" He raised dark menacing brows.

Everett took a moment to gather his nerves. "No, well, yes. In a manner of speaking." If he thought his hand wouldn't shake, he'd lift his mug and attempt a nonchalant swallow. "I can't help you with the second ship. But my proposal is to give you information as to the day, time, and trail of the goods as they are transported from the pier, giving your men an opportunity to lie in wait and relieve them of it. I know the precise place."

He slid a map he'd drawn earlier closer to the men and jabbed it. "The *precise* place, Captain."

Gampo rested his elbows on the table and laced his fingers . "Let's hear it, man."

Everett hunched over the parchment, tracing tiny lines, feeling more confident. "Here is a narrow alley they'll use as a cut-through. There are three recessed doorways as well as an iron stair. It won't be hard to stay hidden in the darkness of the predawn hours. And, I will offer you access to a nearby vacant building where the products can be stored for a time."

He paused, holding his breath. Had he talked too fast? Did he come across as too nervous? The biggest problem would be if Gampo decided to steal his plan and use it for his own means, leaving him out. He must make himself indispensable enough for them to warrant his presence. The impassive expressions on the faces of the three brigands had his stomach churning. Everett dug in his jacket pocket for the key and put it on the edge of the map, but close enough he could grab it back.

The walls in Twin Pines were thin, and it had been easy to eavesdrop on the conversation between Jared Grey, Hart, and O'Brien regarding warehouse rental and transportation. Grey owned several storage properties in Charleston, a few almost empty, due to the time he had to spend at the plantation. There had been only the small matter of unlocking the drawer and borrowing a key from Grey's desk.

Gampo draped his arm lazily across the back of the unoccupied chair next to him. Yet his body stayed tense and coiled. "And what see you as to your part in this plot?"

Everett pulled the items back near his half-empty mug, praying the pirates didn't notice his fingers tremor. He tapped the map. "Along with half the money we get from selling the goods, I need you to apprehend a woman who may not...*realize* that it's in her best interest to leave her current environment. In exchange, I've prepared the base work, found the ideal location, created this map. I know the time of day that will make this stratagem successful."

Pike shoved a piece of meat in his craw, then followed it with a chunk of bread. "'Tis give and take with our lot," he said as he chewed. "Share and share." He glared hard at Everett as he swallowed.

Gampo's smile slowly slit his face. "'Tis the law of the coast. Right mates?"

The two men nodded. Crowe took a long draught of his stout and wiped his mouth with his sleeve before he spoke. "The capt'n and quarter-master gets two shares, the bo'sun and gunner a share an' a half, and officers one an' a quarter. Rest of the crew gets one." He ripped a hunk from the loaf. "That makes ye one of the rest, unless yer one of the other. Which yer not."

Everett's mouth went dry. This venture wouldn't be as profitable as he anticipated. However, the pirates' theft would keep Hart away from Twin Pines thus away from Keelan. If the man was kept busy searching for stolen goods, Everett could continue with his plan to seduce the girl. The best part was that it would cost him nothing.

"Fine, then." Everett pushed the paper and key back toward Gampo. "Share and share. Do we have an agreement?"

Gampo sliced a glance at his men. Crowe gave a nod, and Pike simply shrugged. "On my faith, we have an accord but mark this." Gampo's blade impaled a sausage from the platter. He wiggled the steel tip free from the wooden trencher before raising the sausage to his mouth. He held it there, suspended. Steely eyes locked on to Everett's. "If we're crossed or foul-advised, may I guzzle a bowl of fire and brimstone with the devil if I don't have yer ballocks for breakfast the next day."

CHAPTER FOURTEEN
A SCHEME

C aptain Hart. Would he keep her secrets?

For the next couple of days, Keelan awoke each morning more tense and worried than the day before. Although there were times when her father could rise and move about with less discomfort, his health continued its slow decline. His stomach rebelled against almost everything but a thin broth, and sometimes even that didn't stay with him. Concerned, Dr. Garrison had even traveled to Charleston to purchase a new medicine, hoping it would work better.

To stay busy, Keelan spent the waning morning hours in the kitchen house, learning Ruth's recipes before sitting with the ledgers in her uncle's office in the afternoon. In addition to the plantation books, Uncle Jared had recently asked her to keep his business' records as well. Those activities consumed much of her day, but the distraction pleased her. The most precious time occurred in the minutes following the dawning of each day.

In the small meadow, when she was surrounded by the vibrant scents of late spring, Keelan's burdens fluttered away with the breeze. There, in the subtle light of the Southern morning, she moved through her exercises, thankful for the freedom of movement the boy's garments provided. Only the hiss and swish of blades cut through the tranquil silence surrounding the field hidden in the forest. The escape was rejuvenating, short as it was.

But in the evening, after she slid between the cool sheets of her bed, several nagging concerns blocked the path to slumber.

Had the assassin traced them to Charleston?

How can her father's wellness be restored?

Captain Hart. Too many thoughts about him.

There had been no mention by her uncle of her early training with Daniel. She could only assume the Hart kept his promise of silence. But what of the payment? When would he demand it? Her stomach made an odd little hitch. What would it be?

She clenched her jaw, not accustomed to this wobbly sense of vulnerability. Hart's absence should make her feel more secure. Instead, it caused her to glance over her shoulder several times a day.

Tonight, she opened the doors to the small balcony from her bedchamber and listened to the cicadas while she unpinned her hair. Their song reminded her of a stick clattering along the slats of a wooden fence. Although it was dusk, a moist film clung to her skin.

Which would be worse...to shutter her room against the insects and suffocate in the stagnant air, or leave them open for the occasional puff of breeze, then pray the veil-like sparver draping over her bed would protect her from tiny flying teeth?

She removed the last pin. Her hair fell past her shoulders and blanketed her back. Slaney always said to tame Keelan's tresses was like "trying to still a flame." She walked to the small vanity and dropped the pins into the dish. Pulling her hair to the side, she quickly braided it.

With a sigh, she plopped into bed. Tree frogs joined the chorus of cicadas, creating a woodland cacophony of chirps and twitters, among the undercurrent of humming and clacking.

"What a bloody racket," she muttered. "I'll never understand how the other creatures sleep." She closed the curtains around her bed, then extinguished the candle at the bedside.

Sleep did not come.

Her mind skipped from thought to thought, like a bee buzzing from flower to flower. Too hot to breathe, Keelan climbed out of bed and pulled on a dressing gown. Perhaps her father was still up. She decided to sit with him a while, awake or not.

She crept in bare feet, careful to avoid the creaky boards a third of the way down the hall. The doors were recessed in small alcoves along the hallway. Loud snores emanated from behind Cousin Doreen's, and Keelan suppressed a snort as she slipped past. Outside her father's room, she paused.

The murmur of voices indicated someone else was inside. Curious, she stooped close to the keyhole.

"I would like to see Keelan properly cared for, before I die, Jared."

"Don't talk like that, George," Uncle Jared responded. The hesitation in her uncle's voice drifted under the door.

Her father gave an exasperated huff. "We both know my health is not improving. If anything, I am worse."

"George, as Keelan's guardian, I assure you, I will take excellent care of her," Uncle Jared said. "She's almost twenty. She should wed after harvest season. Pratt is a keen businessman and tripled his family's estates and coffers since he accepted control thirty some years ago. When he dies, Keelan would be one of the largest plantation owners in the state."

Silence.

Keelan winced. The silence meant her father was contemplating Uncle Jared's words. From the duration of the pause, nothing had yet come to his mind that would provide a valid argument against what his younger brother proposed.

Uncle Jared coughed. "Dr. Garrison is interested, but he possesses no experience running a turpentine mill."

"I know," Papa's gravelly voice replied. "He talked to me this morning and asked for her hand in marriage."

An involuntary gasp escaped her lips.

"And did you consent?" Jared asked with the same trepidation that swirled in Keelan's gut.

"I told him I would consider it. I'd almost rather Keelan chose him, since I fear her preferences do not lie with Pratt or country life."

Keelan moved in closer toward the door. He finally acknowledged her desires. It was a small step, but a positive one.

"George," her uncle retorted, "that daughter of yours has sent every young buck in three counties home with their tails twixt their legs. There's a very small pool of fish from which to choose in these parts." Uncle Jared's footfalls paced the floor. "Her husband should be of the ilk who can handle Twin Pines in her best interest. Pratt would see it better done. I cannot continue to split my time between my Charleston business and here for much longer. It's only a matter of time before one of the two begins to show signs of neglect."

Papa hesitated before spoke, "Well, it would be a tremendous comfort to me if she is married and settled soon."

"What about Ahern?"

"Ahern's dead."

Keelan flattened her lips. He *did* lie. Both did. She curled her fists until her nails put tiny half moons into her palms.

Her father sighed. "You're right, Pratt's the better choice. However, I promised Keelan she had until after the ball to make her decision. I doubt another solution will present itself, but I gave her my word. I would much prefer she concur with the decision than object to it."

She leaned back in despair, then froze as the floorboards creaked.

"I will—" Uncle Jared paused. "Did you hear something?"

She clapped her hand over her mouth, whirled and flew down the corridor. The opening click of her father's chamber latch had her ducking into the alcove of Doreen's room. Breathless, she pressed flat into the shadows as the door opened. She dared not move. The dim light fanned out onto the floor. A shadow fell across the floorboards, remaining for several long seconds before it disappeared back into the room. The door shut. When her heartbeat slowed to a more normal pace, she peeked down the corridor. Seeing it vacant, she tiptoed back to her room.

Keelan flopped down on the bed. The sound of her father's feeble, saddened voice tugged at her heart. The past twelve months had been miserable. Her mother's death was so sudden, then Papa's vigor seemed to fail without warning as well. Someone had gone to elaborate lengths to snuff out members of her father's kin in a lethal and gory manner. Only Uncle Jared's family remained whole.

What part did Fynn Ahern play in all this?

She curled into herself. Tears seeped to her pillow. For so many years, she'd prayed for her father to come home, and make more of his time available to her. Now that he was near, it seemed cruel that his tenure was to be so short. Father's death would leave her truly alone.

She swiped the tears from her cheeks. She would not let Uncle Jared destroy her life by demanding she wed a man she didn't love. She desired the opportunity to be independent and pick her own husband, should she decide to marry. She was in America, after all. As Slaney told her, things were different here.

She would *not* create a household mirroring the one in which she grew up. Her resolve locked, she rolled to her back and stared at the ceiling.

She would take the time to study the ledgers first thing tomorrow morning. A willowy idea started to take root in the fertile loam of her mind. As she pondered the situation, a plan began to sprout and blossom. What if she could use Dr. Garrison's interests to her advantage?

15

CHAPTER FIFTEEN
A BETROTHAL

"I will marry you, Dr. Garrison, if my father approves." Keelan fought to keep her voice bright. This plan seemed less crazy and frightening when she was going over it in her bed last night.

If she agreed to marry Garrison, her father would likely give his blessing. He and Uncle Jared would need an alternative plan to finance the plantation. At least that's what she hoped. After reviewing the ledgers, she felt confident she could devise a proposition that all would find agreeable, and may actually succeed in convincing them to allow her to follow her dream. If not, Garrison was far more tolerable than Pratt. She could do worse.

Like marrying Pratt.

Regardless, she would do everything she could to delay the nuptials.

She and Dr. Garrison were seated on the iron bench in Aunt Sarah's garden, near an arbor draped in pale, lavender wisteria blossoms. Hidden from the house by a large magnolia tree, the bench would have been the perfect place for a tryst, or a marriage proposal from the man of her dreams. She fought back a snort.

"Please, Keelan, darling, call me Everett." He reached for her hand. The vision of a chicken's foot came to mind as his cold fingers grasped her own. He tugged her closer. "Your father and uncle can make the announcement at the ball. I should like to marry as soon as possible."

Keelan fought the panic surging in her chest. *Too soon!*

What could she do to prevent his push for an immediate wedding? Fake sickness? Require a special gown be made? That would only buy her a few weeks. She needed more time. "But what about your family?" She finally blurted. "Surely you'll want time to—"

Garrison interrupted. "Not an issue. I don't have a family to accommodate." The frigid, flat tone of his voice made Keelan pause. "Not anymore," he added.

Poor man. "I'm sorry. I didn't know." She waited for him to elaborate, but he kept strangely silent. Perhaps the topic was too unpleasant for him to discuss. Or too new.

"I can see no reason to delay our wedding." Everett smiled stiffly. "Can you?"

Time to take a different tack. Something on which Aunt Sarah would agree. A social faux pas, perhaps.

Clutching her throat in horror, she choked, "I fear people will talk if we rush into a marriage. They will think I have been...*compromised.*" She pressed her palms dramatically to her cheeks, hoping her ruse fooled him. "I couldn't bear the humiliation."

His eyes widened. "Good Lord! That never occurred to me! I would never want to mar my reputation as an honorable gentleman." He reached for her hand and added, "And of course, I would never want to put you through any such embarrassment either, my dear."

Perhaps if she suggested a specific date, he would stop pressing her. "Let's marry on Christmas Day." That might give her enough time. *Might.*

Everett smiled. "Perfect! Plenty of time to spread the word, plan the ceremony, and avoid the gossip mongers." He grasped Keelan's elbow and tugged again, pulling her closer.

She swallowed hard. Good Lord, he was going to kiss her! She clenched her teeth and instinctively turned her head.

"Come, dear Keelan, no one can see us," he whispered. "The bench is completely hidden from view. Grant me a drop of sweet honey from your lips, so I may know what treasures await me in our marriage bed."

His clumsy attempt at poetic prose nearly unlatched the door behind which she had locked away her hysteria, impulsive nature, and reckless tongue. Well, maybe not her impulsive nature.

She squeezed her eyelids shut as his face loomed nearer. Everett's lips pressed to hers in a firm pucker. She could almost feel his teeth behind them. As he pulled away she sighed, relieved it was over.

The doctor gave a contented hum. "My heart is blissfully happy also, my love. Your sigh of rapture warms my soul. I gaze into your eyes, which sparkle like emeralds, and I see such devotion, it makes me weak in the knees."

She blinked, then bit the inside of her cheek. Although she fought to keep her composure, panic-laden laughter welled in her chest like a bottle of shaken ale. Time to flee. *Now.*

She quickly stood. "My dear Everett, you are so eloquent with words." It was all she could do to keep her expression soft. Stoic. Calm. Think doleful thoughts. Recite Ruth's recipe for scones silently in her head... something, *anything* to keep from losing control.

She felt like a butterfly cupped in the hands of a toddler. "I must run this instant and speak with my father. I shall see you at dinner this evening." She hopped up and stepped away from the bench, in case he planned another kiss. Or worse, more nauseating endearments.

"Well, of... of course," he stuttered, smiling sheepishly. "Until tonight then." He reached for her hand, missed, and gave a feeble wave instead.

Moments later, still shaking and biting back nearly hysterical laughter, Keelan closed her bedroom door and leaned against it. God, what had she done? She'd feared Everett would see through her charade, but he did not.

The course was set.

Dr. Garrison believed she wanted to marry him. He'd likely never forgive her deception. Her desperation had climbed to its zenith; she could think of no other way to escape Pratt and plantation life.

Except to run away, which was still a viable option.

Now an avalanche had started, but if she didn't find a way to get out of its path, she'd find herself buried alive.

16

CHAPTER SIXTEEN
A THEFT

Keelan Grey was a *distraction*.

It would be best for Landon if he could push her out of his mind entirely. He had business to attend to in Charleston, the outcome of which could affect the lives of other folks in a most drastic manner.

A wide, damp band of sweat crept around the rim and up the sides of his hat. He wiped his brow again. He'd rented storage space from Jared Grey and wasted no time arranging the transfer of the *Seeker's* cargo. To avoid working long in the heat, they started moving it before sunrise. The last few loads departed the docks, just as the sun rose high enough to add more uncomfortable warmth to the humidity. He was ready to head to a nearby tavern to enjoy a mug of coffee and a small feast with Conal.

He reined his horse down the street where the warehouse stood. Conal took off his hat and waved. Landon returned the salute and spurred his mount to a trot up to the doorway.

"The shipwright started the repairs on the *Seeker*." He dismounted from Orion's back. "The *Desire's* waiting in dry dock. As we suspected, her damage is more severe. After losing Fynn and most of his goods, we can't default on any more obligations. Whichever vessel is seaworthy first, will sail to the next point of delivery and attempt to keep the trade schedule. Is everything secured here?"

Conal dropped his hat back on his head and nodded, "Aye. I'm just waitin' for the last of it to get here, then I'll lock the door and post the sentries."

Landon whirled to face his friend, a tightening in his chest. That meant there was a problem.

"It all left the dock a couple of hours ago," he responded testily. "They should have arrived and been unloaded by now. Damn it all, those wagons carried those bolts of Chinese silks." Their customer paid handsomely in advance for them.

"Perhaps they lost their way," Conal suggested uncertainly. "Who accompanied the last group?"

Landon's paused to think. "Billy was the only member of the crew riding with the last load." His consternation increased and uneasiness churned in his gut. "The rest were locals, so it's unlikely they got lost. I just traveled the same route they would have followed."

He clenched his jaw and inhaled deeply. The boy had left, excited to see his aunt, who lived on the northern fringes of the city. A kind-hearted lad who worked hard for his share, he always seemed eager to show that he was more man than galley boy. No doubt something had gone wrong, and Landon's concern deepened even more.

"I'll rally some men for a search," Conal said.

Landon nodded. He made it a point to take a personal interest in his crew's well-being and livelihood, allowing him to assemble a fiercely loyal group of lads, and his allegiance to them was just as committed. "Choose your men with care," he warned. "If there is foul play involved, you'll need someone in fighting form to guard your back."

Conal rubbed his neck. "It won't be easy, though. I let most of them go on leave. They're likely by now either half in their cups or easing their lust." He gave Landon a wry smile. "And neither puts them in a proper condition to fight."

Hart reached for the door. "Do what you can. I'll retrace my path. We'll need to check the inventory list against the master to determine what's missing."

"I've the list right here." Conal dug a piece of paper from his pocket and handed it to him.

Landon skimmed the list, then put it in his saddlebag. "Mr. Grey should know of other warehouse properties in Charleston besides his own. He might provide advice regarding who might be able to plan and fund a theft like this."

Conal scratched his chin. "They'd have to both provide a hiding place and pay for the dockworkers. Most anyone of significant wealth will be attending Grey's ball."

Landon agreed, his plans following an identical line. "It might be worth my time to inquire later today. We can better prepare to ask the right people the right questions at the ball, in the event we don't locate Billy or the cargo."

Conal cast a sideways glance at Landon. "A visit would also give you ample opportunity to take in more...appealing sights as well, aye?"

He grunted in response. The man had an uncanny knack for reading his mind. Damned if he wasn't thinking how pleasant it would be to see that fiery young vixen again. "Don't you have work to do?" he muttered loud enough for his friend to hear.

Conal chuckled and headed toward the stables. "I couldn't help but notice the regard you took in the lass. Especially since you've never given a woman more consideration past a casual dalliance since—"

"No need to elaborate." Landon cut him off, then shrugged a shoulder. "I can't afford the luxury of anything more than a casual dalliance. Like you, I have a business to run."

Although, there was a time when he rushed back to port from his travels to a wife and a hearth. There was a time when he believed love and marriage between two people was unbreakable. Unfortunately, leaving a beautiful woman home alone while he spent months at sea was a fool's decision.

Conal raised his voice as he walked away. "Well, the lass has spirit. I like her."

He snapped his head around to glare at his friend's back, strangely irritated. "You don't need the distraction, either."

Conal kept walking, but his words carried back to Landon. "I dinna say I was lookin' for one."

Landon adjusted his saddlebags and tightened the girth strap. Truth be told, he couldn't get the chit out of his mind. It was maddening.

Even if he did visit, what then? She was likely by now, betrothed to Pratt, and the rules of polite society demanded he not interfere. Still, he was never one to care much about polite society and their mandates. The only ones commanding his full consideration were those which influenced either his income or his life span.

There was much more to the lady than her obvious beauty and the adventurous side he and Conal witnessed in the early morning mist. She had both a quick mind and rapid reflexes. Sleek and stealthy.

She was brave. The incident with the dog proved it. But it was the look on her face when she observed the interaction between mother and child that gave him pause. For a brief moment, she dropped that shield of indifference, and her expression revealed a yearning like he had never seen before.

Yes, his curiosity had definitely been stirred.

Among other things.

He demanded a kiss in the garden with the good-natured intention of igniting in her a similar shock to the one she gave them earlier. To tease her, to see if he could crumple her confident demeanor a little and expose a bit more of her true nature. He had expected her to turn her head, argue with him or lash out.

It was her reaction to his kiss that had almost brought him to his knees. Her lips had become soft and pliant beneath his, then began responding to his movements and pressure. She had accepted his tongue in surprise, but he also sensed pleasure and passion. Her fingers had plunged into his hair, then moved down over his shoulders to grip his forearms. What had started as a boyish prank to antagonize and taunt had ended in a swirling eddy of dense ardor and roiling desire, well beyond basic physical reaction.

He shook his head in bewilderment. Last night, she prowled through his mind like a sultry green-eyed tigress. He awoke drenched in sweat, hard and throbbing. When he tried to convince himself he had no sincere interest in the girl beyond indifferent curiosity, his body continued to muddle his thinking. The night before, she came to him in his dreams as the waif lunging and sparring, laughing as she removed her scarf...smiling as she slipped out of her shirt. What would it be like to caress the rosy peaks of her breasts? What noises would she make if he kissed the tender skin on the inside of her thigh?

"I said: GIVE MISS GREY MY KINDEST REGARDS."

Conal's shout dispersed the images like a falling boulder to the glassy surface of a lake.

His friend sat astride a roan and had two guns jammed in his belt and several ropes attached to the saddle. A bag of coins jingled at his waist. He was grinning like a damned fool.

Landon scowled. He gave his friend a curt nod and swung up on his horse as smoothly as he could manage, while trying to ignore Conal's chuckles. It was no mean feat, considering the bulge in his breeches. The witch! Even his daydreams betrayed his desire.

"After I recheck the wagon's course, I'll stop and inform the sheriff that a boy has gone missing with the last wagon," Landon stated curtly. "Afterwards, I'll ride out to Twin Pines to speak with Mr. Grey. I expect to be back before nightfall."

"I'll meet you at the Whistling Pig Tavern on the wharf," Conal said as he turned to depart.

"Have the men start from that point and fan out from there. Finding Billy is their primary duty," Landon replied.

Conal's brows furrowed. He nodded, then trotted away. Landon nudged his mount back toward the docks, a knot of worry constricting his chest. He wanted to be hopeful, but something told him Conal's search would be unsuccessful.

17

CHAPTER SEVENTEEN
A STORM APPROACHES

A storm was coming.

In more ways than one. The lunch hour approached, but the events of the day destroyed Keelan's appetite. She had to postpone her plan to discuss her tentative acceptance of Everett Garrison's marriage proposal with her father, because he was sleeping. She hated the effects the medicine had on him.

Keelan fidgeted with her hair; the curtains billowed, inviting her to join the freedom of the breeze outside. As if beckoning, a whinny rent the air from the stables, followed by the angry pounding of a hoof against the stall boards. Her uncle's stallion, Shamrock's Prince, was showing his vexation at being separated from his harem of mares, grazing in the lower pasture.

She brightened. A brisk ride would clear her head and ease her soul a bit. Although she preferred riding in a carriage, she needed to expel additional energy today. Daniel taught her how to handle a mount when she was quite young. There were certain skills the man believed all women should master, even if a cause never arose to put them to use.

Perhaps her father was secretly behind Daniel's tutelage.

Perhaps the commodore had always wanted a son.

A lively stroll through the city would have been more satisfying, but no matter. She would make do with what availed her. She hurried to her room to don her riding habit. Her mind elsewhere, she jumped when a shadow fell across her path.

"Late for another caller?" Her cousin did not attempt to disguise her disdain.

"No, Doreen, there is no caller," Keelan spoke through clenched teeth. Her cousin's spiteful tone grated on her nerves.

"I'm nearly shocked to the point of fainting," Doreen answered, examining a fingernail. "Every eligible bachelor, and even several non-eligible and non-bachelors have found a reason to pay a call on Twin Pines since you arrived." She slid her gaze to Keelan. "Yet, after a few minutes of droll conversation, or a cup of tea, you simply thank them and then depart, leaving me to walk the irate, dejected man to the door. By then, they rarely notice my presence at all."

It wasn't difficult to see through Doreen's vindictive words. Maybe she lashed out because she felt undeserving of a gentleman's attention. Maybe she was just jealous.

"Doreen," She softened her voice. "I'm older. You're only sixteen. Your time will come."

"By that time, no potential husband will want to return." Doreen's voice sounded small and hurt. She raised her chin. "Ladies of the Lowcountry know how to comport themselves. However, I'm not surprised at your behavior, since your upbringing appears to have been somewhat... stunted."

Keelan was determined to control her ire and not cause a scene so close to her father's bedroom door. She refused to let Doreen bait her. "Please let me pass. I'm going for a ride."

Doreen cocked her head. "Your mother's dead. Your father's dying. With no one to monitor your deportment, it's no wonder you act like a rude, uneducated wharf rat. What will become of you when Uncle George dies? A wedding, I think... to Mr. Pratt, I hear."

Keelan squelched the prick of tears at the cold harshness those words brought and brushed past her cousin. As she closed her door, the faint notes of Doreen's humming drifted down the corridor. That girl needed a pastime.

Keelan changed quickly and was heading for the front door when she heard a sudden crash in the study. Wasn't Papa in his room? Perhaps he awoke and decided to read over the ledgers she'd finished. In his weakened state, he would have a hard time navigating around the furniture. She dashed down the hall, fearing father had fallen, or worse.

She rounded the corner to find Dr. Garrison staring at the shattered remains of her father's model ship, scattered on the floor. She paused, startled by his appearance. The doctor's lips were nothing more than a thin slash separating his nose from his chin. He stood rigid as a wooden post, fists at his sides.

"Dr. Garrison?" There was something about his posture that made interrupting him seem like a bad idea. Frightening, even. Stepping into the room, she kept her voice calm and soft. "Are you all right?"

He jerked as if physically prodded. A tattered piece of paper fluttered to the floor behind him. "I... yes. I..." His eyes returned to the broken model. "It seems I have caused your father's ship to break."

"Think no more about it," she said as she inched toward him. "Accidents do happen. My father of all people would understand that."

His nostrils flared in response, but whatever his thoughts, he didn't speak them out loud. He sank to his knees and began picking up the pieces, leaving her to stare at his back for a moment, trying to decipher his mood and find the right words to help lighten it.

The paper he'd dropped when she entered caught her eye and she picked it up. It was soft from frequent handling, the edges slightly rounded, the creases like hinges. The fold on the lower third was in tatters and it flapped open, revealing an elegant script and the faint scent of roses. It said:

... and I look forward to our wedding day with a joyful heart.

Yours Always,

Rachel

Her new fiancee's past was a mystery to her, although he'd informed her he had no family. He'd been educated in London and was born in the United States, but that was all she knew about the man.

The doctor finished collecting the fragments and placed them on the desk. He turned toward her, and his eyes widened when he noticed the note in her hands.

"This was on the floor behind you," she hastened to explain, already feeling guilty at having read part of a very personal note, even if it was accidental. She handed it to him, the bottom flapping back open. "Is it yours?"

"It's torn!" he cried hoarsely, accepting it with both hands and cradling it like a broken-winged bird.

"I... I'm sorry," she replied. "When I picked it up, I didn't realize it was in such a fragile condition."

He gently closed the missive along its creased folds and tucked it into his inner coat pocket. They stood for a moment, not speaking. The doctor cleared his throat, breaking the awkward silence.

"I... yes... the letter's mine," he said, finally making eye contact with her.

The anguish in his expression made her press a hand against her chest. "I can tell it's precious to you." What else should she say to her fiancé?

What else don't I know about you?

She desperately wanted to say those words but didn't dare.

She should feel jealous, at least a tiny bit, but she didn't. In fact, the understanding that he was probably still in love with another woman oddly comforted her.

"Rachel is...was...my fiancée a few years ago." His voice was thick with emotion. "She died tragically."

How awful for the doctor; he had obviously been in love with Rachel. "I'm so sorry for your loss."

"Thank you." His voice sounded detached from his body, as if it came from a ghost standing next to him. "Well." He shoved his hands into his pockets. "I should check on your father. If you will excuse me... "

"Yes, of course." She stepped aside and let him go. A husband like him would never make her giddy with happiness, but now her chest tightened and her stomach swirled in a sickening spiral. His melancholy spirit surrounded her and poked hard at her apprehension. She'd been certain she could suffer this marriage, now she wasn't as sure.

Good Lord, what had she done?

❧ 18 ❧

CHAPTER EIGHTEEN
A WILD DECISION

K eelan needed to do something bold to expend the nervous energy pulsing through her body.

The interactions with Dr. Garrison and her spoiled cousin, combined with the heavy still air of late morning, pulled at her spirits as she left the house. Normally, she'd have asked Slaney to join her, but today she wanted to be alone to sort out her life. She hoped a ride across the farm would buoy her mood, although in the back of her mind she pondered the idea of just riding away and never returning.

She turned in the direction of the barn. In exchange for overseeing the plantation business, her father had granted Uncle Jared use of a substantial tract of land, where he built an impressive stable filled with some of the finest stock in Charleston. They would someday be part of Doreen's dowry.

She paused at the small paddock nearby. Several brood mares stood under the immense oak tree on the far side. She whistled softly.

One of the round-bellied creatures turned her head and perused her for a moment before turning to plod toward her. The mare lifted her nose over the fence and nuzzled Keelan's sleeve.

"Good afternoon, Juliet, my love," she crooned as she stroked the sleek blue-gray neck. "I wish you were able come with me today, but alas, in your delicate condition, 'tis best you reserve your strength."

A voice spoke near her elbow. "She should be droppin' her foal any day now, Miss Keelan."

She turned to find one of the young stable hands staring at the gentle mare. The boy had a nasty welt across his cheek. She inspected the mark, narrowing her eyes.

"Thomas, what happened to your face?"

He stared at his bare feet. "It ain't nothin,' Miss Keelan. Only a scratch."

Unconvinced, but unsure what to say, she returned her attention to the mare. "Juliet is moving slowly today. I don't think she's very comfortable." She gazed worriedly over the mare's bulging sides.

"Don' you worry none, Miss Keelan. Seamus say she lookin' fine, so she is. He been at dis a long time, so he knows things."

Keelan smiled brightly. "I shall place my trust in Seamus then. Since I cannot ride my favorite palfrey, would you please saddle Camilla for me?"

The boy glanced away. "I can't do dat, Miss. She not here. Miss Doreen told me to turn her out in the lower valley."

Undaunted, she shrugged. "I understand." Juliet nudged her arm again, and Keelan rubbed her muzzle gently. "Would you please saddle Uncle Jared's gelding?"

Thomas shook his head. "Mastah Jared rode him this mornin' down to the mill."

She sighed and gestured toward the barn and adjoining pasture. "It doesn't matter, Thomas, you may prepare any one of the other mares."

The boy dug his toe into the dust. "Sorry, Miss Keelan, I can't."

She stopped stroking the horse. "Why not?" she asked.

He mumbled, "Miss Doreen said she'd flog my hide if I let you ride any of her daddy's mares."

Keelan bristled. So Doreen was responsible for the ugly welt. It was within her rights to override her cousin's order, but she wouldn't dare place Thomas in a position that would tempt Doreen's rage.

"Miss Keelan?"

She tried to mask her agitation. Juliet gave up on Keelan and nuzzled Thomas's sleeve. He absently reached into his pocket, pulled out a crust of bread. She delicately accepted the treat from the groom's palm.

"I'm awfully sorry, Miss Keelan. The only ones Miss Doreen say I can saddle for you is Ole Poke, or..." he swallowed.

"Or?" Keelan questioned. She raised her eyebrows suspiciously. There was only one other option.

The groom darted a glance toward the thumping sounds emanating from the rear of the barn. "Or Shamrock's Prince. Mister Jared's stud."

She clenched her jaw and scanned the pasture for Old Poke. He stood lazily in the shade of a large, gnarly tree. The aged mule casually flipped his tail in a half-hearted attempt to shoo the flies from his backside. She shuddered.

No. She might as well sit on a pile of bouncing rocks.

Old Poke was an option she refused to consider. He was no more desirable than the past suitors her cousin escorted to the door.

Keelan frowned. No doubt, Doreen only included Sham on the short list of available mounts because she didn't believe Keelan would dare attempt to ride the beast. It nettled her sorely to think of Doreen's pale, pampered face spying on her from the window.

Gloating.

Keelan set her mouth in grim determination. She'd not give her cousin today's amusement by riding a lumpy old mule. Decision made, she tried to ignore Sham's impatient kicking. The rhythmic pounding against the boards echoed her heart, ramming her ribs.

"Now, Miss Keelan," Thomas said nervously while he peered up at her, expression wary. "Lemme hustle up and saddle Old Poke for you to take on a nice easy, stroll around the plantation. He'll be fine for a spell at a slow pace. Besides, Ruth's bones say we got a big storm a comin'. You might want to stay close by."

"Humph!" Keelan couldn't restrain a snort. If she abandoned the ride and returned to the house, the humiliation of conceding the afternoon to Doreen would be unbearable. She turned and bestowed a radiant smile on the groom.

"Would you please saddle Sham for me?"

Thomas' forehead creased. "Please, Miss Keelan...dat horse is well-trained, but he's a strong 'un. You could git real hurt if he gits a mind to take the bit in his teeth and run."

Laughing lightly, more carefree than she truly felt, she waved his remarks aside. "I'll be fine, Thomas. I've been riding since I was ten years old." Just not recently. And never a stallion. And rarely without a carriage attached.

The young groom expelled his breath in a soft whoosh before ambling to the stable, as if his pace might change her mind. It was several minutes before he led the prancing steed from the barn. He steered the horse to the hitching post farthest away from the brood mares, but the strong-willed stud had other plans. While arching his noble neck and raising his tail like a banner, he trotted toward the pasture, dragging poor Thomas along like a ribbon in the wind. After a few mumbled curses and more than a few stumbles, he finally regained his footing enough to give an irritated yank on the lead, abruptly gaining the stallion's attention.

"Whoa, there, Sham!" he said, annoyed.

The mares paused from grazing as the stallion pranced. Keelan sucked in her breath. Even on this overcast day, Sham's chestnut coat rippled like liquid copper.

Thomas secured the horse and moved to help Keelan mount.

"Sometimes I think the devil hisself sired this cantankerous, mule-headed horse," he muttered, rubbing his trampled foot.

Biting back a smile, she cautiously reached up to caress the velvety nose. "Now, Sham, my good man, do be a gentleman today and provide a well-mannered seat for me."

The horse nuzzled her empty hand then stomped a long foreleg in impatient irritation.

Pausing near the stirrup, she tilted her head up to Sham's back, two hands taller than the top of her head, and took a slow breath. She could do this. He was just a horse.

A very tall horse.

Swallowing hard, she tried to ignore the trepidation flapping wildly in the hollow of her stomach.

The slave stood rigid as Keelan adjusted her feet in the stirrups. Taking the reins in her hands, she finally exhaled. Successfully riding a horse depended on the confidence of the rider. Confidence came with experience, experience came with repetition.

As for repetition, she rode a lot as a child, but not recently. She'd had plenty of experience riding her gelded pony in England. Big horses the size of Sham... well, there was a first time for everything, was there not?

She relaxed her shoulders. Horses always seemed to sense the demeanor of their riders. Just another sunny day on a horse. She peered up at the distant clusters of clouds. Sunny for a time, anyway.

Daniel had taught her skill and trust control a steed. Hopefully she had the skill. She was a little thin on trust with this huge beast.

She carefully reined the horse toward the lane. The stallion's muscles quivered beneath her like threads of contained fire. The opportunity to stretch his long legs was near at hand, and he broke into an impatient trot, then a restless, short-gaited canter. Keelan tightened the reins and spoke in what she hoped was a calm, authoritative tone. "Whoa, sir! Allow me to prepare my seat and hands."

The horse complied, showing his eagerness to fly only by swishing his tail in short, jittery swings.

Keelan fidgeted. She wanted to go for a gallop. Did she possess the strength to slow the stallion if he became stubborn?

Confidence. Yes, she could.

She allowed him to trot again, then pulled him back to a walk. He was well trained, for sure. Repeating the exercise a few more times had her more relaxed and confidant.

Much better.

As they approached the house, she glanced at the upper windows, noticing the curtains at Doreen's window flutter briefly.

"You will not have satisfaction today, cousin," Keelan muttered.

Seconds later, Doreen burst out of the front door, startling Keelan and sending Sham into a startled sidestep that almost unseated her. It took every bit of her concentration to prevent the horse from bolting. An angry admonition on her lips, she turned toward her foolish cousin, but Doreen's gaze focused on a lone horseman approaching from the main road. Keelan didn't need to wait for him to get closer. From the broad shoulders and straight back to the shiny black boots, it was obvious the rider was that arrogant rake, Captain Landon Hart.

She groaned. What brought the man all the way out here today?

I'll collect my due another day, sweet Keelan.

The earlier wiggles of trepidation hatched into a swarm of butterflies that flitted from her stomach to her toes and back. She shook her head. She was making more out of their encounter than she should, certainly.

"Good morning!" Doreen's voice cut through the humid air. "Welcome to Twin Pines!" If the girl knew what a scoundrel he was, she wouldn't be waving and smiling as he approached.

He tipped his hat at Doreen. "A fine morning it is, Miss. And thank you for the kind welcome. Landon Hart, at your service." He turned to Keelan; his white teeth gleamed against his sun-darkened face. "Miss Grey, you look radiant today. It's a pleasure to see you again."

Doreen's smile faded. The glare she threw at Keelan could have burned a hole through a rock. Hart appeared not to notice as he focused solely on the horse and *her*. Keelan fought to keep her expression neutral, not to mention Sham calm, as the man moved his gaze from her perky green hat down to her hem and back up again. The urge to turn her heel into Sham's side and flee almost overpowered her sense of decorum and common sense in general. She may be a tad impetuous, but she was not stupid. Instead, she returned the greeting as politely as she could manage. Slight tip of the head. No smile.

"Good morning, Captain Hart. What brings you back to Twin Pines so soon?" Dare she hope it was simply business?

"Back?" Doreen said, confused.

Keelan rolled her eyes. If the girl got out of bed before lunch, she'd know more.

Hart's expression sobered. "I'm afraid there's been a theft of some of our goods, and I've come to seek your uncle's advice." He dismounted and loosened the saddle's girth strap to allow his horse to cool down.

Keelan stiffened. "Are you accusing my uncle of stealing your cargo?" she asked. That would be a bold accusation.

He shook his head, his mouth set in a flat line. "Not at all. Our shipment was being moved to one of his warehouses farther from the waterfront. At some point, some wagons disappeared, and a young boy is now missing. I merely need to take advantage of his knowledge of the area, so our search has a better chance of yielding results."

Keelan frowned, concerned for the boy. "Have you alerted the sheriff?"

"Yes, and my entire crew is combing the city of Charleston."

A search party of that size should be able to find the child. Hart sauntered over and ran a hand along Sham's neck and shoulder. He gave a long, low, appreciative whistle. "A very handsome steed."

Doreen chirped from the porch. "He's my father's. The plantation might belong to Keelan's, but the horses belong to mine— her uncle. The man to whom you wish to speak." She raised her chin and gave him a condescending smile.

"Is it any wonder why the girl has no suitors?" Keelan mumbled under her breath as she adjusted the reins. She caught an amused grin from Hart and couldn't help but smile back. His eyes sparkled with humor and for a second, she couldn't break eye contact. Maybe she didn't want to.

His responding wink made those annoying butterflies dive to her knees, and she almost had to remind herself to breathe. She hated the way her belly misbehaved when he was near. It would help if he wasn't so handsome. He was likely thinking about the secrets he kept for her. She welcomed the annoyance that last thought brought with it. It was less frightening than the strange pull, which tugged at her earlier.

"Do you ride this stallion often?" The captain's tone was casual, but the humor had left his eyes. "He seems quite spirited for a lady."

She patted Sham's neck. "Although this is our first outing together," Keelan almost spoke without sounding breathless, "I have complete confidence that we will get along fine." Her last few words came out sharper than she intended, but the captain was undaunted, and continued to question her equestrian skills.

His deep blue eyes reflected the concern in his voice. "Don't you think you might better enjoy riding a more gentle mount? One that would offer you a more relaxed experience?"

Yes.

Keelan gave Doreen a pointed stare which was returned with a sly smile. "Unfortunately, there are none nearby." She nodded toward the bank of clouds in the distance. "We might get some rain later, and I wanted to be back before it began, so I don't plan to be gone long."

"If you linger until my business with Mr. Grey is concluded, I would be happy to escort you." Landon ran his long tanned fingers through Sham's coppery mane as he talked. Keelan followed them, remembering the touch of his hands in her hair not too many days ago. It was only the sound of her cousin's voice that broke her concentration.

"I'm sure Keelan is eager to be on her way," she said.

It appeared only Keelan heard the snide undertone, as Landon continued to gaze at her while still stroking his fingers through the mane.

Doreen persisted. "Come inside, Captain Hart, and I'll have Ruth make you some tea while I have Simon fetch my father."

Keelan wasn't sure why it irked her that Doreen did her best to pull the captain's attention away, but she found herself wanting to stifle the attempt. "You can escort me as far as the mill," she said to Landon. "I was told my uncle rode his gelding there earlier. You'll be able to discuss your concerns with him immediately, rather than await him here. You said a young boy is missing, so it appears your need to see him is most urgent."

Hart flashed her an easy grin, returned to his mount and swiftly tightened the girth strap. He tipped his hat to Doreen and settled into the saddle. "Thank you for the hospitality, Miss. A pleasant afternoon to you."

Doreen's jaw clenched through the stiff smile she gave to the captain. "I hope to see you again soon, Captain." She gave Keelan a stony glance before she twirled, snatched the door open, and stomped inside the house.

Sham pranced sideways. She spoke to the horse in what was hopefully an authoritative tone to quiet him. He settled down a bit, but still snorted his impatience in response to her tightening the reins. How she wanted to let the beast stretch his legs!

She chanced a quick glance toward Landon. Perhaps her handling of her mount eased his concerns. Especially, since he'd probably have something annoying to say if she told him her current thoughts, such as *How fast could such a powerful animal run?*

To Shams great disappointment, they walked. A tangy scent of pine and earth wafted from the wood. This particular lane meandered through the entire plantation, connecting the homestead to the fields, mill, slave cabins, and farmland. It was broad enough for Twin Pine's lumber wagons to haul timber from the surrounding forests to the mill, making a ride through the countryside mostly free of strangers and other riders, as well as peaceful.

Stern gray clouds mottled the bright blue sky, giving them some respite from the hot June sun. Landon glanced up. "It appears we will indeed have some foul weather before the day is done."

She followed his gaze. "At breakfast, Ruth predicted rain, and Uncle Jared concurred. He'd originally planned to go into Charleston but decided to wait another day or so, to avoid miring the carriage in the mud near the lower creek crossing again." She shifted in her seat to balance her weight a bit better. "That's why he's working at the mill office today."

"Tis my good fortune then," Landon said.

At Keelan's curious look, he elaborated, "Otherwise I wouldn't have the opportunity to enjoy such pleasant sights." His crystalline gaze never wavered from hers.

He was *flirting* with her. The completely innocent expression on his face didn't fool her in the slightest. He turned his head and looked down the lane lined with oaks, Spanish moss dripping off their branches like a tattered veil.

No quirking eyebrow, no wink, no ornery grin.

He was up to something.

Keelan loosened the reins, and Sham quickly stepped up to a perky trot.

"I'm in no hurry," Landon said, urging his mount next to hers. "In fact, a slower pace allows me to savor your company longer."

She smirked. As much as she'd like to entertain him and respond with some witty cut, she knew better than to encourage him. "Has it occurred to you I might not wish to extend our time together? It seems to me the more we interact, the more trouble I seem to encounter."

"You wound me deeply." Hart's smile was anything but wounded.

Actually, the blue heat in his gaze spoke to a different affect. The warmth pulsing around her neck and chest was certainly due to restrictiveness of her riding habit, not the closeness of Captain Hart. Truthfully, if she were alone, she would have traded comfort for propriety and removed her hat and jacket and tied them to the back of her sidesaddle.

Perhaps later.

She couldn't bite back the smile as she imagined how refreshing it would be to have the breeze comb her hair. There was something deliciously exhilarating about a breathtaking gallop. Now that the thought had invaded her mind, the more appealing a gallop became. She chanced a sly glance at Hart. She loved competition. He must too. What man did not? Other than Dr. Garrison.

"What is your horse's name, Captain?"

He reached down and gave his mount a firm pat on the side of the neck. "This is Orion."

The horse was as tall and elegant as Sham, except he was the darkest black she'd ever seen. "He's beautiful. Is he very fast?"

He gave her a humble shrug. "He's swift enough. According to your uncle, Orion's from excellent stock. I bought him at Mr. Grey's suggestion. He said he was as fine as any he owned."

"Hmm." She perused the horse. "Let's see, shall we?" She patted Sham's neck and crooned, "Now then my handsome steed, lets give the wind a sporting chase." She slid a glance his way. "On the count of three, Captain?"

Surprise blanked his face before he flattened his lips. "I'd prefer not."

"One..." she said.

His eyebrows plunged down. "Miss Grey, I strongly advise——

"Two..."

The next words were a low growl. "I will not —

"Three!"

She relaxed her grip on the reins and took a fistful of mane for added stability. The stallion needed no further urging. His muscles bunched beneath her as he leapt forward, eager to stretch his legs. She faintly registered the angry shout behind her. Soon, they were flying with joyful abandon down the lane. She laughed in giddy delight while Sham's strides beat a steady rhythm on the turf. It wasn't long, however, before she heard Orion's hoof beats getting louder.

Small clods of earth flew up in their wake as they burst out of the woods and raced along the outskirts of one of the fields. A small group of slaves paused in their labors and watched their flight as they thundered past.

Although Sham worked up a lather on his neck and flanks, his breathing wasn't labored. In fact, he still strained against the bit. How fast would he go if she let him set the pace? She pulled on the reins, but the horse did not respond. She pulled back again, harder this time, and tried to ignore the panicked band tightening around her chest.

She threw all her weight back in the saddle and added a shouted command, then another. She expelled a breath she didn't realize she was holding when Sham hitched his gait, allowing her to eventually slow him to an easy canter as they neared the mill.

Thank goodness.

A triumphant laugh exploded from her chest when she succeeded in reining in the animal. "Come now, Sham. I need to catch my breath, even if you do not!"

After a few prancing steps of half-hearted rebellion, the horse heeded her instruction and slowed to a reluctant walk. Hart reined in beside her and shot her a thunderous glare.

"What's wrong, Captain?" she quipped breathlessly, "Not used to being outrun by a woman?"

"Little fool!" His tone was harsh. He reached over and grabbed Sham's bridle. The horse threw up his head, nostrils flaring. The close proximity of Hart's mount agitated the beast, but Landon held the bridle and gave Sham a firm command. When he finally settled, she was once again the recipient of his heated gaze.

"You're just upset that you lost," she countered, trying to divert his anger. It actually *was* foolish. She wasn't sure what she'd have done if she hadn't been able to slow the horse. She bit her lower lip. Her heart was still slamming a staccato in her chest, betraying her act of bravado. She was grateful the captain couldn't hear it, or he'd guess how close she'd been to losing control.

"Your horse could have hit a rut in the trail and gone down with you on him!" Captain Hart's face was dark as a storm. "You could have broken your pretty little neck," he said fiercely.

Pretty little neck?

"Well, he didn't, as you can well see." She adjusted her reins to avoid looking at him. She had to admit that while the ride was exhilarating, it had also been mildly terrifying. Well, maybe a tad more than mildly.

"I'm not some helpless little chit," she added, in case he was thinking so.

"Oh, you have proven that to the point of redundancy," Hart ground out. His eyes practically sparked with blue fire. "It's the reckless nature of your decisions I find most infuriating. Approaching rabid dogs. Riding at a full gallop on a dangerous mount you obviously can't control—"

"Well, that really should be none of you concern, should it?" she snapped back, annoyed at her cowardice.

Stand up to the man. He has no power over you.

Despite lifting her chin and easing back her shoulders, it was hard to keep from shrinking away like a chastised child, even though in hindsight, it was indeed reckless. Perhaps even stupid. His glare scraped her pride like a gravel path to a bare knee just the same.

His kiss had set her on fire. She had to be honest about that. But one kiss would not wilt her. One secret would not control her. "I can take care of myself. Go find some small-minded strumpet from whom to charm kisses. I'll not be a pretty piece for you to use while your boat is being repaired. I'm not looking for a... a... liaison." Mother would be proud of her for saying that.

An odd expression fluttered across Captain Hart's face, and for once, he had no retort.

She nodded toward the mill ahead, her confidence almost refilled. Except there'd be no more gallops for her today. "You'll find Uncle Jared in the office."

He released her, his expression blank, voice flat. "It would be best if you returned to the stables before the rain starts."

Yes, it would be.

"I will when I'm ready," she replied, not about to concede anything at the moment. The thrill left her empowered, strong. She had sole control of her next decision. "I'd like to follow the trail ahead a bit further, first." She reined Sham away before Hart could grab the reins again. "Good day, Captain Hart."

Sham jumped to a quick trot as soon as she relaxed her grip. She allowed the horse to progress into a slow canter as they moved on down the lane. Resisting the urge to check the captain's reaction, she hoped she appeared more confident than she actually felt.

❦ 19 ❦

CHAPTER NINETEEN
A SCANDALOUS DIP

L andon Hart was *dangerous*.
      She may not be very experienced in the ways of men, but she was sharp-witted. Something told her that Hart's charm had been well-honed on young women like her. It made her even more bent on resisting him. At least, that would be the smart thing to do.

The thick air pressed Keelan's clothing against her skin like a damp blanket. A trickle of perspiration carved a pathway down the side of her face and along her jaw, before continuing down her neck. Once she rode beyond the sight of the mill, she doffed both her waistcoat and bonnet and tied them to the back of her saddle. Propriety be damned in this heat. She was thankful Slaney pinned her hair high up off her nape this morning.

That merchant captain was entirely too flirtatious.

Stop thinking about him.

She wasn't sure how to shield herself from his charm, which was a huge predicament. Something about him made her temperature rise, and when that happened, she didn't trust herself to make unerring choices.

When she was a girl, and needed to clear her mind or ponder the solution to a problem, she always took to a horse, dragging along whatever household servant she persuaded to join her. In town, she went by carriage, but when they stayed at the country house, she rode, which was only occasionally.

This ride was no different from the ones in the past, aside from two small exceptions.

She had no chaperone, and she was on a giant horse, not a pony.

She shook her head in self-chastisement. Again, a rash decision on her part had her teetering on the precipice of disaster. When would she learn? If she'd paused long enough to think her actions through, she could've brought Slaney (although the maid would have likely never forgiven her for being left to ride Old Poke).

Perhaps Keelan inherited this particular personality flaw from Papa, who was eccentric in his own right. She frowned as her musings turned toward her father.

His prognosis was terrible, and the thought of losing him dropped a cold ache in her heart. As much as she wanted to squeeze her eyes closed and wish the trepidation away, she could not.

She gripped the reins a little tighter. To stand idly by and avoid preparing for her future would sentence her to years of dull misery with Everett.

The only bright spot was that at least she might avoid old man Pratt now. It was obvious he overindulged in food and wine by his stature and his bulbous red nose. Since servants and slaves tended to gossip amongst themselves, Slaney had been able to provide Keelan with several lurid stories of strange sounds emanating from the master's bedroom at night. Becoming Pratt's bride churned up a wave of nausea.

She'd run away first. She'd—

Her shoulders fell. No, a devoted daughter would stay by her ill sire's bedside. She was tugged in divergent directions of duty and self-preservation. She couldn't have one without forfeiting the other. His health only declined, although he was still lucid enough to plan her future from his sickbed.

If her recent scheme worked, she was likely rid of Pratt, thanks to Dr. Garrison.

If her father and uncle agreed with her proposal, she would break the betrothal. She brushed away the guilt that accompanied that last thought. She truly didn't want to hurt the doctor.

In love. Ugh.

Unbidden, Landon Hart's chiseled face intruded into her mind again. "Stop," she groaned to herself. She had to admit she longed to show Captain Hart she wasn't some boyish twit intent on playing games in a meadow. She wanted him to recognize her as a woman, confident and capable. She squared her shoulders.

And totally in control of her destiny (and her mount—for the most part).

She blew a stray curl from her cheek and gave a resigned sigh. Except acting on that desire would demand she play the same game with Hart as he played with her. And it was a *game,* that was certain. Hart's attentions were based on nothing other than his desire to seduce her.

Even if his intentions were honorable, happiness with a sea captain as a husband would elude her. What woman could stand being abandoned for months at a time, never knowing when, or if, her husband would return, especially one with a vendetta against a pirate?

"Augh!" Swatting the air in front of her as if batting away the image, she muttered, "Leave me be!"

Her stomach grumbled loudly, and she regretted not bringing something to eat. Although the sun remained hidden behind the leaden gray clouds, she estimated it was past noon. Thomas had kindly strapped a canteen to her saddle, and she retrieved it and sipped until it was gone.

Sham flicked his ears forward and back, taking in the surrounding countryside. The stallion hesitated, sampled the wind, and spun around to scan the lane behind them.

"What do you hear, my fine steed?" she murmured. Absently stroking his glistening neck, she tried to peer into the trees.

Nothing.

"Are you seeing ghosts, sir?" A slight breeze shifted the upper branches of the towering pines on each side of the path. "I fear you'd be worthless in a fight. 'Tis fortuitous you have such a swift stride. At least you can outrun your foes."

She reined him back around and they continued along the wide trail. They passed three shanties in various states of dilapidation. One still had most of its roof, but the other two were little more than piles of clapboards, shingles, and sandstone. A sudden scurrying within the weeds near one of the structures startled Sham; he shied away to the side, while keeping a wary eye on the monster in the grass.

"It's likely a rabbit, you big coward." Keelan smiled. "Honestly, for such a grand creature, you really should be a bit braver."

As the soil changed from red clay to sand, Sham's ears twitched, and he sniffed the air again, then huffed. He stopped and pranced a few obstinate paces to the left.

This was new territory for her. How far had they traveled from the mill? It was probably best she head back. Surely Hart was finished with Uncle Jared by now and on his way back to Charleston. Glancing up at the sky, the bank of clouds still crouched on the horizon signaling a storm, but not for a while.

Curious, she allowed the stallion to follow his nose.

"I imagine you'll soon have us both miles away, all because you've discovered the scent of a dainty little filly," she mumbled dryly. A few moments later, they emerged out of the forest to the border of an immense lake.

"Ohhhh!" she breathed. "How beautiful." She gaped at the pristine scene before her. So *this* was the largest lake on the plantation. It was much bigger than she'd imagined.

The balmy breeze rustled through tall pines near the water's edge, making the wispy boughs sway lazily. A purple-tinged haze meandered between the rippling surface of the lake and the solemn sky. Cypress trees stretched gnarled roots toward the water and hunched close to the shore like a cluster of hags sharing a secret. Spanish moss hung from the branches in long, graceful ringlets.

Sham plunged forward. When he reached knee-depth, he lowered his head.

"You were thirsty, too." Keelan stroked his neck. They were standing at the point of a small inlet. Without traveling the entire shoreline, it was impossible to determine how many other thin fingers of land extended into the waters.

A splash shattered her reverie. Water doused her ankles and thighs. She hardly had time to catch her breath before another current of water walloped her full on the chest.

Keelan blinked through the rivulets streaming down her face as the ornery beast lifted his front hoof above the water and slammed it down with determined force a third time.

"You brute!" she coughed, hauling back on the reins and forcing him into a hasty retreat. "If you wanted your belly cooled down, you needed only to take two steps forward!" Her clothes were splattered with water. "You have soaked me to the skin!"

The horse did not act the least bit chagrined and walked forward to take a few more swallows.

How was she going to explain a wet riding habit? Her aunt and uncle would discern how far from the main house she'd wandered. There would be no avoiding her uncle's ire now. Unless she managed to dry before she returned. Keelan licked her lips and gazed at the bright, fresh water as it rippled and twinkled. She plucked at her dampened collar. It had been itchy with perspiration before Sham had soaked it. The cooler water was quite refreshing. It would be lovely to... She glanced around. She was very much alone.

As usual, she made up her mind in a blink. She'd never bathed anywhere but a tub; the anticipation of crisp water against her over-heated skin made her almost laugh aloud. She nudged Sham to the grassy clearing, hopped down, loosened the girth a little, and reached for her new hat and coat.

They were both gone!

She stared for a moment at the empty straps and shook her head, perplexed. She would have to keep a keen eye while retracing her path home. Hopefully, she would find the wayward garments along the route, no worse for wear.

Keelan hobbled Sham and secured the reins where he wouldn't step on them. With a quick pat on the rump, she sent the horse sauntering toward a tuft of sweet grass.

It took an exasperating amount of time to wiggle out of her skirt and drape it over a craggy boulder. Her chemisette soon followed.

Keelan paused. Would she be able to re-tie the stays by herself? Why hadn't that question entered her mind *before* she disrobed?

She huffed in resignation. It was too late to undo her latest rather impulsive decision, so she might as well enjoy herself for a short time and deal with the clothing problem later.

She pulled off her shift. The sun-warmed heat of the stone would dry her clothes before she needed them again. She kicked off her boots, excitement bubbling as she approached the sandy edge. This was going to feel *marvelous*.

The first step into the water was heavenly. She wiggled her toes and waded further. *Sublime*. Moaning, she immersed to her neck then froze. Wearing a sopping garment under her clothes might be more than a little uncomfortable.

However, no lady of the Lowcountry would dare bathe outside completely...naked. She snorted. No lady of the Lowcountry would snort or dare to strip down to her chemise for a dip in a lake.

It was scandalous.

The corners of her mouth tipped up.

But then, she was not a "Lady of the Lowcountry," was she?

It was more a matter of practicality than morality.

Rising out of the water, she wrenched the garment over her head. At least half the pins Slaney used in her hair this morning had fallen out during the ride after she removed her hat. The coiffure ruined, she pulled the remaining pins out and tossed them near the dripping chemise.

Chances were, she was already mired in trouble. First and foremost, she took out her uncle's prized stud without permission. Second, she left with no escort. Third, she went beyond the mill which was supposed to be the limit of her explorations. Not to mention the fact she'd never get her riding habit on correctly, and unless she found a way to sneak into the house unseen, there'd be no way to hide that she'd removed it.

Doubtless there were more reasons, but they didn't carry the weight of the first three. She'd probably be forbade to ride ever again, have to sit with Aunt Sarah in the front room and work on needlepoint, or banished to her room. Maybe all three.

Maybe Papa and Uncle Jared would forbid her to attend the ball. They'd be doing her a favor if they did.

She eased back into the silky depths. She was free for the moment and it was *thrilling*. The water moved over her naked limbs in tender, soothing strokes, like an angel's caress. If she weren't in such an exuberant state of bliss, she might have felt absolutely wicked. Taking a deep breath, she dipped beneath, careful to remain at a depth where her feet still touched. She expelled a lungful of bubbles before she popped back up, breaking the sparkling shell of the lake's surface.

A partially submerged rock a few paces away coaxed her a little deeper. The water was almost up to her neck. She grasped the boulder and leaned on a narrow ledge. It made a perfect hand rest. Lying back, Keelan held on and fluttered her legs from the bottom to float. The sky was darker to the east, but patches of blue still peeked through.

She wanted to arrive home before her uncle and the rain, so she would not tarry overlong. Closing her eyes, she inhaled and released a contented, relaxed sigh. A bird warbled nearby and his mate soon answered. The sun had emerged from hiding; it warmed her cheeks and breasts. Cool air flickered over her body, and her nipples hardened with its breath. The faint, soft thread of jasmine danced on the wind and mingled with the sharp tang of pine and heady scent of earth and water.

Her rumination drifted along as well. She pictured a pair of twinkling, azure eyes and an amused smirk. Her brow wrinkled as her mother's warning echoed in her head.

"There's no settling down for a man of the water. He'll pledge his troth to you to be sure, but his lady is the sea, and she ever beckons him home. In time, he'll leave you for her charms. They always do."

Slaney said as much earlier today.

Certain many women had been lured to Hart's bed by his rakish good looks and charming wit. It would be best to forget about the impression left by his hand on her wrist and his thigh against her own. Forget about the enticing feather of his lips on her palm. Forget about the gravelly sound of his voice.

Her own flesh burned with the memory of the fire that whipped under her skin when his fingers clasped her arms. *Gah*! Even absent he tormented her!

Best to divert her attention to a safer place, like how she could persuade Slaney to run away with her if her sire still tried to push her to marry Pratt after she told him about Dr. Garrison's proposal.

A loud snort, and the clomp of a horse's hoof, interrupted her daydreams. Sham returned for another drink, which was convenient. It meant she would not have to go far to find him when she was ready to head back home. She sighed. She should get out and start struggling with her garments. Heaven knows how long she was going to have to fight to get them back on.

Lazily opening her eyelids, she turned her head toward the bank. There, not a stone's throw away, stood an enormous black stallion. It stomped again and pawed the ground with an impatient foreleg.

Orion!

Oh, no.

On the animal's back, leg casually thrown over the saddle horn, was the very person she had been in the process of banishing from her thoughts.

Landon Hart's magnetic gaze captured her own, and a slow, lazy grin spread across his tanned face. Her bonnet sat at a cocky angle on his head, and he touched the cap in a spry salute.

With an alarmed shriek, Keelan flung her arms across her chest.

And sank.

She couldn't touch the bottom.

Where was the bottom?

She clawed and kicked. Where was the *surface?*

Thrashing wildly, terror seized her body in a deadly crush as her mouth and nose filled with water.

20

CHAPTER TWENTY
A WATER SPRITE

The ominous sky had urged him to seek out Keelan. And something else he was uncomfortable admitting even to himself. When her stallion didn't slow as they'd approached the mill, his stomach shot straight down to his boots and he couldn't breathe. No way she could survive a fall at that speed. It was a long time before that terror-filled moment passed. He had to take a few moments to collect his emotions before seeking out Grey. It wouldn't do to punch a hole in the door of the man's office, although the release of frustration that woman invited would almost have been worth it.

A wall of dark purple-gray clouds moved westward. A gale was not only probable, it was certain. Still, she shouldn't be out alone, regardless. Containing her ride to the plantation land did not mean she stayed out of harm's way. People traversed across Twin Pines when the situation warranted. He was vaguely familiar with the layout of the property thanks to the owners of The Whistling Pig. They'd described it well. He was also aware that fleeing slaves occasionally used the abandoned cabins near the lake.

A lady's bonnet grabbed his attention first, and fearing she'd fallen or had been thrown from her horse, he spent several terrifying minutes looking for her broken body in the brush. Worse, he had to continue the search, since the bonnet could have fallen off at any point during the ride. It was a relief when he found her coat. That wasn't something that could easily fly off unless she'd removed it. At least he found her trail, which prompted him to increase the pace.

He shook his head in wonder as he recalled the prim and proper-looking woman he rode with this morning. Who was the real Keelan Grey? The composed young lady with a quick wit and tongue to match, or the boy-waif who enjoyed sparring in the early morning?

Perhaps she was neither.

Perhaps she was both.

A many-faceted image tiptoed into his mind. Keelan crouching like a tigress, the set of her mouth and stark focus as she blocked Daniel's attack, her glee when she scored first. The corners of her mouth twitching upward, challenging him to a race. Her face flushed and eyes bright with exhilaration and victory.

There. That was the real Keelan.

What would she be like on the open ocean with its unpredictable moods and ruthless privateers?

Orion lifted his head and perked his ears as they neared the lake. Pausing at the edge of the trees, he perused the tranquil and secluded area. There were many places where a person might hide and not be seen.

Although Sham grazed near the shore; there was no sign of the impetuous young vixen who'd challenged him to a gallop earlier. He clenched his jaw; it had been a mistake allowing her to journey on alone. If something had happened to her...

A slight ripple attracted his attention, and when he scanned the lake he almost fell off his horse.

Floating offshore near a gigantic boulder floated the willowy form of Keelan Grey.

And she was completely *naked*.

Now, there was a sight to behold.

So he did.

One hand casually rested on a boulder, the other fanned the water at her side. Her hair swirled around her like a liquid flame. A vision like this certainly called for a more leisurely perusal. Her face, pert nose, kissable lips and the smooth creamy skin of her neck made his mouth go dry. Pink nipples peaked the swell of her breasts like rosebuds.

She kicked her legs up, treating him to a pair of thighs and the triangle of auburn curls where they joined. He shook his head in both amazed disbelief and breathless admiration.

Keelan Grey was a woman who didn't care if she conformed to polite society or not. She went her own way. He liked that about her.

He now faced a dilemma, however. It was doubtful he could alert her of his presence without causing her acute embarrassment. Perhaps he should simply wait and allow her to finish with her bath. He studied at the sky and frowned. If she dallied much longer, they'd be pressed to beat the storm to Twin Pines.

Reaching behind his saddle, he retrieved her bonnet and plopped it on his head. Throwing his leg over the horn, he decided to enjoy the view for a moment more.

Apparently, Orion wasn't as easily entertained, and he stomped his hoof in boredom. The noise startled her, and she opened her eyes and turned her head toward him.

And shrieked.

Then sank.

The water bubbled. Realization hit him like a hoof to the chest.

The chit can't swim!

He jumped down and started to run, then paused to yank off a boot. He glanced up. Her head popped above the surface. He relaxed slightly. Until she gurgled in a breath and sank again.

Dammit. Why the hell was she in the water when she couldn't swim?

Hopping on one foot, he managed to pull the other boot off. He would have rather removed his shirt also but didn't dare take any more time. Plunging in at a dead run, he surged toward the bubbles and reached for Keelan's limp arm.

For the second time today, his heart stopped.

CHAPTER TWENTY-ONE
A DEBT WELL PAID

S he was going to die.

It was impossible to resist the instinct to inhale. Water crushed her chest and the last of her air bubbled to the surface. She battled the urge until her lungs burned and she could no longer resist. As water entered her throat, a strong hand circled her wrist and tugged. She instinctively clutched it. The water moved around her as she was pulled back to the shallower depths. Another corded arm clamped around the back of her waist, and she was hauled coughing and sputtering against a hot, hard body.

It took several moments before she could draw a complete breath of air without breaking into another fit of hacking and snorting. When she managed to open her eyes, she found a pair of flashing sapphire ones locked with hers. Droplets of water still streamed down his thunderous face, his ebony hair glistening with an almost blue light. The muscles in his jaw rippled his shortly trimmed beard. His fingers dug into her upper arms.

Hart's voice was edged with barely contained fury. "Do you have a death wish, or does scaring the life out of me serve as your favorite form of entertainment lately?"

Shock stilled her tongue. He radiated so much heat she wasn't sure if it was due to her lake-cooled skin or the anger pulsing through his. Mortified, she tried to bring her arms up to cover her breasts, but Landon Hart merely growled and jerked her more firmly against his chest.

She became painfully cognizant of her legs pressed against solid muscular thighs. A familiar warmth flushed up her neck and all the way past her eyebrows.

After a moment, he released a long breath and leaned away far enough to sweep her wet ringlets aside. "Are you all right?"

"Y-yes...I...th...th...think so," she stuttered. "C- Captain H- H- Hart." *Gah!*

A slow smile pulled the corners of his mouth up. The twinkle returned to his eyes. "Please, now that our relationship has become more intimate, call me Landon. I insist."

They were in thigh deep water. Her discomfiture deepened. There was no way to extract herself from his embrace without causing additional humiliation. In fact, the only way to keep him from leering further at her naked body was to stay exactly where she stood. How long had he been there ogling?

Keelan opened and shut her mouth in flustered silence. Now, that rash decision to flee the house without an escort seemed like a horribly disastrous one, indeed. As much as she wished she could place the blame elsewhere, this dilemma was entirely her fault. She groaned inwardly.

Why, why, *why*, when in the presence of this man, did she always act boyish, impetuous, and clumsy? Not to mention ridiculously foolish. He must think her an addle-brained child.

Even more vexing was that his opinion even mattered to her.

The only thing worse than returning home with a loosely tied riding habit and mussed hair, would be returning home with a loosely tied riding habit, mussed hair *and* Landon Hart.

That's it. Her life was over.

Unless, by some miracle, she managed to get to her room unseen by the entire household, there'd be no avoiding a wedding now.

Hart's expression, while somewhat masked, did not completely hide the mirth still swirling around the corners of his mouth. Steeped in embarrassment, her anger blazed and she shot him an annoyed look.

"Captain Hart, what are you doing *here?*" Intentionally ignoring his request to be called by his given name, it was better to stay focused on the anger, rather than the current predicament. It seemed easier and less horrifying.

"When our business concluded, your uncle suggested I take a ride through the plantation, since I had earlier mentioned my curiosity." His fingers started making distracting circles on the small of her back.

"You... you, should have made your presence known much sooner." She glared daggers. At least that wasn't a *real* stutter this time.

"I am happy to report that the sights," he continued as if she hadn't spoken, "are impressive indeed."

"You—augh!" she sputtered, giving up the argument. "You are the most frustrating person I've ever met."

"And you are the most intriguing person *I've* ever met." He gave her a mock frown. "I had hoped you would change your mind and wait for me to join you."

"So, you *searched* for me?"

His broad chest rumbled. "It was not difficult, love. I merely followed the trail of departed garments." His eyes sparkled with unbridled humor. "Little was I aware how many had actually... departed."

Her mortification intensified, scorching her cheeks and ears. In fact, it radiated between their bodies in a dangerous wave. "Sir, spying on a lady is indecent." She could hardly breathe out the words.

"It was not my intention to spy. It was simply my unexpected good fortune to behold such beauty that my breath nearly bid my body farewell." His eyes drifted closed and he let out a dramatic sigh.

She scowled at his mocking tone. "You truly are a rake!"

He opened one eye to peer at her, then leaned in and brushed her earlobe with his whisper. "And you, my love, are beautiful beyond words." The circles moved down her lower back to her hip.

All she could think about was the swirls his long fingers made on her bare skin. When his storm-blue eyes paused on her lips, her lungs stuttered and she couldn't draw even the smallest breath. A strange tingling sensation shot from her navel through her belly like a dagger.

His touch affected her in a way she was couldn't define. She became increasingly conscious of the effect the press of her naked body had on *him*. He had to feel her heart ramming against his chest. She needed to put some distance between them, but she was much compromised at the moment. *Obviously*.

Pushing him away would be the appropriate thing to do, but then she'd be utterly exposed once again. Worse, her feet were strangely rooted. How could she possibly win this one?

She expelled a resigned puff of breath. She could only plead her cause and hope for the best. "Were you a gentleman, sir, you would turn away and permit me to remedy my plight."

He gave her a horrified look. "And risk having you fall victim to the raging waters of this lake? I forbid the thought!"

Keelan closed her eyes and groaned, "Must you continue to humiliate me, Captain Hart?"

"*Please*, call me Landon," he repeated in a too-cheery voice.

She groaned louder this time and dropped her head in frustration. She couldn't look into those crystalline eyes one more moment. Her forehead contacted his chest with an unenthusiastic thump.

He chuckled lightly. "Fear not, fair Keelan, for I shall lead you to safety without further injury to your person or your pride, like I did with that poorly mannered shrub a few days ago. You do recall the arrangement we agreed upon?"

Warning bells began to jingle in her head. "I recall our arrangement quite well." Although her knees were liquefying, she forced herself to look up. She didn't want him to notice how weak she really was, what little control she maintained.

The color of his irises deepened to a sultry velvet blue. His gaze never left her face as he took her fingers firmly in his hand and gently kissed the tips. Her breath froze in her chest, and she struggled to calm the shivers that raced up her spine. With his lips, he forged a path to the center of her palm. The best course of action would be to withdraw her hand. Use it to push against his torso and step away. Maybe even slap some manners into him. Although it was quite possible, it might re-ignite his temper, something she couldn't afford to do out here in the wilderness. Alone.

But it was so tempting that both palms itched.

If she moved now, she might be able to catch him off guard enough with a hard shove to send him backwards into the water. It would give her a few precious seconds to dart behind the boulder near her clothes. Her mind nudged her to do so, but the sensations Landon Hart was stirring were also commanding her attention. The kiss she owed him hung over the two of them, drawing them together like a silvery moon pulls at the tide.

If she paid her due now, she'd have no reason to cross paths with him ever again. Surely, the dangerous temptations he had awakened in her would go silent without him so near. Surely, she could focus more intently on her future if she put all this behind her. Surely...

It made sense to kiss him now and be done with it. Heaven knows she wouldn't have the strength to ward off his advances again. Even more terrifying was that it was quite likely she couldn't do it *now*.

Keelan pulled her hand away, but in doing so, her fingers brushed his mouth, drawing a sharp intake of breath from him. Curious, she skimmed her thumb over it and along his jaw, marveling at the roughness of his cheek compared to the pliant warmth of his lips. A sudden desire to plunge her palms into his inky hair had her hand moving past his temple and behind his neck.

She lost the ability to think when she shifted her attention from the shiny black curls to his face. Landon's intense stare smoldered with interest, making her feel like she was melting. Her rational mind abandoned her. It no longer mattered where she was, or what problems weighed on the day.

The last kiss they shared had plagued her every day and night. Were all kisses so heated and heady? She'd been ill prepared for the first one. Now she had an idea what she should expect, and suddenly the overwhelming need to experience it again took over. She pulled his head down.

His lips moved across hers wet and hot. He ignited a fire to her belly, slashed her resolve, and robbed her of thought. Of its own will, her body arched into his. In answer, his hand trailed across the small of her back, then stroked down and grasped her buttocks to press her against his hardness with an almost delicious pressure. A soft moan reverberated from deep within her chest. The contact set flames to every nerve. Her knees grew weaker against the onslaught of his kiss, his proximity. Should he decide to take even more liberties, she would be quite helpless to argue. Because... she didn't want him to stop. And she couldn't keep herself from wondering what those liberties might entail.

She thrilled at the stroke of his tongue moving into her mouth, and back out again, probing, tasting... stirring an ache deeper inside. What was this? Passion or simple lust? Was there a difference?

Did it matter?

Too soon, his lips abandoned her mouth only to ignite a hot moist path to a flammable spot beneath her ear. His husky whisper slid like silk across a polished marble floor. "Consider your debt very, *very* well paid, my sweet Keelan."

22

CHAPTER TWENTY-TWO
A THUNDER BOLT

Landon took a jagged breath. Keelan fought to refocus his kiss was as potent and intoxicating as wine. Past his shoulder, Orion stood grazing next to her bonnet and Hart's discarded boots.

Wait. She'd been drowning, and he paused long enough to take off his...

Her jaw unhinged. It was a moment before she could speak. "How long did it take you to remove those boots?" She almost spoke the words evenly, but couldn't keep herself from leveling a furious stare at him.

He glanced back at the shiny, black boots lying in the grass. "I had those specially made by an Italian cobbler. I find the left one a bit snug, but it'll stretch in time." He turned his attention back to her. "Why do you ask?"

The bewildered words he used didn't fool her. He knew exactly what she'd meant. She spoke through clenched teeth, "I was under water *drowning*. Thanks to *you*, yet you took the time to pull off your boots before coming in after me?"

He tilted back a little more in feigned shock. "Those are my favorite boots! The water would have ruined them." He gave her a wry smirk. "I still saved your life, don't forget that part." He cocked his head and folded his arms around her. "In some parts of the world that would mean you now owe me a life debt and will have to accompany me everywhere as my servant until you are able to save my life in return."

She shook her head, incredulous. "What makes you think when the time came along, I would bother? I imagine it would be much more satisfying to witness your demise."

Landon froze for a second, then threw back his head and laughed. Seeing him so heartily amused made it difficult for her to stay stoic. His laugh rolled genuine and boisterous, with a weight similar to the baritone of his voice, but richer, stronger. It passed along a genial joy and reckless glee, like a sudden gust of wind flings bonnets on a blustery spring day.

He tucked another wet ringlet behind her ear, before tracing a finger across her jawbone. His eyes smoldered. "Ah, but sweet Keelan, I'd take the chance anyway because, for me, just having you by my side would be bliss."

Before she could retort, he pulled her against his chest again and kissed her soundly on the mouth before turning and sloshing from the lake.

She did not trust herself to speak and instead stared in disbelief at the man who was walking toward his horse and precious boots. What was it about this infuriating scoundrel that made her stomach tingle and her heart hum in her chest? And why in the world did her body ignore her brain when he was near?

Again, he'd mocked her and used her for his own arrogant entertainment. Or was it she who had used him? She snorted in vexation and splashed toward her clothes, her eyes locked on his retreating form.

The white shirt on his back was almost invisible from the effects of the water, and it stretched tightly across his broad muscular shoulders. Landon's torso was lean and tapered. His breeches clung to his buttocks and powerful legs, leaving nothing to the imagination. Keelan marveled at the way his muscles rippled with every movement. Smoldering lava still churned in her belly.

Hopefully her clothes were now dry and warm from the sun-baked rock. She scampered behind the boulder to dress. Drawing a shaky breath, she tried to cease her trembling, while her fingers fumbled with her clothes. What had she been *thinking*? She pursed her lips in irritation. How many times must she remind herself of the danger he presented to her virtue and reputation?

Apparently once more.

Even her own body betrayed her.

Again.

And now, she stood perched on a precarious edge. They were alone together, far away from a chaperone. She was dangerously close to putting her recently hatched plan in jeopardy. Here, without Slaney or suitable companion, she deserved no better, she supposed.

Unless she could make it back to Twin Pines before Landon Hart and before Uncle Jared arrived home from the mill.

Keelan twisted her hair into a braid, unable to replace her locks in the manner Slaney had so skillfully arranged them earlier this morning. A new idea sparked in her mind. She could hide in the kitchen house until the maid could come and put her in more presentable shape.

She might be able to salvage her future after all.

No doubt, Hart would wed her, bed her and then sail off to other ports, other women. She'd seen this happen time and time again in Chatham, England, the small naval town where she'd grown up.

Was it so wrong to desire love?

Or a husband who desired her company beyond their marriage bed?

Reaching behind her back for the skirt stays, she huffed in exasperation. She was an idiot. What had she been thinking? She had been so very over-heated and sweaty. The cool lake had called to her and lured her in with its sparkling surface and cleansing water. She didn't regret it.

She should have enjoyed it *without* disrobing.

She should have paused long enough to deliberate the difficulty of dressing herself. Her cheeks flushed anew at the growing realization that she must ask for Landon Hart's assistance. She squared her shoulders and clenched her fist around the stays. *Reckless.*

Again.

When she emerged, Hart had already removed the hobbles from Sham's legs and tightened the saddle straps. He led the horse to her.

Sham tossed his noble head at the sight of Landon's stallion tethered nearby. Nostrils flaring, he pranced sideways; Hart spoke low and commanding until the horse quieted to a more docile walk. He secured the reins around a branch and patted Sham's neck before turning to approach her. He was no longer the smiling jester. He'd shifted to a commander.

"Keelan, this is a fine steed but not an appropriate mount for a lady." His voice was even, but she still heard the chastisement. She stiffened as he pressed on, "I understand you are an accomplished equestrian. However, this stallion requires a rider with much more strength."

She lifted her chin. "I am quite capable of keeping my seat. So far, this creature has given me no trouble."

Almost no trouble.

Approaching Sham, she caressed his velvety nose. "He has been the perfect gentleman today." She chanced a sideways look at Landon. "Unlike some males with whom I am acquainted."

He smiled down at her. "'Twill be interesting to see how well you keep your seat while also maintaining mastery of your garments." He raised an ebony eyebrow while leaning over to glance at the back of her skirt. "Or would you like some assistance to that end?"

She took a breath and prepared for more mockery. "I have done the best I can do," she stated, "but I worry my efforts at tightening these might lead to my continued embarrassment." She hesitantly turned her back to him and peered over her shoulder. "Would you mind...?"

Without hesitation, he nimbly grasped the ribbons. In a matter of seconds, they were deftly tied, neither too loose nor too tight. Slaney could do no better. It made her wonder, how many times in the past this same opportunity had presented itself to the rake.

"You seem quite good at this," she quipped.

"Aye," he said. "But I am much more skilled at removing them." He reached up and playfully tugged. "Would you care for a demonstration?"

She whirled away from his reach. "Certainly not!" Seeing his amused visage, she let slip a sheepish grin, relieved for once that he was teasing her because heaven knows how hard it would be for her to refuse one more advance from him. She attempted to regain a more composed countenance. "No doubt, you have much experience to that end."

He grinned as he untied Sham's reins. "I never kiss and tell, fair maiden."

She couldn't help but roll her eyes. She was painfully aware of her tousled appearance, certain she looked nothing like the ladies of the captain's past.

Landon's joviality faded when he shifted his steely gaze up and scanned the darkening sky. "The other reason I followed you, was because the storm that's approaching is likely to turn violent. It appears it'll soon be upon us. If we're to make it back to Twin Pines before it hits, we must make haste now."

She followed his gaze and caught her breath at the sight of the purple and green hues coating the sky above them. She hurriedly wrapped her braid into a twist at the nape of her neck, and began to place the pins by feel alone.

"Would you hand me my hat, please?"

He shook his head as he retrieved her bonnet. "My dear, the gesture is valiant. Still, I'm afraid the ride and the wind will destroy your efforts."

He obviously had no idea how precarious her situation had become. It would have been easier to take the admonition from her father and uncle for leaving without a chaperone than it would be for arriving home with Landon. Doreen might have already gleefully informed Papa that the two had ridden to the mill together. In fact, she'd bet on it.

She exhaled in irritation. "First, I am not your *dear*. Second, were I to return with a proper escort in this disheveled state, my reputation *might* remain intact." She lowered her brows at him. "Returning with you as an escort will certainly tarnish it beyond all hope for repair. My uncle and my father will undoubtedly believe you seduced me with your handsome face and irresistible charm."

She poked him in the chest. "You might take this lightly, but I assure you, I am most serious. I do not want to be shackled in marriage to a lecherous sea captain, an old codger, or a bumbling doctor." She gestured to him. "I must do what I can to preserve my integrity as well as my unsoiled state. Now if you don't mind, please give me my bonnet and my jacket."

He gave her a resigned sigh, willing to retreat. "As you wish." He held her coat as she shrugged into it, then gave her the hat. He cocked his head and studied her for a moment. "Do you truly believe I have a handsome face?"

She choked back a laugh. "I truly believe that *you* believe it."

He grinned, revealing those dimples again. It was hard not to stare at them. They gave him a more boyish appearance, more innocent, which of course, made him more dangerous.

He took a step closer and whispered, "You think I'm handsome and charming. You just said so."

She secured her bonnet on her head. "Just because someone might say you're handsome, doesn't mean they want to marry you."

Hart stepped closer and stroked his finger across the back of her exposed neck, causing her skin to zing with the contact. "You want to marry me?"

She was momentarily speechless. For one thing, it was impossible to talk because the sensation he was creating with a single finger was completely unsettling. Was this the game he played...to charm and seduce? It might amuse him, but he'd no longer find her an easy mark.

As long as he didn't kiss her.

Or come near her.

Ever again.

Or touch her.

Ever again.

Finally, her voice returned. "I didn't say I wanted to marry you. If you recall, I specifically said I *didn't*."

He clutched his heart and staggered backward. "Woman, you wound me with your sharp tongue and harsh words. But to describe our sweet bond as *shackled*, leaves me broken-hearted."

He gave her such a sorrowful look that for a moment, she nearly took pity on him. Keelan turned her face away and chewed her lip to stop a smile. He would likely consider her amusement as encourage-ment. It was best for him not to see it.

"You are a strong, healthy man with a thick shield of arrogance, Landon Hart." She almost succeeded in keeping the laughter from her voice. "I'm sure your heart will recover at a record pace."

His head perked up. "But I'll be forever scarred," he replied, laughter lacing his words. "Besides, you called me Landon. You *do* love me."

She rolled her eyes and searched for a stump or a rock she could use as a mounting block.

"Allow me, love."

She quirked a brow. "With the exception of your aid in saving me from the depths, I am quite certain you have 'helped' me enough today." She perched her fists on her hips. "Exactly what do you plan to do? Throw me across the beast's back like a sack of rice?"

Tossing her a cagey grin, he sank to one knee and laced his fingers together. "My intentions are more chivalrous, I assure you. I mean only to give you a step up."

There appeared to be no other option, so she relented and placed her boot into his waiting palms.

He helped her into the sidesaddle, and boldly guided her foot through the stirrup, ruining her intention to evade his touch from now on. She should thank him for rescuing her. If only he wasn't such a scoundrel, and an arrogant mocker of impulsive young ladies, then the words wouldn't stick in her throat so tenaciously.

But it had to be done.

Even though it was his fault she'd lost her grip on that rock.

"Captain Hart," she said, touching his shoulder. She caught herself too late. Now her hand burned. She curled her fingers into her palm.

"Landon," he corrected, lifting his eyes to her face.

"Landon." She swallowed her pride and hoped her voice wouldn't falter. "Thank you for saving my life. It was foolish of me to go in to begin with. I would have drowned had you not pulled me out."

"It was my *greatest* pleasure, my lady." A spark flared in his eyes and ignited her cheeks. She should have expected that response. She adjusted the reins. Sham seemed to sense her tension and pranced and fidgeted.

The low, angry rumble of thunder echoed through the pines. The gentle breeze of the afternoon had dropped in temperature and picked up speed. A fat drop of rain splattered on her hand; she'd have to hurry home to beat the storm. The ground was already spotted with large dark blotches where raindrops plopped and tumbled in the soft thick dust. They began to fall with more frequency. A rivulet of water dripped off the back of her hat and down her neck.

"Keelan." Landon's expression was serious now. Both his hand on the bridle and his tone made her pause. "It would ease my mind if you would allow me to lead your mount. I can tether him to my saddle and keep him better controlled if the weather worsens and unsettles him."

She eyed Landon warily. "I think not." She lifted her chin. "I appreciate the offer. However, I am perfectly capable of handling a horse." She reined Sham away from him and gave the stallion a smart heel. She had to make an effort to get back in time. She could act as if she didn't know Landon had been riding about the plantation.

She didn't expect him to attempt to stop her.

He lunged for the reins and succeeded in getting a couple fingers on one of them, jerking it from Keelan's hands. His quick movement startled Sham, who spun away, nearly unseating her in the process. She grabbed at the saddle, an angry admonishment on her tongue. As she tried to jerk her body upright, her heels clipped against Sham's side, which sent him leaping forward.

A scream erupted from her throat before she could stop it. The panicked shriek only spooked the horse more, and he took off at a dead run.

Without warning, a bright flash of lightning and earsplitting crack of thunder ripped through the air around her and shook the ground. There was a loud snap, then the screech of ripping wood. Sham skidded stiff-legged to a stop, squealed, and reared up in fright. Keelan clawed at the horse's mane in a frantic attempt to keep her seat. Landon's warning shout echoed behind her as a large pine to her right toppled.

A bone chilling terror banded around her chest, and she instinctively thumped Sham's flank. The horse jumped forward, dislodging her lower foot from its stirrup, and jolting her off-balance again. Only by twisting her hands tighter into the mane, did she manage to keep her seat. The powerful stallion flew down the lane at breakneck speed, and the next loud thunderclap almost drowned out the drumming of his hooves as well as the tree crashing to forest floor behind them.

23

CHAPTER TWENTY-THREE
A WILD RIDE

Terrified, Keelan clutched a bigger handful of Sham's mane and held on until her knuckles whitened. Her hair again whipped free from her bonnet and slashed across her face and neck, impairing her vision. Seized by panic, a new horror gripped her when she realized she'd dropped the other rein in the fight to maintain her seat.

She now had no way to control the beast or slow him down.

"Stop!" she screamed. "Whoa, Sham!"

Unheeding, the stallion continued at a bone-jarring gallop with Keelan powerless to halt him. He sensed her fear and reacted in kind. She choked back a terrified sob and again shouted the command to stop, but the rising wind swallowed her voice. The furious storm-chased drops pelted her face in a blinding assault. Her insides churned with cold dread; she clenched Sham's mane as tightly as her trembling fingers would allow.

"Keelan!" Landon's shout was close, and she cast a wild glance over her shoulder. His horse was only a length behind. Orion soon stretched up alongside them.

Landon leaned to the side, reaching toward her. His arm shot out and clamped around her waist like a steel band, plucking her off Sham's back like a rag doll. He pulled her sideways across his lap; she impulsively wrapped her quivering arms about his neck and buried her face against his shoulder and inhaled the scent of rain and leather and Landon Hart. Tears threatened, and she tried to close her mind to the image of the toppling tree or of her crashing head first to the ground. His muscle-hardened arm tightened, providing comfort and safety.

The swirling wind dipped and danced about them and the hail, like small stones, stung their flesh. He reined his horse to a soft canter, then a light trot, and finally a walk before he turned from the path. She numbly heard his voice vibrating in her ear. "You're safe, Keelan. I have you."

The words passed her lips before she had time to think, "Landon, please don't let go of me!"

"I won't let you go, love. I promise. Not ever."

Her shoulders were quaking uncontrollably, and she fought to take a deeper breath. A crash of thunder shook the earth, and another bold streak of lightning split the heavens. Blinded by the flash, disoriented by fright, she threw her arms up to shield her face. Her entire body trembled with racking, hysterical sobs. The rain's nearly horizontal attack was lessened by the huge pines, which made up most of the forest on either side of them. With a low curse, Landon trapped her wrists in his hand and forced her arms away from her face.

"Keelan! Look at me. You're safe. I have you." He scowled, slipped his hand behind her neck and pulled her face to his. His mouth collided into hers with the same fierce intensity of the tempest raging around them. A shock coursed through her body as if lightning had struck her. Unconsciously, her fingers curled around the wrist of his hand cupped firmly at her nape. A sudden heat consumed her right breast, and the dull understanding that the sensation was caused by his other hand crept into her brain. He can't. He can't touch her like this —or kiss her like this—she wouldn't have the strength to guard her heart. A few days or weeks of joy weren't worth the months and years waiting alone for a man who may never come home.

With a shocked gasp, she opened her eyes and jerked away. Before he said another word, she landed a stinging slap against his cheek. She was rewarded with a lopsided leer and a burning palm.

"There you are," he said with unmasked satisfaction.

"How dare you!" What kind of man takes advantage of a woman when she's hysterical?

Ugh.

What a ridiculous question to ask herself. Landon Hart, of course, was the kind of man who'd be so bold. It had taken her a moment to register the kiss, but it was glorious, and the lure of this man could very well be her undoing. Embarrassment seeped through her at that hysterical display he just witnessed. Why was she so *weak*?

Now they were about to arrive home on the same mount. She was *doomed*.

A warm finger touched her chin, and she glared up at the source of her own personal storm. The man stirred such a turbulent tide of emotions in her heart, that it pitched and rolled hither and yon like a small dingy in a roiling sea. She had no control over it, and that petrified her.

Landon's eyes clouded with concern and stared intently back at her. His nearness unnerved her, and her senses reeled again from the manly scent of him.

"My apologies love, but it was the only thing I think to do to shatter the state of near hysteria that took you." He grinned. "I am extremely pleased with the results, although somewhat worse for the effort," he said, touching the red outline of her hand on his cheek.

"You'll not get an apology for that," she retorted. "You most certainly deserved it."

His grin widened. "Well worth the price paid."

She pressed her lips together and glanced away. He was so... irritating. She didn't enjoy his absurd admission. Not one tiny bit.

"I blame myself." His mood sobered. "I should have never let you get on that horse. Instead, I should have damn well thrown you over my saddle and tied you there!"

She gave him a cool smile. "It would have been interesting to see you try."

His eyebrows jumped up; his chest rumbled with a chuckle. "A fascinating physical engagement, that would be." He leaned forward. "I would have enjoyed the win immensely."

She managed a feeble smile. Hard, dense rain soaked her clothes, and the wind howled around them. She shivered. Animals had a gift for finding their way home, but she still worried about Sham. They stopped at the cluster of abandoned cabins she'd passed earlier in the day. What was he doing? She turned her questioning gaze toward him.

He spoke into her ear over the howling wind. "The gale will be upon us before we can return. We need to find shelter *now*."

Alarm exploded in her chest. "Nay! I cannot!" She glanced wildly at the sky. "We must get back. It can't be very far, and Sham is still running loose. We must find him!"

He ignored her tirade and urged Orion forward to a shanty near the edge of the clearing. Wind gusts began to hiss through the pines with frightening ferocity. The torrent hammered down so hard it hurt her head.

Even as she realized the lunacy of her demands, she pushed against his chest and tried to raise her voice above the roar. "Please, Landon, please take me home!" There was still a chance they could get there before Uncle Jared if he waited out the storm at the mill. If they delayed, her absence would become obvious. They'd be watching for her. Papa would worry.

He grasped her shoulders, shouting over the wild storm. "Keelan, can you see what's happening?" He swept an arm wide. "The wind has picked up several knots, and soon it'll be strong enough to pick up debris as well." He slid his hands down her arms until he could grasp her elbows. "Your safety is more important to me now, than your precious reputation. Surely your family will be in agreement." His voice strengthened into a commanding tone, which allowed for no further argument. "We shall seek refuge now. My decision to protect you is firm in this regard."

She hid her agitation by lashing him with her words. "A comfort, to be sure, Captain."

But who will protect me from you?

His eyes darkened to the blue-gray of a chaotic sea. "Your virtue will remain intact while you are under my protection. I give you my word, as a gentleman."

She couldn't hold back a snort. "Gentleman? Do you even understand the definition?" she asked, unable to break his stormy gaze.

Captain Landon Hart's mere presence was dangerous. Reason and logic seemed to disappear faster than Ruth's pecan pie when he was around her.

He cut her a wry look. They'd halted beside a structure with one corner of the roof missing, giving her cause to wonder how many creatures their visit would disturb. The front door hung askew by the bottom hinge, and both windows lacked shutters for protection.

She peered through the deluge and raised her voice above the wind. "I don't understand how this feeble structure will protect us."

He dismounted, then lifted her down. "This one has a cellar." He gestured to the entrance near the side of the cabin. He turned to remove the saddle and pack, speaking over his shoulder. "We'll be safer here." He placed the tack on the ground, then reached up for the blanket.

She opened her mouth to argue, but a wave of dizziness crashed over her, cutting off her retort. A loud roar filled her ears and her world began to swirl and dip. Flashes of sensation hovered just out of reach from the fringes of her consciousness. A numbing pulse seeped into her skin, darkening her vision, followed by the jarring impact of the rain-soaked earth.

爨 24 爨

CHAPTER TWENTY-FOUR
A STORM SHELTER

Landon's scent, mingled with leather and fresh lake water, awakened her in the semi-darkness. Confused, she searched for a familiar sight before she remembered she was in a cellar below the shanty.

On the dirt floor, a cheery fire crackled merrily, the smoke escaping through a yawning hole in the ceiling above them. Only about half the main floor remained intact; the rest was gone. Up there, the dark gaping maw of a brick hearth loomed in the shadows, standing quiet and cold at the far end of the first floor room. Farther up, cobwebs coated the rafters, obscuring the shaggy remnants of several abandoned nests tucked in the corner eaves. Her surroundings smelled of neglect, mice, and damp dirt. Straight ahead were steps built into the side of a wall, leading up to a small hinged door, which appeared to open next to the hearth. The cellar was oddly larger than the cabin itself.

She couldn't see into the alcove on her right. Probably another storage area.

The structure was deserted, still she had an uneasy sensation she was intruding. There were old burlap bags stuffed with straw and a basket of turnips and potatoes, along with a couple of well-used blankets, as if the occupants had tried to live in the root cellar, rather than up in the old cabin.

She had been resting on a saddle blanket; Landon's coat had been rolled into a makeshift pillow and placed beneath her head. She lifted it to her nose and inhaled. Glancing about, she spied his saddle leaning against the far wall.

Keelan's skin crawled at the sound of the angry wind lunging and clawing at the tiny cabin, causing the frail structure to shudder and groan. A loud thunderclap made her jump, and she glanced up through the hole in the ceiling toward the open windows. The rain fell harder and blew through to the floor. She was immediately grateful for the fire's comforting glow.

The furious slapping of the crippled front door, with its single hinge, couldn't drown out the hailstones clattering on the porch and against the clapboards. The faint clip of boots was nearly drowned out by the whistling gusts of wind and pelting barrage. The hinged door in the ceiling opened and Landon ducked, stepping down the cellar ladder, then closed the hatch behind him, his pack slung over his shoulder. He deposited everything near the saddle and glanced about, as she had done a few moments earlier.

With every movement of his shoulders, muscles rippled beneath the dripping shirt. The confident set of his jaw and the sinuous fluidity of his stride added to that now familiar air of authority which seemed to surge toward him, envelop him, radiate from him. He was used to leading men, and obviously comfortable with the responsibilities that went hand in hand with such a position.

He began to step closer, but stopped when he saw she'd awakened. "How are you?" He seemed oblivious to the fact he was soaked and water still streamed down his face and neck.

Caught staring, she could only give him a blink and shrug. She brushed her hand across her brow in a vain effort to wipe away the cobwebs from her mind before she mumbled thickly, "A bit muddled."

Landon picked up his pack and moved to kneel beside her. He loosened the straps and withdrew a cloth-wrapped bundle and a flask.

He unwrapped it, revealing a loaf of crusty bread. Using the cloth, he wiped the water from his face and hands. "When did you last eat?"

Keelan couldn't quite remember. She'd meant to grab one of Ruth's muffins at dawn, prior to training with Daniel, but in her haste, forgot. She missed breakfast. Of course, after Everett's proposal, she'd lost her appetite for lunch and soon after went for a ride.

"Last eve," she said.

"Keelan." He eyed her sternly. "Going without water or food in this climate can be taxing. Add to it the shock you've had, no wonder you're faint."

She bristled at his chastisement. She was not some weak maid who swooned at every turn of events. Even if it had become obvious that she had less control of her actions and decisions when this striking captain was near, with his cobalt eyes and broad shoulders. It all added to her frustrations. "Not as taxing as fighting off your roguish advances."

Landon's storm blue eyes smoldered with a silent challenge. "That remains to be seen, my sweet Keelan."

He gestured to the flask and bread he had removed from his saddlebags. "There is more than enough here for two." He had a mischievous gleam in his eyes. "However, the rules of the high seas demand you earn your share."

She pushed herself upright and tossed her storm-combed hair behind her. If this arrogant man expected she would "earn" her share, as would a doxy from the docks, then he had a lot to learn about the daughter of Commodore George Grey.

"I will not be manipulated." She narrowed her eyes. "If you think I might serve you favors in exchange for a crust of bread, then your senses have taken flight. I would choose to starve than bend to any more of your prurient whims."

He cocked a quizzical brow. "Aye." He nodded. "I believe you would." With a dramatic flourish, gave her an exaggerated, albeit seated, bow. "I humbly beg your forgiveness, my lady. I only seek to barter for pleasantries. I resolve to halve my share with you in exchange only for warm conversation and your beauteous presence." He placed his hand over his heart. "Put away your barbed tongue for the rest of the day, and I'll gleefully starve myself instead."

She couldn't keep from smiling; still, she gave him a wary look before responding in kind, "Dear sir, your price is too steep, for I can think of no other way a lady can fend off your rakish tendencies, unless you pledge your protection in addition to the treasures you would provide." She pretended to examine her nails. "I shall demand protection from all rogues, including and most especially...you."

He dipped his head and gave her a crooked grin, making the dimple in his cheek deepen. The firelight gleamed off his dark hair, still wet from the rain. "The bargain you demand is a rigid one, my lady, but I pledge to you my fealty. I shall fight for your love and honor until death removes me from your sublime presence."

Gah! He should have taken to the stage.

Keelan feigned a tight-lipped smile, while patting the space beside her makeshift pallet. "Come then sir, and sit, for my throat is parched and my stomach rumbles louder than the storm outside." She'd never conversed in private so casually with a man before, other than Daniel, but he didn't count. She found it oddly pleasant and relaxing. Had her parents shared a similar relationship, did they talk and tease each other when they were alone?

Somehow, she didn't think so.

Landon moved near her and reached for the flask. He broke the seal and handed it to her, "Sip this slowly," he warned. "It's water heavily laced with rum."

Heeding his advice, she sipped cautiously. She guessed the water was from his ship's supply, where they mixed rum with it to keep it drinkable while at sea.

He pulled out a round of wax-coated cheese and several odd crispy rolls. He handed one of them to her and smiled at her curiosity. "Marcel, the ship's cook, learned to make these while we were trading in the Orient."

She took a bite. "Delicious," she said gratefully. "Ruth makes something similar, but not as delicate. She calls it a fried pie."

Landon broke off two chunks of bread and used his knife to cut into the cheese. The fire cast quick, sprite-like shadows, which flickered and danced on the walls. Late afternoon had fallen, but the day had darkened to an eerie blue-green hue of dusk. They shared the small corner of the cellar, seeking comfort in whatever small amount of protection it provided. As they sated their hunger, the gale continued to rage.

He cocked his head and listened. "It's gaining strength. 'Tis good we found shelter when we did."

She eyed him, curious. "How is it you know so much of storms?"

"Over the years, I have sailed around many and through even more. Although we map our routes and time our trips to avoid the worst tempests when we can, one cannot often second-guess the elements."

Keelan picked up the flask and reclined against the rough cellar wall before taking a sip. "You must enjoy the sea very much to spend so many years upon the water."

Landon shrugged. "Everything good that's ever happened to me took place on the water. I've made my fortune crossing oceans and have seen many strange and amazing sights." His eyes turned a molten blue. "However, none can compare to the vision of exquisite beauty I witnessed today."

A flush crept up her neck. *The blackguard.* He enjoyed making her blush. "Should I one day hear tales of you becoming a pirate, or a priva-teer, scouring the high seas for weak merchant ships to plunder, I would have no trouble believing them." She took another careful sip and studied him warily. Captain Landon Hart certainly was *not* a gentleman, and that particular character defect was sure to cause trouble for her.

It already had.

"Slaney says men of the sea have women in every port and isle. How many maidens have you tarnished in your conquests?"

Landon paused, his fried roll partway to his mouth, then threw back his head and laughed. The genuine sound was contagious. Amuse-ment lingered in the corners of his eyes for a moment, then he sobered and leaned toward her.

Her smile faded as she pressed her back against the wall in a vain attempt to keep a fair distance between them. Landon's eyes glittered dangerously, and she squirmed, now slightly unsure of her choice of topics.

When he spoke, his voice was low and smoky, making the air in the room thin, and she caught her breath. "If I became a pirate, my love, you would be in dire need of a champion. I'd deem you a most valuable conquest indeed, and wouldn't wait long before claiming you as my own."

Keelan swallowed. This maddening talent he had, turning her words to his advantage, both vexed and heated her, spurring the urge to deflate his ego to a more manageable level, and her trepidation at the possible consequences of doing so.

She plunged stubbornly on. "You must have no desire to take a wife or start a family, or surely you would have done so. How long do you stay in a harbor? A few weeks? That's not nearly enough time to court a prospective bride. I can only conclude, you have no wish for a family of your own. Do you enjoy the freedom? I know I would."

Landon reclined against the adjacent wall, rested a hand over his bent knee, and finished chewing his fried roll before answering. "Aye. 'Tis true in part. I don't normally stay for long when I run the trade routes." His gaze locked with hers. "While I would treasure having a family, marriage does not seem to suit me." His gravelly voice dropped.

How would he know unless he tried it? It dawned on her. "You've been married before," she observed. Curiously, he must have tried to keep a life on land while also maintaining one on the water. But like any sailor, the temptations are too many. The ability to stray with no repercussions had to be hard to resist. No union can weather the battering of that kind of storm unless neither spouse cared.

"Aye," he whispered to the flames. "I was married, once."

"And?" she prompted. For some twisted reason, she wanted him to prove her right and say it was impossible to remain faithful, that the sea would be his only love.

"She died in childbirth," he stated numbly. "While I was away."

His words jarred her as if she'd been stuck. This wasn't what she expected to hear. A dark cloud of guilt settled on her shoulders for her faulty assumptions. "I'm sorry for your loss, and for my insensitive questions."

He shrugged, then reached over and tossed a broken clapboard on the fire. "But, you are correct," he mused. "Courting a worthy bride cannot be accomplished in the span of time I'm in port." Leaning forward again, he traced a finger along her jaw, tilting her face toward his before lowering his voice to a husky whisper. "I must admit, my lovely Keelan, your beauty, spirit, wit, and courage have all given me pause to consider *making* the time."

Her breath froze her lungs. Keelan tore her eyes from his and busied herself, cutting another small slice of cheese, annoyed she was once again flustered by his frankness, so much so, her hands were shaking. She wished she could attribute it to the lack of food and the recent terror she experienced. She must look as wobbly as a new foal. Even the dagger became an awkward tool, and she fumbled with it.

Landon's warm fingers closed around hers and gently removed the rebellious utensil. He cut a chunk of the cheese and impaled it upon the tip of his blade. He passed it to her, and she plucked it from the knife and sent him a small, embarrassed nod of thanks.

His damp, black curls fell forward around his face, giving him a roguish countenance, and she wanted to reach over and brush them away. She occupied her fingers by wrapping them in her skirt. What was it about this man that drew her to him? Her body foolishly defied her common sense at every turn.

It was so frustrating.

He'd been wed before; he should know that it requires more than spirit and wit. "Beauty doesn't make a marriage. Nor do riches or passion. I will marry only for love or not marry at all." *Not at all* was preferable given her current options. She'd not live in another house made lonely by a husband's gaping absence. And she wouldn't marry a man she didn't love. As soon as she safely could, she'd break her engagement with Dr. Garrison, and pray he'd forgive her.

She passed the watered-down rum back to Landon. "I witnessed what my father's leaving did to my mother. "She rested her head back against the wall and stared at the web-thatched ceiling far above them. "I'd prefer to stay unmarried and open a shop in Charleston where I could sell all kinds of exotic fabrics, spices, and goods from across the ocean. I could never be lonely doing that."

She flicked the back of her hand at him, as if swatting a swarm of gnats. "And no matter how handsome or silk-tongued he is, I would never wed a man who comes home for a few weeks' time, only to get me fat-bellied with child, then leave for months. And months."

He remained silent.

Oh, dear. She was an idiot.

That was a heartless thing to say after he just admitted that his wife died in childbirth. She should have bitten her tongue. Now, she felt like a cruel harpy. "I'm sorry, I didn't mean... It wasn't my intention to—"

A gentle finger on her chin cut her off and guided her gaze back up to his. A liquid flame sparked in his eyes. The humor had left, and in its place was a smoldering blue fire glittering with a mesmerizing luminosity. The intensity of his stare made her ears ring. He leaned forward until his face was inches from hers.

"Any man who would leave you alone for even an hour would be a fool," he said softly.

Landon lowered his lips and her heart slammed violently against the sides of her ribs, sending tremors straight through her chest. They stopped below her belly and exploded, creating a dense heat. Her mind screamed for her to retreat, but she wanted the touch of his lips against hers again, and the power of his strong arms pressing her against his body.

She no longer cared what she should or shouldn't do.

❧ 25 ❧

CHAPTER TWENTY-FIVE
A RARE JEWEL

Landon inhaled the woman who had stirred his interest so strongly and his passions so wildly and pulled her closer still. She was like a sprite flitting and dancing beneath the wide, waxy leaves of a magnolia tree; sometimes still and pensive, others quick and carefree. He thought he'd discovered the real Keelan earlier at the lake, but now he wasn't as sure. Was she the boyish imp dueling so bravely? Was she the stunning, yet haughty maiden preparing to dash his heart into the flames? Or the beautiful fire-haired water nymph who drew him to her like a fish on a string? The mystery only stoked his curiosity, making him even more determined to solve it. For reasons he couldn't fathom, he was drawn to her. He longed to taste the skin on her stomach, run his fingers over her ribs, and down her hip and caress the soft creamy skin of her inner thigh. It went beyond human desire, too. He wanted to make her laugh, shield her, and keep her safe, fulfill her dreams.

In the twilight of the storm-darkened afternoon, her eyes glowed a jeweled green. It was like looking into the untamed gaze of a dragon, shimmering with fire and energy, ready to erupt into heat and flame. His need to kiss her was fueled by an unexplained urgency to capture without conquering, to yield without surrendering, and to protect without imprisoning.

She hadn't hidden her distrust of him. The barrier she fought so hard to build slipped only in the height of an impassioned kiss or during a sparring match of words and wit.

Yet it slipped.

For a few brief moments, she allowed him to view something more than aloofness in the depths of those emerald eyes. A competitive spirit. Humor. Longing. A thirst for motion. Ambition. She was not afraid to take risks. He liked that.

But her assessment of him was accurate.

He would never abandon his business or his crew and leave the sea for a married life on land. Adventure and the thrill of experiencing new things was like air. He needed it. It was as much a part of him as his skin.

Could a young lady like her possibly care for a man who offered love, but not marriage; loyalty, but not lands; riches, but not lineage? She'd admitted she cared nothing about titles and wealth, but could love alone truly satisfy her?

Could love alone, really win her heart?

Could a lifetime of devotion, loyalty, and protection be enough to claim her? His heart jumped at a new thought. If he asked, would she join him, share a life with him on the water? Her eyes flared with a passionate light when she spoke about her shop. Would she give up her dream for him? It was selfish to even consider asking such a sacrifice from her. He couldn't bear to be the brunt of her resentment later.

He'd known her a few days, yet it seemed they'd known each other for years. She wanted him even as she tried to refuse him. Her drive for independence was as strong as her spirit. He could never tame that part of her, nor would he ever want to.

She pulled away to stare at him. He stroked the soft skin of her cheek and neck. The little noise she made deep in her throat vibrated lightly against his fingers, and he sucked in his breath. Self-control was almost impossible with her so close that he could see the burning flecks of gold in her irises. She was a siren, and he was helpless.

He stared at the beauty who gazed at him with raw, wild passion. She had no idea the affect she had on him, the power she wielded. A throbbing pressure shot through him. Was he strong enough to keep himself in check? He wanted nothing more than to lay Keelan down and make love to her, but common sense urged restraint. Here was a rare jewel, one he must earn. To take her this moment would only provide fuel for her hatred later.

Normally, there wouldn't be a later, and now he surprised himself by looking forward to it. Hungered for it like a starving man hungers for bread.

Keelan's lips parted, and she took a ragged breath. Gone was the mistrust and regal wall of indifference, replaced now by the vulnerable wonder of a virgin, and the heated desires of a woman. His need for her intensified, and with a low curse, he pulled her against his chest and eased her back down onto the saddle blanket. The mere thought of kissing her tore at his control. He lowered his head and pressed his lips against the sweet skin of her neck.

He was weak.

⚓ ⚓ ⚓

☙❧

KEELAN HUNGERED in a way she couldn't describe. The taste of his lips on her mouth, the hard, warm press of his body, the air she could hardly draw into her lungs left her *intoxicated*. She craved the sensations his kisses created, like she'd craved air below the surface of the lake.

He moved to that impossibly tender place behind her ear, and she lost all sense of time and space. She wasn't sure of anything except that she didn't want this to end. A strange thrill fluttered just beneath her skin, tingling and vibrating. She put her hand under his jaw, brought his lips to hers, and kissed his lower lip before sucking gently. He drew in a harsh breath and slid his palm around the back of her neck, cradled her head and crushed her to him.

His mouth ravaged her, stealing her breath, leaving her swirling somewhere high above the storm. The shock of his hand on her breast was quickly replaced by a torturous bliss when his thumb began to rub circles around her nipple. It hardened under the fabric of her gown, and she covered his hand with her own, before pressing it more firmly against her.

More, she wanted *more*.

And he gave her more, pinching her nipples lightly and then a harder tug, making her moan at the unexpected pleasure. The caress of his fingers as they traced a trail down her ribcage lured her closer, and she arched toward their heat. His hand found her hip and pulled it flush against him. He was hard and hot, and she craved his touch more than anything.

Her tongue danced with Landon's. How could anyone tire of kisses like *this*? Kissing him was like breathing; it was a requirement.

She should want to move away. But she didn't.

She wanted more. Needed more.

She wanted to pulse against his hand and beg for another caress.

She... *wanted*.

His hand stroked her calf. Her breath hitched when his fingers carved an invisible line up her thigh. The intense throbbing at the juncture where her legs joined made it impossible to think of anything else.

It was impossible to even think at all.

HER HAND CLOSED around Landon's forearm, stilling his fingers inches away from the moist heat he sought. He would not push her beyond her desire. For a reason eluding his logical mind at the moment, he needed her to crave his touch, even demand it. It baffled him. God, how he wanted her. He raised his head and searched her face for the command he needed. Her breath came in light pants.

"Landon...I..."

"Tell me you don't want me to touch you and I'll stop," he whispered hoarsely. He kissed the place that pulsed wildly on her neck and she whimpered. His hand stayed in place, but he moved his thumb in tiny patterns on the inside of her thigh. Her grip on his arm tightened, and her pupils widened with desire. She inhaled sharply as he brushed over the fine curls covering her womanhood.

"Touching your skin is like touching the sun and the rain. So warm —" She moved against his palm. "So wet."

Because she had intrigued him, he'd wanted to lure her to his bed and seduce her. Fool that he was, he'd thought he could enjoy a tussle or two and be on his way. Just the thought now sickened him and writhed sour and twisting in his gut.

More. That was what he wanted.

More.

She opened her eyes, and he lost himself in the darkened pools of green. They were filled with need, hunger, and bewilderment. The pull was impossible to resist. He could barely find his voice. "What is it that makes me want to breathe you in as if you are the last breath of air on earth?"

"Sometimes," she breathed, her eyes still locked with his, "the same thought flows through my mind."

His heart jolted and his mouth went dry. For once, he had no words. She reached up and pulled his head down and kissed him, and he fell into a pool of fire and emeralds.

He lightly slipped his fingers into her soft silky folds and made languid circles around her opening before moving up to that sensitive spot and repeating the movement. Her reedy gasp against his lips sent a surge of pleasure through him.

"You were made to be worshipped, Keelan," he rasped. "I want to show you how a man should pay homage to a goddess."

"Landon..." she breathed. "What is— It... oh!"

He increased the pressure against that small sensitive nub until she moaned his name. Her cheeks flushed with passion and her eyes went limpid. Her full, lush lips parted, and he had to taste them. She entwined her fingers in his hair and opened her mouth, accepting his tongue, hot and slick against her own.

He wanted to devour her.

Taste her.

Please her.

Claim her.

He caressed her, and she ground her hips into his hand until he slid a finger inside.

"Please," she said in a ragged whisper. "I don't know why, but Landon, please."

"Soon, sweet." He pushed down the shoulder of her dress enough to expose her breast, and he cupped it while he traced his tongue down her throat. She smelled of rain and sunshine all at once. The musky scent of her pulled at him, and he struggled to keep himself from breaking his earlier promise. Every beat of his heart made his body pulse and throb with need, and he was harder than he'd ever been in his life.

He trailed kisses along her collarbone, then licked the pink peak. She shuddered and breathed his name, then arched against him, pressing urgently into his palm, clenching his fingers inside her.

"Landon," she gasped.

He sucked her nipple into his mouth. "Let go, Keelan."

Her lids fluttered shut, and she tilted her head back, revealing the creamy skin of her neck as he slowly sucked her nipple. She clenched again as a small cry burst from her beautiful mouth.

❧ 26 ❧

CHAPTER TWENTY-SIX
A WEEK MOMENT

S anity had abandoned Keelan's mind. Even as warning bells began to bang harshly in her head, her body continued to fight them. She wanted to experience more of this; she wanted Landon to be the one to teach her how to make love. And she was only a caress away from begging him to do so.

What next, then? Her mind asked sluggishly. *A wedding? Followed by a farewell? Would he still make you happy, then? Or perhaps no wedding for you and no commitment from him. Remember his game; you may be nothing more than a pawn, insignificant and expendable.*

Did she care?

Where was her *head?*

Her weakness around this man was appalling

She finally caught her breath enough to speak. "Landon, please stop. We can't..."

He brought his lips to hers and kissed her. She should've moved away before she lost herself again, but this kiss was different. Gentle, lightly probing... tender. It was *tender*. It mesmerized her like a cobra to a lute. It took a long moment, but she managed to brace her palms on Landon's chest and shove. A little. It wasn't particularly hard, but it worked and he released her.

"I can't let this happen," she gasped. "No matter—"

"No matter how you feel about me?" His words were soft and quiet, but they hit her like a stinging slap.

"I... I don't know how I feel about you." She lied as she scooted away from him. Her chest heaved as if she had run for miles. Heat still smoldered in the center of her body. His touch had done things to her that she never imagined were possible. She couldn't even slow her breathing and compose herself.

She had acted like an addle-brained fool. Was a moment of bliss, the rapture of a caress worth the cost of her future happiness? Who was she to him, anyway? All he wanted was to seduce her. He had accomplished his goal, then.

Shame and anger seeped through her.

She choked, struggling to form the words. "You lied."

He quirked a brow. "I promised your virtue would remain intact. It did."

"You promised to protect me from—" Embarrassed by what she had permitted him to do to her pulled hot tears from her eyes. "You took advantage."

He peered at her closely. "Are you saying I am solely responsible for what happened between us?"

"Yes. No." Keelan sat up and inched further toward the wall behind her. Thinking back to the way he gave her such intense pleasure made her heart limpid and vivacious at the same time. "No, not entirely. But, I let you manipulate me, and that was a mistake. I know to never trust your kind. I knew that, and I still—" Anger at her own stupidity had her hissing through her teeth.

"My kind?" Landon's eyes narrowed. "What is my *kind*, exactly?"

Her embarrassment had reached its peak. A harsh laugh clawed from her throat; she whispered hoarsely, "You know what type of man you are, one who seduces women for sport. It's a *game* for you. I'm well-aware I'm nothing more than your current fancy, a way to bide the time while you're in Charleston." She dropped her chin and flattened her lips. "And I'm embarrassed to admit that I'm soft-headed. And gullible and apparently easy to seduce."

Somewhere in the back of her mind, she wanted him to deny it, convince her how wrong she was, tell her that she meant more to him than anyone he'd ever met. That he loved her as much as she—

Instead, his stormy eyes turned flinty and his expression chilled.

Hope twisted into a black shard and sliced her heart open; the sharp, searing pain stole her breath.

She didn't want to be right. But apparently she was.

She willed the tears burning the corners of her eyes away, then tucked a loose strand of hair behind her ear. "That's not a role I want to play." She turned her head and spoke before he could cast his spell on her again.

He heaved a sigh. "You're not a part of a game of seduction, Keelan. I care about you—"

"I wish I believed you." She gave a dry laugh that burned the back of her throat. "But I don't. Your sweet charm and easy smile are very seductive, but it's not real, it's an act. A lie. Find another to warm your bed. I'll not sacrifice my virtue for your simple, primal pleasures. I want you to stay away from me." She choked out a whisper. "Please, Landon, I beg you."

Yet, she was aware that even as she said the words, the image of him touching another woman the same way he had touched her twisted her stomach. As hard as she had tried to avoid it, she allowed her heart to slip and tilt her center of logic.

Soon, he would sail away from the port of Charleston, and she would be left bearing a yoke of misery because she wasn't strong enough.

He'd already created a raw, bleeding wound.

Damn him.

His voice dropped. "I see."

The chill in his tone made her wince. She lifted her nose and ignored the bite of his words. She combed through her storm-blown hair with trembling fingers, doing her best to banish the thoughts and images of the exuberant sensations he stirred.

"Boy, girl, temptress, lady, now shrew, the many faces of Keelan Grey." The quiet words he spoke affected her more than if he had shouted them. "Which will you show next, I wonder?"

He had no idea how each word sliced off another chunk of her heart.

"Our lives follow different paths," she whispered. "You're a man of the sea. I could never love you," she lied. "I'm a woman who enjoys the busy atmosphere of the city. I want to run a shop and have a family someday." She wanted more than that, now, thanks to him, something she'd never attain.

His voice was low and hoarse, "Then 'tis a dangerous course you tread now, my sweet." He leaned back against the wall and closed his eyes, dismissing her from his sight.

She turned her back to him and wiped away the hot tears before they traveled too far down her cheeks. Disappointment, hurt, and humiliation smothered her like thick smoke.

They sat in silence as the wind wailed forlornly; branches and debris hit the outer walls. Gusts clawed and slashed at the shingles around the damaged corner of the roof. The pelting rain found its way further into the small structure, causing the fire to sputter and hiss angrily at the intrusion. Landon jumped up and quickly doused the flames, which extinguished much of the light.

"Why did you put it out?" she cried, thinking there would be no way to dry their rain-soaked clothes.

Landon answered from a few feet away. "The hole in the floorboards above served as our chimney, but if it becomes covered with debris, the cellar will fill with smoke," She could almost make out his silhouette in the diminishing light.

Seeking something solid for support, she groped for the wall behind her and scampered backward until her spine pressed against it. The storm was a giant, angry beast and when it ripped away another portion of the cabin, she screamed. The force yanked away a large section above them and tossed it straight up into the sky. She let out a strangled cry and ducked her head as splintering wood shrieked into the howling wind.

Landon's hard arms gathered her close, his deep voice firm in her ear, "I have you, Keelan. Don't be afraid." He murmured something else, but a loud screech drowned out his words. He pushed her back to the ground against the wall and covered her body with his, as shards of planking and rubble rained down on them. She squeezed her eyes closed, wrapped her arms around him, and clung with every ounce of strength she had. She shouldn't be so relieved to be this close, but it would be useless to pretend otherwise. Truth was, she'd rather be the recipient of his anger instead of that cold indifference she felt moments ago.

More of the shanty collapsed above them, plunging them into complete darkness, and muffling the sound of the storm outside. He held her tightly, and she prayed the structure wouldn't completely fall into the cellar. They stayed that way for a long time, while the wind and rain lashed the land. His hard chest, hips and thighs blanketed her, creating searing warmth where they touched. She nuzzled her face into the pulse on the side of his neck and when she opened her eyes, her lashes flickered against his skin. He started and then chuckled.

"I remember my mother doing that to me when I was a young lad," he said, a smile in his voice.

"Doing what?" she asked, confused. It was too hard to ignore the lovely pressure of his body long enough to figure out what he meant.

"This." Landon blinked against her cheek, drawing a surprised giggle from her. "She called them 'fairy kisses.'" He dipped his head and did it again.

"I like fairy kisses." She was unable to contain her laughter at the ticklish sensation his lashes created. "Have you told her how you cherish that memory?"

"My parents died of a fever during the voyage from Ireland to Boston when I was young."

"Oh," she said, saddened. "How awful for you. What did you do? Where did you live?"

He shifted his weight to the side. "Conal's uncle took me in and taught me about sailing ships and bartering for goods. Eventually, Uncle Fynn rented a small space in his hold to me, and I would purchase cargo and sell it at a profit. When I saved enough money, I bought my own brigantine, the *Desire*. Conal took over the *Seeker*. After a few years, Fynn turned his trading company over to four of us: his sons, Ronan and Brendan, his nephew Conal, and me. Brendan was Fynn's first mate on the *Reward*."

"What's the name of Ronan's ship?"

"Ronan is only fourteen. The fleet was running a new trade route together a few weeks ago when we were attacked. We came here to try to complete Fynn's original plan while our ships were repaired. Brendan Ahern and the *Reward* are awaiting us in Harbour Town."

Keelan already suspected Fynn's reasons. She took a resigned breath, wishing she didn't have to admit to him something that might have horribly affected his adopted family.

"I might be able to clarify why Uncle Fynn wanted to speak with my father." She was now grateful for the darkened cellar; he wouldn't be able to see the embarrassment in her eyes, although it was uncertain if she could keep it from her voice.

"My father inadvertently gave orders to sink a vessel off the coast of Ireland about two years ago. He assumed it was a French privateer being duplicitous by flying American colors. Unfortunately, it *was* an American passenger ship. Almost everyone drowned or was killed. There was a large public outcry. He was court-martialed, and if it hadn't been for the influence of one of his old war comrades, he would have even been hanged."

Her mother had to close and board up the shop after stones had been thrown through the front windows on two different occasions. Less than a week later, she was dead.

"We suspect it's the reason our family was targeted by an assassin. Someone seeks revenge against my father. My mother was murdered, then my aunt and cousin. Papa's friend managed to help us escape to Charleston, where we hoped we'd be safe."

"So you're wondering if Fynn Ahern had a family member aboard," Landon stated.

"Yes."

"No," he mused. "I don't think that was the reason. Fynn was like a father to me, so I know Conal's entire family. They had no such a tragedy. I doubt Fynn journeyed here for retribution," he added, as if reading her mind.

She made a mental note to speak with her father about it at the first opportunity.

The wailing wind eased, and the fierce din of angry hail changed to the gentler slap of a spring rain. How long had they been talking?

"It seems the worst has passed," he said, echoing her thoughts. "Let's see if I can push the hatch open."

As soon as he lifted his weight from her, the cool air blew away his warmth, leaving her chilled and exposed. A moment later, she heard the sound of his shoulder pushing against the door, then a grunt. No creaking hinges followed. He tried again and was delivered the same result.

"It won't move even a little. If I had to wager on the cause, I'd say the chimney wall above has collapsed on it," he said.

They were trapped in an abandoned, now demolished, shanty miles from the mill and the main house. The chances of anyone finding them soon were tiny. And there was nothing they could do about it.

"Maybe if I help you, we can open the door together." She did a horrible job of hiding the tremor in her voice, as she scrambled to her feet. Keelan reached out and when her hand found the wall, she began to grope her way along the rough, damp surface toward Landon's voice.

"There's not enough room for both of us to stand on the step," he answered. "But, I fear our efforts would be in vain. I noticed no give at all."

The thick air invaded Keelan's chest, and her breaths shortened in response. The walls loomed around them in the murky blackness. Something brushed against her hand and she jumped, unable to restrain a surprised squeak.

Landon's long, firm fingers twined with hers and he gave a squeeze. "That was just me, trying to find you."

She allowed him to pull her into the comforting circle of his arms. "What now?"

"An opening exists above the remnants of our fire, but the floor here drops sharply and I can't reach high enough to move the debris enough to fit through." Landon's words were carefully even.

"Then we're trapped here," her voice quavered, and she swallowed. She really should have just stayed in the house this morning rather than take her problems on a ride through the countryside.

"There is one thing we could try," he mused. "But it won't be easy for either of us." Was that a smile she heard in the dark? Was he *smiling?* She could think of nothing that was even the tiniest bit humorous.

"What is it?"

"If I lift you, and whatever covering the opening is moveable, you might be able to shift it enough to squeeze out."

He waited patiently while she mulled over his plan. Surely, she could think of something that would work better. But nothing came to mind.

Think of something. Anything.

She let out a beleaguered breath. There was no alternative to even consider.

"Tell me what to do," she said resignedly. She had a feeling the captain would be more comfortable with the situation than she. The only satisfaction for her was that she would be spared seeing his rakish leer.

Suddenly, the darkness seemed less intimidating.

CHAPTER TWENTY-SEVEN
A FREEDOM RUNNER

"Ready?"

No.

"I'm ready." She tried to sound nonchalant, but her voice came out lumpy with trepidation.

Landon had explained how he would wrap his arms around her legs and lift her up. He was strong enough to do so effortlessly, but she still wasn't comfortable being hoisted off the ground in total darkness.

Holding her hand, he picked his way through the stifling darkness, stopping when his boot crunched on the charred wood remnants of their fire. She heard him move behind her, the heat from his large body pulsed against her back, and the tiny hairs on her arms and the back of her neck twitched.

Perhaps this wasn't the best idea after all.

She trembled slightly, but still managed to stay mute as his hands moved down her ribs, over her hips. Keelan wasn't about to give him the satisfaction of knowing how his touch affected her, or a reason to mock her for chastising him for it. She'd had enough for one day.

His hands continued down the outside of her upper legs with agonizing slowness. She tensed in response, about to lose the fight to remain silent. Before she could open her mouth to snap at him, he hugged her knees and lifted her off the ground.

"Oh!" She gasped and flung her arms wide. There was nothing to cling to. Good Lord, she now sat on his shoulder. He had one arm over her thighs and the other on the small of her back, dangerously close to her bottom. She reached down and grabbed the fabric of his shirt.

"Stay still," he grunted.

"Get your hand away from my backside!" she hissed. He was intentionally trying to irritate her.

"Keelan—"

"Now!"

He released a frustrated sound. "As you wish." He slid his hand up her back and around her ribcage to rest right beneath her right breast, nearly covering her entire side.

"Landon Hart!"

"If I don't hold you, love, you'll fall," he said with a hint of exasperation in his tone.

Keelan rolled her eyes. He could find a way to keep her secure without all this groping. "This is your way of protecting my well-being? Surely it can be done with your hand somewhere less improper."

He glided his hand around her ribs so slowly it felt like a caress, heating her skin and making her want to close her eyes and savor it. Not that she enjoyed it. Well, she shouldn't have enjoyed it, considering the predicament they were in at the moment.

He stopped between her shoulder blades. She wobbled without the protective band of his arm. A startled yip escaped her throat. His hand jumped back to the front of her ribcage, and it was a moment before she realized she was gripping his forearm with both hands, pressing his thumb into her breast. It would be better if he slid his giant hand an inch lower, but she didn't dare ask. Who knows where it would end up?

"Don't do that again!" Her breath came out in short pants. "Stay this way, it's safer."

He chuckled. "Yes, my love."

"Stop that." Irritating man.

"Stop what?"

"Calling me your 'love.'" It was entirely too unsettling, too intimate, and too wonderful.

And too false.

"But sweet Keelan, you—"

An unintelligible murmur of voices filtered through the rubble above. Keelan's heart leapt. Someone was out there! They would soon be discovered and rescued. Thank goodness!

Landon gently lowered her to the ground and slipped his hand over her mouth before whispering, "Let's listen before we alert them to our presence, in case they are not well-intentioned."

Of course, how naïve of her. She did her best to swallow her fear, but it was impossible with a dry mouth. They might be vagabonds or worse. She'd been ready to shout out, which could have put them in danger.

She nodded, and he removed his hand. Footsteps sounded on the planks above, but the voices remained muted and she couldn't make out any words.

"What should we do?" She wanted to yell for help, but what if the strangers were indeed highwaymen taking advantage of the chaos following the storm?

He slid his hand down her arm in the darkness and before she could question his motives, the handle of his dagger pressed into her palm.

"Keep the knife handy in case things go awry."

Before he could proceed with his plan, a dim glow appeared from within the small alcove. It took only a second for her to conclude that it was an entrance to a small tunnel, rather than a storage area, and the people who were outside a moment ago were now on their way *in*.

They were trapped.

Landon moved swiftly, dragging her with him. He pressed her against the wall adjacent to the tunnel's mouth and touched his finger to her lips to remind her to be silent. In the slow dawning of light, he withdrew a pistol from one of the saddlebags. Her breath froze.

The glow grew brighter and a brown arm holding a lantern appeared. A young man, perhaps in his early teens, crawled from the opening. As he straightened, he locked gazes with her, and his eyes widened. Landon crept up behind him, put a hand over his mouth and pressed the pistol into his side. He pulled the young slave away from the lantern and into the shadows.

A woman emerged next. She stood and brushed her skirts, then turned to help a man crawling behind her. As he straightened, she could see he was cradling his arm, and blood had seeped through the sleeve of his shirt. The man froze in place, but he seemed to coil like a viper, every muscle active, eyes fixed on Landon and the boy. The woman reacted to the tension of the man next to her. She whirled and stifled a scream with her hands, as her gaze fell upon Landon's pistol and the young man he held.

The last person to emerge made Keelan gasp.

It was little Joseph's father.

"Simon!" she said with surprise and relief.

He jolted as if struck. His head whipped up, and he spun to face her. A multitude of emotions fluttered across his face. Shock, relief, fear.

"Miss Keelan! Praise the Lord, you all right! Ruth an' yo family has worried themselves sick."

The enlarged root cellar made more sense, now. The baskets of vegetables, the small sacks of rice, the tattered blankets and straw pallets, were enough provisions for a few people who might need a place to rest without drawing any attention.

"What are you doing here, Simon?" she asked quietly, already knowing the answer. She had heard of a secret society who helped slaves escape to the north. What were they called? Freedom Runners?

The house slave shifted his weight from foot to foot for a moment. Landon had released the boy, but still had his weapon pointed at the group. He changed position to stand next to her.

With trembling fingers, the woman reached over, grasped the boy's arm, and hugged it to her stomach. Finally, with watery eyes, Simon appealed to her. "Miss Keelan, these folks here... they jus' need a short stopover on their way... along." He gestured to the other man's bleeding arm.

"Along where?" She really didn't need the answer.

She already knew.

CHAPTER TWENTY-EIGHT
A RIDE HOME

Runaways.

Simon stared at his toes. The woman began to weep softly; the boy stood stiff as a statue. The wounded slave put his uninjured arm around the woman's waist. "Hush, now, Nettie," he murmured.

Landon whispered in her ear, "I think it's best for us if we don't know their destination." He holstered the gun. "'Tis obvious they're runaways. Unless you wish to force them back with us, the less we know, the better."

She wondered what Simon's part was in all this. Unlike her father and uncle, she hadn't been able to adjust comfortably into the Lowcountry society of plantation owners and their families. If she were a slave, she'd run away too. She might still, depending on what transpired when she returned home.

She jerked her chin toward the other man's wound. "Let me see your arm."

He straightened and gave a sideways glance to Simon, who nodded. He peeled back his bloodied sleeve to show a deep, jagged slash. She glanced at Landon. "I'll need your rum-laced water, unless you have straight whiskey?"

"I do have a small flask of whiskey," he replied. He rummaged around in his saddlebags and pulled it out.

She addressed Simon. "Please see if you can find some garlic in those bags in the corner."

While he searched for garlic, she took the dagger and slit strips from her shift. Remembering Slaney's words in the kitchen house, she doused the wound with Landon's whiskey. The slave had a stronger countenance than she, and showed no sign of pain, except a slight hissing intake of breath. Simon handed her a needle and thread, and she glanced at him in surprise.

"Found it near the garlic," he said, not meeting her gaze.

Stopover, indeed. She wondered what other supplies were hidden in the cellar.

Keelan stitched the wound. When she finished, she perused it smugly. Her needlepoint might be horrendous, but she could stitch a wound quite effectively. She poured a bit more whiskey over it, then crushed the garlic, using the blade's handle. She pressed it over the cut, then wrapped everything securely. She gave the left over strips to his wife, along with the rest of the clove.

"Use these later to change the dressing."

"Yes'm." Nettie took the items and placed them in her apron pocket. Her eyes were still wary.

Keelan calmly studied Simon. "Will you be going with them?"

He gave her a surprised look. "Why no, Miss! I wouldn't leave my family. We together. I ain't runnin' Miss Keelan."

Family. She recalled Ruth and Joseph, and how they had clung to each other in the kitchen yard. She came to a conclusion. Hopefully Landon would go along with it. Turning to him, she handed him the blade. "It has been an exhausting day, and I'd like to go home." She spoke to the runaways before she exited. "We'll make no mention that we saw you. God speed on your journey."

Landon's face softened. "Go on ahead, I'll gather my gear and meet you outside."

The tunnel itself was cleverly hidden within a cluster of shrubs and rocks, several paces from the old shack. She climbed out and perused her surroundings. In the aftermath, an eerie, golden, pink veil had settled about the countryside. The evening sun began to peek from behind the dark purple clouds now moving northwest.

She stared at the remnants of the small shanty that had been snuggled into the grove. A massive tree had flattened it. Her throat constricted at the devastation surrounding them. A path of trees, snapped midway up the trunk, trailed away from the cabin as if a giant had stomped on them. The ground was littered with shaggy tresses of Spanish moss, dark prickly pine cones the size of her boot, and a carpet of twigs and green leaves. She couldn't restrain a shudder. They were lucky to have escaped injury. Thoughts of her family had her eager to head home, concerned for their well-being.

Landon emerged, then dragged an old plank across the entrance to hide it.

"I'm glad your knowledge of storms is sound, Milord Pirate," she murmured.

"Been through enough to see them coming, most times," he replied, taking in the demolished structure behind them.

It was as if there was an unspoken agreement between the two of them to avoid discussing Simon and the runaways, almost as if ignoring them made them invisible and kept them safe. It would be nice to forget the harsh words they exchanged too. Although it might be better for her to stay distant.

Worry churned in her stomach and she prayed that the horses made it through unscathed. "Where did you hobble Orion?" That horse now held a special place in her heart.

"I didn't," he responded. "In conditions like these, it's best to allow the animal's instincts to see it safely through. I trust Orion found adequate shelter." Glancing at her, he added, "Sham would have, too." He gave a loud piercing whistle and waited.

She heard the pounding hoof beats before she caught sight of the stallion. He rounded the toppled shanty and skidded to a muddy halt before snorting loudly in greeting. Landon spoke to his horse in soft tones, while he moved his hand over the mud-streaked shoulders and quivering flanks. Aside from several twigs tangled in his mane and tail and a few streaks of red clay, the steed had weathered the elements well enough.

Satisfied he was sound, Landon quickly saddled him and turned toward her. "At a leisurely pace, it shouldn't take long to make it back. Come, I'll help you mount."

She stepped into his waiting hand, and he hoisted her easily. It'd been many years since she'd had ridden astride a horse. Her father insisted she learn how to control a well-trained mount with her knees and heels before she attempted to ride sidesaddle. Even so, it still seemed strange and unfamiliar as she wiggled in her seat. Her short-ened shift hindered her ability to keep her legs open enough to straddle Orion's back, so she pulled it up and allowed it to bunch above her waist beneath her skirt.

Landon secured his bags and swung a leg up behind her. Keelan's back went rigid at the shock of his hardened thighs against the backs of her own. His arm looped with bold familiarity around her middle. Even more shocking was the scalding heat of him against her backside. She squirmed forward as far as she could.

His chest rumbled behind her. "Methinks the ride back should be a pleasant one."

She made a point of removing his arm and placing it on his own leg. "Keep your hands to your own person, Captain. I'll not tolerate your oafish groping. Despite your roguish conduct today, I will continue my efforts to preserve my reputation and my virtue. Being seen in your presence will do enough damage to my good name as it is."

He gave a short laugh. "My touch did not seem to tarnish your reputation during the violence of the gale. Indeed," he continued in a thoughtful, yet mocking tone, "the high and haughty Miss Keelan seemed to desire the warmth and protection of my arms, making me wonder what other services I might provide."

There it was. He probably didn't mean to reveal that information, but he'd just admitted to her that the intimacy they'd shared was driven by lust. *Services, humph.* He spoke as if he was a stud and she a brood mare. Now that she understood both his place and hers in their relationship, there was no need for her to say more. It didn't matter, and it would change nothing, not the way he felt about her or the different paths their lives would soon take. There could be no satisfaction in bringing it all to light. If anything, it would only cause pain. Well, *more* pain.

His warm breath against her nape flashed across the skin on her neck. She shivered involuntarily and annoyed with her body's response to his proximity, she brought her hands up to her hair.

"Thanks to a spring rain, my appearance has been much damaged." She groaned. "What will my family think?"

She felt him shrug as he nudged Orion into motion. "This was not a mere rain shower, Keelan. If they care about your safety, they will welcome you home, relieved you were able to weather such a fierce tempest. I'm afraid many others may not have shared our good fortune."

She pondered his statement as they plodded through the clearing. The other abandoned shanties hadn't survived the ravages of the winds either. Shingles, clapboards, and splintered planks littered the earth. The horse picked his way nimbly through the debris. Landon steered them toward home. He shifted slightly, and Orion leapt into a slow, easy canter.

She almost squealed at the unexpected change in gait and grabbed the mane with both hands. Landon's arm snaked around her and settled her firmly back into the seat. This time she did not remove it, choosing safety in exchange for pride.

The rest of the journey back was uneventful, and she couldn't help but enjoy the easy conversation she had with Landon. He was a talented storyteller, keeping her holding her breath in suspense or holding her side from laughter.

"It is no wonder you love sailing the ocean. If I were a man, I think I would choose the same profession. It would be fascinating to see such exotic sights and live such extraordinary experiences."

"Just say the word, my lady and I will be your most devoted escort."

She sighed and became quiet as her thoughts churned. He spoke the words lightly, but their weight was palpable. Circumstances with her father and her own troubles made such a life appear no more than a childish dream. Remaining practical and following her plan of opening her shop should stay in the forefront of her mind.

Everything else should stay distant.

Exposing her tender desires to a charmer like Landon would only add more torment to an already broken-heart. She had to steel her emotions from the potent lure of the man and somehow maintain a cool and aloof demeanor. Keeping a snowflake from melting on a hot July day in South Carolina would be easier.

Both marveled at the destruction. The storm had cut a swath of devastation through the forest along the southern side of the trail. Entire trees had been uprooted. Some looked like broken broomsticks; their trunks twisted and snapped several feet from the ground.

"It headed northwest," Landon quietly observed.

She chewed her lower lip.

Toward Twin Pines.

CHAPTER TWENTY-NINE
KEELAN'S CHOICE

The stable roof was in shambles.

From what she could see, it lay in pieces scattered about the barnyard and as far as Aunt Sarah's garden. Men, women, and children dotted the landscape, picking up the debris. Somehow, the main house had escaped damage. Keelan expelled a thankful sigh.

Thomas worked hitching horses to Uncle Jared's carriage. Nearby, additional mounts were saddled and tethered to the fence.

They rode into the yard. Upon recognizing them, the young groom let out a whoop and ran off into the house.

Landon dismounted. "It appears we have caused a bit of a tizzy."

She blew a curl from her face. "A search party has been assembled." She glanced worriedly toward the house, wondering if it was for them or the runaways. "I worry Simon won't make it back before his absence is noticed."

Landon wrapped the reins around a fence post. "He is a very resourceful man," he answered, his expression shuttered.

She shot him a narrowed glance. "How would you know that? You have only seen him twice."

Landon shrugged. "He left a strong impression." He reached up and circled her waist with his hands, then pulled her from the saddle.

There was a fierce tug on her train accompanied by a violent rip making both freeze. She was suspended, held in part by his extended arms, as well as the trapped skirt snagged on the saddle horn. With a wary swallow, she peered over her shoulder, then gasped. The back of her skirt had been separated from the seam, exposing her twisted shift. The result unveiled a pair of ivory-white legs and from the draft, most of her backside as well.

Landon followed her gaze and his eyes widened. She wanted to smack his hard and horribly unyielding shoulder, but she settled for glaring at him. He leered back, crystal blue eyes brimming with humor.

"Put. Me. Down."

His grin expanded. "As you wish."

He began to lower her to the ground, but paused again at the sound of another rending.

"Wait!" she shrieked, immediately regretting her command.

The corners of his mouth twitched. "What will it be, my love? Shall I put you down or not? I enjoy having you in my arms but would desire a more private spot."

"This is no time for jest!" she hissed. "Nor the time to play the rutting stag. My hem is caught, and you know it."

He tilted his head and leisurely scrutinized her exposed limbs. This time, she thumped his chest with her fists.

"Landon Hart!"

"Would you like some help to that end, my love?" he asked solemnly.

His calm, confident demeanor, combined with his ornery teasing, made it hard for her to focus on the issue at hand. She expelled an exasperated breath and hoped she sounded intimidating when she spoke through clenched teeth. "If you are quite through being a scoundrel then, *yes*!"

Landon easily lifted her higher and to her shock, put her over his shoulder like a sack of sugar. His left hand rested boldly on the small of her back, if you could call it that, since its position was either at the lowest part of her back or the highest part of her bottom. Stepping forward, he reached up and disengaged the train. That feat accomplished, he lowered her from his shoulder and released her, allowing her to slide against his body with a speed similar to cold molasses. He was a rake to the *core*.

Her body instinctively arched toward him. Her mind and body were both traitors. She shoved against his chest, which was like shoving an ox. With what she hoped was a chilling glare, she struggled to wriggle the stubbornly tangled shift free.

"Look what you've done!" She swiveled and reached for the torn waistline. She grasped a handful of fabric and tried her best to preserve her modesty. How humiliating. At least no one was near enough to witness her mortification. She decided to ignore the hot flush burning her cheeks. Let the cad think it was anger instead of acute embarrassment, which welled inside her like an overfilled pitcher.

The entire day had been one compromising event after another, and Landon Hart had witnessed or participated in every single one. Embarrassment and shame turned to anger. His proximity made him an easy target. Scowling, she raised her chin to meet his carefully subdued gaze, and poked a slender finger hard on his chest. She stalked him when he stepped back, narrowing the space between them.

"Since I have been in your presence, I have been insulted, ogled, mauled and now, practically had the clothes ripped from my body."

Landon managed to look appalled. "My sweet Miss Grey, I never insulted you."

At no time in her life had she repeatedly felt so discomfited, desirable, passionate, and scandalized as she had since meeting Landon Hart. Why must she ever be the ninny in his eyes? She painted herself into a very unladylike portrait; and repeated it every time they saw each other. It annoyed her even more that Landon had gleefully witnessed every dreadful moment. She'd even allowed him to seduce her.

And enjoyed it.

Gah. She was so weak. To be placed in a category with all the other ladies he'd charmed had her stomach tossing acid up her throat. Even now, she ached for his touch and craved his kisses.

She longed for it to mean more.

The horrible understanding that she'd acted like a lovesick girl, rather than a young lady of grace and integrity grated her pride. Worse, was the way her body reacted when he was near, beyond the annoyance and anger. Part of her wanted to be close enough to breathe him in, run her fingers over the hard ridges of his ribs, and thrill in the way his presence energized her.

Another part of her was frantically clanking gongs and tin kettles in her head.

She wasn't a daft, pampered child of the aristocracy. She'd grown up as a commodore's daughter. Her mother had made sure she understood the ways of men. She'd be wise to avoid letting her reckless emotions override those lessons. If only she could trust her own self-restraint.

Seemingly undaunted by her reprimand, the sea captain was rudely avoiding eye contact as she spoke. His attention was directed over her shoulder.

"Keelan, my sweet—"

"Do *not* attempt to ply me with tender words in hopes of dampening my vexation." Unwilling to yield him the opportunity to toss about any more of his apparently bottomless supply of mockery and charm, she continued, "I am not your *sweet*. I am not your *love*. You act like a charming gentleman one moment and a pirate thief stealing kisses from me the next." She wished she could find the words to slice his overconfident ego and dispel that infuriating grin. She gestured to her person. "Look at me! You have literally ripped the clothes from my body."

His eyebrows lowered in warning. He spoke softly. "Keelan, love, 'tis best to continue this conversation another time."

Her jaw unhinged. Did he think he could simply tell her to be quiet and postpone the admonishment until such a time it was convenient for *him*?

She flung an arm in the air in exasperation. "Do you really think I give a damn about whether you want to hear about what a scandalous debaucher of women you are?" He might be lord, master, and captain of his ship but this was not his domain, and she would not let him bully her into silence. She would speak her mind!

"And you should know, Sir Pirate, if you think your groping and pawing will have me soon falling, willing and lusty, into your bed like a common street trollop then you, sir—" She jabbed his chest again. "Are an arrogant *ass*!"

There. He deserved every last word of that chastisement.

She dropped her hand and tried to better gather her tattered skirt. "Oh, for pity's sake, let's speak no more of it. I'm afraid it's been a trying afternoon, and my patience has been worn too thin." She brushed her hand over her renegade curls. "We should be thankful the worst thing that happened was that I lost my—"

A startled gasp behind her hit Keelan like a cold blast of water.

"... Favorite bonnet." She finished weakly.

Landon's face blanked as he fought to remain painfully composed. Who was behind her? Slowly turning, she saw Thomas standing with a small contingent of family and servants. To her horror, Mr. Pratt, Doreen, Aunt Sarah, and Uncle Jared stood on the porch at the forefront, their eyes wide and unblinking. Her father sat on a wheeled chair. Thomas and Ruth did their best to find other sights to peruse, like toes, trees, the sky. Behind them, Everett stuttered out the front door, making matters truly abysmal.

Her aunt managed to find her voice first. "Keelan, dear child," she choked. "When that beast of a horse returned without you, we feared the worst!" She scurried forward and lightly hugged her. "I am so relieved you are home safe. You appear to be..."

Doreen dug her fists into her hips. "Running around the countryside like some loose floozy!" she sneered, her perusal raking Keelan from nose to toes. "Look at her. Riding hither and yon without a decent escort! It's shameful." Doreen turned toward her father. "Our name will be the laughingstock of the Charleston area, if it's not already, thanks to her!"

Keelan stiffened at her cousin's harsh outburst.

Uncle Jared scowled at his daughter, quickly grabbed her arm, and pulled her behind him. "This is none of your concern, Doreen."

Landon addressed her cousin; placing a hand over his heart, he bowed slightly. "I assure you, Miss Doreen, Miss Keelan was on her best behavior. My reputation as a gentleman has remained intact and not been tarnished in the least by today's events."

Keelan's jaw dropped as the meaning of Landon's words sank in.

Her aunt made a strangled choking sound; her eyes flickered nervously between her husband and the other onlookers. Her uncle actually appeared to be fighting back a smile. He coughed into his hand, then scratched his neck and glanced at her father.

But it was Mr. Pratt who acted first, his face a mottled red. His glower shifted between her and Landon. "I came here before continuing on my search for three runaways, to make sure my intended hadn't been harmed by the storm." He turned to her father and uncle. "However, in light of the current situation, consider my previous offer of marriage rescinded!"

Horrible man. Keelan sent up a silent prayer that Simon helped the family get away safely. They were already at a disadvantage. It's harder to run with three.

Pratt shouldered past the two men and strode down the steps without another glance in Keelan's direction. After snatching his horse's reins from the hitching post, he mounted and dug his heels into the gelding's side. At his shout, two other figures near the stables galloped to join him in his flight down the lane toward the mill.

The family stood in horrified silence, except for Keelan, of course. She wanted to laugh with relief, but didn't dare try to appear anything but grim. Doreen clapped a hand over her mouth. Although, by the gleam in her eyes, she had to assume her cousin enjoyed the entertainment immensely.

Her father was stone-faced. "What have you to say for your actions, Captain Hart?"

She went from sudden elation to instant terror. Her chest turned to hard, jagged stone, weighing her down and making it difficult to draw an even breath. What had she done? How much had they heard?

Landon answered smoothly, unruffled, "I acted with your daughter's best interests in mind."

Liar.

Of course, Landon didn't have the courage to look at her as he continued. "After speaking with Mr. Grey, I took his advice and toured the plantation. I came upon Miss Grey and offered to escort her back to the house. We were unable to make it back in time, so we sought shelter and waited for the hurricane to pass. Unfortunately, the lightening frightened off her mount. I did my best to return her to you, unharmed in every way."

Should she correct him? Should she tell her father Hart had saved her from a runaway horse in addition to the fury of a horrendous storm? Would Papa think it was a ploy to show Landon in a more positive light than what he deserved? Sadly, the damage had already been done, thanks to her regrettable tirade. As hard as it was for her to do so, she slammed her mouth shut.

"According to my daughter, your conduct was unbecoming," her father growled, leaning heavily on the arms of the wheeled chair. "I assure you, knowing Pratt, the sun will barely rise on the morrow, 'ere the rest of the county will be buzzing with the news you have *ruined* her!" His last words ended in a near roar, causing both Keelan and Aunt Sarah to cringe.

Landon didn't flinch. In fact, his face showed no emotion at all. "I have no desire to see your daughter ruined beyond repair, Commodore. As amends, I respectfully request her hand in marriage, sir, if that will remedy the situation."

"It would certainly help," Jared interjected. "And sooner rather than later."

"Wait!" Everett fell forward, tripping over Ruth's foot as he squeezed between her and Joseph. "I... I also offer my hand in marriage. I have spoken to both the commodore and Miss Grey, concerning such. Keelan and I are in love and are, in fact, already betrothed."

She could only stare at the doctor in shock. What had he just said?

In love?

In... *love?*

She opened her mouth to object, but all that would come out was an odd squeaking noise.

That beautiful plan, the one that started out as a delaying tactic, had turned on her like a rabid dog. To make matters even more deplorable, she'd inadvertently moved up the wedding date.

Everything was now completely out of her control, and she didn't do well when she had no control. Papa slammed down his eyebrows, then glared at his brother, who remained stoic. Her mind worked furiously, tossing away one idea after another, but she could find no quick way out, other than fake a complete faint, but that would mean letting go of her skirt. Drat.

Her father crossed his arms. "My daughter will decide now which of the two she will wed."

Decide *now*?

Marry Landon Hart or Everett Garrison? Choose either a rogue like Landon who flirted with the strings of her heart better than the best trained violinist, or a benevolent, but meek man like Everett, who while kind, stirred no passion in her soul at all.

Good Lord, she lived a nightmare!

She finally found her tongue. "Papa, can we not take some time to discuss—"

Her father swiftly raised a pale, trembling hand and stopped her. "I need no time. My decision stands. You will marry immediately. The only question you must answer is, which man will you take as a husband?"

She could only gape at her father. Her heart screamed Landon's name, but her voice would not. Her body hungered for his touch, but her heart feared he'd feed it lust rather than love. Then a wicked image crept into her mind of her standing on the pier with a swollen belly, and the women of Charleston talking behind their fans about her husband, who left his naïve little wife behind while bedding every arduous beauty between here and China.

Everett had a growing practice in Charleston. It was likely he would return to it when he was no longer needed at Twin Pines. Already, he'd made several trips back and forth each month. The fastest way to see her dream of owning her own boutique fulfilled would be to choose Everett. Better to chain herself to the one she didn't love, than the one who would shatter her heart and leave her bitter and lonely.

It would be safer, less painful in the end.

Her shoulders sagged, as if Orion had just climbed on her back. She stared at her father and swallowed. "Fine, then. I'll take..." She closed her eyes. "Dr. Garrison."

Doreen inhaled sharply before she whirled, wrenched open the door, and ran into the house.

Next to her, Landon released the slightest expulsion of breath. A sigh of relief. Her stomach took a sickening plunge.

So, she'd made the right choice after all. The right choice, not the most desired one. Not her heart's choice.

Now that the decision was made, she hated herself for allowing Landon to shred her stupid heart. How dare her father force her choose now, in front of everyone? She couldn't stand there a moment longer. When she started for the porch, Landon touched her elbow.

"Keelan—"

The world turned red. She reacted instinctively with a fury fed by regret, heartbreak and humiliation. In one smooth motion, she jerked her elbow away and with her other hand, landed a slap on his cheek that could be heard all the way to Jamaica. Whirling back toward the house, she gathered her ruined skirt and stomped up the stairs, people parting a path for her like the red sea.

Damn that man!

And damn her silly, foolish, *foolish* heart.

$$\text{❈ } 30 \text{ ❈}$$

CHAPTER THIRTY
A NEW PROPOSAL

Landon adjusted Orion's reins and prepared to mount. He'd probably dodged a bullet, both literally and figuratively. Grey would have been perfectly within his rights to demand he marry Keelan today, and at gunpoint. He lifted his sleeve and wiped the small beads of sweat from his hairline. If he ever married, it would be too soon. His line of work didn't accommodate wives very well. And he enjoyed his freedom. He couldn't help looking back toward the upper windows of the house. So why did he feel as if something thorny scraped the inside of his chest?

"Hart."

He turned toward Commodore Grey, who was alone with his brother on the porch. The commodore's pallor was more pronounced, now that his anger had diminished. The veins on his stark hands glared like blue ink on white parchment.

"Yes, Commodore?"

Sighing heavily, the old man cleared his throat. "Thank you for taking my daughter under your protection and seeing her home. We've been sick with worry over her welfare."

He gave the commodore a slight nod, thinking back to his earlier blunder that made Sham bolt away with Keelan on his back. "I'm glad

I was able to help, sir. However, I have a distinct feeling that even if I hadn't been, your daughter would have managed well enough on her own. She appears to be most resilient."

Commodore Grey gave him a wry smile. "Indeed."

"Godspeed in finding the missing boy and your stolen property," Jared said.

"I appreciate the information you shared. Our search will continue until we find both." With that, he swung a leg over Orion's back. "Good day, gentlemen."

As he rode back to Charleston, it was easy to explain away the dull ache in his gut to hunger. That fiery-haired forest imp of a young woman was better off wed to a bland man like Garrison. The doctor might be able to rein her in and settle down that wild spirit of hers. Keep her safe before she set the country on fire.

The chit was bright, but reckless.

She took risks without considering the impending consequences.

She was fearless. Strong-willed.

What would it be like to have her with him? Would her fire consume him like embers to paper, or would they both plunge headlong over the edge of the universe in a torrent of passion and flames?

He shook his head. It did no good to ruminate over it; she and Garrison were *in love.*

He was better off sailing solo with the wind at his back and the world solid and faithful at his feet.

KEELAN LEANED over her father's shoulder as he sat at the desk in the study, perusing the figures she'd prepared. She'd spent the entire day yesterday studying the ledgers and writing down her proposal for Twin Pines based on her engagement to Dr. Garrison.

It had been a daunting task. Not so much because of the

complexity of the financial aspects, but because her mind kept drifting to the memory of Landon's mouth curving up at the corners in that sensual, knowing smile. The press of his body on hers. His palm on her thigh traveling up to that sensitive spot which sent her crashing through wave after wave of pleasure.

She had made the right choice. Right? Yes, of course she had. Yet, the base instincts driving the woman in her to deeply desire Landon Hart were crying foul.

And would not *shut up*.

Her father glanced up at Uncle Jared, who was sitting in a chair. "What do you think, Jared?"

"I think leasing Twin Pines to Pratt is a sound idea. The fact that after five years, he'll have an option to buy the plantation will appeal to him." He ticked off his observations on his fingers. "It'll allow him to generate revenue for the purchase. It will provide Keelan and Garrison time to establish the business, and expand his practice. Pratt's regular lease payments will give you enough monthly income to live in Charleston, as well as enable you to garner a line of credit to provide them the funding to open and stock the store."

George Grey sat back in his chair. Keelan placed her hand on his shoulder. "Papa, you know there isn't anything like this in town. Not the way I envision. I know my boutique will be a success." Bolts of colorful fabric, lining the walls near the ceiling, would draw a patron's gaze from across the street. Shelves of jars filled with exotic spices and teas would stir an aroma just as enticing. Beautiful pottery and china would glitter brightly in the front window on a bed of luxurious, deeply hued silk.

He reached up and patted her hand then squeezed. "I believe you. If anyone can, you can, my dear."

Uncle Jared had unexpectedly become her grudging ally. "Between Keelan's knowledge of your late wife's boutique and my connections on the waterfront, we should have no trouble getting things underway in town. Our entire family would be able to reside and conduct business there. I'll always be close by to help Keelan, should she need it, George."

Jared paced the study. "Garrison can focus on his practice as well. I concur with Keelan's reasoning. Pratt has been coveting Twin Pines since you arrived. I think he'll agree to a lease, contingent upon an outright purchase within a limited time frame." He rocked back on his heels. "When I met with Captains Hart and O'Brien regarding the rental of one of my warehouses, I had an opportunity to review their inventory list, which I have to say, was quite impressive. They trade rare items which would have the people of the Lowcountry salivating."

Her father stiffened. "There are many reliable merchant companies to choose from. I'm sure we can find someone similar."

Jared sighed. "You must admit the men have very keen business sense. Their company is sound, even after losing part of their cargo. Although I doubt they could recuperate from another loss. They only have to sail along the coast and deliver goods to their buyers. If their journey was to the Caribbean or South America, there'd be a greater risk."

Although she was leery of Captain Landon Hart when it came to his personal intentions, he would indeed be the perfect supplier of out-of-the-ordinary items she'd want to sell. She wasn't sure she'd be able to tolerate any kind of business arrangement with him. Seeing him each time would be like pulling a scab off a partially healed wound over and over. And over.

"Papa's correct. I'm sure we can find another shipping merchant to work with," she said, hoping she sounded as certain as her words. If father would allow her to enjoy a long engagement to the doctor, rather than insist on a hasty wedding, she'd have the opportunity to show she could accomplish both *without* a husband.

Without a husband to disrupt things. And kiss with his teeth.

She'd already succeeded in moving the wedding date to five months hence. If she delayed enough, surely Dr. Garrison would lose interest and break their engagement.

She could at least hope. She harbored no yearning to marry, especially now. How could she tolerate an intimate relationship with someone who could never arouse passion in the way Landon Hart could with a single kiss? Anything less was bound to be a tremendous disappointment. She'd rather remain a spinster.

"It's settled then," her father replied. "I'll pen a letter to Pratt to include with the proposal."

Keelan faced the window and allowed herself a victorious smile.

She should feel relieved, but there was a nagging sensation deep in her belly. Something still wasn't quite right, like a table with one short leg that wasn't noticeable until you leaned an elbow on that one spot that made it tilt.

CHAPTER THIRTY-ONE
A SECRET OUT

"Quit yer fidgeting, lass, or I'll never get this right!" Slaney, huffed. "Ye be squirmin' like a wee minnow in a child's fist." For the second time, the maid tried to pin a wayward strand of Keelan's hair.

The night of Doreen's ball arrived all too soon.

Keelan sighed apologetically. "I'm sorry. It's just that—"

"You canna wait to be in the arms of yer betrothed?" She couldn't miss the sarcasm in her maid's voice.

Keelan snorted. "Had poor Pastor Braun and his chapel not been blown away by the storm, I'd be a married woman by now. At least it's an announcement and not a wedding ceremony that will take place later this evening." She picked up a mirror and studied the maid's handiwork. "Lovely work, Slaney."

Still, she had an intense desire to don her waif's clothes and stuff the hidden bag of coins into a pillowcase, and slip out the back a final time.

Run.

The chamber door opened, startling both women.

Slaney made a small, strange noise.

Perplexed at the sound and assaulted by the overpowering aroma of rose water, she shared Slaney's reaction. One glance at Doreen's attire, and she understood the maid's response.

Doreen's evening gown was a magnificent, pale yellow silk creation. Obviously a talented seamstress tried hard to take the latest style and mold it to Doreen's skinny body. On a more endowed woman, the dress would have been stunning. On Doreen's scant frame, it was obscene.

It almost covered what little Doreen had in the way of breasts by showing a daring plunge in the neckline. Uncle Jared would be horrified. How did her cousin persuade Aunt Sarah to buy it?

Doreen pushed her skirts to the side as she walked past the bed and scowled, shaking her strawberry blond locks in disapproval. "You've ruined my soiree."

Keelan smiled humorlessly at her sulking cousin, although she was careful to add a cheerful lilt in her voice. "Good evening, Doreen. That is a beautiful gown. Has your father seen it yet?"

The young woman sniffed as she gestured to the garment. "I had it made by the best dressmaker in Charleston. She assured me it's all the rage in Paris." She patted a carefully placed curl on her shoulder and lifted her chin higher, while her gaze scraped up and down Keelan. She added snidely, "Papa would want me to have only the best."

That raised a brow. So Uncle Jared *hadn't* seen it.

Her cousin continued. "Since you arrived, all the eligible beaus have come to call and after a few minutes with you, they bolt out and never return! They always want *you*. Please tell Miss Keelan I have come to call," she mimicked. Doreen's face imploded with disdain, "Yet, you toy with them like...like...a common strumpet!"

Keelan's temper flared at the lewd words. She hadn't intended to reveal her reasoning, but it escaped before she could stop it. "I was not toying with them, Doreen. I was rejecting them in an attempt to turn their attention to you."

For a moment, the girl was speechless. Her composure shifted and transformed her expression from jealous spite to deep humiliation. Her face paled, and her hand shook a little when she reached up to brush a curl of hair from her eyes.

"Well, it didn't work, did it?" Doreen responded in a choked voice.

Her lower lip trembled. A dark flush started to creep over her cheeks. "You have managed to draw all the attention to yourself, instead. Again. My party, *my* night, and Father insists on making your betrothal announcement to the whole of Charleston." Doreen's voice cracked, and she whirled away and stood facing the window.

A long moment passed before Doreen composed herself enough to turn back to face them. Her eyes glistened. "You're now engaged to marry the one man about whom I care the most." She swallowed a jagged sob. "Why didn't you simply choose the captain and go away with him? Why Everett? You don't love him. I know you don't!"

No. Keelan froze in stunned silence. Doreen was in love with Dr. Garrison? She took a hesitant step forward. Oh dear. Why hadn't she noticed?

"Doreen, had I known I would have—"

"What, Keelan?" Tears started to spill down her face. "You would have what? Turned his attention toward me like you claim you did with the others, as just another one of your cast-offs?"

"Yes," she said, then regretted the response. She hadn't meant to sound as if she agreed with Doreen's assessment, that she would leave Everett as one might do with an unwanted possession. "No, I mean—"

"I know what you mean." Doreen cut her off, her breathing harsh and jerky. "You are so selfish! Do you do this for amusement? Do you enjoy playing with a man's affections like a child with a doll? Can't you see he was trying...to save your stupid, worthless, reputation?" Doreen stuttered the words between sobs. "What's it like, Keelan? What's it like to be so beautiful that every man who lays eyes on you falls in love with you? What's it like to play your game of seduction and then, when they are smitten and vulnerable, shove them aside?"

Keelan was shocked into silence. The raw, heavy weight of Doreen's words slammed into the accusations she'd thrown at Landon back in the cabin. Fingers of regret raked across her heart. Her intention was not to steal the man Doreen loved. Given a choice of two evils, she just chose the lesser. How did she miss Doreen's affection for Everett? Had she been so wrapped up in pursuing her own schemes she hadn't caught the most conspicuous tells?

To give her something to do other than watch her weep and feel wretched about it, Keelan went to the tallboy and pulled open drawers until she found a handkerchief. She silently pressed it into Doreen's palm. The best thing for the girl to do now was to cry it out.

"Don't try to be kind," Doreen said at last, snatching the handkerchief and dabbing the tears. "You don't deserve Everett. He is kind and chivalrous and generous. He's not only been seeing to your father but also the children on this plantation. I've been helping him. He's been teaching me how to mix up medicine and treat injuries. He's even taught me how to administer your father's. I was hoping..." She choked back another sob.

A horrible guilt seeped into Keelan's chest. Her intentions weren't to toy with anyone's heart. She'd done just that with Dr. Garrison, hadn't she? She'd taken advantage of his besotted devotion for her and used it to bolster her cause.

She was no different from Landon. The irony hit her like a hard punch to the chest.

Now, more than ever, she wanted to devise a way to avoid this marriage. But the wheels were already in motion, and the chances of stopping them were very slim.

Run away, whispered a voice in her head. *Just go.*

Her cousin sniffled about the room, picking up objects and absently putting them down again.

Keelan felt like an idiot. "Doreen, I'm sorry. This isn't something I want either. Maybe things will change for the better for both of us."

"Better? How can anything become better?" Doreen clenched her fists at her sides and stomped her foot. "This should be my engagement celebration, Everett's and mine! But you stole him from me, and the worst part is that I know you don't even love him!" She flung the mirror on the bed. Doreen glared at her. "I hate you."

Keelan felt horrible about the deception, but this needed to end before Doreen lost her composure entirely. "Doreen, you should go."

Snarling, Doreen grabbed a water goblet off the nightstand and flew toward her. "Don't ever speak to me again, you greedy, spoiled bitch!"

Doreen drew back her hand and swung the glass. In two quick movements, Keelan instinctively blocked with her left forearm and snatched it away with her right hand. The momentum of the charge carried Doreen forward. Being disarmed threw her off balance and she crashed to the floor. Keelan stared down at the fluffy pile of silk and petticoats.

Doreen wailed and floundered around like a drunken trout. "My arm! This will bruise for sure, I just know it!"

"Slaney, please help Doreen up so she can leave."

The maid warily moved behind the girl, slid her elbows under Doreen's armpits, and heaved. After stepping on the stiffly starched petticoats several times, Doreen stumbled to her feet and jerked her arms away. Her curls looked like they'd been combed with a kitchen whisk.

She tromped from the room, yelling for her maid at the top of her lungs.

For a moment, both Keelan and Slaney stood frozen. Waving away the still pungent scent of rose water, the maid moved to close the door. Slaney brushed her hands on her apron, then reached for Keelan's gown. "Come now, lass, let's get ye dressed. Guests are beginning to arrive." Leaving the obvious unsaid.

Keelan doubted she'd be able to act the part of a happy fiancée in Dr. Garrison's presence this evening. However, her father's health seemed to improve slightly in the past few days, and he planned on attending for a short while, so she'd do her best. Perhaps she could find the doctor and have a brief word with him before the festivities start. She owed him the truth, that she didn't love him. If he cared about Doreen, he'd jump at the opportunity to break the engagement. She couldn't marry him out of convenience. Papa and Uncle Jared already sent her proposal to Pratt. There was no need for this charade to continue.

Slaney's sympathetic voice broke the quiet of the room, "Perhaps ye could feign a headache and retire early."

"I won't give Doreen the satisfaction of thinking she's bullied me away." Yes, her pride was overriding every thread of sense, but she was too upset and angry with herself to care. She stepped into the shimmering ocean-blue ball gown. Slaney pulled it up over her breasts and shoulders and began working the fastenings. Keelan tried to swallow the lump expanding in her throat.

When she finished, Slaney gave her a warm, soft hug and spun her toward the door. "At least the other gents will be leavin' ye be this evenin', since yer betrothed now."

She rolled her eyes. Wonderful. "That's a *colossal* comfort."

CHAPTER THIRTY-TWO
A BALL BEGINS

L aughter and music rose from the ballroom below as Keelan left her room. Every window in the house had been opened to enjoy the cooling effects of the light winds. The aroma of roasted meats from the fire pit mingled with the heavy scent of magnolia blossoms. Her aunt's voice carried up the stairs as she greeted guests.

Normally, the opportunity to attend such a gala made her giddy. However, the somber blanket of reality smothered any excitement or anticipation. Keelan's mind was bombarded by images of shackles and grey mist.

Melancholy seeped deep into her bones.

The only bright spot of optimism came with the comfort that she didn't have to worry about Pratt. Even thinking his name made a cold, murky hand clamp her stomach.

Twin Pines had a glorious two-story foyer. The staircase split partway down, much like a wishbone, to hug the side walls. Upon entry, visitors were ushered straight ahead, through the tall archway under the grand stair. She began her descent with deliberate steps. The last thing she wanted was to roll to the bottom in a tumbled heap.

The hard edge in her uncle's voice stuttered her next step. "Captain

Hart, welcome." Her stomach plummeted to her feet at the thought of seeing the mocking countenance of Landon Hart again.

Not him!

Not here!

She sensed his perusal even before she lifted her head. She fought to maintain her attention on her slippers, otherwise that amused, mocking smirk would destroy her concentration. Would he ever treat her as a lady, or would he always see that boyish chit beneath?

Not that it mattered anymore.

There was no way to delay it any longer, so she allowed herself to look at him. Even as tension tightened her lungs, a slow, swirling sensation pooled in her belly. Landon's shiny, ebony locks were secured in a queue. A matching light gray waistcoat complimented the dark charcoal breeches. The black silk shirt accented the sun-darkened skin of his face and neck. His eyes glowed with a blue sheen.

That was definitely not a mocking expression. Instead, he regarded her with a warm glow of admiration. Or lust. Probably lust. His perusal sent a wave of pure heat from the hem of her gown to her hair, causing a shiver to whip across her shoulders. A furious blush crept over her cheeks, as the captain's sapphire stare lingered overlong near the neckline. It took almost all her strength to keep from crossing her arms over her chest and fleeing back up to the safety of her chamber. Instead, she slapped what she hoped was a cool, serene smile on her face and continued down, despite the Albatross flapping hysterically in her stomach.

Breathe. Swallow. Swallow and breathe. No, blast it, not at the same time. Her mouth had gone dry. She clutched the banister more firmly and gave herself a mental tongue-lashing.

Concentrate on the steps, you ninny.

Now was not the time to lose her footing. Before she could take another step, Landon ascended two at a time and offered her his arm.

"Allow me to escort you, Miss Grey." He gripped her elbow. A warmth zipped through her arm and all the way to her toes.

Ignore the touch of his fingers. Focus on the steps.

Good Lord if she tripped now the humiliation would vaporize her like boiling water in a teapot.

"Quite honestly, I don't know how you ladies cope with steps and full skirts. Were a man in your shoes, he'd already be a crumpled pile of arms and legs down in the entryway."

Her laugh came out more as a weak warble, betraying the state of her nerves. "It appears men are wise enough to avoid wearing them in the first place," she muttered. "We women bring this all on ourselves."

He dipped his head and chuckled. "And we men are most grateful."

Really, what kind of mindless banter was this? Was he actually trying to calm her with this banal conversation? Perhaps this was an attempt to lure her into a false sense of security. She resolved to stay away from the man, as soon as she descended the stairs safely, for her own sake.

When they reached the foyer, she disengaged her hand from his arm to greet her aunt and uncle by the door, her palm still radiating heat. "What a beautiful night for your daughter's ball."

Her aunt kissed her cheek. "Isn't it simply perfect? We are so fortunate to have this refreshing breeze." Aunt Sarah's eyes twitched from Landon to her husband and back.

Apparently, more droll observations were needed to keep Uncle Jared from making a scene.

Her uncle's perusal traveled approvingly up and down. "Might I say you look stunning, my dear?" His face softened. "I just came from your father's chamber. I'm afraid he's feeling too poorly to join us. He would have been proud to be the one announcing your forthcoming nuptials."

Landon stiffened. She still managed to smile woodenly at her uncle. If she met Landon's gaze, he'd read it in her eyes.

A lie. It's all a lie.

Keelan's heart fell hard enough to pull her shoulders with it. Papa had improved dramatically over the past few days. He even took a walk with her yesterday to inspect the stable repairs.

Her face must have betrayed her heartache as well as her despair. Aunt Sarah gave her a light hug. "I'm so sorry, dear."

Keelan quickly decided to excuse herself as soon as possible to sit with her father for the rest of the evening.

After pulling Garrison aside to break their engagement.

Landon turned, pulled her hand toward him, and pressed his lips to her fingertips. "I wish you a happy, loving marriage, Miss Grey. Although I am sure several young men will go home this evening much saddened by such news."

A happy, loving marriage. Everything she wanted. Nothing she'd experience. She focused her attention on the vase of flowers on a nearby table.

Don't look at him. Don't look.

As badly as she wanted to tell him everything, she didn't dare.

Hart turned his attention to her uncle. "If you'll recall, one of our galley boys went missing during the theft of our cargo. When you and I talked at the mill, you gave me several names of a few who might know about the local men I hired. So far, none provided helpful information. I hope you can introduce me to others tonight, who may have the information I require. I'm most concerned for the boy's welfare."

Uncle Jared clasped his hands behind his back and pursed his lips. "Ah yes. The storm hindered those efforts more than a little, I'm sure. As soon as all our guests arrive, and the ball is underway, we shall meet in my study."

"Thank you, sir." Landon inclined his head.

Simon stepped forward and smiled. He held a tray of unfilled wine glasses. Joseph stood at his father's side, carefully holding a half-filled carafe.

Simon removed a stem, a kind crinkle in his eyes. "Would you care for a glass of wine, Miss Grey?"

She smiled. "Yes, please, I would. Captain Hart?"

Landon's response was curt. "No, thank you."

She flinched at the coolness coating his demeanor. She deserved it.

Guilt enveloped her. She didn't think she could ever hurt his feelings in any way. He'd played his game with her. And now it was over. Although she hadn't planned on using Landon to ignite her scheme to prevent matrimony to Pratt, everything fell perfectly into place.

Everything but the truth.

CHAPTER THIRTY-THREE
A SIP OF WINE

A feminine cough broke the temporary silence. Everyone's attention turned to the top of the staircase.

Doreen posed on the landing, smiling sweetly at Hart.

Keelan raised her glass and took a sip. Doreen's hair had been repaired, her face no longer reddened by tears and anger. She tried to act nonchalant, but the flirtatious gaze Doreen had fixed on Landon fired Keelan's irritation.

She was annoyed even more by the fact that it bothered her.

Immensely.

Then she heard her aunt's small gasp behind her. Apparently, Aunt Sarah hadn't seen the dress either, and cast a horrified stare over the rim of her glass at her husband. A wide-eyed look of panic seemed to have paralyzed Uncle Jared's normally stoic face. His jaw clenched and began a convulsive quivering. When he found his voice, the words fell out like a cup of nails on a tin plate.

"WHAT IN GOD'S NAME?"

Aunt Sarah's elbow shot out from her side and she gave her husband a merciless poke which sent him into a fit of coughing.

"Captain Hart, you remember my daughter, Doreen," she said thinly, waving a weak hand at the stairs.

Uncle Jared stood like a wooden pillar; his stare dark under his thick, slashing eyebrows.

Since no other gentleman were nearby, and her uncle struggled to breathe, Hart once again ascended the steps and graciously offered his arm. He'd better love the fragrance of rose water, otherwise a pungent trip up and down the staircase awaited the lethally handsome Captain Hart.

As he neared Doreen, he stifled a low cough. Keelan grinned into her glass. Rose water wasn't a favorite, then.

"It is a joy to see you again, Miss Grey." Hart said cordially. "You look lovely this evening."

Doreen gazed dreamily at Landon. "Thank you," she drawled, as she batted her lashes demurely. "It's refreshing to converse with a man with an astute sense of style." She slipped her arm through Landon's and pulled it tightly against her ribs, which smashed a breast up enough to almost fall out. "My! Such strong arms. I truly appreciate your kind escort."

A larger gulp of wine was needed to keep from snorting in disgust at her cousin's shameless and downright blatant attempt at flirtation. The pair descended, and this time Landon accepted refreshment from Simon and Joseph. Doreen continued to cling to his arm while she tried to steer him in the direction of the music.

"Captain Hart, you must come and listen to the musicians my father brought in from Charleston. They play a divine waltz."

Landon smiled politely. "My apologies, Miss Grey, but I have urgent business with your father. I'm sure your dance card must already be quite full."

Aunt Sarah hopped forward and draped her fichu around Doreen's shoulders. "Here, dear," she said, "it's a little drafty this evening." She swiftly tied the garment.

"Mother, I do not need—"

Uncle Jared's voice growled from behind his wife's shoulder, "Daughter, you'll do well to obey your mother!"

"But Papa..." Doreen whined.

At her sire's warning scowl, she gave a soft exasperated sigh, and grasped Landon's arm tighter. "Come, Captain Hart, allow me to show you the way to the ballroom where the draft is not so cool." She stared pointedly at her parents and gave them a triumphant smile.

"Keelan!" Dr. Garrison's voice froze her spine. "My darling, you are a vision from heaven!"

Lord, help her.

She tipped her glass and finished the wine in a solid gulp, ignoring the raised brow from Landon. At the moment, she didn't care what he thought of her. Her most immediate mission now was to escape from dancing with the doctor. More importantly, she needed to find a way to speak to him privately. And soon.

She raked a cheerful tone into her voice, "Good evening, Dr. Garrison."

Keeping his eyes fastened upon her face, he plucked her empty glass from her fingers and held it out in Simon's direction. The servant took it without a word.

Dr. Garrison leaned in and whispered, "Please call me Everett, my dear." Then louder, "Come, sweet Keelan, grant me the pleasure of dancing with my betrothed in my arms."

It was hard to swallow the groan. She did her best to keep a bright smile frozen on her face, but her toes cowered in her slippers.

She endured the first two dances of heinous torture. After he tromped on her foot a fourth time, she begged leave to get some air. "Really, Dr. Garrison... Everett... I guess I'm not used to this heat. Allow me to sit a moment and catch my breath."

"Of course, my darling. Rest while I get you a glass of punch."

"You're very kind."

"Not at all, my sweet. Perhaps we could take a stroll outside. It is most beautiful on a night like this, with the full moon."

The stroll would also give her a chance to speak with him privately. It couldn't come soon enough. The urge to banish her charade grew stronger with each passing second Landon Hart was in the house.

Dr. Garrison made his way toward a buffet laid out with food. Halfway there, a short, stout woman, who was fanning herself madly, heralded him and pointed to a place on her arm. Keelan moved out to the veranda where she'd have the opportunity to speak with the doctor in a more secluded spot.

If only he wasn't so kind and empathetic, it would be easier. She didn't deserve it, but she hoped one day he'd forgive her and maybe even understand her motives. Having her hand in marriage would never be same as having her heart.

After she accepted Dr. Garrison's hand and presented her proposal for Twin Pines, her father consented to give up the plantation. She was relieved both Jared and Papa understood it would benefit the family better and even enable her to have a livelihood that could provide for them to a greater degree than country life ever could.

In spite of that, her recent actions still left a bitterly ironic taste on her tongue. For all her efforts to prevent walking the same path as her mother, she still fell into the quicksand mire of a life without love.

Keelan would end up exactly like her; she would put all her time and focus into the shop, to distract from the loneliness. She had been foolish to think she could control her life entirely.

She was her mother's daughter, after all.

A young serving girl holding a tray of wine-filled stemware stepped close, and Keelan removed a glass. Perhaps the wine would dull the torment, as well as the pain of her bruised toes.

"Miss Keelan! You look beautiful!"

She turned. A petite blonde woman waved and wove her way toward her.

"Margaret! It's nice to see you again." She managed to smile. Margaret Hampton loved conversation, and if one wanted to know all the happenings in the Lowcountry, one needed only a short chat with Margaret.

Margaret opened her fan and spoke behind it. "What's this I hear about your engagement to the handsome Dr. Garrison? Is it true?"

"Well—" What should she say?

Margaret saved her the decision by jumping ahead. "Wonderful! I can only—"

Margaret froze, and Keelan turned to see what had attracted the young woman's attention so thoroughly, she'd stopped in mid-sentence.

"That must be the wealthy merchant captain I have heard so much about," Margaret breathed.

Landon was chatting with a stunning woman. Tall and slender, her hair gleamed like blue coal. The sapphire gown sharply contrasted with her ivory skin. Together, they made quite a handsome couple.

Keelan's voice caught in her throat, and she took a quick mouthful of wine to clear it. "Yes, it is. Captain Hart's here at my aunt's invitation," she said.

Margaret's whisper bounced with glee, "I've heard some very interesting things about him. When he was a boy, he emigrated with his family from Ireland, but his parents died on the way over. The ship's captain took him in and raised him as an apprentice of sorts." She paused for effect. "I've also heard the old man once was a pirate who fell in love with a woman he took captive. He eventually gave up the pirate's life but even now his old ship mates continue to engage him on the open sea, in retaliation for his poorly timed departure."

O'Brien's uncle Fynn Ahern had been a *pirate*? All the more reason to avoid Landon Hart. "Goodness, Margaret, you do tell the most entertaining stories." Keelan tried to laugh, but it came out stunted.

"These are no stories." Margaret's voice climbed to an excited hiss. "The old captain's nephew and Captain Hart now own an entire fleet of merchant ships. Captain Hart may not have come from old money, Keelan, but I'd wager he's just as rich as any titled lord."

"And pirates still seek him out," she murmured, recalling Landon's partial telling of the tale during the storm. And the solid comfort of his arms. And the heat of his kisses. An odd flutter skittered across her stomach.

Margaret frowned. "I wonder if he remarried."

Keelan choked on her wine. That young woman really was privy to all *kinds* of information. What else did she know about Landon?

"I was told that while he was at sea." Margaret lowered her voice again, and Keelan had to lean closer to hear. "His wife became pregnant with another man's child, but the pregnancy went bad. Both she and the babe died."

A tight, prickly gasp filled her chest. "How terrible," she replied in a hushed tone. Her assumptions couldn't have been more wrong. She felt like a bitter, shallow, shrew.

"Marriage does not suit me..."

Margaret fluttered her fan. "Well, he's done quite well, with the exception of his current choice for a partner."

The lady dancing with Landon was beyond beautiful. Her movements were as fluid as water over polished marble.

"Who is she? We haven't yet been introduced." Keelan couldn't take her eyes off the woman.

Margaret snorted. "Annette Camsby. She tried to sink her claws into the captain a couple of years ago, but he wouldn't let her. She wanted him to sell his shipping company and invest in land, specifically her daddy's failing plantation. He refused and left Charleston. Although, he occasionally returns, or so I've been told."

The woman laughed and pressed her hand to her heart before reaching over to stroke Landon's shoulder in a very familiar manner. If Keelan needed confirmation she'd made the right choice by refusing Landon's offer of marriage, then she certainly had it. She would be a simpleton if she believed he'd bind himself to her, if he would rather sail the seas, then marry a woman as alarmingly exquisite as Annette Camsby.

And why marry a man who regularly engaged in hostilities with pirates? How horrible would it be to wait for a husband who never returned and not know whether he'd been killed by brigands, lost at sea, or just chose to not come home?

The two conversed as if they were old friends, or lovers. "Mrs. Camsby seems quite comfortable with him."

Margaret harrumphed. "Her late husband left her *very* wealthy. Maybe she's trying to get Captain Hart to reconsider her last offer, now that she's no longer in financial duress."

Keelan felt slightly queasy. Still, she couldn't drag her gaze away as they walked toward an open window, the Widow Camsby's hand resting possessively on Landon's arm. He lowered his ear down to her lips and nodded as she spoke. Keelan found her cousin standing near one of the food-laden sideboards. Aunt Sarah's fichu had fallen unnoticed to her elbows. Doreen's arms were crossed as she glared at Annette.

Well, here at last was something on which the two of them could commiserate. Although it pricked her pride to do so, she had to admit she was no less bothered.

"Please excuse me," Margaret said, "I see Mother and Aunt Alice have taken a seat. I am going to see if I can get them anything. I'll be back soon." She gave her a shy sideways glance. "Perhaps you can introduce me to Captain Hart later?"

Absolutely not.

"Of course," she murmured, careful to keep her voice expressionless. For her own peace of mind, she was determined to put as much distance between herself and Landon Hart as possible. In fact, it would probably be best if Margaret couldn't find her after she got her mother and aunt settled.

Keelan took in the activity around the room. Everett was completely surrounded by a cluster of elderly gentlemen and appeared to be involved in a very animated discussion. Doreen had managed to convince some poor young fop to dance. Annette Camsby chatted with several eagerly attentive men whom, like her, found the raven-haired beauty hard to ignore.

Landon was nowhere to be seen. Good, hopefully he left.

A servant wandered past with a carafe.

"Blackberry wine, Miss Grey?"

"Yes. Thank you," she said, allowing the girl to refill her glass. The last thing she wanted to do was watch Landon and Mrs. Camsby waltz again. She sipped the drink and glanced toward the open doors. The gentle whisper of solitude beckoned to her. Perhaps she could wander unseen for a while and enjoy a bit of the moonlit evening in peace. She'd wait for Dr. Garrison to find her in the garden.

She sauntered outside and down the steps. The strains of music from the ballroom drifted with her. She ducked beneath the wisteria blossoms dripping from the arbor and followed the path lined with moon shadows and tiers of herbs until she reached the small lake. It shimmered in the moonlight, like midnight blue silk sprinkled with diamonds. She recalled her naked swim and how the crisp water had cooled her heated skin, and smiled to herself.

Sleek black locks and steely arms intruded into the memory, followed by hot, wet kisses and hard, lean thighs. Her breath came out in a puff, and she quickly swallowed another deep sip. When it didn't expel the image, she raised the glass to her lips again. A warm hand closed around hers and gently removed the stem from her grasp.

"Careful, Keelan." Humor laced the resonant timbre of Landon's voice. "Stairs are much harder to navigate when drunk."

CHAPTER THIRTY-FOUR
A DANCE

Keelan tried to sound disinterested, but her words came out thin, breathy and weak. "Spoken from experience, Captain?"

He gave her a boyish grin, his face savagely handsome. "You could say that."

Landon placed her hand on his arm, solid and warm beneath her palm, slid his other around her ribs and before she could object, they were waltzing in the garden, his fingers scorching her skin. Fragrant blossoms no longer permeated her senses. Instead, the scent of leather, fresh ocean breezes and sandalwood, intoxicating as the blackberry wine filled her to overflowing. The shiver bolting up her spine could be pleasure or unease. Both?

"I don't want to dance with you!" It was a lie, but she'd do better if she listened to her head while it still managed a coherent thought. Her body betrayed her long ago.

Weakling.

Although she stopped and tried to pull away, he trapped her hand against his broad chest, and she wondered what the skin felt like under his shirt.

"Come." Blue eyes brimmed with humor. "At least help mend my broken heart by dancing one waltz with me before you wed yon gawky heron." He nodded toward the house.

"I can't—" Near panic spasmed in her chest. Absolutely not. "I shouldn't even be alone with you." Let him think it was because she was engaged, rather than the real reason. Rather than admit that she had an impossible time thinking clearly when he was close. Or that his touch made her stomach flutter like a newly hatched bird.

Stupid bird.

His right eyebrow jumped up. "One waltz will not harm you, Keelan."

Oh *yes,* it will. She slammed her lips together and tried to glare at him, but mirth circled the dimples in his cheeks like whirlpools. Terribly distracting. His teeth flashed in the moonlight and her nipples hardened, remembering the scrape of them over the tender flesh.

"Will you cause a scene at your cousin's ball?" Both inky eyebrows lifted. The answer twinkled in his sapphire eyes.

Yes, she was tempted to say she didn't give a horse's tail if she caused a commotion or not.

"Cause a scene? Here in the garden? Heavens no. I would simply return to the house," she retorted. *If* he released her. And *if* she could get her feet to propel her in that direction. Already warmth crawled through her veins, igniting her blood.

"What makes you think I'll let it be that easy, love?"

He wouldn't dare bring about another scandal.

Her eyes jumped to his, but saw no jest in them. Why waste time considering such a thing? Of course he'd dare. "Haven't you done enough damage?" Her voice sounded reedy and desperate.

His face became shuttered, and his voice dropped to a growl. "Damage? I thought I did you a *favor*. You managed to create a perfect situation where the man your father would've had you wed rejected you, and the man you wanted only had to announce his intent. That was your plan, was it not?" His eyes flashed like blue steel; his words clipped through the night air sharply, like horses' hooves on a paved street. His arms, an iron cage. Had he followed her to the garden to have a row with her?

"Yes. No!" Her insides twisted into a tangled knot, while he spun her words, making her appear mean and devious. His nearness warped her reasoning. The guilt she felt over the effect her actions had on Doreen made everything worse. Or did it clarify things? There'd been no other option that would have helped her attain her objective.

None.

At all.

His hand was turning volcanic. The fire from his palm had to be melting the fabric of her gown. Her breath thickened and became stuck as his gaze shifted from flinty blue to something heated. And lethal.

The hard angles of his jaw relaxed. In an easy silk-coated voice, he murmured, "Were you in your cousin's dress, I would strenuously object to the addition of a shawl, fan, or any other obstacle to my view."

The words barely crawled from her knotted throat. "That's because you are a lecherous rake."

He molded her hand to his chest, she could feel his heartbeat jarring her palm. Or was that her pulse jarring his chest? She studied his ridiculously attractive face and expected again to see mockery, but instead saw something hooded, almost feral lurking in his eyes. Her breath stilled. For a moment, she teetered. Should she flee or allow this to continue? It was fairly harmless, was it not?

That was *not* a clear head talking.

Many words described Landon Hart. *Harmless* wasn't one of them.

His voice rumbled from his chest like a waking volcano. "Relax, it's only a waltz,"

Relax, *ha*. "Fine, then let's get it over with!" she snapped, proud her voice cooperated, unlike her lungs, which were refusing to expand enough.

He sensed her tension so easily. Nothing disguised her frayed nerves. Curse the overpowering effect his very presence had on her peace of mind! Why was she so weak and gullible? She couldn't deny she craved his touch anymore than she loathed the misery its absence would bring later.

As they danced, the distant notes from the strings penetrated her senses and soothed her a little. They glided around the arbor. Their movement had no beginning and no end; it was a constant, fluid motion, moving to the rhythm of the music.

He was quite talented. After being the brunt of Everett's clumsy attempts, it was refreshing to waltz with a partner who seemed to anticipate the next note to float from the string. The night air was bright and alive and in spite of everything, she relaxed in his arms. Gone was the strain from acting her ruse; gone were her fears and concerns. She danced in the moment, and she felt free and safe and vibrant. Landon's long, lean fingers curled around her waist and squeezed gently, almost tenderly, sending that baby bird in her stomach flapping again.

"Dancing is like a passionate kiss," he said, his voice a slightly rasping caress, like callused fingers on sensitive skin. "It's much more pleasurable when you relax, and let the natural movement guide you along, like the kisses we shared."

Just the sound of his voice turned her stomach into lava. "Dancing is nothing at all like kissing, and I don't think you should speak of sharing anything with me." That sounded confidant and commanding, although she was still unable to keep the visions from flooding her senses. Good Lord, she would surely go to hell for all the lies falling from her tongue tonight. She closed her lids, which did nothing to make those sultry images go away. If anything, it nudged her imagination up a tempo. Fiery hands on her skin, torturous mouth on her breast, fingers strumming inside until the crescendo made her implode.

Humor laced his tone again. "No? Spoken from experience, I gather?"

She pursed her lips. At least she made the attempt to purse them. She wasn't quite sure if she actually succeeded. He was teasing her again. When she let down her guard only a little, he pounced like a panther. Strong, sinuous and sleek. Dripping wet and walking from the lake. Muscled thighs and powerful shoulders that rippled when he moved.

Molten, indigo eyes captured hers. They mercilessly refused to release her. In those clear pools was an image of the two of them fused together by a kiss radiating blue heat. Her pulse quickened with the memory. Could he feel it pounding in her fingers? She realized, with some chagrin, he awaited her answer.

"Yes. No. I mean..." her voice trailed off. What was the question? Something about a kiss? Drat that man. Now her cheeks were blazing. "I have kissed plenty of men to know how to kiss." A tiny lie. Just add it to the others.

Tally away.

He leered, as if she'd just shed every last article of clothing. "I seriously doubt that," he said, something like a challenge heating in his eyes.

"Believe what you want, I don't care," she shot back. She almost didn't care. That was fairly close to the truth.

Sort of.

"Show me."

꙳ 35 ꙳

CHAPTER THIRTY-FIVE
A KISS

"*Show me.*"

No two words could have been more destructive to the fragile hold she had on her emotions. Her heart kicked into a more frantic rhythm, slamming against her ribs. "You've stolen enough kisses from me to know. You don't need me to show you anything."

"Oh, but I do." His voice draped over her like blue velvet on naked skin. He gave her a slow mocking leer "You can *respond* to my kiss, but can you initiate the spark? Your mouth is sweet and moist. How could it not be, with lips like these?" His thumb traced her lower lip, it tingled; making it almost too sensitive to touch. "But hear this, my love. It's your passion, spirit and zest for life that I crave to taste, breathe and experience." His gaze fell to her mouth, and she struggled to swallow. "Still, you have much to learn, and I have much I can teach you about the fine art of kissing. And making love."

His last words, spoken lethally soft, jolted her like a lightening strike. The fever abandoned her cheeks, tore down her neck to crash and swirl deep in her belly.

She tried to sound calmer than she felt. "You must have kissed many, many women to consider yourself so knowledgeable on the subject, you raise it to the glory of an art."

"A few," he replied, apparently enjoying her discomfort. "There is more to it than placing your lips against a stone."

"I have not—" Garrison's kiss snapped her mouth shut.

They glided down the garden path. "Nothing fills the heart like a kiss born from passion and love," he continued, "It's extremely difficult to act as if you're in love, when you're not."

Landon aroused a new worry. When Everett revealed she had already accepted his proposal, did she appear to others as if she was in love? People married without love all the time. Not that it mattered, she would not marry the doctor now. She wouldn't marry anyone. Ever.

"I... was not acting," she scoffed. Nicely said. That didn't even convince *her*.

He leaned forward until his lips almost touched her ear. The light caress of his breath wrapped around her neck, and a shiver slid across her collarbone. "Then, were you acting in the cabin? When you cried out my name after I stroked that sweet, moist spot between your thighs?"

Crazy things were going on in her lower belly. She stared over his shoulder to avoid that sultry cobalt gaze. Places inside her ignited, the intensity driving every drop of moisture from her mouth, pushing it down to her core.

That moment had been haunting her dreams every night. Now she was having trouble controlling her breath. She should be ashamed of allowing him to be so intimate with her.

But she wasn't.

And she didn't regret it, either. No one would ever be able to stoke such fierce desire in her; she didn't regret experiencing it with Landon.

This conversation was moving along a dangerous path. She tried to change the direction.

"Love and passion aren't as important as other elements of marriage. Fidelity. Honor. Trust. Respect. Those traits create the foundation required of a solid union," she countered.

"Commendable attributes." He agreed, squeezing her fingers and brushing them with his lips, hatching a thousand butterflies. "But what good is building a strong base if there is only an empty shell perched upon it?" Landon twirled her around a rose bush. "Love and passion give a marriage substance and purpose. Combined with your keystones of fidelity, honor, trust and respect, no empire could ever possess greater wealth or strength."

Her throat tightened. He didn't sound at all like the scoundrel she'd accused him of being. Did Landon Hart, the man who admitted marriage didn't suit him, truly believe his own words?

Was he simply telling her what she wanted to hear in an attempt to seduce her? He wouldn't assume that since she was already engaged, he could do so with no repercussions, no firm entanglements. Unless he was trying to destroy the betrothal. She was unsure of the answer, but she'd keep her guard up.

His warm breath caressed the tender skin behind her ear, and a hungry tingling moved down her spine. She was weak and vibrant simultaneously. It was a sensation she could have enjoyed, if he was her husband and not a man only concerned with adding her name to his long list of conquests. He played with sugary words and hypnotic touches in ways that made her feel helpless and hungry for more.

In fact, he stirred such a tumultuous whirlwind of desire inside, she ached for him in places that had grown warm and dewy.

"What would a man like you know about love?" The knot in her throat doubled and tightened. "Ardor may flow through your veins, your kiss might leave young maidens breathless, but can you love only one woman?" Annette Camsby floated to the forefront of her mind along with the image of them conversing earlier, heads close together, her hand stroking his shoulder like a lover. Landon had appeared as comfortable with that woman as he was here with her. How could she possibly believe she meant anything more to him?

She locked her eyes on his. "Can you stay faithful to your wife when other beautiful women offer themselves to you without demanding the bindings that a marriage vow dictates? Can you love the same woman day after day, year after year?"

Landon's eyes had a fierce light, like a midnight fire. "If she captured my heart and trusted me with hers... yes."

She laughed. "Forgive me if I find your words hard to believe."

"Has Dr. Garrison offered you the same?" Something treacherous gleamed in those smoldering blue eyes, shuttered by thick dark lashes, tempting her to fling herself headlong into certain disaster.

"He has offered all I... require." Her voice betrayed her flimsy confidence. Stupid voice. Stupid confidence.

"So you do not require to be loved." He twisted her words as easily as a string.

"Of... course... I do." For some reason, that response triggered her chest to clench in panic; she wasn't sure why.

"So you love him?"

That's why. It was a trap. "Well..." She sought to find some threads of truth to mend her irritating conscience. She could love someone without being in love, couldn't she? She repeated Slaney's earlier comment. "Sometimes, love comes later."

His voice was carefully level and soft. "So you are willing to take the chance that it might not? Even though you just admitted you want it?"

Blast. She'd dug herself a hole. She couldn't confirm his statement, because she didn't believe it either. Her own words sounded stoney and false, even to her ears.

What she needed was another change of topic. This exchange was dangerously close to revealing the plan she had recently set into motion before she had the opportunity to end it without causing additional chaos.

The grey and silver tones of the roses blurred. The pressure from his hand had already burned into her waist like a red iron against bare flesh.

She had to get away from him. He made her feel like a flustered little girl. She stopped moving and tried to disengage her fingers, but he was not cooperating.

"Wouldn't you prefer be kissed every day by a man who passionately loves you? Or would you rather kiss someone made of wood?" The corners of his mouth hitched up. "Like your Dr. Barn Door?"

"You are an arrogant..." Her words tripped over her tongue as she wrestled to pry his fingers from her side.

How much did Landon know? Or thought he knew? She spun away from him, away from those eyes that could read her mind easier than a children's reader. Away from the touch that left the scorched imprint of every finger. Away from leather and brandy and Landon's spicy soap.

The heavy, sweet fragrance of magnolia blossoms floated lazily in the night air. Nocturnal creatures added their song to the evening breeze, bringing the night in like a collapsed canopy. The moon was luminous, and her gown glimmered in its light. And things were still spinning even though she'd stopped dancing.

He finally released her. She twirled away and inhaled deeply, swaying with the soft evening air. His presence at her back rippled through her like a physical pulse. His scent taunted her memories. Trapped together while the thunder raged around them, she'd felt both hunted and safe. Then. Now, he was only inches from her and the hair at her nape stood on end.

"You are a vision," The gravelly tone made her entire body hum. "Garrison is a dolt. He has no idea he is betrothed to a goddess. Your skin outshines the moonlight, and you smell sweeter than a jasmine blossom in full bloom." His fingers traced a line up her arm to her shoulder, heating a trail that made her vibrate. She should protest such boldness, but couldn't bring herself to speak. Or move. She stared at the lake, but saw only Landon's fiery blue gaze, intense and commanding.

"I would love you with the passion you deserve, Keelan. He would never worship you with the devotion I would. He could never sate your hunger or feed your desires as well as I." His fingers skimmed along the back of her neck, making her blood simmer. The tension inside her wanted to fracture and explode like a volcanic fissure.

Despite her desperate attempt to erect a thick emotional barrier to protect herself, an overwhelming need enveloped her. It pulled at her like the moon pulls the tide. A throaty moan escaped from deep in her throat.

His lips brushed her shoulder softly, leaving behind hot impressions on her bare skin. Gooseflesh rose on her arms.

More.

Yes, he spoke honeyed words and made promises she longed to hear, but what about when he boarded his ship and went back out to sea? What then?

The caustic image of Landon waltzing with Annette, her hand on his shoulder, leaning in to whisper something intimate pushed itself into her mind in a bitter rush. How could a man possibly stay loyal when beautiful women practically fell at his feet everywhere he went? He was too handsome, too desirable, too charming. What woman on this earth could ever resist him?

How could she live that kind of life, living alone, wondering if her husband was remaining faithful during the months he was at sea?

It was then she realized it wasn't that she didn't think he could love her more than another woman. There was something else standing between them, glaring like a red-eyed demon. It was beyond jealousy.

She didn't *trust* him.

She didn't trust his fidelity. She didn't believe him when he said he thought she was beautiful. She didn't think for a moment that once he seduced her into his bed, he would ever want her again.

The craziest thing about it all was that it would be worth the price.

Because she was in love with him.

Hysterical laughter bubbled in her chest and threatened to escape. All she'd ever be to Captain Landon Hart was a light of love he had one summer in Charleston. He would sail off to the next port and to the next woman to catch his eye, and she'd still be here. And her heart would still be irreparably damaged beyond all hope of repair. It already was.

Don't just stand here. Walk away from him.

Walk away.

"Yield to me one last kiss, Keelan."

❧ 36 ❧

CHAPTER THIRTY-SIX
A VICTORY

The moon could have fallen from the sky, and she would have been less unnerved. She couldn't kiss him! She'd lose whatever tiny grip of control she still possessed.

Swaying slightly, she turned unsteadily to face him again. She'd drunk too much wine. One kiss? It was, in light of everything else, a small price to pay, was it not it? Was she ready to abandon her pride completely and allow him to see she'd fallen in love with him? Could she stand to give him the satisfaction that he'd won his foolish game? Did it matter now?

"One kiss for your silence?" Did she just say that? It sounded as if she was actually considering it.

He grasped her shoulders, branding the flesh on her arms, and turned her to face him. "My silence concerning what exactly, love?" A corner of his mouth twitched; eyes flickered with mockery. "Would it be regarding your habit of sparring in boy's clothes in the early morning hours?" He paused and appeared to be pondering a very important thought.

She crossed her arms. "I already paid for that one."

"So you did." He scratched his chin. "Or maybe, 'tis the more treacherous pastime you play with Dr. Garrison's affections." His lips were moving against her temple. "Or Pratt's runaways? Which secret will you be silencing, dear, sweet Keelan?"

Pratt's runaways? Was he actually attempting to blackmail her? She took an unsteady breath. How could he betray Simon and his friends? How could he betray *her*? Her heart pounded in her ears so hard they went numb.

It truly was all a game to him. He had no care for whom it destroyed. Would he really reveal her secrets, or was this simply another ploy? She should call his bluff and make him admit he wouldn't, but it didn't matter now. It was a ruse, a sport. She no longer cared.

Another tiny lie. Maybe she cared a little.

Why couldn't he be honorable, loving, and passionate toward her instead of a duplicitous, scheming, scoundrel? Both versions of Landon Hart warred with each other in her mind. She desperately wanted him to be the former, but was terrified that in reality, he was the latter.

In fact, she was convinced of it.

"All of them," she sighed in defeat. "I wish to silence them all."

A victorious light gleamed in his eyes. "Then pay the toll, my love. A kiss." He stepped away and clasped his hands behind his back. "Whenever you are ready, then."

The conceited lout deliberately moved so she would have to approach him! Well, she could be just as sly. He asked for a kiss, but didn't specify any details.

She would beat him at his own game.

She closed the distance between them, placed her hands on his chest, rose up on her toes and plopped a quick kiss on his cheek. *Ha.*

He frowned. "That was not a kiss. It was a re-enactment of a chicken pecking corn."

She smirked and arched a brow. "You said to yield you a kiss, and I have done so. My debts are paid."

He smirked. "Is that why Garrison wishes to take you to wife? I imagine he must be a simple man with simple needs to require no more than that pathetic version of a kiss. If it's the best you can do, then you are his perfect match."

Walk away.

Chin high, shoulders back.

She bristled at the insult and shushed the voice in her head.

Walk. Away.

Stepping forward, she threw her arms around his neck and crushed her lips to his, curving her body into his hard, angular planes. In response, Landon's hands slid down over her waist, feather light, propelling multiple sensations to spiral through her spine.

It wasn't enough.

Her belly tightened with longing. His heady scent threatened to drive away any sanity she had left. She moved one hand down over his chiseled chest, then his ridged ribcage, before sliding it up the indentation along his spine to join her other hand already entwined in his inky hair. She pulled him closer until her breasts pressed against him. A savage vibration rumbled in his chest.

His lips began to move more insistently; an exhilarating blend of soft pressure and unyielding strength. Her heart abandoned a rhythmic beat and pounded erratically; her fingers dug into the skin atop his shoulders.

It wasn't enough.

She slipped her tongue tentatively into his mouth. With a throaty groan, he crushed her to him. A white-hot bolt shot through her body as his tongue responded.

Tasting. Exploring. Beckoning. Igniting.

His hand moved up over her ribs, leaving a trail of lava in its wake. He cupped her breast and her body instinctively arched into his hand. He rubbed his thumb over the peak until it hardened, making her moan softly.

More.

The late spring night, leather, blackberry wine, the whisper of fingertips brushing silk, the velvety strength of his mouth... all assaulted her consciousness and melted her knees. Thoughts swirled into a reckless whirlwind. The rigid barrier of indifference she had fought so valiantly to place between them crumbled at her feet.

All the warnings and rules she had given herself, regarding this particular sea captain, had been drowned by a tidal wave of emotion too powerful to stop. Her trepidations were no match for the intoxicating, physical lure of the man himself. She'd been captured by his seductive charm. Tormented by his hot fiery kisses. Enslaved by the waves of heat and desire, his presence stirred in her.

Captured, tormented, enslaved... but not loved. Seduced, yes, but not... loved. Did she care?

An angry shriek broke through the haze. "Keelan!"

The shocked undercurrent in her cousin's voice hit her like an icy torrent. Startled, she gasped and opened her eyes in time to see Doreen whirl and run back toward the ballroom. Worse still, standing there staring with a deadly snarl on her beautiful face was none other than Annette Camsby.

She shoved against Landon's chest and to her surprise, he immediately released her. Appalled, she pressed her trembling fingers against her swollen lips and stared at him. His expression made her face burn with embarrassment and humiliation.

It was one of triumph.

He'd won.

37

CHAPTER THIRTY-SEVEN
A CONFRONTATION

Something was still not right.

Everett Garrison's pain and anger should've diminished somewhat when Keelan agreed to marry him.

Her presence at his side should be giving him peace.

Taking the commodore's daughter should be giving him *peace*.

New wealth in the form of Keelan's inheritance, Twin Pines, should be giving him peace.

He'd expected it to be easy to help Keelan conform, to be more like Rachel.

More docile.

More pliable.

Instead, since Hart showed up, she'd become more distant over the last few days. She'd taken to spending time in the kitchen house or on rides around the plantation with her maid. He could never find her alone.

She continued to evade him, just like tonight. He searched the area near the veranda, peeking into corners, and peering at silhouettes in the semi-dark of the moonlight, but didn't see her anywhere. Maybe the garden? Had she already fled to her chamber?

The iron bench wasn't visible from here, but she seemed to favor that spot. He reached into his pocket and caressed Rachel's letter.

Soft, sweet Rachel.

So demure, so willing to please him.

Keelan would learn. He'd help her become the wife Rachel would have been.

He headed toward the steps leading down to the stone path which meandered its way across the back lawn and toward the arbor.

⚓ ⚓ ⚓

CHOKING BACK A TORTURED SOB, Keelan whirled away from Landon and his victorious smirk and ran.

Arrogant, conceited horse's ass!

Angry tears pricked her eyes and threatened to spill down her cheeks.

She was an idiot. She'd known from the very beginning that he'd do this to her, yet she let it happen.

He toyed with her emotions like a sated cat. Hadn't she predicted it? She'd done her best to guard herself against him, tried to discourage him, but her best was as flimsy as ash.

He was much more experienced at this game. No doubt, he had played it many times before with other less gullible maidens. Fury welled inside her, along with the ever-present embarrassment and humiliation that always followed an encounter with that rogue. Even the cicadas taunted her with their chatter.

Fool! Fool! Fool! Fool!

Under the moonlight, the hedges and shrubs shone a silvery-green, casting ebony shadows. She stopped and sat down hard enough on the metal bench to jolt the breath from her lungs. Hidden by the wisteria vines, she rubbed her temples, willing her ridiculous heart to slow and those stupid butterflies and birds to settle.

She had no one to blame but herself. She had been naïve. He had goaded her into that kiss, and she had been completely distracted by his diversion. The embarrassment set her face on fire, likely evaporating the tears.

"Miss Keelan? Are you all right?" Dr. Garrison stepped into view.

She tried not to groan aloud. "I'm fine. I think perhaps I drank too much wine," she said lamely, waving a hand in the general direction of the ballroom.

"Apparently, so." There was an icy edge to his voice, "Miss Doreen sought me out with this ridiculous story about you and Hart..."

Oh no, there would be *no* discussing Landon Hart.

In fact, she would not even utter his name. Her mortification had reached its zenith, and she was unwilling to revisit it.

Yet, for some odd reason, a giggle escaped, and she batted the air as if swatting a giant fly. "Oh, Everett, it was only a little kiss. He didn't think I knew how, you see, so I showed him I did. It was nothing."

Oh dear, why had she said that?

Everett's jaw dropped. "Nothing?" He sputtered like a soup pot with its lid on, left to boil too long. "Do...do you realize what you've done? It's not decent. You have compromised your reputation! Again! I chose to put aside the ignominious circumstances between yourself and Hart after the storm, because your safety and well-being had been my foremost concern at the time. But I will tolerate no more of it. Your cousin is already telling anyone who will listen that you were acting like some sort of, of...*Jezebel*." His words echoed sharply. "What will people think? We are engaged to be married, and you are kissing another man like a common whore!"

For a moment, she sat in stunned silence. Gentle, serene Everett Garrison now faced her, his face dark and furious.

Jezebel? *Whore?*

She sprung to her feet in outrage, her fists clenched at her sides. "How dare you speak to me that way!" She tried to glare at him, but her vision blurred.

She blinked.

Now there were two Everetts. The ground was uneven and her head was floating.

It would be best to retire now and discuss this in the morning. They needed to have a conversation, but she didn't have the fortitude at the moment. Landon had completely upended her plan and unsettled her nerves too much to concentrate right now.

She whirled away, teetering slightly. She was unsure as to the reason why, but suddenly, she had a strong need to release the guilt plying her conscience.

Hadn't she just decided to postpone this?

Even as her mind silently fumbled to scream an objection, she began to speak, "Everett, reconsider your offer of marriage if you want a wife who loves you, because you should know I do not." She started for the house, then paused and turned back, unsure if she'd spoken clearly enough. "Love you, I mean. *I don't.*"

Time to go to her room before she got herself into any more trouble with her overactive mouth. Kissing, talking, it didn't matter. It always caused problems.

He snatched her wrist and twisted it, yanking her back to him. She cried out in pain, and tried to pull away again, but his grip was cruel and tight. His face darkened, and an angry leer sliced his lips open. "I will *not* reconsider."

Keelan's belly gave a sick twist. This man had never shown anger or even frustration toward her in the past. Her own actions were deplorable for a woman engaged, but of course, the wine was mostly to blame. Wicked drink.

"You're hurting my wrist." Her voice shook a little. For the first time since she'd met him, she feared him.

His face flickered and his expression changed to a more neutral one, though his nostrils flared as he spoke. Releasing her, he narrowed his eyes. "I will forgive your little indiscretion. It's obvious the drink addled your mind. Perhaps it's best you retire. We can talk in the morning."

He nervously glanced toward the veranda. "Allow me to escort you to your chamber." He gripped her elbow. "We should go up the rear stair. I'll see you to your room and settled, then I will smooth things over down here with Doreen." He began to steer her to the servants' door.

No. He could not just dismiss her words then lead her away like a misbehaving child. She wasn't going to go with him to her quarters, unescorted either. If Landon could so easily toy with her reputation, she could only imagine the story Garrison would create about his time within the confines of her bedroom. A wedding would definitely occur sooner rather than later. She jerked her arm from his grasp, backing away from him.

"Dr. Garrison." She spoke slowly, both to make sure he understood and to prevent slurring too much. "I would prefer to go alone. So please, leave me to suffer the consequences in solitude."

Everett's mouth flattened, gaze turning steely. He stepped nearer, bringing his face close. His eyes had an almost rabid sheen. "You know nothing about suffering the consequences of another's actions," he spat. "So much tragedy has occurred during the last two years in the Grey family, no?"

His ominous tone hit her like a blow to the stomach.

His fingers dug into her arms. "I lost my family too, Keelan. I know the heart wrenching pain caused by such a dreadful event." He shook his agony into her flesh. "Surely you know your father is dying. When he is gone, you'll be entirely alone." He gave her a brief, humorless smile. "Until you become my wife."

It could have been hearing him put a voice to the dark, silent fear roiling in her own mind.

Entirely alone.

If her father died soon, how would she live? Could she really take care of herself?

His lips drew back in a snarl. "I will have you, regardless."

She narrowed her eyes, which seemed to clear her vision a bit.

"I refuse to be treated like a possession." She shook her head, jaw tight. "I will not permit anyone to decide how I will live my life. You will find, that I do have a say, and I say *no*."

Maybe it was Garrison's words, maybe it was Hart's ruthless assault on her pride, or maybe both, that ignited the powder keg in her chest. He would not *have her.* She'd had enough, already.

She balled her fist and punched Everett Garrison in the stomach as hard as she could. He doubled over and gasped for breath, then lifted his head and stared at her, slack-jawed.

A muscle in his cheek twitched and rolled, betraying his effort for control, as he slowly straightened. He spoke through clenched teeth, and a frigid hush seeped into his voice while his stare pierced her like a spike. "Your father has apparently neglected his duty to see you properly tutored in women's arts. Even so, I will maintain my position and accept you as my betrothed. I'll see to it your father's estate and his coffers are well supervised, he owes me that much. I'll make sure your transformation from a wanton young woman to a docile wife is absolute."

His face twisted into shadowed crevices, and he took a step toward her, stalking. "One thing is for certain, my dear, dear Keelan, you will learn to treat me with more respect."

A sudden, chilling dread crept through her chest. She'd obviously pushed him too far. In the past, he had always comported himself in a gentlemanly manner. However, even a man as passive as Everett must have his limits. She started toward the house.

Time to go.

"Do not turn your back on me!" He reached out and grabbed her sleeve. On the edge of panic, she snatched her arm away, and to her horror the seam ripped then separated from her bodice. Her heel slipped off the garden stone. She teetered for a brief second, then stumbled and fell.

The quiet night was broken by a savage growl and before she could move, Everett was flying through the air like a spidery rag doll. He crashed into a nearby birdbath. With a muffled groan, he collapsed.

❧ 38 ❧

CHAPTER THIRTY-EIGHT
A PROPOSAL

B *last it all.*
Furious, Keelan tried to scramble to her feet, but her legs were entangled in her gown. She'd lost a slipper. A slight headache began to throb behind her eyebrows. A rebellious sob escaped, and she rubbed her eyes with the heels of her palms. What a horrible night.

The cruel scent of sandalwood drifted into her nose just as steely arms lifted her from the ground and placed her gently on the bench. A warm hand replaced her slipper. She opened her eyes.

Sleek and lethal, Landon stood in front of her. His eyes were thunderous, face stony, all marbled planes and angles, every one of them livid.

His voice, although soft and gentle, still vibrated with fury. "Are you hurt?" He scanned her tear-streaked face, eyes softening as he wiped a tear from her jaw.

"This is entirely your fault." She hiccuped. In vain, she attempted to tug her tattered sleeve back into place.

"Yes." He withdrew his handkerchief and dabbed at the trails on her cheeks.

Through the cloth, she muttered, "Why are you here? You won

your infernal game, proving that I am weak and stupid around you. What more is there?"

He studied her intently. "There's you."

She turned her face away, but it didn't deter him. He blotted another tear and brushed his fingertips along her jawline. She closed her eyes. Why wouldn't he stop tormenting her?

"Better to admit you don't love Garrison before the wedding, don't you think?" His voice was thick, soothing, almost hypnotic.

"I never loved him, nor did I intend—" She bit her lip, realizing she had let her last secret escape. She huffed a resigned sigh. Her charade had ended; she had nothing to lose by being honest with him now. She fiddled with the torn lace, and plunged on before she dissolved into a soggy, weepy mess.

"My father is still very, very ill, and he fears he will die soon. That has led him to take steps to properly secure my future to his satisfaction. I accepted the marriage proposal from Dr. Garrison to ensure I could live in Charleston and run a shop while he runs his practice if all else fails. Truthfully, I planned on delaying the nuptials until Papa was well again, or I turned twenty and one, or found a more suitable solution."

She met Landon's knowing stare, then unable to keep eye contact, dropped her chin and stared at her hands. "But you knew, didn't you?"

"I didn't know for certain until we kissed this evening," he admitted gruffly.

Puzzled, she peered up at his face. "What do you mean?" He was even more handsome in the moonlight, like a carved statue, hard jaw, aquiline nose, eyes like a surging ocean, amazing mouth.

Very talented tongue.

He helped her to her feet. "You can't kiss one man like you just kissed me, when you truly love another," he said, voice remaining low and gravelly. "Nor would you have willingly kissed me if you were in love with him."

A wobbly moan drew their attention to Garrison. Thank God he wasn't dead. He'd raised himself to his hands and knees next to the toppled birdbath. Etiquette dictated she should inquire as to his well-being, but she honestly didn't care.

There. A solid truth.

He tucked a stray curl around her ear before cupping her face, directing her attention back to him. "You don't really love Garrison, do you?" The look on his face made her heart stutter.

The deep pools in his eyes were mesmerizing. "Nay," she said softly. "I do not love him." She closed her lids, the rest shouting in her head. I love *you*.

He tipped up her chin, drawing her eyes back to his, voice dropping to a ragged whisper, "What about me, Keelan? Will you deny wanting to be with me, even when your lips tell me otherwise?"

Did he jest? Did it matter to him what she desired?

Didn't he realize he had conquered her weeks ago?

He trespassed upon her dreams at night and seized control of her thoughts during the day to the point of dangerous distraction. Sure, she tried to convince herself for days it was all simply a girlish fascination and lust for adventure, not actual feelings for him. However, would she want Dr. Garrison were he in this captain's shoes? No, she wouldn't.

She flicked a sideways glance to the birdbath. The doctor was gone. Good. With any luck, she'd be able to avoid him the rest of the evening.

Her heart was already too mangled to bother protecting it anymore. It was time to shrug off her pride for once and be honest. Her voice was no more than a wisp of air. "I can't deny that I wish to be with you."

Potent desire swirled in his azure eyes. "I have wanted you from the moment I first kissed you." He stroked the back of his fingers down her cheek and along her jaw. A heated shiver followed their path.

She let out a small sigh. "It's not the wanting, and it's not the passion, Landon." His eyes clouded with confusion and she looked away.

Now he was torturing her in a different manner. Forcing her to put words to her emotions? He might as well strip her bare and make her say it in front of the entire city of Charleston. "It might sound petty and vain to your ears, but I can't—I won't—marry a man who beds other women or has mistresses in every port town. I'm not willing to live that life. I'm prideful, I know, but—"

Keelan's breath caught as he silenced her with a single finger on her lips. He lowered his head. "Sweet, sweet Keelan, I want no one but you," he murmured against her mouth. "*Ever.*" His lips brushed against hers, causing her heart to give a hopeful lurch. This time, the caress contained such tenderness her tears flowed anew. Time stopped as he slowly and claimed her mouth. She couldn't move, nor did she want to.

He finally broke the kiss and took both of her hands in his. She couldn't tear her gaze from his now if her life depended on it. The cobalt stare deepened. "Even when you chose another, I cursed myself for allowing the opportunity to have you slip away. I resolved that before the week was out, I would return for you and ask you to break your engagement and choose me instead." Voice husky with emotion, he urged, "Join me, Keelan. Leave behind your secrets and schemes and let me show you what it's like to be loved and worshipped for the woman you are."

She sucked in a frail, reedy breath. How cruel of him to say something so beautiful to her. This time, she didn't doubt his words or intentions. In his crystalline irises, she saw nothing but a burning intensity, flaring with determination.

Emotion roughened his voice. "You do want me, want to be *with* me, don't you, love?"

How could she not? His thumb was making distracting circles on the top of her hand. "Desiring you, being with you, has never been a problem, Landon." His expression shifted. Guarded, anxious. She reached up and touched her palm to his cheek. "Loving you is the easy part."

There. She said it.

It was painful, but now it was out. Her heart was leaden, thick with sorrow, already grieving for something she never had in the first place. "The problem is the torment you'd cause with every departure." She gestured weakly toward the house and Annette Camsby. "It's the beautiful women who are naturally drawn to your charm and handsome smile and—well—*you.*" Her heart had been scraped raw; she had nothing more to protect, so she stumbled on. "I could never stand to be away from you so long, and the distance will always prevent me from completely trusting your fidelity."

"I know." His face softened even as something primal flashed in his eyes. "But, Keelan, love, I promise—"

She hushed him with a finger across his lips. "Don't make promises you can't keep." She lowered her hand and turned her face away. In the light of the moon, the wisteria blossoms looked like drops of silver cascading from the vines. She didn't trust Landon and that hurt him, which made her hurt for him, but it didn't change anything between them.

Passion coated Landon's voice, making it husky and raw. "You once told me you'd never want a man who comes home for only a few weeks' time."

She nodded.

"Do you recall what I said in response?" He brushed away tear with a callused thumb. "I told you that any man who would leave you for even an hour was a fool." He cradled her face in both hands, storm cloud blue eyes drank in her features like he was memorizing every facet. "I am many things, but I'm not a fool."

For a moment, it was impossible to breathe. Her heart slammed into her ribs. "What are you saying?" It would be foolish to read a message in his words that wasn't there. Hope surged. Would he do that for her? Would he leave his seafaring life behind? She could never ask such a thing. He loved the sea. Never would she ask him to abandon the source of his joy for her. But what if he chose it of his own volition? "Are you staying in Charleston?"

He shook his head, sending her world plummeting to shatter on the jagged rocks of disappointment. "I cannot. I have responsibilities and obligations to a great many people who count on me."

Her heart constricted painfully. "I would never ask you to abandon them."

He gave her a slow, painful smile. "Sweet, brave, honorable Keelan. That is one of the things that pulls me to you." Heated blue eyes held hers with a charged intensity that made it impossible for her to even blink. "Keelan, I need you. I can't imagine setting the sails without you by my side. You've stolen my heart, lass."

By his side? "Do you mean—" Her voice came out thin, tremulous. She searched his eyes for any trepidation. Only warm conviction and a promise of fire swirled in his gaze. "Are you saying you want me to go *with you?*"

The fire flamed, brightened. He dragged his fingertips down her throat, then rested his hand over her heart. "I'll always crave that reckless courage and untamable spirit in here. I can't live without them. I want you beside me every day for the rest of my life."

Every day.

A surge of pure joy cascaded down her ribcage, healing her heart and sending those birds and butterflies on a wild, gleeful flight.

He took both her hands in his. "Keelan, love, leave behind your schemes and plots. Break off your engagement with Garrison and marry me instead. Come with me now, tonight."

God, yes.

She flung her arms around his neck, earning a satisfied growl from him. Here was a solution that hadn't occurred to her. To be able to both love a man of the sea and never be parted. It was *perfect*.

"Oh, Landon, yes! I will marry you."

He crushed her mouth with his. From their first meeting, she was drawn to this man in a way she couldn't explain. It was as if, when she breathed, his essence flowed into her chest and surged through her veins. It permeated her being, invaded her mind, surrounded her heart, and enveloped her soul. Simply being next to him energized her and brought her senses sharply into focus. She craved the strength and freedom and vitality he stirred in her. Her mind stilled even as her heart soared to the heavens and time hung suspended in a mad twirl among the clouds.

Landon's voice rasped low and gravelly in her ear. "My light, my love, my beautiful tempest, I shall show you the world."

⚓ ⚓ ⚓

A TWIG SNAPPED NEARBY, and both froze in place, listening. She clutched his forearms, the corded muscles tensing beneath her hands. He gave a slow shake of his head, telling her to remain silent.

"Miss Keelan! Are you there?"

She immediately recognized the voice and gave him a reassuring smile. "I'm here, Slaney. On the bench near the roses."

The maid rounded the hedgerow, breathless, her face pale and drawn. "I've been looking for ye everywhere, lass. I'm afraid, it's yer Da."

Cold talons of dread clenched around Keelan's throat at her maid's next words.

"He's taken a bad turn, and he's askin fer ye." Slaney twisted her apron in her hands.

Her startled gaze jolted back to Landon. He took her hands in his and planted a gentle kiss on her forehead. "Tend to your father. I'll wait for you on my ship. In the meantime, we have cargo in the *Seeker* to deliver to Harbour Town. The *Desire* should be able to leave dry dock in the next week. I'll hoist a Blue Peter—a blue flag with a white square in the middle—when the ship is preparing to leave port. As soon as I locate our stolen freight, we'll be ready to sail. Join me when you can." He bent his head and captured her lips in another fierce, tender kiss that set fire to the winged creatures in her belly. She marveled at the way slick thrusts of his tongue combined with the dominating movement of his lips liquefied her bones.

He held her a moment longer and inhaled deeply, as if he needed her in order to breathe. She melted against the forged heat of his chest.

"In a few days we'll be together," he whispered in her ear. "I'll wait as long as it takes."

Keelan looped her arm through Slaney's. "We'll take the back stair. It's longer, but I'd rather not be seen in such disarray by the guests."

Slaney flattened her mouth as she took in the ripped dress, then glared at Landon.

"This isn't his doing. I'll explain everything later," Keelan promised.

The maid flicked one last warning glance to Landon before patting her hand. "We should hurry, lass. I heard a couple on the veranda mention taking a walk this way," she said, tugging on her arm. "I'll take you to your Da, then I'll go make you a nice strong cup of tea."

⚅⚅

LANDON'S CHEST felt twice its size. The world around him settled. Keelan was *his*.

He couldn't think of a better way to live out his days aboard the *Desire* than with Keelan by his side. He slid around chattering guests, searching for Jared Grey. Instead, he spied Conal, his shoulders taking up most of the space at the ballroom doorway, scanning the room. His rigid stature put Landon immediately on alert.

Beside Conal stood a crewman, Henry, holding his hat in his hands like he would rather be eating it than standing there among Charleston's finest dressed. Landon weaved his way through the jovial crowd, then nodded a greeting to the men.

Conal shifted his stance, and apparently finding no other words which would make the news less harsh, blurted the facts, "We found Billy near The Whistling Pig Tavern in an alley off Meeting Street." His voice dropped, "He was hit on the head and left tucked in the shadows behind the building. He wouldn't fully wake. We put him in his aunt's care. I don't think he'll be up for another voyage for some time yet, if ever."

Landon took an angry breath. He'd find those bastards.

Conal continued, "Did ye learn who went with him and the last wagon load?"

Landon nodded, "All three were local lads. Robbie Crowe, long scar across his shoulder and missing the ring finger on his left hand, Orvis Pike, shorter and stouter, and a tall, thin man named Hawkins. I am waiting to speak with Jared Grey, regarding their possible whereabouts and employer."

Henry spoke up. "We could start at the pubs and boarding houses. They are bound to have a favorite tavern, woman, or place to sup."

Landon lowered his voice. "Be discreet. I don't want them to get nervous and disappear. I want their employer." He scrubbed his hand over his face. "I'll see Billy's aunt compensated before we sail. We'll have to hire another galley boy to help Marcel."

Conal and Henry departed to carry out his orders. With luck, they would be able to glean some useful information without causing much suspicion. They'd never find his stolen cargo either if the thieves went silent and dark. He scanned the room again for Grey. He had some questions about the buildings closest to the docks.

Grey was surrounded by four other men, chatting. As Landon approached, he excused himself, and gestured for him to follow down the hall.

"Captain Hart," Grey said, when they were away from the music, voices and ears. "I have some news for you. If you accompany me to my office, we can discuss it more discreetly."

Once in the study, Grey poured him a glass of port and they sat in chairs flanking an unlit fireplace. A model of a frigate was piled in pieces on a lower shelf.

"I appreciate your efforts to help my cause," Landon said, hoping the man had the information he needed.

Grey waved his hand in dismissal. "I'm afraid it might not be worth much, but you should know what I learned."

Any information was better than none.

Jared leaned forward, forearms on his knees. "I heard an unfamiliar group has been frequenting a tavern near the docks. I noted this only because one name mentioned sounded familiar, then I recalled hearing the same name during our conversation a few weeks ago, when you and Captain O'Brien joined us for breakfast."

Landon's stomach tightened.

"The leader's name is Gampo," Jared finished.

AFTER HIDING behind the hedges to eavesdrop on Keelan and Hart's conversation, Everett stumbled into the ballroom and elbowed his way through the guests and up the front stairs. It was hard to focus, and his head ached. The anger at Keelan's betrayal and Hart's interference roiled in his gut. Tonight's events necessitated an adjustment. He had planned to finish Commodore Grey after the wedding, but his haughty daughter made it necessary to alter the timing.

Two years ago, the bastard sealed his own fate when he sunk the ship carrying Everett's family and beloved fiancée, Rachel. The memory made him trip up the last step.

Rachel.

So loving, so devoted, kind, and gentle. In his dreams, he still heard her whispered promises...to love him forever, and give him a family. Children. Now, without her, he was a spinning compass with no true north.

What else could he do?

What else would ease his despair?

He owed her more. She deserved more. Rachel deserved to be avenged.

Don't fret, Rachel, my love. The result will be the same. The commodore will resign his life, racked in pain.

Vengeance would release his mind from the torment of her absence. It had to. It was all he could think about. She came to him at night, crying in despair for the children she would never have. Her tears filled an ocean, rising up above her ankles to her waist, and neck; it swallowed her down into its depths, her mouth open, her arms wide... pleading... sinking.

It took considerable willpower to restrain himself from simply killing the commodore and be done with it. However, the man who murdered his family and his love didn't deserve a quick, painless death. The gallows were too good for him, and while Everett was furious at the time, now he was glad the idiot was rescued and shipped off to America. He had time to coordinate and execute a slow, agonizing poisoning coupled with sharp, steady grief. One murder at a time.

Justice.

Sweet Rachel would have her revenge.

Hoping each death would chip away at the painful stone encasing his heart, he vowed to eliminate Commodore Grey's family members one by one. It was easy to spook the well-bred, but spirited horses pulling the commodore's carriage. The accident was spectacular; the wife died instantly.

Excellent news arrived earlier this week. He received word the assassin he hired in London recently succeeded in eliminating the eldest brother, and that information lightened Everett's mood considerably.

Keelan was a jewel. Beautiful and kind, she'd make a suitable wife, after he polished her a little. He would teach her how to be more like Rachel... daintier... softer... reticent.

Obedient.

She would put his needs and desires before her own and see to his comfort. She would give him children. She would commit her life to making him happy. A fitting patch for the gaping hole the commodore tore open.

Keelan could never replace Rachel.

Never.

But he'd make sure she'd come very close.

Like a clay mold.

A replica.

Keelan would learn how to be more like his Rachel. Then his life would be fulfilled and whole again. The dark, sad days churning with wretched loss would be behind him, forgotten. The world would be as it should be once again.

But Keelan must *love* him. She must love him as Rachel loved him.

It was bothersome to hear her say she didn't. That would change. He developed a plan to fix that element, which meant he required Gampo's assistance, again.

39

CHAPTER THIRTY-NINE
A CONFESSION

"This entire night is a complete disaster." Doreen tossed her fan on a nearby chair in her Uncle George's bedroom.

"Doreen!" Aunt Sarah gasped, pausing at the doorway with Keelan.

"Well, it's true," her cousin pouted. She flounced onto the chaise and stared at the ceiling. "As the guest of honor, I should be downstairs entertaining my beaus."

Uncle Jared had been standing near the bed, but at his daughter's tirade, he stepped over to where she sat brooding. He frowned down at her. "Out of respect for your uncle, you will stay."

Doreen turned her head to stare at the tapestry hanging on the far wall.

Keelan scanned the room for Garrison. No sign of him, thank God. She had taken a few moments to change her damaged gown. She also wore Papa's gift, the signet ring, on a ribbon around her neck. Slaney had made her drink a cup of strong tea. Thankfully, she was feeling less woozy. She took a step toward her father's bedside.

"Gracious, Keelan! Whatever happened to you?" Uncle Jared gaped. She caught her reflection in the window. In her rush, she'd forgotten about her hair. Several ribbons had come undone and the braided coif sagged crazily near her nape.

"You should ask the good Captain Hart." Doreen folded her arms and smirked.

"What?" Her uncle's jaw tensed, and he stared pointedly at Keelan. "If he abused you..."

Keelan spoke through clenched teeth. "Doreen, this is not the time." To her uncle, she said quietly. "Dr. Garrison and I had a bit of a disagreement, and I called off the engagement."

Doreen jerked like she was poked with something sharp and sat upright.

"Oh, dear." Aunt Sarah cast a worried glance at her husband.

Uncle Jared's eyebrows furrowed in confusion. "He did not mention it earlier."

When was that? "You saw him?" she asked.

He nodded. "Yes, he came in to tend to George and realized his time was... short. He found me a few minutes ago and told me we should say our goodbyes."

⚜

KEELAN'S HEART clenched within grief's cold grip as she took in the form on the bed. She didn't think Papa's color could pale any further. Shallow cheeks, sunken eyes, and white lips. He looked nothing like the stocky, vibrant, jovial man she remembered. His once broad shoulders were now thin and bony.

Papa was dying, and all she could think about was that she'd never really known him. Even after his retirement and her mother's sudden death, her father still had not spent much time with her. She hoped she would be able to nourish a stronger bond with him, but he had remained distracted and detached, spending most of his days and attention on Twin Pines, then later indisposed with his illness.

Aunt Sarah sobbed into her handkerchief. Uncle Jared leaned into his wife, put his arm around her shoulders.

Keelan moved to sit at her father's side, then clasped his cool, limp hand.

"Papa?" She placed his hand upon her cheek. "I'm here."

Her father focused on her; his mouth turned upward in a weak smile. "Keelan, child," he rasped, "I must speak to you. I must tell you something very important." He winced as a spasm rippled over his body. "I must talk to...you alone."

He sounded so parched. Sh poured him a small glass of water.

"Wait." Her cousin hopped up and nudged her out of the way. "I can help him. Dr. Garrison trained me to administer his medications. I'm to mix one of them with water to subdue his pain." She opened a drawer in the bedside table and selected a vial. Using a dropper, she added the medicine to the water glass.

"Thank you, Doreen." Keelan gave her a fleeting smile. "Here Papa, sip this." She cradled his head in the crook of her elbow and pressed the rim to his lips.

Doreen hovered a moment, then returned to stand by her parents.

He took a small swallow and scrutinized his daughter's face. "I remember that dark, rainy night when I first picked you up and held you in my arms. Where have the years gone?" He lowered his head back to the pillow. "Memories float through my mind on wispy tails of a smoky haze. Death is near, Keelan."

Her eyes welled with tears. "Don't say that, Papa."

He released a dry, thin sigh. "Sweet girl, it's true. I've made some terrible choices. I hope if I confess my indiscretions and try to make things right, you might have a chance to repair the damage I caused, and perhaps even forgive me. I owe you the truth."

Keelan shook her head. There was nothing to forgive. The medicine must be interfering with his mind. After setting the glass back on the table, she tucked the covers around him. She didn't want him to see her cry.

"It's been twenty-five years, and time has tempered my hatred." He reached for Keelan's hand, and she enveloped his knobby fingers with hers. "Keelan, you will not be left alone."

She smiled through her grief. "Oh, Papa—"

He interrupted. "I must tell you something extremely important. A secret... a treasure which I kept from you and your mother for far too long."

He made no sense. "A secret—treasure, Papa? To what do you refer?"

His voice faltered. Her father stared with watery eyes at his brother. "Please... leave us."

"We want to stay with you," Jared objected. "We are family, George." He grasped his brother's other hand and patted it. "We are right here beside you."

Her father lifted his head and raised his feeble voice a bit louder. "This is a private matter I must discuss with Keelan." He collapsed back on his pillow and closed his eyes, breathing raggedly. "Please, Jared."

A little bewildered at her father's demeanor, she reluctantly rose to guide her aunt, cousin, and uncle toward the door. "I'll come get you as soon as he is through speaking to me."

Doreen hooked her arm through her mother's. "Come, Mama, I'll walk with you to the sitting room, then I'll get Tilly to bring us some tea." Uncle Jared took a single step, then another, before expelling a breath and following his wife and daughter. Keelan moved her chair closer to her father's bed.

"Try to conserve your strength." She stroked the hair from his forehead.

He sighed. "'Tis the way things go, my dear. There is no stopping it. My life has been cursed. Ever since I... all because that Irish rake stole her from me, I've lived a cursed life! *Cursed*!"

"Papa, why would you say such a thing?" She spoke softly to ease his distress, and because her throat felt as if it were filled with stones.

"I would have cherished her forever, but she fell under his spell and broke my heart." He heaved out a sigh. "I hated and punished them a long time. And that bloody ship—all those souls lost." He rubbed his hand across his face in anguish. "Now, God is punishing me—and I deserve it."

His fingers shook as he reached for her hand, his voice sounding like old sticks blown across a barren field. "Keelan, I need to make things right for you. Listen carefully."

A fit of coughing followed, and she gave him another drink. "Papa, please rest a moment. Try not to talk for a while."

He shook his head. "I must. Keelan, something of significant value awaits you back home at Wind Briar. I hid it away all these many years." He inhaled a ragged breath. "You have kin in Ireland. You must find them."

"Ireland?" Keelan's jaw unhinged. "But—"

He pointed a bony finger to a wooden box on the nightstand, "That box, get it for me."

Baffled, she handed it to him. Rather than take it, he ran his trembling fingers along its side. "A small compartment is hidden..." His quaking hands would not cooperate, and he handed it to her. "Release the latch near the hinge in the back. Press it."

His eyelids drooped. She turned the elegantly carved box over in her hands, found the latch. There was a tiny click, then a drawer glided from the right side. She removed a bag of coins and a large egg-shaped locket.

Papa's hand shook as he pointed to the locket. "That's him, the debaucher. The man who stole my darling's heart," he whispered harshly. He spoke between short gasps. "At the time, the repercussions of my actions didn't matter as much as punishing that arrogant Irish lord who seduced the woman I'd loved since I was a young buck. But now, as I face the portal of death, those repercussions terrify me." His watery gaze drifted to hers. "I ask your forgiveness, Keelan."

She wanted to understand him, but his words made no sense. "Papa, I—"

"Remember the ring I gave you? Look at it," he urged. "On the side is a family crest, *your* family crest." His breathing became more labored as he coaxed his withering body to draw yet another murky breath. "What you do with the information I am about to confide, will either ruin you or save you, dear girl."

She pulled the ribbon holding the signet ring from around her neck and peered at it more closely. The way he had skirted her questions when he'd given it to her some weeks ago, signaled that there was a story behind this ring then. Perhaps she would learn its secrets now.

His voice trembled with regret. "The locket belonged to her. He had gifted it to her. I took it. I was jealous, angry, and spiteful. She was mine! My own love. But he seduced her and warped your mother's mind against me..." He nodded toward the ring. "That same crest is on both."

The ring displayed her family crest. Keelan was puzzled. Her father had never talked about any other kin. She studied it again. It showed a lion in each corner. Three bundles of wheat crossed the middle. Above was a knight's helm. The other indeed bore the same image, although larger.

Her father's words chipped away at her composure like a ticking clock chipped away the time. What exactly was he saying?

With shaking hands, she turned the piece over in her palm then sucked in her breath. It held a tiny portrait of a young man, perhaps ten or so years older than she. There was no denying this was a relative. Although he had black hair, he had her long, slim nose. His expression was impish. Amusement glittered in his eyes even though he wasn't smiling. If it wasn't for the ebony of his hair, the man could be her brother.

"Your Uncle Fynn suspected. He wrote and demanded a meeting, but died en route, I was told." He gestured to the ring and locket. "Both belong to you."

Wait, *her* Uncle Fynn? During the conversation at the breakfast table, the two merchant captains had mentioned Fynn Ahern's name. Uncle Jared had denied the name was familiar to him. Yet, there had been something suspicious with Jared's manner that morning.

He'd been lying.

Papa's next strangled words fell like stones, "Keelan." He dragged in another short breath. "You must understand...you are not really *my* daughter."

Not his daughter.

"Child, please listen. Go back to Wind Briar and search through the old wooden trunk in my library. Inside, you will find a letter." He exhaled loudly and struggled for another rattling breath. "Daniel?" he wheezed.

A figure approached from the dark corner of the dimly lit room. The valet had been so quiet; she didn't notice him. She smiled sadly. Of course, he would be here to see to his master's every last need. He was a most faithful servant to her father. Daniel walked to the bed and dipped his head in greeting. Keelan stared numbly at his cheek, where a tear's path still glistened.

"Yes, milord?"

"Daniel. Enough coin is in the box for the journey. Take it. See her safely home."

Daniel immediately nodded. "I will, sir. I give both you and Miss Keelan my oath."

"Papa, I'll return to the country house and seek your trunk." She swallowed tightly as she fought back her own tears. She wanted to reassure him, so he would rest easier. As it was, he flailed his arm as if he were batting away an invisible demon.

He paused in his thrashing and finally calmed. "Keelan, the contents are of... immense value... to you." His expression turned to one of reluctant regret. He wrestled with the confession. "I couldn't give my Catherine a child, she so wanted a baby. It was a fitting punishment for the man who took everything from me."

She tried to remember a trunk in the library. Perhaps it was the one draped with the lion's pelt? His next words whisked her back to the present.

"Your mother and your father..."

"Good Lord!" She gripped her father's hand tighter. *Her mother?*

Like an earthquake deep beneath the surface, the meaning rumbled through her consciousness. She stared at her father. No... at the man who was *not* her father. A loud ringing echoed through her ears. It pierced her mind and shattered her thoughts. Her mother... desperate for a child... what had she done? Taken a lover?

His gaze left her face and roamed around the room, as if he were seeing it for the first time. It was a moment before he focused once again on her. "Oh, Keelan! How I loved her. He took her from me!" He shook her hand with each word. "Don't cry. My next trip to London, I shall bring you some bright ribbons for your hair. Would that cheer you?"

Tears streamed down her face; he was fading into a realm where past and present swirled together in a grey mist.

"Papa..."

"It was wrong, the way Catherine acted." He flopped an arm across his eyes. Somehow, even in his broken state, reliving the torment the secret had caused.

"It wasn't the right thing to do, but after the deed was done, it could not be undone without serious repercussions."

Keelan heard the blood rushing through her head. Her heart pounded and tried to beat back the word thundering over and over in her chest. But her mind screamed it louder.

Bastard child.

Her mother was an adulteress. She had an affair with another man, a married man, and became pregnant with his child. Since Catherine and George were childless, he raised her as his own.

In a burst of energy, he reached for her and grasped her arm. He searched her face, as if hoping for some confirmation she understood him. "Please forgive me, but I named Jared as sole beneficiary of my estate." He pointed to the miniature. "I had to make sure you had no other choice but to locate the man in the locket. Your real father should know you, your mother too, would want it." He thrashed his head from side to side. "I loved her. I have always loved her. I *still* love her."

He moaned his agony and drew another jerky breath. His lips moved. As she leaned over him, his faint plea stirred the air like a faint breath through the sheer muslin curtains.

"There is nothing here for you, Keelan. Find your family. Tell them I am... sorry for keeping you. Promise me, Keelan. Promise."

"I promise," she choked out the words. This new information strengthened her decision to leave Charleston with Landon. She hadn't wanted the burden of the plantation.

Now, she was free of it.

As heavy as her heart was for him, the weight of the encumbrance crumbled and fell away. As for finding her real father, she could call upon Landon for help. They could sail together to Great Britain.

It would be an adventure.

George Grey turned his head toward Keelan. "Light a lamp, child. I can't see your face."

Tears streamed unchecked down her cheeks. She stared at the brightly burning oil lamp at the bedside of the stranger she had called "Papa" for the last nineteen years.

"The lamp is lit, Papa."

CHAPTER FORTY
THE DECEIVER

E verett tucked his watch back into his pocket. It wouldn't be long now. Keelan had excused herself to her bedchamber earlier, promising to return soon.

He closed the bedroom door behind Doreen. At his instruction, the young lady had administered the last bit of the "medicine" to George Grey a few seconds ago.

When the old man died, he would be there to comfort his daughter. She'd see then he'd make a good husband, wouldn't she?

"George." He reached down and roughly shook the old man's shoulder.

George opened his eyes. He winced and Everett leaned in close. He wanted to make sure the old man didn't miss his next words.

"Doreen just gave you a potent dose of the serum that has been slowly poisoning you over the past several months," he said in harsh satisfaction.

George's eyelids flew open and widened in shock.

"Why did your niece do it, you're wondering?" He took a deep breath but couldn't contain his shudder. "I am a healer, not a killer, like you." He stared at his hands. "Still, my fingers are coated with blood, even though I had Doreen do the deed. She was unaware, of course.

She believed she was giving you *medicine*." He clenched his hands into fists. "Have you heard of Rachel Hornsby? Robert Garrison? Martha Garrison? Emmett Garrison?"

George shook his head, a confused frown on his face.

"They were my family, my parents and younger brother, my fiancée... sweet, darling Rachel. You murdered them. You sunk their ship, and you killed them."

The pain in the dying man's eyes would not affect him. It was too late for that.

He continued, "I vowed to her, my Rachel, that I would serve you the same dish you served me." He leaned closer. "You have been feasting on it for months. Now you know what it's like to lose the people you love."

The old man's brows furrowed, as if he was trying to decipher his words. An understanding began to dawn across his features.

"Yes!" Everett nodded. "Your wife, nephew, sister-in-law, all dead. Before we left England, I hired a man to kill your older brother. It took longer than I anticipated, but it was accomplished quite successfully."

He wanted to witness the old wretch's expression when the final most horrendous realization occurred.

"And now, your beloved daughter is my betrothed."

The old commodore's frantic eyes darted to the door and back. He struggled to raise his head. "No!" he rasped, the fear choking his voice.

"Oh, yes indeed. You were there when she chose me, remember? Although we had a little tiff tonight, I will still make things work to my satisfaction. She *will* become my wife."

The old man's mouth opened in a silent scream. Bony hands reached to claw at him, but he was now well out of reach.

"Papa?" Keelan knocked, then entered "Dr. Garrison, how is he?"

He gestured for her to come to the bedside, and she approached and kissed her father's forehead.

Everett gave her a sympathetic smile. "He's nearing his end now, my dear. The hallucinations are worsening." He took her hand and patted it. "Speak to him, let him know you'll be fine so he can...let go." He ignored how she pulled her hand from his grip.

Grey's eyes twitched frantically between him and Keelan. He made a low hissing sound. She quickly grasped his hand.

"Papa, I'm here. It's all right. I'm here." Her eyes welled with tears.

The commodore's lips cracked as he tried to form words. "Keelan... don't... he is...." A slight whimper escaped from his mouth.

The old man's chest rose and fell, and rose and fell, then stilled. Keelan's head sank. She wept softly, still holding his hand. Everett squeezed her shoulder in sympathy. "I'll go inform Mr. and Mrs. Grey that he has passed on."

Keelan nodded and blotted her face with a handkerchief.

Everett stepped into the hall, then pulled out his watch. He gently opened it to stare at the small portrait wedged inside the lid.

"For you, Rachel, my love," he whispered. He snapped the case shut. If Keelan Grey thought she was going to elope with Hart, she'd thought wrong. She'd never arrive at that ship.

He'd make sure of it.

⚓ ⚓ ⚓

KEELAN gently placed Papa's hands on his now still chest. Shock and grief left her numb and immobile. She was not his daughter, but another's. Who was the man who'd sired her? How would Landon take the news that she was not the commodore's child, but her mother's illegitimate daughter?

Somehow, the captain didn't seem the type of man to allow such things to sway his course. Still, she would give him the opportunity to rescind his offer of marriage, although her heart would shatter if he did.

Was Landon Hart the type of man to take on this new adventure of hers? To seek her father?

Her heart stirred, shifting to accommodate the surge of warmth and strength brought by a certain truth.

Captain Landon Hart was just that type of man. His love for her was as fierce as hers for him. They would sojourn together on Hart's *Desire*. Adventures were life's breath to Landon Hart, and she couldn't wait to stand at his side for the next one.

A new beginning.

A new life.

A new adventure.

Landon's words echoed in her heart. *"My light, my love, my beautiful tempest, I shall show you the world."*

IF YOU GIVE A RAKE A REASON
HE'LL CRAVE A CARESS TO PLEASE HIM...

Book Two

❧ 41 ❧

CHAPTER FORTY-ONE
THE PERFECT CRIME

Charleston, South Carolina
June 1811

I f they were going to steal it, tonight would be the perfect time.
The pirates watched.

And waited.

The moon was nothing more than a sliver in the sky, leaving the night almost as dark as pitch. A single sentry strolled along the street in front of the warehouse. He passed the main doors and continued until he reached the far corner. He yawned, stretching his arms out wide. Removing his floppy hat, he scratched his head vigorously and then jammed the hat back on. After a lazy glance up and down the street, he pulled a bottle from his pocket and took a swig before he leaned against the wall and yawned again.

A dog barked in the distance, provoking a shouted curse from one of the city's sleepy residents. The sentry sank to his haunches, tipped the bottle to his mouth and then rested his head against the bricks behind him. Once more he looked around. Finally, with a bored sigh, he sat on the ground and placed his bottle within reach before resting his arms on his knees. Within minutes, his head slumped to his fore-arms. The gentle sea swayed against the pilings with the easy rhythm of a rocking chair. The street was quiet except for the gently breaking waves and the soft snoring of the sentry.

Drago Viteri Gamponetti, Gampo to his men, leaned around the corner and gestured to a pair of wagons waiting behind him. A few men slipped down to lead the teams forward. A loud 'clop' on the cobblestones made everyone freeze in stunned silence.

"One of the mufflings has fallen off," whispered a driver.

"Crowe, you'd best check them all before we head on," he hissed. "And check all the wheels!"

"Aye, Cap'n Gampo, sir." Crowe muttered, as he scampered hastily about doing as he was told. All metal parts should still be wrapped in strips of dark cloth to keep them from jingling with the horses' move-ments. He ran his hands over the strips of oiled leather covering each wheel. As soon as everything was secure, Crowe motioned for all to move out. The caravan stopped near the warehouse doors.

With the stealth of a shadow, Gampo descended from the lead wagon. Producing a key, he placed it in the lock and turned it until it gave a dull 'click.' After a quick glance toward the end of the building and the sleeping sentry, he pulled a glass bottle from his pocket and squatted by the door hinges, then removed the cork with his teeth. After the hinges had been fully doused with the oil, he stepped back and gently pulled one of the doors open a bit and then closed it again, testing. He repeated this procedure several more times. Satisfied he'd eliminated any squeaks, he opened both doors wide.

One of the men gestured toward the snoring sentry near the corner. Gampo studied the man, noted the whiskey bottle next to him and gave a slight shake of his head. The other shrugged, stepped down and grabbed the halter of one of the horses, then led it inside. Gampo followed and pulled the doors shut.

Once inside the warehouse, the men remained motionless while Gampo struck a match to the candle wedged between the boards of the wagon seats.

"Take the blankets and cover the windows facing the street," he directed in a dry whisper. "Once they're secure, light your lanterns and get to work."

"Aye, Cap'n."

The men went about doing what he'd ordered. They all were well aware there was no room for error. Failing to execute even one small detail could get them caught. Getting caught would get them hanged. It gave the men strong impetus to do the job correctly.

An hour later the wagons were loaded with casks of brandy and whiskey, rolls of silk fabric, boxes of spices, ammunition and countless other treasures from across the sea. They snuffed out the lanterns and removed the blankets from the windows. Gampo was the last to exit. The sentry hadn't moved. He chucked to himself. The poor tar would have a great deal of explaining to do when his employer arrived in the morning. Still smiling, he reached into his pocket, pulled out the key and locked the warehouse.

That ought to give 'im something to think about.

❧❧❧

THE SENTRY SHIFTED SLIGHTLY. Steel blue eyes glinted from under the rim of his hat as he watched the wagons pull away. After giving a slight nod to the roof of the boarding house across the street, an oil lamp flared in answer. Landon Hart rose and headed in the direction taken by the wagons seconds before.

"THEY TURNED east down the next street," Landon whispered to his friend Captain Conal O'Brien, as they followed the path of the thieves, staying near the darker shadows. "They're heading in the direction of the warehouses we scouted earlier."

Conal nodded. "Hopefully they take it to the one containing the rest of our cargo. It'll be harder to find the first half if they put this load in a different place."

It was a risky venture, but the only way to find out where their goods were taken was to leave the rest vulnerable. Conal had bragged at the pub near the docks that they had rented the most secure warehouse in the city and had complete confidence in the quality of the locks. They were so convinced, he'd boasted only one man was needed to guard the lot.

The thieves swallowed the bait, and now Landon had his hook embedded deeply.

An ugly image of Keelan in the brutal arms of one of those leering pirates nudged its way to the forefront of Landon's daydreams. He couldn't get the fiery-haired vixen out of his mind. His chest felt twice its size. The world around him settled. Keelan was *his*. He couldn't think of a better way to live out his days aboard the *Desire* than with Keelan by his side.

This was no time to be preoccupied with thoughts of a woman, but this wasn't just any woman, it was his heart, his love. It was difficult to avoid thinking about how sweet her mouth tasted or how she smelled of jasmine and sunshine...

Stop it.

An entanglement was the last thing he'd wanted when they made port in Charleston. He and Conal had suffered a major loss, Conal's Uncle Fynn at the hands of Gampo. Bloody, ruthless pirate.

Fynn planned a trade route to include a stopover in Charleston so he could meet with Commodore George Grey, who'd turned out to be Keelan's father. Fynn had been very secretive about the reasons why he wanted to meet with the commodore. So, following the run-in with Gampo, they tucked their ships in dry dock for repairs. Landon and Conal kept Fynn's mysterious meeting out of curiosity more than anything.

While visiting Twin Pines plantation, he'd met Keelan, who was masquerading as a boy and dueling with swords with her father's valet. It was only after he'd had given her a brief lesson in knife throwing he'd learned Keelan was actually a young lady. Conal found it highly amusing and had retold the story several times at The Whistling Pig Tavern, where they'd rented rooms.

What Conal hadn't seen occurred later the same morning. Landon had caught Keelan eavesdropping from the depths of the garden bushes. At the time, he didn't know she was the commodore's daughter. He saw her as a curiosity. Up close, she was more than that. She was smooth and sleek with the quickness of a cat and the curves of a woman.

Eyes wide like a startled doe and lush lips parted in surprise, she'd have bolted if her hair hadn't been severely tangled in the branches. How could any normal man possibly *resist* the opportunity to kiss her? So he did.

She froze in shock at first, of course, but after a moment her lips softened. His boyish prank soon became something over which he nearly lost control, especially when he pressed his hips against hers and instead of pushing him away, she slid her hands over his forearms and pulled him closer.

Enough! Focus on the task at hand. Retrieve the stolen cargo without getting killed.

Then, he'd locate Keelan and find out why she had not yet arrived. Less than a week ago, she'd promised to sail away with him on the *Desire*. The Blue Peter was flying above his top gallants, signaling the ship was preparing to sail. She should have already arrived.

Unless... she'd changed her mind. Life on the sea could be hazardous and hard.

It could also be invigorating and prosperous.

Running away with him was a risk for Keelan. She'd have to leave behind the shelter of what little family she had left: an uncle, aunt and cousin, as well as the possibility of marriage. Dr. Garrison had already asked for her hand. Her uncle would have her marry Pratt, a wealthy plantation owner old enough to be her father.

To accompany Landon on the *Desire*, she would have to accept that there'd be a certain degree of uncertainty with each dawning day. Danger presented itself in many forms: British warships, pirates, privateers and tempests. Had she changed her mind and decided to stay within the protective embrace of the Charleston Lowcountry? Had Garrison convinced her that she'd be better off married to him, a country doctor, rather than a merchant ship captain?

Stop.

There was work to be done.

Landon pulled a bottle from his pocket and took a mouthful of the amber liquid. He sloshed it around, then spit it into his hands and rubbed it on his face and shirt. He handed the bottle to his friend.

"Seems a shame to waste it," Conal muttered sadly, as he repeated the same procedure.

Landon grinned. "Leave it to an Irishman to mourn the loss of a mouthful of whiskey."

"Look who's talkin'."

Landon threw his arm over Conal's shoulders. "Let's go."

The two men staggered down the alley.

Conal broke into song:

Oh, my wee lass is a fine, young lass if ever a lass there be...
Her bosom's as big as a bowl of figs,
Hips broader than a wil... (burp)... low tree,
Oh my wee lass is a fine young lass I hold in high regard,
I know she loves me because her bannocks
Are shaped like me cock,
...and just as hard!

They burst into bawdy laughter and stumbled past the first warehouse with no incident. However, as they passed the entrance to the second building, a wide bulk blocked their path.

"'Hoy there, mates. Where're ye headin'?"

Landon and Conal halted, each swaying slightly.

"Why, we be headin' to Miz LeBlanc's housh, my big man," Conal slurred. "Gonna bed me a strong Irish lash wi' the biggest breasts in Charson. Char-lesson." He shook his head numbly. "Town," he finally stated firmly.

Landon jiggled the bottle enticingly. "Ha' yersef a slosh and join us, man." He thrust the bottle at the burly guard. "But we git firs' choice of the wenches, since it's our idea."

The man frowned and shook his head. "Ye couple of drunken sots can't find yer way to a wench if ye was locked in a room full of 'em. Madame LeBlanc's be two blocks west of here."

"Two more blocks, ye say? Wish way is west?" Landon scowled and squinted over the tar's shoulder. The windows were covered, but there was a sliver of light shining from the side of one, along with a bright red bolt of fabric. *His* silk, he'd wager.

Conal made an exaggerated turn toward his friend. "Did not the wench say three streets north and two streets east?" he said with arms crossed and fingers jutting into the air.

"Aye. She said two streets east and three streets south," Landon bobbed his head then staggered a couple dizzy steps sideways.

"Ha' we been goin' east or wes'?"

The warehouse guard rolled his eyes. "Listen lads," he said impatiently, pointing back up the alley. "Turn yer arses around and go two blocks that way and turn left." He waved his left arm and pointed. "Madam LeBlanc's be the white house with the red front door. Ye can't miss it."

"Two up then left ye say?" Landon repeated, blinking.

"Yes, man. LEFT. Turn LEFT," the sentry confirmed in an exasperated tone as he batted his hand to the left yet again.

Conal brightened. "Oh, well then. It's not sa far from here. We thank ye verra mush, me good man." He clapped the man on the back and nearly fell down.

Landon made a show of helping Conal regain his balance, then wrapped his arm over his friend's shoulders and spun him around. "Let's be off then. Ahead and to the lef'!"

"The left!"

Conal thumped Landon on the back and pointed up the street. "To the wenches!"

"The wenches!"

They staggered a few steps before pivoting around again to face the surly guard.

"Ye sure ye won't join us for a romp?" Conal shouted, although he was only ten feet away.

The man gave a wave and shook his head. "Nay lads, I'm workin' this night. Have a warehouse to guard." He pulled aside his vest to show the handle of a pistol sticking out of his waistband. "Ye go on."

"Suit yershelf," Landon slurred. They swung back around and shuffled away.

The guard chuckled as the drunkards staggered down the alley and paused a moment before making a right turn. Leaning against the warehouse door, he gave a dry laugh, shaking his head. "Ye'll not lay a lass this night, lads."

CHAPTER FORTY-TWO
PLANS TO ELOPE

K eelan Grey stood at the foot of the grave, gazing at the sharply chiseled marks on the stone without really seeing them. This afternoon, they'd buried Papa in the Circular Congregational Church cemetery on Meeting Street. The death bed confession still had her stunned. What would Landon think of it all?

She'd made a promise. Two, actually. The first, to elope with Landon Hart. The second, to find her true father.

She intended to keep both.

Aunt Sarah patted her shoulder. "Keelan, please walk with us," she prodded in a quiet voice. "Your uncle has arranged a luncheon at Rosewood's boarding house."

"I'm not hungry now, Aunt Sarah," she responded, giving her aunt a small smile. "I need a few moments alone, then I'll return home."

And gather my things and go.

The afternoon sun was obscured by a layer of gray which threatened rain. Aunt Sarah hesitated a moment. The older woman glanced around. Probably worried Captain Hart would appear from behind one of the large oaks lining the cemetery, or Dr. Garrison would show up and cause a scene.

A valid concern.

Keelan had been entangled in two terribly scandalous events, one involving Captain Landon Hart and the other involving...Captain Landon Hart.

First, there was an outing without a chaperone. Then there was a kiss in the garden the night of the ball, resulting in a broken engagement with Dr. Garrison, who'd taken the news badly, and she couldn't blame him. While that seemed like a very casual and abbreviated chain of events, it really wasn't.

Although wildly handsome and devilishly charming, Landon Hart was everything Mother had described when she spoke of 'men of the sea'... men who could seduce a woman with a look and leave her the following day, off to the next port, the next woman, the next adventure. Keelan understood this; Mother became bitter and lonely while Papa had been away sailing with the Royal Navy. She never wanted to live her mother's life, married to a man who's mistress was the sea, therefore, she'd instead reluctantly accepted a marriage proposal from Papa's physician, Dr. Everett Garrison, a few days before her cousin's ball.

Dr. Garrison was a quiet, practical man with a quiet, practical life.

Landon changed all that with three short words:

"Sail with me."

He had no intention of leaving her behind, and that changed *everything*.

They would be together aboard the *Desire*. There'd be no lonely life of waiting for a ship to bring her beloved home. The thought sent a comforting warmth swirling in her chest.

If Papa hadn't worsened that night, she'd have run away with Landon that moment he'd asked. Now, with her uncle as her guardian, things were more complicated. He'd not approve, so she couldn't reveal her plans.

Didn't dare.

Aunt Sarah fidgeted with her bonnet ribbon a moment, then said, "Don't stay too long. I'll ask Slaney and Daniel to wait for you. You shouldn't walk home alone."

"Thank you, Aunt Sarah."

Her family was always vigilant. An assassin had murdered her mother and Papa's eldest brother and his family back in England. She suspected it had to do with Papa's court-martial. He'd fired on the wrong ship; it sank, killing innocent passengers. After a huge uproar, Papa had been court-martialed, the family the main gossip topic for weeks.

After a word from her aunt, Keelan's maid, Slaney waited a few feet from the grave site. Daniel, her father's valet, joined her.

Daniel had been Papa's valet when he was home, and her tutor when Papa was at sea. He taught her not only to read, write and mathematics but also how to defend herself. She was quite proud of her skills with a blade. She had Daniel to thank for that.

After making his daily trip to the pier and back early this morning, Daniel had informed her that Landon Hart's ship, the *Desire*, was flying the blue flag signaling it was ready to depart.

It was the signal she'd been watching for. He was ready to leave port.

Fluttery ripples of anticipation spread through her stomach. Soon, she'd be away from here, away from plantation life and on toward unknown and exciting places with Landon.

Daniel held out a hand for the maid, Slaney took it, allowing him to help her rise to her feet.

"It's hard to believe he's gone." Keelan took one last look at the grave of the man she'd called "Papa" all her life.

"Yes, mistress. I know you'll miss him. As will I," Daniel said, voice cracking.

"We all will, lass," Slaney added, blotting beneath her eyes with a handkerchief.

"What will you both do now?" Keelan asked. Slaney and Daniel had been like family to her since she was small. With Papa at sea most of the time and her mother in Chatham, England, running their shop, Daniel and Slaney had practically raised her.

"We'll fulfill our obligation to the commodore and accompany you safely back to the country cottage in England, as promised," Daniel said. "Unless you have decided to remain here, instead."

"No." She shook her head. "I have no wish to remain on the plantation. You heard what Papa said. He's left me nothing. His entire estate has gone to Uncle Jared. I no longer have Twin Pines as my dowry."

Which was fine with her, she wasn't angry or upset at this sudden turn of events. In fact, it was a relief. A small smile tugged at her mouth. She had other plans involving Captain Hart, a wedding, a ship and a life of adventure.

"By removing you from his will, the commodore thought he was forcing you to act on his request to find your real father," Daniel said gently.

Although truly, it was unnecessary; her curiosity and longing to find out who she was and where she came from would have driven her to search for the man, anyway. But Papa hadn't known that.

He hadn't known her well at all.

"I made a promise to find him, and I will," she responded. They strolled along the cobbled street, the scent of damp soil and salty air hinting a spring rain.

"Then Daniel and I will be ready to join ye," Slaney said. "Yer like a daughter to us both. We'll not leave ye unless ye wish it." She looped her arm through Keelan's and gave her a secret smile.

The words tugged her heart; she swallowed past the lump in her throat. "Thank you, Slaney. Hopefully the contents in Papa's trunk will help my cause and not hinder it."

He'd mentioned an old trunk tucked in the library of the country house near Chatham, England. Apparently it held the answers to all her questions. She looked up at the valet. "You heard what he said. My mother and that man..." Daniel had been there, the night Papa revealed his secrets.

Daniel's eyes softened. "Yes, I heard. But the commodore said the man, your real father, would *want* to know about you."

She sighed, her heart and head in turmoil. It's rare a by-blow is ever welcomed into a household. The scorn of her sire's wife might be more than she could take.

Slaney stepped over a puddle, then peered at her closely. "But what about Captain Hart? Ye fancy the man. Will ye leave him behind?"

She chewed her lip. How much should she tell them? It wasn't that she didn't trust them. She did, with all her heart. But she'd never ask them to lie for her. The less they knew of her plans, the safer they'd be.

"What about Dr. Garrison?" Daniel looked back and forth between Slaney and her.

Of course the two servants had talked. What had she been thinking? She might as well tell them everything.

"I broke the engagement. I never wanted to marry Dr. Garrison. Without Twin Pines as a dowry, I'm sure the doctor's interest in me would have dropped drastically, even if I wasn't born on the other side of the blanket."

Daniel's voice carried a note of relief. "Begging your pardon, Mistress, but I've never cared much for the man. He has a dark air about him sometimes, makes me wonder if he's hiding something."

She gave him a quick glance, thinking about the doctor's uncharacteristic behavior toward her the night of the ball. It had looked as if he were about to strike her. "I have had the same concerns, especially recently. And sometimes I wonder..." A thick foreboding seeped into her thoughts, questions she'd asked, but no one seemed to be able to answer while Papa struggled with his health. Why he would have a few days of improvement, then drift back into the illness sending Dr. Garrison in search of new medication? Why were there days he would eat voraciously and days he could keep nothing down?

Daniel furrowed his brow. "I remember your mother's funeral when Dr. Garrison introduced himself. The commodore had been grieved, but robust, then." The valet jingled a couple coins in his pocket and stared pensively at his shoes while they waited for a wagonload of casks to pass before crossing the street.

The shame of Papa's court martial had always lingered about his countenance, adding to his depressed state, but Daniel was right. He hadn't been ill back then, only sad. He and Dr. Garrison became friends and spent many hours together, engaging in various activities to distract Papa from his grief, but still it consumed him. He ate less and lost weight. He slept more and became sickly.

A shudder skittered across her shoulders. She met Daniel's gaze. "I've been wondering if Dr. Garrison might have recommended the wrong medicine, or made the wrong diagnosis."

Daniel was silent for a moment. "It's possible he made a mistake."

A mistake.

Everett was young, right out of university. Perhaps he was too inexperienced.

"I've wondered the same thing..." she murmured.

Daniel straightened. "Then it's good he's out of your life."

Keelan plucked at a loose string on her cuff. "Captain Hart asked for my hand and I accepted," she finally said, unable to prevent the blush tingling her cheeks at the anticipation. "I plan to marry him and sail with him aboard the *Desire*."

A startled look flashed across the valet's face, but he recovered quickly. "Is that something which appeals to you?"

Slaney smiled. It truly was impossible to hide anything from them. Both had heard her mother's lectures and her own vows to find a husband with feet firmly planted on solid ground.

"Very much." She smiled, but a dark thought rose to the surface. "In light of recent events, I hope his offer will still stand," she murmured. What if it didn't? What if he wouldn't want to marry a woman who'd been born out of wedlock?

Daniel became thoughtful. "Mr. Hart doesn't seem to be the type of man to let social inclinations dictate his actions. If he changes his mind, we'll simply book passage on the next passenger ship heading north, if you wish to do so."

Slaney harrumphed. "Well, a choice like that would brand him a fool, I says."

Keelan swallowed. Daniel made it seem like the decision had no real significance, but it wouldn't be so easy for her.

Sailing away with Landon had been the only thing keeping her own shadow of grief from blanketing her in darkness over the past two days. A niggling fear had shadowed the anticipation as well. Given her current requirements, would Landon assist her? What if he wanted no part in her quest to find her true father?

"I'm glad you'll both be with me. It gives me comfort knowing I'll not have to make the journey on my own should things change between me and Captain Hart."

"We wouldn't ever leave ye at a time like this, Mistress. We'll help ye find yer Da," Slaney squeezed her arm.

With fresh eyes, she took in the ocean in the distance, blending into the infinite blue of the South Carolina sky. Worrying about it would not bring the answers to her questions any sooner. "First, we must gather our things and take them to Captain Hart's ship. We don't have much time to finish packing our trunks, hire a livery and depart before Uncle Jared and Aunt Sarah return home from the luncheon." Uncle Jared would try to stop them. He expected her to marry and stay in Charleston. He certainly wouldn't approve of her eloping with Landon Hart.

Daniel nodded his agreement. "I'll arrange for transportation to the *Desire* while you and Slaney have the trunks brought down."

"It shouldna' take long," Slaney said. "I haven't unpacked much yet, seein' how we just got to town yesterday."

"Good." Keelan had a little more confidence now. A shiver of excitement shot through her chest as her uncle's townhouse came into view. She fingered the red ribbon holding the signet ring around her neck.

The coat of arms bore four lions, a knight's helm, shafts of wheat. She had no idea what it meant or stood for. What was her real surname, if not Grey?

Who was she?

❧ 43 ❧

CHAPTER FORTY-THREE
EDGE OF MADNESS

The man who murdered his family and fiancée was finally dead.

Yet Dr. Everett Garrison still waited for the thick, suffocating burden of grief to lift.

But it didn't.

A brief swell of panic surged against his chest. Once Commodore Grey was dead, things *should* have changed. The rock in his stomach should have disappeared, the sharp pain clenching his heart every time he inhaled should have subsided, and the black emptiness filling his soul should have receded.

The morning light was still dull, his feet were still heavy, the air still empty, and his hands still stained with blood. No matter how many times he washed them, it lingered.

He had committed a heinous sin.

Commodore George Grey undoubtedly deserved to die, but Everett was more familiar with saving lives, not taking them. If Rachel hadn't screamed for vengeance in his dreams every night when he closed his eyes, he would never have considered it.

Anguish clawed through his voice. "Rachel... I miss you."

Everett didn't bother to brush away the tears or dry his cheeks.

How he missed her smile and adoring gaze. Her quiet words. Why was he still so tormented?

He stared down at the letter on his desk. And now, the bank was unwilling to extend him any more credit.

This presented a problem.

In exchange for Dr. Garrison's personal medical care, the commodore and his older brother, Jared Grey, had given him money to set up a practice in Charleston. Instead, Everett had used it to fund his plan for revenge. The slow poison he carefully dosed to the commodore had been very expensive to procure in a discrete manner.

He tossed a bundle of papers on his desk. It had been worth every cent he paid for justice to be done. That idiot had given the order to sink the ship carrying his parents and brothers.

And his fiancée, Rachel.

It didn't matter that the commodore had claimed to have mistaken the passenger ship for some devious French privateer. He deserved to be punished, and Everett had complained loudly and frequently to those in charge of his court martial. But, before justice could be done, the commodore's friend, an aristocrat, had used his wealth and influence to whisk away the disgraced Navy commander and his daughter, Keelan, to Charleston, South Carolina. The man even purchased a small plantation for them. A place for them to hide... far away from the gallows in London where the commodore belonged.

Everett slammed his fist on his desk. "Did he not deserve to suffer the same pain as I?"

Last fall after murdering the commodore's nephew, the man he'd hired in England also arranged the carriage accidents killing the wives of both the commodore and his older brother. According to the assassin, the women were low-hanging fruit, easy to pluck. Everett didn't have the stomach to do it himself. He was a physician trained to do his best to preserve life, not take it. Besides, such things were best left to a professional. He had no desire to risk botching the job and getting himself hanged in the process of attaining justice.

But the loss...the agony. He tried *everything* to relieve it. Brandy and opiates wore off, left him groggy and sick, didn't solve the problem, and only delayed the execution of a solution. It was, however, during one of those binges when he came up with the brilliant idea of hiring a man to exact revenge *for* him.

Less guilt to deal with if they didn't die by his hand. A deed he could live with, so he'd thought.

Everett opened the desk drawer, cradled a pale lavender handkerchief, then pressed it to his lips and inhaled. Rachel's perfume grew fainter each time. Soon, like her, it would be gone forever.

"The commodore needed to feel the same suffering," he murmured into the scented cloth. "He had to understand that his transgressions had *consequences*." He hadn't expected he could actually go through with it. The first time he had dosed the commodore with a small amount of poison, the man complained of an upset stomach and went to his cabin. Everett had vomited over the side of the ship. His hands quaked for an hour afterward.

The assassin he'd hired in London had been thorough. He'd finally sent the announcement of the death of the commodore's eldest brother, along with a letter requesting the last and final installment owed for his services.

Everett returned the handkerchief to his drawer and then picked up the missive next to the one from the bank. He reread the letter from the assassin. His gut clenched. The words blurred. His heart thrummed in his ears, sounding like a drum of war signaling death to the enemy.

Doctor Garrison,

We agreed that upon the notification of completion of the duties required of me, that payment would be available for me at your barrister's office. Unfortunately, according to the documents your barrister showed me containing your signature, it appears you withdrew the funds prior to traveling to Charleston. This is not acceptable. I request you rectify this immediately. Should I not receive your payment in a reasonable amount of time, I will consider you in breach of our contract and will contact a man in Charleston to perform the same duty for me, which I have so diligently performed for you.

❧

REGARDS,
   Munsford

❧

THE PROBLEM WAS, Everett had to use some of Munsford's funds to keep up appearances here in Charleston and to handle a slight problem in the form of Captain Landon Hart.

The gaping hole Rachel's death left in his life didn't shrink with time; it grew. If he didn't find someone to fill it soon, it would continue to grow bigger and bigger. It would eventually consume him until there was nothing left but the edges of his soul.

It seemed like poetic justice to have Keelan Grey be the one to fill the void.

He'd not been prepared for the ripples Captain Hart had caused. Everett's scheme had been progressing well until the man showed up at Twin Pines. Everett sat heavily in his chair, gripped the hair on each side of his head and rested his elbows on the desk.

It had taken him *months* to court Keelan to the extent where she'd agreed to marry him. Then the captain interfered with his courtship, distracted her, and made it difficult to regain her full attention and affection.

He'd had been at the table one day when Hart explained the attack by Gampo's ship. Apparently, Hart's fleet and the pirate had some sort of ongoing feud. It only took a couple inquiries in the pubs near the wharf and a meeting with Gampo's first mate to get a message to Gampo himself.

The pirate and Hart had a history of clashes on the open sea. Gampo helped Everett develop a scheme to distract Hart. In exchange, Everett was supposed to find out if a woman named Marisa sailed with Hart's fleet. How was he supposed to obtain that information? It was almost impossible. However, he had indeed tried. One bright morning he'd walked to the pier, up the ramp, and asked the first mate. The man looked at him as if he was daft.

"Having a woman aboard is bad luck, mister. Any sailor knows that."

He couldn't very well approach Hart, his adversary, and ask him, could he? Surely Hart would lie to him. Gampo wouldn't accept that answer, however. Unfortunately, he still had no information for the pirate, and that was disconcerting.

Thankfully, the plan they managed to execute may yet generate additional funds. As soon as he found the right buyers for the cargo the pirates took from Hart, there would be enough money to pay the assassin.

Hopefully.

The bloody pirates had some sort of hard and fast rule on dividing things into "like shares."

Even after they stole the goods, Hart had seduced Keelan, and she broke her engagement to Everett. Their plan could still move forward, but now, he would have to make a few adjustments, since it appeared Keelan was not going to come to him willingly. He didn't dare ask Gampo, but he'd found two of the pirate's men who were willing to work a side job while at port.

But it was going to be costly, because getting to Keelan was going to be more difficult now.

Keelan Grey, the commodore's daughter...

Beautiful, cold, and distant, he understood she wasn't the type to enjoy country life. More than once he'd overheard her plead with her father to sell Twin Pines and move to the city of Charleston. She was not the soft, gentle woman Rachel had been. Keelan was bold and impetuous; Rachel had been quiet and reliable.

Rachel was water.

Keelan was fire.

Everett recalled that night when the commodore had spoken privately with the young woman. A glass placed against the wall in the next room allowed him to hear much of their conversation. The commodore spoke of a treasure he'd hidden for Keelan back in his country cottage.

A thought struck like a lightning bolt. Everett straightened. Why hadn't he thought of this earlier? Obviously, his grief muddied his mind. Rising, he began to pace the floor and tried to recall the commodores words.

"The contents are of great value... promise me you'll go back to Wind Briar and find my old trunk..."

There! The answer to his financial woes rested in a trunk at the Wind Briar estate. They only had to find it. Then he could leave the assassin's funds with his barrister. Everett spun on his heel and snatched his hat from the hook by the door. He had to change his strategy, which left behind a few frayed ends he'd have to clip. Soon, his sword of justice would do its duty. He'd already sacrificed significant time, money, and energy to this endeavor.

He deserved to reap the rewards from his service.

It was his due.

And Keelan would share it with him.

As his wife.

🕸 44 🕸

CHAPTER FORTY-FOUR
OLD EMBERS

Landon waited in Annette Camsby's parlor, choosing to stand by the window rather than take the seat offered by the house slave. He didn't plan on being here long enough to relax in a chair. Instead, he gazed down the narrow side street in Charleston.

Frustration still had him grinding his teeth. His visit to Twin Pines had answered some questions, but raised others. He'd been informed the commodore had been buried earlier in the day, which explained Keelan's delay in meeting him. He'd not known of the commodore's death, although he'd been aware the man had been ill for some time. With the hot, humid temperatures in Charleston in June, there was not much time for long wakes. Bodies had to be buried as soon as possible. He'd stop by Jared Grey's town house and offer his condolences when he returned. Hopefully, by this evening or tomorrow morning, Keelan would be able to join him aboard the *Desire*. If not, he'd either wait, or make a quick run up the coast to Philadelphia, then return for her.

A small bag of coins clinked in his coat pocket, making him frown.

"Why, if it isn't Captain Hart!" Annette Camsby floated into the room as if transported by an invisible stream. "What an unexpected, but delightful surprise." Beautiful, rich and once again widowed,

Annette captured his gaze with eyes the color of dark coffee. She sank to the deep gold velvet sofa and leaned forward just enough to provide him with an unhindered view of her cleavage as she reached for a cup. "Join me for tea?"

Landon's throat was dry, and he had to clear it before he could trust his voice. He could use a drink, but hot tea wasn't what came to mind. "Thank you for the invitation, however, I can't stay. I came to refund your fare for passage to Philadelphia. Henry should not have accepted it. We're unable to take on passengers this time." He pulled the bag of coins from his pocket and placed it on the desk.

Annette's gaze chilled. Full, ripe lips thinned to a flat line. "And why, may I ask, do you feel obligated to do that?"

He hadn't expected Annette to make this easy.

It was bad enough Conal had thrown up his hands in mock terror when he'd asked him to return the fare, leaving Landon to ride to Annette's town home to return it.

She'd been a tigress in bed once. Every trip to Charleston had been enhanced by her attentions. Normally, she'd accompany them to Philadelphia or even as far as New York and then occasionally make the return trip back to Charleston with them, keeping his bed warm and active. Now, the thought no longer held the allure it once did.

He'd have never guessed he would marry again. But Keelan was like no other woman he'd ever met—spontaneous and reckless, yes, but also clever, passionate, and witty. And luscious. He inhaled deeply and allowed himself the luxury of taking time to expel his breath. Otherwise, he feared his more primal reaction would rise to the forefront, especially when he recalled the sight of the lithe, young Keelan Grey floating naked upon the lake at Twin Pines. It would certainly be misinterpreted, fighting an erection while standing in the middle of Annette Camsby's parlor.

"Well?" Annette cocked her head to the side, her deep black ringlets dangling near her ears. She raised a brow, but her expression was accusing and wary rather than inquisitive.

Landon clenched his jaw and forced a tight smile upon his face. "I'm afraid I've cancelled the journey to Philadelphia for now. A large portion of my cargo has been stolen and until it's located, I cannot depart port." A cowardly way to put it, but he wasn't in the mood for one of Annette's tantrums.

Her eyes widened, and she placed a hand to her chest. "Oh dear! How terrible! What will you do?"

He clasped his hands behind his back to keep himself from crossing his arms in frustration. "Make every effort to find it. When we do, we'll have to reassess its condition, which might take time. If we don't locate it, then we'll have to change our trade route. Either way, I'm afraid our departure will be delayed, at the very least, and likely to be cancelled. I'm not sure at this time what our plans will entail going forward." That was mostly true. His plans going forward included spending a lot of time with Keelan on deck and in bed.

Annette rose from her seat and glided over to him, a slow sultry smile playing upon her face. She stopped an inch in front of him and then leaned in, running a bold hand up his torso, over his chest, and down his arm.

She took his hand and entwined her fingers with his. "Well, then we should make the most of your time while you're here. It would be a shame to come all the way to my home and leave... empty-handed." She placed his hand on her breast.

In the past, he'd have needed no further urging. He would have locked the parlor door, and they would have sated their lust on the large Persian rug he'd given her. However, today there was no stirring, no passion aroused to drive him into her open arms and thighs.

"I'm sorry, Annette," he said, removing his hand and dropping it to his side. "I cannot. I will not."

Her smile slipped from sultry to sad. "Such a shame. I hope you remember to send word to me when you are ready to sail." She was testing the barrier he was building. "You know how fond I am of our sojourns together." Her gaze shifted to a doleful hurt. Her lips in a full pout.

She'd guessed he had another woman of interest. *Good.*

"I'm afraid my next destination will not be one you'll be willing to travel, Annette."

"I see," she said, turning toward the window Landon had stood near earlier. "Well, if the winds shifts in my favor, do send me a word."

"They will not."

There was nothing more to say other than farewell, and he hated those. "Stay well, Annette. I wish you the best. I'll not call again." He spun on his heel and left the parlor. A house slave opened the front door, and he strode to Orion and unwrapped the reins from the post near the steps just as Dr. Garrison and Miss Doreen Grey were sending their mounts with a stable boy.

He nodded a greeting to the doctor and tipped his hat to Miss Grey. Keelan's cousin had been accompanying the doctor on his calls and assisting him with his patients. It appeared, thankfully, she had diverted the doctor's attentions away from Keelan.

He turned his horse toward Jared Grey's town home. Now, to find his betrothed.

❦ 45 ❦

CHAPTER FORTY-FIVE
TIME TO GO

The early summer heat in the Charleston Lowcountry had become oppressive. As she'd quickly become accustomed, Keelan dipped her handkerchief into a basin near her bed and patted the base of her neck with it. The black garments she wore for mourning did nothing but absorb heat, and the dress itched like the devil. The now familiar trickle of sweat ran between her breasts and she pushed the damp handkerchief down her bodice to absorb the moisture.

Her stomach quivered with a thousand butterflies. The night of the ball, when Landon had taken her into his arms in the moonlit garden and asked her to sail away with him, he'd given her hope that she'd spend her life with someone of her choosing. Her uncle's choice, Pratt, was an aging plantation owner. Doctor Garrison was a colorless, bland physician. Hart had offered her an opportunity to flee from her father's and Uncle Jared's scheme to be certain she was "properly" wed and cared for before the start of the harvest season.

What Papa and Uncle Jared didn't realize was over the years while Papa was at sea, her mother spent every moment in the shop, leaving no time to develop any kind of relationship with her daughter. Keelan had learned at an early age how to take care of herself. Unlike many women, Keelan did not *need* a husband, and until Landon, she hadn't wanted one.

Early this morning, Slaney had started to pack their things. It was important for them to depart quickly, before Uncle Jared approached the topic of her future. Only Slaney and Daniel knew of her plans. The rest of the family simply assumed she and Garrison had a tiff, but were still engaged. Dr. Garrison hadn't mentioned anything either.

"I wish we didn't have to sneak away," she muttered to Slaney. "Uncle Jared and Aunt Sarah were kind to move to Twin Pines to help Papa and me. We had no knowledge of running a plantation, and Uncle Jared's management was a godsend. I would have preferred to be able say goodbye properly."

"I know, lass," Slaney replied, closing the trunk. "But yer uncle is responsible for ye now, and he promised your Da' to see ye married to Dr. Garrison. Both took a likin' to yer suggestion to rent out the plantation to Mr. Pratt and use the rents to help ye open yer shop in town. If yer uncle caught wind of your promise to go back to Wind Briar or run off with Captain Hart, he'd marry ye off this instant, instead."

Aunt Sarah would want her to stay and marry Dr. Garrison and start a safe, placid life in Charleston. But after Papa's death and her aroused suspicions of Dr. Garrison's choices, marriage to him would have been out of the question even without Landon Hart in her life. Her uncle would have been happier if she'd agreed to marry Pratt, because of his wealth and landholdings. The neighboring plantation owner not only had a penchant for overindulging in food and drink, but was heavy-handed with his slaves as well.

Keelan shuddered. She'd rather be a spinster than marry either.

"Well, after we're gone, Uncle Jared can sell the plantation to Mr. Pratt outright. I'm sure he'll be happy to be rid of the responsibility. I'm simply not comfortable with it." She closed the lid on the smaller, worn trunk, looking longingly at her dagger, sword, and waif's clothes. She normally wore them in the early hours each morning when she trained with Daniel, another activity of which her uncle disapproved. She always suspected the commodore had secretly been proud of her skills with both sword and blade.

She sighed. It was hard to stop thinking of Papa as her father and instead as a man who played the role. He was never around very often or for very long, but still, she was fond of him and he'd acted fond of her.

It would have been easy to simply ignore the promise to him and go on with her life, but Daniel had taught her a promise kept built on one's integrity. And drat it if curiosity wasn't driving her crazy, anyway. Sending Daniel and Slaney was a satisfying compromise for all of them.

The day Hart had bartered a kiss from her in exchange for untangling her hair from a briar bush had changed her.

Her heart tripped at the memory of his wet, fiery kisses, and glacial blue eyes that looked at her as if they knew every secret she'd ever possessed. She let her lids drift shut and savored the sensation of his arms around her waist, his palm capturing her breast. He had left a mark on her heart she'd never be able to erase.

She pulled out a bag of coins before lowering the trunk lid. After providing for their passage to Boston and enough for emergency supplies, little remained. How she managed beyond that would depend on Landon or the information contained in the letter her father had placed in a chest in their country home, Wind Briar.

There was also the ring and the man in the locket to consider.

She wandered to an open window, greeted by the sickly sweet scent of aging Magnolia blossoms in the dense, humid early summer air. Heat had settled over Charleston, turning the dirt to a fine dust and coating everything, muting nature's colors to various shades of red tinted gray.

Even if she found her father, there was no guarantee he would want her. According to the tale she had been told, he had a wife and other children of his own. Thinking back to the conversation a few weeks ago between her uncle and Landon, she still wasn't sure she would be able to make it back to England. With an inevitable war approaching, the crossing became even more treacherous because both countries had unleashed privateers, who were little more than pirates with permission to plunder. Landon's merchant fleet would be a prime prize. As badly as she wanted to finish her quest and find her father, she'd never ask Landon to take such a risk.

Daniel, true to his promise to the commodore, had slipped away and booked passage to Boston for himself and Slaney. She'd heard the northern colonies were more tolerant of the British, and more likely to offer safer passages to Great Britain. From there, they'd find a vessel bound for England. Both Daniel and Slaney had family there, and with the letters of recommendation she'd provided, both should easily find employment. Daniel had promised to locate the trunk and keep it safe until she could retrieve it.

A light knock sounded upon her door. At her summons, it opened, and Dr. Everett Garrison poked his head in.

The doctor glanced curiously about the chamber, noting the trunks in the middle of the floor.

"Are you going somewhere?"

Slaney exchanged a wary look with Keelan.

"Dr. Garrison, would you join me on the porch?" she asked. "We can discuss my plans in private. The heat is overwhelming in here and I could use some air. I'll be along in a moment."

He nodded and retreated.

She huffed out an agitated sigh. So much for leaving unnoticed. As much as she dreaded it, she'd have to face Everett once more. Everything was packed and ready to go. "Slaney, please have our trunks brought down to the street. The carriage should be here shortly."

The maid nodded and Keelan went downstairs and out to the veranda, pondering the best way to tell Dr. Garrison she still would not marry him. Nothing came to mind to add ease to the task, making her stomach churn.

Jared Grey's house was typical of most Charleston homes. Since they were taxed by frontage, houses were built close together. Residents also built them narrow and deep. It was as if they took their home and rotated it ninety degrees, so the side faced the street. Long covered porches, which normally embraced front doors, instead ran the side length of the house. The proximity of their neighbor added shade to the porch during most of the day. A hedge along the street front didn't do as much to muffle the city's noise, as it did to offer a bit of privacy for those enjoying a respite outside on the long side-porch.

Dr. Garrison was looking over the foliage at the activity out front. The street wasn't a particularly busy one, but there was the occasional rider or carriage passing by, as well as people bustling along the walks. Keelan sat, her back toward the road and the clop of horses hooves and the jangle of carriages. There was less chance of being overheard out here.

Dr. Garrison pulled his hands behind his thin, rigid back. He leveled a flat stare at her. "Please tell me what is going on."

"I leave for Boston in a few days," she lied. "Slaney has packed our things. We're going back to England."

He jolted as if struck. "What—why—" he sputtered a moment before he continued. "Miss Keelan, I have no objection to returning to England, but first we are to be *married*."

"Dr. Garrison, we discussed this the night of Doreen's ball. I cannot marry you. Going home to England is my decision. I am going at the request of my... at Papa's request."

His chiseled expression hardened further. Muscles rolled in his jaw. She waited for him to continue. She'd not spoken to him alone since the night in the garden, after she privately broke their engagement. That was when the doctor's darker side had surfaced. He'd become almost violent. Even now, there was something a little off in his demeanor, a cut in his gaze, a stark parlor on his face, which made her even more uneasy in his presence.

When he finally spoke, his words tumbled together in a clumsy rush. "Miss Keelan, my behavior at the ball was abhorrent, and I am here to offer my sincerest apology. I wish to mend our relationship. You were—well—the wine was..." He shrugged tightly and dug his thumb into his palm. "Perhaps you weren't quite yourself, and you said some things you did not mean, and I said some things I certainly did not mean."

Oh dear, this was going to be harder than anticipated. He'd seen her kissing Landon. It would have been best if his pride forced *him* to break the engagement, which was apparently wishful thinking on her part.

Indeed, she had been slightly tipsy at the time. Seeing Landon waltz with the stunningly beautiful Annette Camsby had affected her recollection of the amount of wine she'd sipped. It had given her the courage to tell the doctor she didn't love him, and she'd rather not marry him. Unfortunately, she'd done so rather bluntly. The doctor didn't take the news well.

"Dr. Garrison." What could she say now, without hurting or angering him further? A multitude of expressions crossed his face. They moved across at such a pace, she struggled to follow them. Shock, anger, confusion, fear.

"Please, *please* accept my apology, Miss Keelan." He approached her with his hands spread and palms open. "I don't want to break our engagement. I truly want to marry you. I've no one, *no one* but you, now. My family—" He coughed and blinked a few times. "They all perished at sea a few years ago. I've been so lonely. I... I need you with me. Believe me when I say I will take care of you. I promise." He reached forward and grasped her hands.

Her heart lurched in sympathy, stirring her guilt at distressing him further. This was going to be more difficult than she'd anticipated. She shook her head. Maybe a different tack will work better. She shook her head. "Dr. Garrison, you don't want to marry me."

His eyes widened. "I do! Yes, I do. I will marry you and take you all the way to England." He sank to one knee. "If the commodore wanted you to go back to Wind Briar, then I'll take you as soon as we're married."

How could he know about Wind Briar?

Her heart gave a hard jerk, then began to pound more closely to her skin. She'd said nothing about Wind Briar, and there was no reason he should have known about the country house.

Keelan thought back to when her mother died. She and Papa had been staying in Camden when they'd met Dr. Garrison. She shivered. An uneasy feeling, like a cold finger trailing down her spine, raised gooseflesh on her arms, although the day was already suffocatingly hot.

She swallowed, doing her best to block the tremor from her voice. "For reasons I cannot explain to you at this time, Dr. Garrison, a marriage between us is impossible." She couldn't tell him about her plans to run away with Landon. He'd tell Uncle Jared and then Uncle Jared would have an apoplectic fit and probably insist she marry the doctor today.

How did Everett know about Wind Briar?

Dr. Garrison slowly stood, a vein jerked erratically at his temple. He drew his hands down and clenched them at his sides. Although he tried hard to hide it, Keelan couldn't ignore the anger flashing across his features, like heat lightening before a storm. Her guilt at hurting his feelings added to her burden, but his response fortified her resolve. Perhaps a more financial perspective would help.

"Dr. Garrison, Papa left everything to Uncle Jared. I don't have a dowry. I can't return to Wind Briar to live. I'm not even George Grey's kin by blood."

Everett jerked as if shot. He stared at her like he was seeing her for the first time. "Not blood kin," he repeated so softly she could barely make out his words. "Not blood kin!" His eyes lit with something almost feral, and he pulled her to him, enveloping her in a stony hug, startling a frightened gasp from her throat.

His arms banded hers to her sides, preventing any opportunity to push him away. There was no delicate way to extract herself from his embrace without inciting his anger again. Thankfully, the hedges blocked the awkward embrace from view.

He swayed with her in his arms, mumbling into the hair on top of her head. "I knew you could never be like *him*. I knew it. This is perfect. You will be *perfect*. Everything will be as it once was, perhaps even better!"

That last cryptic sentence sent another chill skittering down her spine. Bells clanged in her head to the tune of *something is not right*. She shifted, hoping her movement would cause him to loosen his hold. No luck there.

Without releasing her arms, he stared into her eyes, smiling wildly. "I know of the treasure chest the commodore hid in his country house. Together we'll find it, and everything will be as it should be."

"Treasure chest?" What in the world was he talking about? Before Papa died, he'd mentioned only the trunk containing information about her real father, no treasure.

And I was alone with Papa at the time. Everett had been eavesdropping!

"Yes!" His eyes were wide. Maniacal. "I heard the commodore talking about it. He said it was extremely valuable and wanted you to have it, so it's not as if we'd be stealing. It's yours. We need only to retrieve it."

Whatever he heard the night Papa died had planted a seed in the doctor's mind that would bear no fruit. She needed to clear up this misunderstanding now. It wasn't the items inside which were valuable, it was the information, and it was valuable only to *her*.

"Dr. Garrison, you are mistaken."

"Please call me Everett, my love."

Before she could say another word, he lowered his face and kissed her. The pressure of his mouth on hers took her by surprise and she gasped. He took the opportunity of the slight opening of her lips to plunge his tongue inside.

Her stomach took a sickening dive. Locked in the harsh embrace, she couldn't move. She couldn't breathe. The more she tried to arch away from him, the harder he kissed her until she was sure her teeth would break through the skin of her lips. His thick tongue swirled in her mouth, and for a second, she thought she might gag. This helpless feeling churned up both anger and panic.

At this point, she cared not a whit if she angered him or not. She kicked him in the shin, eliciting a pained grunt. Enraged, she tried to twist away. Before she could say a word, a voice stilled every muscle in her body.

"It wasn't my intention to interrupt a tryst." The deep baritone behind her pulsed with an undercurrent of fury, like thunder from a far away, but fast advancing storm.

Garrison broke the violent kiss and sliced his head toward the voice.

Landon! *Thank God*. Her relief immediately dissipated by the realization of what he'd just witnessed. Oh no... her stomach lurched. He'd obviously misinterpreted the stolen kiss. Everett held on to her like she was anchoring him to the earth. She wiggled and jerked and when she stomped on his foot, he finally released her, stepping away, although he twisted her hand behind the small of her back. Pain sliced through her wrist and she was forced to sink into a chair.

Everett glanced at her, the warning pulsing in his eyes shocking her into temporary silence. Her mind was too slow to process the meaning behind the erratic behavior. It was too tangled up in denial. This was not the Everett she knew. *Nothing was making sense.*

Everett looked up, still clasping her hand in a painful vise. "What brings you here, Hart? I daresay, unless you have an invitation or a summons from Mr. Grey, it's my understanding you are not welcome." Acid dripped from his voice. "Isn't that so, my love?"

"You know that's not true," she hissed to Garrison, wishing she had her dagger. Her hand shook as she reached up and wiped her mouth, then glared at the doctor, speaking through her clenched jaw. "Release my hand this instant, Dr. Garrison." She wanted to slap him hard enough to make his ears ring, but was unwilling to start another brawl. The last one ended badly enough. Surprisingly, he let go. She jumped to her feet.

"Landon!" She scanned the street.

He wasn't there.

Lifting her skirts, she dashed down the porch steps and rounded the corner toward the street. Landon, already astride his horse, was trotting back toward the wharf, well out of earshot. There was no way she could hail him without luring unwanted attention, even if she could raise her voice above the din of the activity on the street. A livery carriage slowing in front of the house soon blocking him from view.

Damn that man! How could he possibly think she'd ever willingly kiss Dr. Garrison? Surely he'd noticed her predicament. She glanced over the hedge, pursed her lips at the sight of Garrison staring at her, and then understood.

Only the doctor's upper chest was visible over the hedge. Her pinned arms had been out of sight from Landon's view. When Garrison forced her to sit, it must have looked like she was trying to hide from him.

She groaned. Landon's ire was understandable. He'd been betrayed before; his first wife died giving birth to another man's child. Landon himself had once said to her: "Marriage doesn't suit me."

That was before the ball, before the kiss that revealed her secret, before she'd admitted she loved him, before he'd asked her to marry him and sail aboard the *Desire*. Things had changed, hadn't they? He'd told her he loved her. Landon Hart had made her feel cherished, energized, strong, and weak in the knees.

She expelled an annoyed breath and resisted the urge to stomp her foot. Well, this issue could be resolved with a simple, civil conversation. As soon as Garrison was gone or occupied, she'd slip out and head straight to the *Desire* and speak with that stubborn sea captain.

She'd make him understand.

Keelan clenched her jaw and straightened her shoulders. He'd listen to her if she first had to clobber him over the head and tie him to a chair in order to say her piece.

She quickly tried to walk past the doctor. He grabbed her arm, and the glare she gave him should have frozen him solid. Pausing, Keelan dropped the temperature of her voice enough to the chill a harsh winter wind. "If you touch me again, I will chop off your hand with a hatchet."

Eyes widening, he lowered his arm and took a couple of steps back. He opened his mouth to say something, his Adam's apple jerking up and down. Rather than extend the torture of his presence, she flew down the hall and up the stairs to her room.

Slaney was closing the lid on her trunk when she entered, winded and furious.

"Did ye square things away with Dr. Garrison?"

She shook her head. "Things are worse, actually. He seems to think we are still to be married." Keelan grabbed her quill and a piece of parchment. "And Captain Hart seems to believe so too."

"What?" Slaney stepped back as if someone flung cold water in her face. "Why in the world—"

"Our course is set," Keelan answered swiftly. "The livery carriage Daniel summoned is here. We must leave *now*."

46

CHAPTER FORTY-SIX
CAUGHT

Keelan signed the letter to her uncle stating her plans, saying goodbye and left it on the dressing table. She grabbed her reticule and bonnet and slipped down the servant's staircase; the aroma of toasted pecans and raisin scones wafted up the passageway. She would miss Ruth, the soft, brown kitchen slave who loved cooking and all things spicy-hot. Under Ruth's tutelage, Keelan had learned to cook and also dress meat and fish, and prepare a good many household remedies from removing rust stains to making lard candles. Things that could come in handy, depending on her future.

They quietly exited the back door and made their way to the side street where the carriage waited. Her uncle and aunt were hopefully still at the luncheon. Thankfully, there was no sign of the doctor.

Daniel helped both women step into the carriage. As she settled herself on the seat, the sound of running feet and a shout drew her attention. To her horror, Uncle Jared was approaching the carriage. Dr. Garrison was close behind. When her uncle took in the trunks strapped to the back and the three of them, his expression darkened.

"What is the meaning of this?"

"Please, Uncle Jared. Allow me to explain—"

Her uncle's brows slammed down his face thunderous. "No need.

Garrison has explained everything to me. I *forbid* you to leave on this fool's journey."

"But Uncle—"

"Have you forgotten why you and your father fled England?" His face turned a mottled purple. "Someone has a serious vendetta against our family. Your mother, aunt, cousin and uncle were all *murdered* within weeks of each other. In addition, our country is but a hair's breadth away from a full scale war and I'll not permit you to endanger your life by attempting a return to England now."

"Please her me out." She couldn't explain her reasoning about Garrison while the doctor stood there, listening. Better to explain her suspicions in private. She gave the only lame excuse to pop into her mind. "Captain Hart said a passenger ship would be able to make it safely from Boston."

Uncle Jared's expression darkened further. "I don't give a damn about what Hart said. I made a promise to your father that I would make sure you're safely married, and so I shall."

Keelan reached out and grasped her uncle's arm. "I made a promise to him, too. He made me give my word to retrieve something vitally important." This was the wrong place to have this conversation. She needed comprehension and understanding from Uncle Jared. Instead, his face showed an even more hardened resolve, making her shoulders tighten, and her stomach dive to her toes.

She lowered her voice. "It was his dying request, Uncle Jared. Please."

His expression softened slightly, and for a moment, it appeared he understood. Then he shook his head. "I'm sorry, Keelan. Such a journey can never be made safely by you or anyone in our family. I cannot let you go in good conscience. It's now my duty to see to your welfare, and so I shall."

Horrified, Keelan glared at Everett, who stood a little straighter at Jared's words, but wouldn't meet her angry gaze.

Everett stepped forward. "Sir, I am prepared to marry your niece as soon as you deem necessary."

Uncle Jared glanced at Everett and uncrossed his arms. He frowned and lowered his voice to a more soothing tone, one that had warning bells sounding in Keelan's head. "I'll consider your offer with Pratt's. We shall discuss particulars in the study."

No!

Keelan could only stare in disbelief at her uncle. A marriage to Pratt was a prison sentence. How could he even consider such a thing? She certainly would not.

"Uncle Jared, please don't do this. I will *not* marry Pratt. He is unsavory and cruel—"

He batted her words away. "Keelan, those rumors are typical of those spread by the house slaves. You'd do better not to listen to them. They carry no credence." He managed to look a little sympathetic. "He's older by more than a bit, but trust me, Keelan. You'll live quite well."

Tears burned in the back of her eyes. She couldn't let this happen. She simply couldn't. It was time to admit her plans. "Uncle Jared, I cannot marry Pratt. I... I have a confession."

Uncle Jared's brows rose. "I don't doubt it. You tried to sneak away, rather than confer with me about your plans, so obviously you knew I wouldn't approve."

She hoped if he understood her true motives, he'd let her go. "If truly your motive is for me to be happily wed, then let me go. I will be fine. I've promised Captain Hart I would marry *him*. He's waiting for me. I'm on my way to his ship. Daniel and Slaney will go to Boston and then on to England. They will secure Papa's trunk for me. He told me there is important information within it which I must secure." She moved closer to her uncle and murmured, "I believe I've discovered who is behind the assassinations."

"Really?" Her uncle looked at her in surprise. "How? Who?"

She stepped down from the carriage, pulled him out of the doctor's earshot, and told him her suspicions about Everett Garrison. "The 'accidents' began after the sinking of the ship," she whispered. "Then Papa got sick and died while under his care." She tilted her head in the doctor's direction. "It makes sense, don't you see?"

Jared inhaled deeply, then let his breath out in a sympathetic whoosh. "Keelan, my dear, I understand your reasoning a little, but it doesn't quite fit with the events."

"It does, Uncle Jared, think about—"

He held up his hand and closed his eyes. "He can't be responsible, my dear. I received a post today from my eldest brother's barristers. Edmond was found murdered in his home. The assassin is in England. Dr. Garrison has been with us for *months*, Keelan."

Everett coughed and raised his voice, "Miss Keelan, you might consider that you have been duped by Captain Hart. On my way to retrieve your uncle, I passed by the docks and witnessed both the *Seeker* and the *Desire* departing the port for open sea. For South America, I was told by the harbormaster. I'm sorry, Miss Keelan, but perhaps you misunderstood Captain Hart's intentions?"

His words hit her like a blunt blow to the stomach. A sharp jolt pierced her chest. Her tongue was paralyzed; she could only stare. No, it had to be a lie. She did not misunderstand Landon. He wouldn't leave without her.

Would he?

⚜

"Come away with me, Keelan," he had whispered. "Leave behind your secrets and schemes, and let me show you what it is like to be loved and worshipped for the goddess you are. Let me take you aboard the Desire *and show you the world."*

"I'll meet you as soon as I can," she'd promised. "I will slip away to Charleston within a fortnight for certain."

"I'll await you aboard my ship."

⚜

Landon had told her the *Seeker* had to deliver cargo to Harbour Town and then meet the third ship in their fleet. By the time the two returned to Charleston, the repairs to the *Desire* would be complete. He'd hoist a blue flag with a white square in the middle when they were ready to depart. All three ships would then sail north to Philadelphia. He'd told her this. He'd promised to await her aboard the

Desire. Why did he leave her behind? How could he possibly leave without allowing her to explain?

She fingered the handle of her reticule. Had she let Landon stir her passion so strongly with his kisses that she'd been that blind?

Had she been nothing more than a diversion for him?

The bitterness in her mother's tone remained vivid in her mind:

"There's no settling down for a man of the sea. She's his mistress and forever calls him away from the arms of those on the land. A sailor will eventually leave you alone and lonely. Mark my words, girl."

Jared's face smoothed and his eyes flooded with pity. "Come child, I'll have Ruth make you some tea."

A small voice in the back of her mind needled her, *"Had he not told you marriage didn't suit him? Hadn't you been afraid something like this would happen? That he might use you as nothing more than a dalliance while at port? That he'd never trust another woman to be faithful?"*

And he'd seen Garrison kissing her!

She and Landon hadn't known each other long. It would be understandable for him to question her fidelity, just as she was now questioning his promises. Numbly, she followed Jared into the house. By leaving, he'd made sure there would be no happy life for her sailing the seas with him. No exotic places to visit. It was as if a curtain had been pulled to shut out her view of the outside world. Allowing nothing to be visible, except four plain, lonely walls.

How could they live a happy life together if he couldn't trust her love for him?

Do not cry. Do not cry.

Jared's voice was soft and compassionate. "Keelan, my dear, you've had a heartbreaking week with the death of your father. I'm sorry your plans can't be put into action. I gave George my word to care for you as your guardian." He glanced at her uneasily as they walked, then cleared his throat. "I'm well aware he raised you in an unconventional manner, dear girl. Therefore, I will not give you an opportunity to run away." Jared swallowed and continued, his voice solidifying to granite. "And, as added security, you will remain locked in your chamber until the wedding."

She stumbled, felt her eyes widen in horror. "Uncle Jared," her voice came out as a dusty whisper. "Please don't do this. I was raised as your brother's daughter, I don't think he would want—"

"Stop." He was already shaking his head. "I will hear no more. I've already penned a missive to the family barrister in London to auction off all holdings owned by my two deceased brothers." He sliced his hand through the air. "There will be no journey to England. My family and I prefer life in America, and I do not wish to endanger anyone by allowing them back into that assassin's lair, or subject them to such a dangerous journey in these uncertain times."

Her uncle opened the door to the house and nodded at Simon, who dutifully held the door.

"Miss Keelan is not to leave her chamber for any reason. Do you understand?"

"Yessuh." Simon's eyes shifted from her to Uncle Jared, then to Garrison.

"You are to lock the door and keep it locked except for the normal care and cleaning of her room and delivery of meals."

"Yessuh." Simon's voice sounded very small.

Uncle Jared grasped her elbow, dragging her upstairs, despite her protests. When they reached her room, she tried to beg her uncle once more to reconsider, but he quickly shut the door. The key clicked in the lock.

Keelan took a seat near the balcony doors and stared out the window. Jared's footsteps grew faint and soon all she heard was the silence of the air, still and hovering in the room. Despair clawed at her throat, its weight crushed her heart. She expected to break down and weep, but strangely, no tears came. Landon Hart had seduced her with his kisses and caresses. She'd fallen in love with him. And he had broken her heart by leaving without demanding an explanation, without giving her a chance to even offer one.

She was a fool.

A few minutes later, the scrape of a key in the lock drew her attention back to the door.

"Miss Keelan?" Simon spoke through the door.

A tear finally broke free and crept down her cheek. She quickly brushed it away. "Come in."

Simon stepped across the threshold and paused. His voice dropped to a conspiratorial whisper, and she had to strain to hear him. "If there's anythin' I can do to help you..." He toyed with the keyring he held. "I mean *anythin'*, Miss Keelan. You saved my boy's life, and I'll never forget dat, an' you helped the others runnin' for their freedom after the storm."

At her questioning look, he whispered, "Mister Pratt never caught them, they free now." The servant leaned in. "Well, you jus' say the word, Miss Keelan." He quietly swung the door wide and stepped back, waiting.

Her heart jumped. The slave offered her freedom, but she couldn't bring herself to take it. At least, not yet. Where would she go? Until Slaney or Daniel came to see her, they couldn't devise a plan. If she left now, Simon would be whipped for sure.

"Thank you, Simon, but I will not jeopardize your position in this house."

The slave started to argue, but she silenced him with her hand. "There is one thing you can do for me. Find Daniel," she said. "If we require your assistance, he will tell you when and how."

"Yes'm. I can do dat. I'll be happy to do dat." Simon gave her a firm nod and retreated, closing the door behind him.

Less than a minute passed before the door opened again.

Keelan ground her teeth as her cousin Doreen bounced into the room.

"Daddy is sending a letter to Mr. Pratt, I hear."

Doreen's taunts and gloating observations were the last thing she wanted to hear right now. She pressed her lips into a hard line. "I have nothing to say to you, Doreen. Please leave."

Doreen's cool laugh echoed in the room. "This is no less than you deserve for trying to take Everett from me."

Keelan rolled her eyes, but held her tongue. Doreen began to saunter about the room. "Thank goodness Mr. Pratt is available to take you." Her cousin gave a dramatic shudder. "I have heard he is quite heavy-handed with his slave girls. Although, with you as his bride, they might suffer a reprieve."

Keelan's dug her fingernails into her palms to keep them from trembling. There was rage, yes, but also fear. That dark, ragged monster invading her brain, forcing her to writhe and flail under its cold, contemptuous shadow. It was something she kept pushing frantically to the far places in her mind when the topic of a marriage to Pratt arose. Only her anger at Landon Hart kept her from covering her ears, collapsing into the corner, and becoming nothing more than a limp pile of pathetic mush.

Keelan's shoulders tightened as her cousin walked up and stopped in front of her. Doreen pretended to study her intently. "This might be the last time I view your face unmarred." She whirled and skipped from the room.

Her cousin would *not* crumble her pride and throw her into hysterics. Still, it was a long time before her body stopped quaking. The uncertainty of her future mauled her mind and spirit. She desperately wanted to believe Everett lied to her about the ships leaving port. Was it so far outside the realm of possibility that hurt and anger drove Landon to make a sudden decision to just *leave*?

A ship bound for Boston currently anchored in the Charleston harbor, set to sail tomorrow at sunrise. If Landon had indeed left her behind, was still her intention, and now perhaps the sole purpose of her life, to be aboard.

❧ 47 ❧
CHAPTER FORTY-SEVEN
NEW PLAN

"I'll not leave without ye!" Standing in the middle of Keelan's chamber, looking like a silver whirlwind, Slaney crossed her arms.

"Neither will I," argued Daniel. He stepped away from the doorway where he and Simon were keeping watch for Jared or Doreen. "I made a promise to Lord Grey, and I don't intend to break it." He walked over to the maid. "Slaney, you *must* go."

"I will not!" Slaney countered. Her eyes flashed in defiance. "Who's going to take care of me mistress?"

Daniel sighed softly, taking Slaney's work-toughened hands in his own. "*I* will. I promise." He rubbed his thumbs over the top of her fingers. A slight blush suffused the maid's cheeks. "Slaney, if you are safely gone, then I can concentrate all my efforts on getting Keelan away. If I have to worry about the *both* of you..." He shrugged his shoulders and left the rest unsaid. "Miss Keelan and I shall meet you aboard the ship. We'll have to wait until we can slip out unnoticed, which will probably be late, hours before dawn when the house is still abed. We can move faster with only two."

Keelan's heart tugged with affection for the two people who'd cared for her for the past nineteen years. To think for most of her life, she'd taken their loyalty for granted. Gratitude radiated in her chest and emotion closed her throat.

She added to Daniel's logic with her own. "Slaney, I'm grateful for your concern, but if something prevents me from boarding to the ship in time, *someone* has get to Wind Briar and retrieve the chest. I need those papers inside if I am going to find my real father."

Keelan took a breath and willed the thought of failure away. She *would* make it. "If Uncle Jared's instructions to auction everything are carried out before we can get to it, I might never get a chance to read them." She pressed an envelope into Slaney's hand. "Here are letters of recommendation to help you find employment and give you permission to stay with your sister at Wind Briar."

Slaney's shoulders slumped. "All right then, I'll go on," she muttered. She shook a finger at Daniel. "Ye best bring her safely home and yerself too, or ye'll be answerin' to me." She sniffed and rubbed her nose.

Keelan held out a small purse. "Your passage has been paid. The receipt is inside, along with enough coin to get you to Wind Briar. Go *now*. Daniel told Simon to gather your trunks and wait for you in the stables. I want you away before Jared finds a reason to detain you."

With a soft sniffle, Slaney circled her arms around her in a warm hug. Keelan held her tightly and kissed her cheek.

"Everything will be fine. You'll see. Don't worry." Her own words sounded thin, meager, even to her.

With forced bravado, Slaney heaved in a deep breath. "I'll go then."

"God speed, Slaney," Daniel said, squeezing her arm.

Slaney let out a choked sob and then threw her arms around Daniel's neck. He stood stiff and shocked for a second then slowly wrapped his arms around her, hugged her fiercely then kissed her forehead. "We'll see you soon." He released her and stepped to the door.

Slaney opened her arms and perhaps for the last time, Keelan walked into the safety and solace of the familiar embrace. Warmth curled in her chest and her throat tightened. She prayed she'd made the right decision, and she wasn't sending Slaney into danger. The uncertainty of the future, the ease of the journey, even the weather all weighed heavily upon Keelan's conscience.

Slaney pulled away and wiped her eyes with the corner of her apron. "Well, then. I'm away." With a last wave, she slipped from the room.

Keelan prayed she would see her again.

CHAPTER FORTY-EIGHT
EVERETT RETURNS

A loud commotion broke the post-dawn silence downstairs and Simon slipped up to whisper through the door that Doreen had run off with Doctor Garrison, and Master Jared was in a rage. Sarah was still in a state of shock and Ruth was on her way to the herb garden to make her a special tea.

This was an unexpected surprise. Hopefully Uncle Jared would be so consumed with locating his daughter, that he'd postpone corresponding with Pratt long enough for Keelan to make an escape. Still, she nervously paced in her chamber. The afternoon sun had begun to warm her room, and still no sign of her uncle, or Daniel.

She waited out the day in solitude. No matter how hard she tried to drive thoughts and visions of Landon from her head, they persisted. Broad, masculine shoulders, clear blue eyes, strong, corded arms, and full, urgent lips.

Damn her naïveté and her weak, weak heart.

And damn Landon Hart's stubborn Irish temper.

How could he believe she would choose Everett Garrison over him? Was he not convinced of her affections? She had told him she wanted to be with him. She had agreed to elope with him. A single thought rose to the surface of her mind.

She'd never admitted to him that she loved him.

Admitted. As if it were a crime. What was *wrong* with her? Was her pride so powerful that she could only confess to herself the effect Landon had on her?

A key clicked in the lock and drew her away from her musings. The door opened to reveal Uncle Jared and Simon. Her uncle entered the room with short, agitated steps. Simon shifted from foot to foot in the hall, looking worried.

"Your maid has disappeared." Uncle Jared snapped, pacing the floor. "Your father's valet has refused to tell us her whereabouts. He claims he doesn't know where she went." He whirled back to face her, his eyes thunderous and his scowl making Keelan's belly twitch with fear for Daniel. "I expect he's lying. Where has she gone?"

Keelan's mind jumped quickly to various explanations which might keep Daniel out of trouble. Slaney went to the apothecary, for... what? Slaney was delivering a letter... to whom? About what? None would keep him safe enough. It was simpler to tell the truth.

"I sent Slaney back to England to secure the documents which I promised Papa I would retrieve."

Her uncle paused, his face reddened. "Keelan, we discussed this."

There was no reason to keep her secret any longer. Perhaps, if Uncle Jared understood that she wasn't actually a blood relative, he'd relinquish his guardianship.

If he believed her.

"He said they'd explain the identity of my true sire." The words seemed to stick in her throat and she paused a moment to clear it before continuing, "You see, Uncle Jared, Papa confessed to me that I'm the illegitimate child of my mother and another man. I'm not even his kin."

A small vein pulsed in his temple and he sliced the air with his hand. "Nonsense!" He stepped forward and clenched his hands into fists before grasping her fingers. He expelled a thick sigh and closed his eyes, the obvious battle for calm raging behind his lids. "Keelan, my dear, you must understand, your father was not in his right mind at the time of his death." He finally met her confused stare. "He'd been babbling the night he died even before Sarah came to get you, of revenge and a stolen love." He gently squeezed her hands. "Of *course* you are his daughter. I have a document signed by him stating I am *his daughter, Keelan Elizabeth Grey's* legal guardian in the event of his death. He also left a will in his desk stating Twin Pines goes to you as your dowry."

What?

That was so far from what she'd heard from Papa himself, she couldn't reconcile it being any sort of misunderstanding. Keelan drew her brows together in confusion. "Before he died, he told me he left everything to you. He instructed me to return to England and find my father."

Jared's composure softened a little more. "Don't take the ramblings of a dying man as any more than what they actually were: simple ramblings."

The night Papa had died, he *did* seem to have trouble staying in the present, but she had the signet ring he'd given her weeks earlier, and the tiny portrait of the man in the locket who bore such a striking resemblance to her. Those were tangible things that fortified his claims. Why would he possess those items if the tale was false?

They couldn't be explained away. If she showed Jared the ring and the locket, he'd probably believe her story. But what if he took them from her? She'd have no way to prove who she was to her real father when she found him, if he even existed. No, she must not give up hope. Everything had all become too confusing.

Jared must have taken her silence as acquiescence to his way of thinking. He let her hands go, leaned in, and gave her a cool kiss on the cheek. "Your father cared about you, Keelan. He wanted you to have a secure future."

Secure future. That meant marriage to money. "I cannot, I *will not* marry Pratt," she whispered. Her heart belonged to another. Even if the stubborn oaf had left without her.

Jared expelled a loud sigh. "I'll not force you. Although I pray, please take the time to contemplate the security of a life with him against the alternatives. You may, of course, stay with us as long as you wish. We can sell Twin Pines to Pratt outright, then do what we can with the funds to see to your comfort, or continue with the plan to lease it. Let's discuss this when I return. I should like you to assist me with the draft of the purchase proposal before I take it to my barrister, should we decide to sell."

"Thank you, Uncle Jared." He'd understood. Hopefully, he'll leave quickly and she and Daniel could still escape to the wharf and find Slaney's ship.

He turned toward the door. "I must find my daughter first. Once I locate Doreen and that rascal, Garrison, I will deal with Pratt and Twin Pines." He paused, then addressed Simon. "Keep her here until I return." He spoke to her, although he didn't dare make eye contact. "I'm sorry, Keelan, but I have to assure that you'll be here when I return, and not make some impetuous decision that will endanger your life."

He knew her too well.

"Uncle Jared, I beg of you—"

He left, locking the door behind him.

She stared at it, not quite believing what had just occurred. For a moment, she'd thought she'd convinced him to allow her the freedom she desired. Now it would be harder to accomplish her goal, but not impossible. The worst thing that could happen would be if she and Daniel missed the ship.

"I'm sorry, Miss Keelan," Simon said through the door.

"I'll be fine, Simon." She hoped. "Will you please tell Daniel I need to speak with him?" All was not lost.

"Yes, Miss Keelan."

◊◊◊

SOON, Daniel entered carrying a bucket of water. After Simon retreated into the hall, the valet leaned forward and whispered in her ear, "Simon has agreed to leave the key out for us." The valet continued, "We'll go in the predawn hours. I've rented a room tonight at a pub called, The Whistling Pig."

She raised a brow. "Rented a room? Why?"

Daniel's mouth pressed into a straight line. "The ship to Boston departed at high tide today. We missed it."

"Slaney—"

"She boarded just in time."

This made things harder. Not impossible, but definitely harder.

He straightened his jacket and plucked a piece of grass off his sleeve. "The tavern is near the docks. We can hide there and wait until we can board the next vessel sailing north... if you still wish to do so." He fidgeted with the bucket handle before clearing his throat.

Still wish to do so? Why wouldn't she? She narrowed her eyes. "What is it, Daniel?" Even a blind man could tell the valet had more to say.

"The *Desire* and the *Seeker* are still anchored out in the harbor, Mistress. Both are flying Blue Peters."

The Blue Peter signaled for the crew to return to the ship. Her hand flew to her mouth. "He lied. Everett *lied*!" A surge of relief hit her so hard she sank to a chair. Landon had not left her. He was still here. Would he let her explain? Even now, was he waiting for her to come to him? A more terrifying thought invaded her mind. What if this delay made him think she'd changed her mind? She flew to the desk and took out a piece of stationary, then grabbed the quill.

"Daniel, would you please deliver this note to Captain Hart?" She wrote furiously.

"Of course, Mistress." He paused and cleared his throat. "I must warn you, the accommodations at The Whistling Pig might be a bit rough, but I fear we might be easily found by your uncle if we stayed at a better boarding house."

She nodded, quickly sanding and sealing the letter. "You made a wise choice. Please don't worry about me, I'll be fine. I hope to confer with Captain Hart at his earliest convenience."

Daniel caught her gaze and held it. "I'll come for you tonight. Be ready to flee. Wear your shirt and breeches, we'll move quicker and draw less attention." He hefted her smaller trunk. "I'm sorry to say you'll have to leave the bulk of your things behind, unless by some miracle Mister Grey allows me to return and take procession for you."

She didn't care. If given a choice between all the riches in the world or the opportunity to set things to rights with Landon Hart, she'd take the latter in a blink. She was almost giddy with relief. Surely, he'd at least allow her to explain. A thought hit her like a ringing slap. What if Everett had lied to Landon as he'd lied to her? Suddenly, the sun couldn't set fast enough.

When it was nearly dark, she doffed her dress, glad to free her body from the sweaty, prickly mourning gown. Keelan dipped her hands in a bowl of tepid water and splashed it over her face.

If only she could change into her waif's clothes, she'd be better prepared when Daniel returned. However, if Uncle Jared made an unexpected visit after supper, she would be hard pressed to explain her wardrobe. It was best to wait. She slipped on a clean chemise and dressing gown, then sat at the small table and nibbled on the cold supper Simon had delivered earlier.

Her tray held chicken, bannocks with brandied peaches, a glass of wine, and some of Jared's prized boiled potatoes. No doubt, Simon gleaned more than a small bit of pleasure, giving Jared's favorite dish to Keelan. She ate every last morsel.

She had a few short hours to get some much-needed sleep. She climbed into bed, only to stare at the ceiling. Nothing seemed right. Her mattress was too hard. The tree frogs sang too loudly. She tossed and turned before her lids became heavy enough to resist her twitching and worrying.

She must have finally dozed off, because she was awakened by the prickle of hair rising on the back of her neck. It took a moment while she waited for her vision to adjust to the darkness. Had Daniel signaled her from the yard below?

She rose quietly, turned up the oil lamp at her bedside, and slipped on her dressing gown. Pulling the curtain aside, she scanned the ground below. No signs of Daniel. Yet something had disturbed her sleep.

A barely audible click behind her made her whirl to face the door. It eased open inch by inch.

"Daniel?" she breathed, afraid to speak any louder.

The tall, lean shadow of a man moved into her room. The figure was too tall to be the loyal valet. Her heart began to hammer in her chest. A scream caught in her throat, and without thinking, she snatched the heavy pitcher next to the washbasin and held it high, ready to bring it crashing down on the intruder's head.

"Keelan," the man whispered hesitantly. "It's me... Everett. I have come to take you from here. I cannot let you be married to that brute, Pratt!"

Relief washed over her like a clear, cool rain. "Good Lord, you gave me such a start!" she clutched the neckline of her dressing gown as she sat weakly on the chair, still holding the pitcher.

He hastened across the room before dropping down to one knee and peering at her. His voice was low and urgent, his frame slightly illuminated by the low wick of the lantern. "Please, Miss Keelan, you must get dressed so we can depart immediately."

Perplexed, she peered at him closely. "Uncle Jared said you'd run off with Doreen. I am quite shocked to see you here. Surely you must realize Jared is determined to seek you and his daughter out."

Everett gave a derisive snort, "Mr. Grey will not find her, of that, you can be certain."

Something beyond Everett's words unnerved Keelan. He sounded almost emotionless. The detached, dead tone of his voice was wrong, like a string out of tune. He spoke with an unusual iciness. As she stared at him, her throat dried, and the air seemed to leave the room.

Something was wrong. She could sense it.

"Dr. Garrison..." she said. "What are you saying? Did you not take Doreen away to marry her?"

He snorted. "No, although she seems to wish it. She is hiding... for a little while longer, anyway." He paced the room, grinding his fist into his palm. "I'm still angry with the way she acted the night of the ball. I worry for your reputation, my dear. If we are to be married soon, I want to make certain you have the respect and admiration you deserve." A slow, thin smile creased his gaunt face. "She thinks I'll return to marry her, but in truth, I want her out of our way for a while. It distracts her father."

Icy fingers of trepidation slid across Keelan's throat. The faint glow of the lamp cast dark, quick shadows, making Everett's face appear contorted and hard.

"Wh—what..." she stammered, "What exactly have you done to her?"

He gave a harsh laugh. "She's staying with Mrs. Camsby." Everett walked to the window and peered out, casually clasping his hands behind his back. He turned to face Keelan again. "When we arrived, Captain Hart was just leaving. And Mrs. Camsby seemed a bit disheveled. Did you know they were lovers?"

She froze, then fought to keep her expression blank. Dr. Garrison had lied to her earlier. This time she wouldn't be so gullible. She'd finally made the decision to trust Landon, and she would continue to do so.

He moved to the small table and lit the candle, casting the room in a faint, yellow glow and sending shadows clamoring up the walls. "Your cousin needs a respite." He lowered his voice to a more soothing tone, one he used when addressing his patients. "She's upset with herself for giving your father too much pain medicine. It likely killed him, you know. Seems she misunderstood my dosing instructions."

Doreen? Could that be true? She clutched the arms of her chair while mind twitched from thought to thought. If she fled from the room, what then? He would catch her. She'd be faster in her sparring clothes. Somehow, she needed to get him to leave her alone in the room to change. "Dr. Garrison, did you explain any of this to Uncle Jared? He's frantically looking for her."

He stepped forward and knelt before her again. "Of course he is. That was my plan. He is too distracted to worry about *you*. We shall leave tonight." He reached over to take her hands in his. The skin over his knuckles was thin and icy white. "I am doing this for you. My dear, you deserve a better life. I'm going to take you away and marry you." His eyes glittered in the dim light, voice lethally soft. "Think of our future. The two of us will live the lives we were meant to live, happy and prosperous. We'll have the children we always talked about. Please Rachel, leave with me, now."

Rachel? She stood and backed away. "Dr. Garrison, you just called me Rachel," she whispered, horrified at what she was hearing. It was as if he was having a conversation with someone else... not her.

Everett paled. "I... I...." He stood and reached for her hands again.

His white lips seemed to just stretch over his teeth. A grim smile. "A silly slip. Come, we have to go."

His manipulations of Doreen and Uncle Jared seemed so uncharacteristic of him on the surface. Yet, when she thought back through the events over the past weeks, his demeanor had slowly shifted from charming and docile to unpredictable and angry. She should have noticed. She shook her head and tried to keep the panic from her voice, "Uncle Jared and Aunt Sarah—"

"Will not be a concern," Everett finished. "There will be no one to displace our claim to Twin Pines or any of your father's other properties. You and I will live out our lives surrounded by wealth. We can even live at Wind Briar, if you'd like."

"Wealth?" He went from calling her 'Rachel' to *this*? And he'd never been to Wind Briar. "Papa left nothing—"

He pressed his fingers over her lips. "Shhhh. Enough, my love. We must go *now*. There will be time enough to discuss our plans later when we are safely away. I have everything perfectly planned." He pulled her from the chair and toward the door.

"Stop."

It was as if he hadn't even heard her. Not one word. In his mind, she was acquiescent and willing. That mind was no longer functioning as it once did. Her heart thrashed in her chest like a small fish jerked out of the water. Something was terribly wrong with him.

She had to dissuade him. Keelan furiously worked through her options. She could go, and hope to make an escape later, or refuse and then alert the household which would likely make it impossible for her and Daniel to slip away tonight. Uncle Jared would probably not even believe her. She'd already accused Garrison of being an assassin. Her uncle would probably think she was being melodramatic or—

"I cannot go with you." The words fell out of her mouth before she could stop them.

He froze. "What... *what* did you say?"

Her knees were trembling, and she hoped her voice wouldn't tremble too. Perhaps if she simply refused him, he'd leave.

She spoke again, slower this time. "I can't go with you," she repeated. "My life travels along a different path now. I cannot do it. I will not do it." Cautious and tense, she stated it in a tone that was both firm and confident even though she was not in the least.

Everett stared at her. His breathing was quick and shallow, as if his lungs merely quivered instead of expanded and emptied his breath. He stood quietly for a long time, studying her before he responded.

"The events of the past few days have put a tremendous strain upon your ability to think clearly. Don't fret, it's normal for a woman's mind to become a bit maladjusted when dealing with a tragedy and loss." He reached out and gripped her shoulders, his fingers like talons. "I'll help you through this. We love each other, my dear. You will be well-cared for, as your father wanted. We'll be happy, as we've always wanted. We'll have the children you've always wanted."

She almost laughed at the irony of Dr. Garrison diagnosing her with a maladjusted mind while his own was fracturing to the point of changing his entire personality. He stepped closer and traced his fingers along her jaw, and she barely suppressed a shudder.

His next words sent icy tremors down her spine. "I will not let you make a decision that is detrimental to your future. You must think about what I've said. When you do, you'll understand it as I do. I think you only need time to let my words sink in. Time and rest." He caught her hand and raised it to his lips. "Get dressed. I shall return soon."

He slipped out the door.

Weak-kneed, she sank back to the chair. It was a moment before her breathing slowed to a normal pace and her brain kicked into action. The door! She jumped up and tried the handle, but it wouldn't budge. Drat. She needed to change into her boy's clothes and search for Daniel. First, she would pen a letter to Uncle Jared, explaining where Garrison took Doreen. Pulling the quill and parchment from her desk, she sat down and scribbled another note.

After completing it, she knelt on the floor and opened her trunk to change. Keelan paused at a small scratching sound outside the door. Just as she stood, it swung open.

Two cloaked figures swiftly entered her room and headed toward the bed. Finding it empty, it was only a second before they noticed her. She opened her mouth to scream, but could only clutch her throat in terror, desperately willing her voice to work.

It was then she noticed the ropes.

With a frightened squeak, she darted toward the open door. The shorter man reached out and grabbed for her wrist. She ducked and dashed under his arm, sending an elbow into his kidney as she passed. Releasing his breath in a loud grunt, he stumbled forward. The tall one was quicker and grabbed her hair as she sped by. She spun and kicked at his shins with her bare feet.

"Dammit! Grab her, Orvis!"

She let her legs buckle and fell away backwards. Her head slammed into Orvis's nose, causing him to let out a howl.

"Quiet, idiot! You'll have the whole house upon us!" The taller assailant still had his hand in her hair, and he jerked her head painfully forward. Keelan swung her forearm up in an arc and struck him in the throat, eliciting a strained hiss of breath. His hand loosened slightly. She opened her mouth to scream as a wide fist made contact with her chin. Little white dots exploded in front of her eyes, then vanished into utter darkness.

❧ 49 ❧

CHAPTER FORTY-NINE
IN THE PIRATES' LAIR

Keelan woke to a dull throbbing pain in her jaw and moaned.
The sound came out raspy and choked. Her mouth tasted like
she'd chewed on a horseshoe and gargled with sawdust. She opened her
eyes to inky darkness. In a panic, she squeezed them shut before carefully opening them again.

Was she *blind?* She was in a heap on a hard floor. Rough planks
pressed ridges into her cheeks. She wrinkled her nose at the stench. It
smelled like a barn. The faint *chink* of metal links when she moved
quickly brought her to the realization that she was chained. Panic
swallowed her breath, and she sat up quickly. A blunt rush of dizziness
crashed into her, and she braced her hands on the floor to keep from
collapsing. Her head was throbbing.

Where was she?

Slower this time, she straightened. Flexing her fingers and rotating
her wrists, she winced. The manacles were heavy and roughly made.
She tugged at the shackles, which was futile. It might be possible to
wriggle her wrists out, if she could collapse her knuckles enough, but
the links were securely fastened to the wall about knee height from the
floor. Twisting her hands only managed to make her skin chafe and
burn.

A sound disturbed her work, and she stopped moving to listen. The lumbering shuffle of heavy footsteps grew louder. They stopped, and the door creaked open, swinging on under-used, rusty hinges. A faint light from a low lantern fanned into the room. At the sight of dozens of empty shackles hanging from the surrounding walls, a renewed wave of panic crashed through her chest. She glanced frantically around, trying to get her bearings, and find for something to use as a weapon.

There was nothing.

Aside from the manacles on the walls, the room had two doors. One was nestled in a far corner. The other was obscured by the form of a short, round man carrying the lantern. He moved forward to the center of the room and held the light high.

"Yer awake, finally. Feared I might've hit ye too hard." He eyed her smugly before placing a bottle of ale and a small bundle wrapped in a bit of cloth within her reach, then warily stepped back.

"Who are you?" she demanded sharply. Her voice was almost commanding. Almost steady. "Why have I been chained?"

The man cocked his flabby head to study her, then chuckled. "None o' yer business who I be. You're locked in 'ere for safe keeping until yer new master comes to fetch you."

"New master?" A sharp jolt of panic tightened the skin across her cheeks.

Keelan struggled to her feet, tried to ignore the wobbly dizziness, and leaned against the wall. She held her pounding head until the spinning subsided enough to focus on the hulking form in front of her.

Fear twisted in her stomach and the only way to keep it from totally taking over her body was to funnel it into anger and indignation. Otherwise, the hysterical scream churning in her chest would surely burst out.

"Release me at once!" She fought to keep the terror from shaking her voice, but failed.

He shrugged his broad shoulders in indifference. "I do the bidding of me employer. He'll deal wi' ye."

Her voice shook with barely contained fury. "What's his name? I demand to see him." Her words echoed in the chamber, thin and weak.

"Gampo will see you when he's good an' ready."

Gampo. That was a familiar name. Conal O'Brien and Landon Hart had told a story about the man during breakfast several weeks ago. Gampo was a *pirate*, with whom they had an ongoing feud. He was the one responsible for killing Conal's uncle, Fynn. The trouble she might have thought herself in a minute ago had just increased a thousand fold.

He pointed at the bundle he'd put on the floor. "I brought you somethin' to eat. You'd best get at it before the rats take it."

"I demand you release me!" She raised her voice, but it sounded more like a warble than a shout.

Instead of responding, he backed quickly to the door.

Keelan reached down, grabbed the knotted piece of cloth, and angrily threw it at him. He flung his pudgy arms up to protect his face and ducked. The bundle opened and a piece of bread and two chunks of molded cheese rained down. The cloth floated crazily to the floor at his feet.

Realizing the worst was over, he straightened and pointed at the scraps. "Them is all the rations you get, woman!" He stepped nearer, careful to stay just out of reach. "You're lucky I brought you anything at all after you cracked me bloody nose!"

She studied his face. Both of his eyelids were purple and the man's nose was indeed slightly askew. The sight was grimly satisfying. "What kind of reception do you expect when you enter a lady's chamber in the middle of the night and attack her?"

He touched his nose gingerly. "Well, it hurts like the devil."

"Good."

Added irritation darkened his features. Growling, he opened the door, pausing first to slam the lantern on a large iron hook on the wall. He scowled at her over his shoulder then stomped out, pulling the door behind him, and muttering words that were probably best she couldn't clearly hear.

A spinning head forced her to sink back to the floor and close her eyes, unable to fight off the wave of fatigue that descended. She must have managed to doze off for a short while because she was awakened by the low rumble of hunger from her stomach. She stared longingly at the cloth still crumpled in a small heap.

The bread and cheese had disappeared.

The ale still sat nearby, and she quenched her thirst gratefully, then placed the bottle close to her blanket and hugged her knees to her chest. An overwhelming waterfall of despair unfurled within her heart. She choked back a desolate sob; she shouldn't allow herself to cry. If she started, she might never stop.

CHAPTER FIFTY
STOLEN CARGO FOUND

I t was nightfall when Landon and Conal met Commodore Hall and Sheriff Pinkerton outside a pub near the waterfront. The air was still thick with humidity, even though the sun had set over an hour ago. They walked along the pier rather than meet inside. Spies were everywhere, and extra cautions had to be taken to avoid being overheard. A small sliver of a moon occasionally darted from between quick-moving clouds. The wind had picked up and was caressing the land below with gentle gusts hinting of rain.

Sheriff Pinkerton's voice was steady. Confident. "We have a total of sixty able seamen and deputies between the four of us, Commodore Hall." He checked the priming of his pistol. "If Captain Hart is correct about the men in the warehouse, we'll have them outnumbered. Let's hope they're smart enough to surrender without a fight."

Landon wouldn't bet they'd be *that* smart. "We'll meet there in an hour's time with our men," he said. "With only the night watch up and about, we should be able to catch them off guard."

"I like the odds." Commodore Hall clasped his hands behind his back. "In an hour then." The three men walked along together for a short distance, then the Commodore parted company.

Landon and Conal walked for several moments in silence.

His musings drifted to Keelan Grey.

Again.

He'd tried to banish the woman from his consciousness, but the memory of their time together in the abandoned cabin cellar during a fierce storm last month haunted him in both sleep and wakefulness. Keelan's soft curves and passionate kisses left him hungry. Many nights he lay awake wondering what it would be like to make love to that fiery tigress.

When they'd reached the plantation after the storm, her father and uncle were understandably furious that he and Keelan had been together without a chaperone.

He'd offered to marry her that day, to appease her father and do the honorable thing.

Certainly for no other purpose than that.

On the surface, he supposed it looked as if he did so to save her reputation. Truth was, he spoke without contemplating the consequences of his words. It was as if his reasonable, mortal mind shrugged off its duties and allowed his blind, foolish heart to take the helm. He'd vowed to *never* tie himself to another woman in marriage, but the idea of waking every morning to Keelan's soft warm flesh pressed against him had pushed out any trepidations he would normally have had with regard to the bonds of matrimony. Something about her drew him like a parched man to water. She was impetuous and reminded him a bit of Conal, who acted first and asked questions second. She was compassionate. She'd not hesitated to rescue Simon's boy from a rabid dog, even at her own peril. She was daring. Training to fence in boy's clothes, swimming in a cool lake with none...

In the end, she'd saved him by choosing the physician, Garrison.

Or so he'd told himself over and over and over.

And over again.

He was bound only to the sea. The freedom of the open ocean and the thrill of finding exotic treasures to trade and sell along the shores of the Americas had nourished him as well as any plate of food. Perhaps even better. He was sated. Content. Happy.

Lonely.

Which is why he'd tried to gain Keelan's favor while in Charleston.

Never would he permanently weigh anchor and retire to a land-locked life. Keelan seemed to sense that from their first meeting. She'd made it very clear his "type" would never make her happy, and she'd not marry a man who would sail off for months at a time, leaving her behind, lonely and alone.

He knew too well what lonely women did when their husband's left them alone for too long.

Her decision to accept Garrison's proposal had been a relief. Certainly.

His freedom had been preserved.

As soon as they recovered the cargo and brought to justice, the band of thieves who took it, he'd set sail north along the coast to trade the rest of his goods, make a tidy profit, and enjoy his riches.

Alone.

However, after a month had passed, the desire to be with Keelan again had nearly driven him mad. Her decision grated against his peace of mind. She came to him in his dreams, floating naked on the water, sparkling drops of sunlight dancing all around her, light pink nipples flowering on her supple, round breasts and her hair flaming like rays of a burnished sun. He could still feel the velvety warmth of her lips on his neck, and the touch of her slender fingers twined in his hair.

He had indeed goaded her into a final kiss the night of the ball. He'd found her in the garden, away from the dancing and the guests. She didn't... *couldn't* love Garrison, and he'd intended to prove it to her. A person doesn't agree to kiss one person when they are in love with another. If they do kiss someone else, especially someone they find undesirable, they couldn't possibly do so with passion and heat.

But *that* kiss... even the memory of it made his pulse quicken.

No woman could have kissed him with that kind of fire and been in love with another. It wasn't possible.

Her lips, soft and eager, stirred a heady passion from deep inside, leaving him hungrier rather than sated. It was at that moment, he couldn't imagine sailing for the open sea without her.

He'd asked her to join him and his heart had flung itself at the walls of his chest when she'd accepted, promising to come to him by today. Yet she'd not arrived, nor had she sent word to him.

So, of course he'd sought her out.

Landon clenched his fists. The image of Keelan and Garrison locked in a long, passionate kiss burned in his gut. *Why* had she changed her mind? How had he been so wrong about her? His chest tightened and his heart railed and thrashed. He tried to divert his thoughts elsewhere, but his mind wouldn't obey.

Originally, Keelan had revealed her desire to live in town and open her own shop. Perhaps she'd changed her mind about life on the sea with him? Did her desire to be a woman of substance and independence outweigh her desire for him?

But why choose *Garrison*? That bastard had been violent when he confronted her in Twin Pines' garden. How could Keelan go back to him knowing the kind of man he was?

Only one answer made sense.

She wouldn't.

Unless he was more wrong about her than anything or anyone he'd ever been wrong about in his life, she would *never* bind herself to Garrison willingly.

It would be a mighty blow to his pride if he was mistaken, but he'd speak to her one last time before he left port. He wanted to hear the reasoning from her own lips. The ones he wanted to devour.

On the morrow, he would call on her and wouldn't leave port until they spoke, and he heard a worthy explanation. She might tear his heart open further, but he had know if she ever wanted him, or if she had been using him all this time to spur Garrison into marriage.

"I wish I coulda rounded up more men," Conal said, interrupting his thoughts.

Landon struggled to force the images of the fiery-haired beauty from his mind. "I'll not take a drunk man into battle," he said firmly. "Only those with clear eyes and a steady hand can help us." He clapped Conal on the shoulder. "We'll do fine with what we have. The good Commodore Hall has offered his assistance. The odds weigh heavily in our favor."

"Aye," Conal agreed. "Let's go gather the men." He fingered his pistol. "Been too long since the last brawl. I'm ready for a fight."

Landon grunted in agreement. So was he.

CHAPTER FIFTY-ONE
NEVER DEFY A PIRATE

A large rat sat in the middle of the floor, sizing up Keelan with a cocky, jaundiced stare. She grabbed the empty ale bottle and cracked the bottom against the brick wall. It shattered, leaving a long shard protruding from the bottle's neck. Ha! She had a handy blade now.

"Come any closer, you bloody rat, and I'll have *you* for *my* supper." She picked up a piece of glass and threw it at the filthy creature, causing it to scurry into the shadows of the far wall.

Scuffing footsteps outside the cell door broke the quiet, and she tossed the blanket over her new weapon.

"Slow down, Orvis. It's dark on these steps."

Orvis was back, and he had brought a friend. She wrinkled her nose. By the stench, neither had bathed in quite a while and at least one, if not both, had been drinking. They confirmed her suspicions when they staggered into view.

"She's awake now, Crowe." Orvis gestured at her with the bottle in his hand. "Little Miss 'igh an' Mighty." He managed two steps toward her, but the third strayed to the right.

Her skin gripped her flesh as Crowe stared at her, a lusty sheen in his eyes. She returned his stare with a frosty one of her own. As she sat up, the filmy white dressing gown slipped over her right shoulder, baring her pale skin.

Crowe's lewd grin revealed several brown, broken teeth. Keelan glanced down. The curve of her breast peeked enticingly from the silk chemise. Firm nipples stood erect against the thin fabric in the cell's chill. With bravado she did not feel, Keelan put every bit of malice she could rouse into her glare as she slowly and deliberately reached up and pulled the dressing gown over her shoulder and clenched it in her fist, links clinking softly with the movement. Her heart gave a terrified jolt, its beat turning erratic with fear as she eyed the two. If they came closer, she'd make sure they'd regret it.

Crowe swallowed, his Adam's apple jerking as he licked his lips. "God, what I wouldn't give ter have a taste of that." He strode forward and Keelan scrambled to her feet.

"Are you Gampo?" Though she tried to sound authoritative and stern, she failed mightily, and she barely kept her shaking limbs from crumbling beneath her. He looked about as scared of her as he'd be of a church mouse.

Crowe gave her an extravagant bow. "Crowe at yer service milady, I be his brother in arms. His first mate."

"I want to speak with Gampo," she retorted, inching backwards until the wall pressed against her shoulders.

He grinned. "Soon enough."

Orvis leaned against the far wall and gulped a mouthful from his bottle. Keelan sliced her gaze between the two men. Her heart was now racing, her palms damp with sweat. Frigid fingers of fear threatened to paralyze her.

It was obvious their intentions were dark and ugly.

As Crowe continued to swagger toward her, he removed his belt and began to unfasten his breeches. "Methinks 'tis you who will do the service."

Orvis spoke up from the far wall. "The Cap'n said—"

"I heard what the Cap'n said," Crowe snapped, cutting him off. "I thinks she needs ter learn different ways ter please her new husband." He reached down and pulled his hard erection from his breeches.

Keelan felt the blood flee from her face and she recoiled in horror, a scream frozen in her throat.

He grinned, reeking of sour ale. "This here is Beauregard. He wants a li'l kiss."

She gave a warbled shriek and swung a fist which he easily blocked. Grabbing her fingers in his meaty fist, he bent them back until she sank to her knees.

Biting her lip against the pain, Keelan lanced him with a deadly scowl. "Hurt me and I will kill you."

Crowe stared at her a moment, then tipped his head back and roared with glee. "A wench with spirit!" He leaned nearer, smirking. "It will be a fun to break you like a li'l pony."

Orvis Pike snorted, then touched his nose, wincing. "Give her a li'l lesson, Crowe."

The barrel-chested man released her fingers, but before she could move, he grabbed her hair with both hands and twisted his fingers into her curls. His eyes glowed with a cold, cruel light.

"I said he wants a kiss," Crowe sneered hoarsely. "Be sweet and gentle now. If ye be stupid enough to bite me, I will break yer neck."

Panic seized her. What she wouldn't give for a nice sharp rapier or even a dirk right now. Remembering the bottle, she groped madly for the blanket. Her palm closed around the cool, smooth glass neck. Gripping it tightly, she thrust it upward with all her might. He would learn that she was not some dainty, weak little woman. Until she ran out of strength to lift her hands against him, she would fight like a hellcat.

The sudden, high-pitched shriek emanating from Crowe could have shattered a sherry glass. His face darkened with fury; he shoved her backward into the wall. The bottle flew from her grasp and shattered. A thick, red stream of blood oozed from a deep gash on the inside of his upper thigh, less than an inch from where Beauregard dangled, suddenly limp.

"Where the hell'd she get *that?*" he cried, his voice racked with disbelief and pain. "The bitch nearly gelded me!" He staggered back, tore off his shirt and quickly wrapped it around his bleeding leg. He snarled, "I'll teach ye what happens to them that defies me."

Fear scraped the inside of her ribs. She was defenseless now. Keelan's mouth went dry when he limped over to his fallen belt and wrapped the end in his fist. The metal buckle dangled menacingly, inches from the floor.

"Orvis, hike her up!" Crowe spat.

The rotund man lumbered over and grabbed one of the chains. Her insides churned with a thick, dark dread. She gritted her teeth and tried to pull the chain from his grasp. Unprepared for such a reaction, Orvis crashed into the wall. He reeled away, cursing with his hand pressed hard against his left eyebrow.

"Firs' me nose, now me eye. Dammit, woman!"

He brought his hand away, his brow now sporting a rather large knot, which was quickly deepening in color. Unfortunately for her, the drink apparently dulled the superficial pain, as Orvis was not swayed from his mission. He snatched the chain and hooked the right link over a spike in the wall, grabbed her shoulders, spun her face first into the boards and crushed her body into the hard planks with his own, while he fastened the left chain on a similar spike.

Her heart pounded frantically as the sound of Crowe's footsteps neared. There was a hard yank on the collar of her dressing gown. The delicate fabric was no match for his strength and rent down to her waist. Every instinct screamed at her to fight. She pulled frantically at the cuffs, but they held fast. A renewed sense of panic seized her, and she tried to twist her hands out of the manacles. Pain shrieked through her wrists as the malicious metal bit into her skin.

"Ye shouldn't have fought me," Crowe growled in her ear as he squeezed her buttock hard and then caressed it roughly.

Keelan tried to swallow, but her throat froze and would not obey. She squeezed her eyes shut and silently began to pray.

Crowe swung the belt.

52

CHAPTER FIFTY-TWO
FINDING KEELAN

"On my mark, we'll charge." The lanky sheriff checked the priming of his pistol. "Hopefully we'll surprise them and avoid bloodshed, but don't hesitate to defend yourselves."

Landon turned to the waiting men and growled low. "Ready your weapons."

Swords and sabers were drawn, pistols held at the ready.

A muffled scream pierced the night from deep within the warehouse. The men froze at the unexpected sound.

"That's a woman's scream!" Conal hissed to Landon in surprise.

Landon clenched his jaw, fury building in his chest. Gampo had gone too far this time. Their past skirmishes had consisted only of shots across the bow on open sea until Fynn was killed by falling spars. Everything had elevated since then; severely wounding young Billy and now abusing women. It stopped here and now.

"Now!" Sheriff Pinkerton roared.

The men crashed through the doors. A warning shout from the sentry inside was cut short by the heavy fist of one of Commodore Hall's sailors. The guard sank into a limp heap as the men swarmed into the building.

Shouts of surprise and panic arose from a small group of warehouse occupants who had been playing cards on a barrel near the door. The disturbance drew an additional dozen or more thieves from the rear of the building, their roars of alarm mingling with the hoots and yells of Hart's sailors and Pinkerton's deputies. A stray pistol shot shattered a glass oil lamp. It exploded into flames, scattering a shower of blazing oil on several rolls of silk. Thin fingers of fire licked hungrily at the lamp oil dripping down the table legs and over the floor.

Landon shouted over his shoulder, "Henry! You and Marcel contain those flames before they spread. Save that silk!"

Henry's eyes widened as Landon motioned to several crates a few paces from the fire. "Captain, those are sittin' next to munitions crates!"

Landon paused and glared at Henry. "Then you had best be *quick*!"

Henry grabbed Marcel by the arm and together they knocked the bolts of silk to the ground, stomping madly at the ravishing flames. Thick black smoke began to spread through the warehouse.

That silk had cost him a small fortune, dammit. Would his luck never change? Half of Fynn's cargo was ruined during their confrontation with Gampo last month, then Landon's cargo had been stolen from under his nose. Although he'd found it, some of the most expensive items were now on fire. How many more setbacks would he be able to take before he was back to where he started seven years ago?

Conal pointed through the smoky haze to the second floor, and an open loft currently stuffed with part of their stolen wares. "The screams might have come from up there."

He glanced up at the thick timber door, which stood ajar above them. The faint glow of a lantern, somewhere within, illuminated the end of the passageway. He bounded up four steps before a dark form blocked his way. He barely raised his own weapon in time to deflect the first blow from the tar's saber.

Landon blocked the second strike and returned a parry of his own, neatly disarming his attacker. The man jumped the railing to the floor below but stopped short to avoid the tip of Commodore Hall's sword. Since the thief was in good hands, Landon continued up the stairs. He'd made it halfway before a bellowing war cry made him turn.

Conal stood on the first step, his back to Landon, holding a sword with one hand and a dirk with the other as a large man carrying a broadsword and a pistol ran directly at him. Conal roared and raised his blade.

While normally, he'd leave his friend to his own very capable defense, in this case Conal was holding a dagger instead of the pistol he needed for a balanced fight.

Landon fired. A bright red blotch seeped through the ruffian's shirt. The man cried out in pain and his weapon clattered to the floor. Conal brought the point of his sword up to his assailant's throat. Things seemed to be in order; time to check out the upper level.

He spun around, but his forward progress was halted by the cold gray barrel of a pistol inches from his chest. The twisted face of a scarred, balding man with a toothless grin met his gaze.

He'd fired his last shot to save Conal. This one was too close to fight off with his sword. Perhaps, if he was quick, he could strike out at the gun, and hope to dislodge it before the bullet discharged into his chest. It was a stupid plan, but it was the only one he could come up with at the moment.

A whisper of sound, slight as a fawn's breath, skimmed past Landon's ear. The man's snarl was replaced by an odd bewildered look, the hilt of Conal's dirk protruding from his chest.

Now *that* was a much better plan. There was no better man to have his back than Conal O'Brien. They'd fought shoulder to shoulder since before they sprouted their first whisker.

Landon stepped aside as the cutthroat tumbled forward down the steps. Exhaling with relief, Landon tossed his friend a grateful nod then bounded up the remaining steps, two at a time.

❖

"There's a commotion of some sort goin' on below," Orvis slurred.

"Probably another fight over cards," Crowe said. "Kinda figured we'd have trouble after we opened another bumpkin of that wine." He gave Keelan a swift lash with his belt.

Pain seared across her back and sank its talons into the deeper depths of her consciousness. She gritted her teeth against another scream as the buckle bit into her shoulder. A fine, warm trickle of blood crept down over her ribs, backside, and inside of her leg. The steely bite of the iron cuffs temporarily drew her attention from the sting of her back as she twisted her wrists within the bindings. Staying focused was her priority now. She couldn't fight if she was unconscious.

Focus on getting out of the manacles. Leave no room to acknowledge pain. Get at least one hand free.

With the rest of the crew downstairs drunk, she might have a chance to escape during the confusion.

CROWE DREW THE BELT BACK, ready to deliver another blow. This little diversion made his gut clench with lust, the sting in his thigh almost forgotten. Half a dozen welts crossed the haughty bitch's back and shoulders. Four of them, he noted smugly, had opened her flesh. He swung the strap again, but to his surprise the buckle cracked harmlessly against the wall. Where her bloody back had been, a manacle dangled empty against the planks.

After managing to slip one hand from its iron cuff, she worked furiously to get the second chain off the spike. The links fell to the floor with a metallic "clink." Her left hand remained shackled to the wall, but now she could dodge the lashes with better success.

The wench faced him with a glare containing such hatred and contempt, he was taken aback. He'd expected pain and fear. Submission. Instead, the small victory of freeing one of her hands had bolstered her courage; she appeared even more defiant.

He shook his head at her, chastising. "You still haven't learned the lesson yet, dearie."

He drew back for another blow, but the forward momentum of his arm was abruptly halted. When he glanced over his shoulder to determine what had impeded the progress, he screamed. Standing behind him was a man dark and sinuous as a panther.

And death glinted in his eyes.

LANDON LET OUT a feral snarl and with a vicious jerk, pulled the leather belt with his left hand, and crashed his right squarely into the pirate's jaw using the pommel of his sword.

The woman's tormentor crashed to the floor, motionless.

Landon stepped over the prone form and looked at the lady crouched in the shadows, backed against the wall. Pale legs, fiery hair… His heart lurched in shock, then contracted with a sharp spasm, squeezing all the air from his lungs.

He barely choked out her name. "Keelan?"

What was she doing here? He wanted to go to her and gather her up into his arms, but instinct made him pause. Her stare was wide and wild, like a caged animal with a fevered gaze. Her breath seemed to come and go in short hollow gasps, as if it was afraid to stay in her lungs.

Sounds from the battle downstairs had ebbed. Sensing the danger had passed, he gently placed his sword on the floor and held open his palms, anguish seizing his breath. As badly as he wanted to crush her to him, he stayed still, calm. She'd not recognized him yet. He kept his voice soft and even, despite the thudding of his heart that jarred his entire body. "Keelan? It's me, Landon."

Her jittery gaze jumped around the room and landed on the prone figure on the floor. Widened. Her throat convulsed.

"Keelan. Look at me, love."

Please recognize me.

She finally lifted her head and wild, wide, green eyes locked on to his face. A shudder shook her shoulders like a violent quake. Landon's heart wrenched tighter in his chest at the sight of her tear-stained cheeks and pale lips. He stepped closer, until he was an arm's length away, careful not to make any sudden movements.

"Keelan, I can take you out of here. Will you let me?"

At last, relief washed over her features and with a choking sob, she threw herself into his arms. He closed his eyes and inhaled.

Jasmine and spring rain.

Keelan.

He held her like a starving man clutched a loaf of bread. When he crushed her closer, she let out a pained gasp, and he quickly released her. His arms were blotted with blood.

With an enraged oath, he stared over her shoulder at the lash marks running across her shoulders and back. Fury boiled through his veins. "That bloody bastard!" At least four gashes were oozing blood. Raw anger roiled in his chest, and he tossed a murderous look at the still form sprawled on the floor. "I should have killed that maggot-ridden piece of filth."

More gently this time, he pulled her into his arms. A terrible ache gripped his chest. She'd chosen Garrison, and the bastard didn't protect her. He shouldn't have allowed it. He damn well shouldn't have let anger and jealousy drive him away from her. Part of him wanted to toss her over his shoulder and carry her back to his ship like a savage. He took a strangled gasp of air, and tried to speak, but his words came out strained. "He hurt you. Keelan, love, I'm so sorry." She buried her face in his neck, hot tears dampening his skin. "I won't let anyone hurt you ever again. I'm here. I'll always be here. You're safe with me. I have you. I have you."

❧ 53 ❧

CHAPTER FIFTY-THREE
RETURN OF GAMPO

W hen the haze of pain and terror finally thinned, Landon's handsome, chiseled face came into focus. The lack of food and sleep was probably causing her to hallucinate. His hands slid up her arms, leaving trickles of heat in their wake. She reached out and pressed her palms against his warm, hard chest. Except he was solid. He really was here.

"Landon?" This would be a cruel trick for her body to play on her mind. She moved her hand, her fingers bumping along the ridged muscle across his chest. *Please God, let this be real.*

He sucked in a ragged breath, going still. His skin quivered beneath her fingers. "Aye, love, it's me." Relief washed over her like a cool rain. He was here. He was really here.

Landon tenderly stroked her cheek, then ran his thumb gently along her jaw, frowning at the angry purple bruise near her chin. "How did you come to be here?"

Despite fighting for calm, her voice trembled as she told him about the two strangers who had kidnapped her from Jared's home. "At first, I suspected it was Dr. Garrison. He visited my chambers earlier in the evening and asked me to elope with him, but I refused." She still suspected Garrison. Her stomach clenched, both anger and shock weaving a tight knot at the thought of what the doctor had revealed.

He eyed her cautiously. "So, you refused Garrison?"

Of course. He was thinking about that stupid kiss.

Foolish man.

How could he think she would ever choose any other man over him? A spark ignited the latent anger and frustration inside her, and shoved past the trauma-laced panic. She poked him in the chest and glared through her tears. "If you think I would ever *willingly* kiss that awful man, then Landon Hart, you are a bigger fool than he was for attempting it."

Landon's brows jumped up. There was a slight relaxing of his face, the corners of his mouth lifted, but only a little. She threaded her fingers in his. "If I had eloped with him, I'd not have been in my room when those men came for me." She understood his reluctance to nurture another relationship of the heart. He needed to trust her. Trust her love.

They needed to trust each other, which wouldn't be easy for either of them.

"What you saw today, was Dr. Garrison kissing *me*, even though I did not desire it."

He studied their entwined fingers and released a tightly coiled breath. "I would not have left without you, unless you wished it," he closed his eyes briefly. "I had planned to return to speak with you about your decision." His voice caught, then dropped to a rasp. "I shouldn't have left you behind at all." He trapped her with those sapphire eyes, making her breath catch and her stomach tingle. "All I can think about is having you with me."

He dipped his head and kissed her lightly. Her lips burned with the impression, slight as it was, against her own. Her body curved into his, relishing his heat and strength. She wanted to cling to him and tell him she was already his. But would he still want her after she told him about her heritage? Unwilling to destroy the moment, she hesitated.

Landon gestured to Orvis and Crowe. "Do you have any idea who these men are?"

"That one is Crowe," she pointed, hatred crawling hot and acidic up her throat. "The other is Orvis." There was something else they said that was familiar. What was it? Her mind was still fuzzy. Her head ached. A name they mentioned...one she'd heard before.

Gampo.

"They work for the pirate whom you spoke about, Gampo."

Landon froze, eyebrows slamming down. "Why would he come after *you*?" A muscle ticked in his cheek. Tension radiated from him like heat from red coals. "How would he know to come after you, to get to me?"

Something about that admission made her chest warm. It was strangely pleasing. "I'm not sure," she said, bringing her hands to her pounding temples. None of this was making much sense.

"It's too big a risk for them." His frown deepened.

She shook her head. "Perhaps he's here for the same reason you are. His ship needs supplies or repairs."

Landon shrugged, unconvinced. "It's possible..." Landon smoothed a rebellious strand of hair from her face, before slipping his hands around her waist, carefully avoiding her wounds this time. A tingling warmth raced under her skin.

"You're here, that's all that matters now." She pressed her cheek against his chest, where his heart thudded solidly. She inhaled him, her tremors easing, filling her with the scent of leather and sandalwood and sunshine.

His voice rumbled in her ear. "I was following our stolen property. This is one of Jared's warehouses." His thumb rubbed tiny circles on her hips. Soothing and at the same time terribly distracting. "A different portion of my cargo was stolen from another one of Jared's properties. It's too big a coincidence. Especially now, with Gampo involved."

Gampo and Jared? She tilted her head up. "Do you suspect *Jared* had me kidnapped?" Somehow, that didn't seem probable. He'd always acted in a way he believed to be in her best interests, even if, as far as she was concerned, it often was *not*.

Landon's face darkened dangerously. "Either it was him or someone who had knowledge of his business or access to his warehouses." With a grim set to his jaw, he murmured, "I wouldn't eliminate Garrison as suspect yet."

Neither would she. In fact, she was convinced he was at the center of *everything*, even if Jared didn't believe it.

Landon gently released her and grasped her hands, eyes flashing blue fire at the sight of her raw, bloody wrists. After a quick search through Crowe's pockets did not produce a key, he turned his attention on the bolt securing the chain to the wall. "I'm afraid the best I can do for now is to separate the tether from its moorings." He grabbed the links, put his foot against the wooden planks and pulled. Muscles bunched, cords in his neck and arms stood out in hard lines under the strain. The fabric of his shirt stretched across strong, broad shoulders. Just when she thought they were going to have to think of another solution, there was a mournful creak followed by a loud crack; the wood splintered apart around the bolt, leaving her with four feet of chain. It was infinitely better than four feet of chain *and* a wall.

"I'm afraid, this is the best I can do for now." Landon said, a rueful slant to his lips.

"It's enough. Thank you." A tremor ran up her spine, reminding her how badly her night dress was torn. She shuddered, unable to control the shiver clamping around her neck, then winced as fire zipped across her shoulders. Landon removed his coat, picked up the end of her chain, and dropped it down the left sleeve before helping her shrug into the garment.

The warmth was welcome, but the rasp of fabric against her tender wounds sent flames of pain skittering across her back. Landon cupped her chin, turned her face up to his, and studied her intently, heated blue eyes catching hers. Her heart jerked in her chest as his touch warmed her skin from the inside out.

Suddenly she had to know.

"I need to tell you something I learned, the night Papa died," she blurted. For some reason, getting this out and over with took precedence over everything else. Taking a deep, shaky breath, she plunged on before her courage failed. "On his deathbed, he told me I'm illegitimate—not of his blood." She almost kept her voice firm. As shameful as her position was, she was determined to keep her pride from crumbling away entirely. She wouldn't hide the truth, but neither would she live out the rest of her days in shame. Still, she couldn't look at him, fearing she'd see scorn in his eyes.

She inhaled a swift, fragile breath, and picked grit from her fingernail with her thumb. "He made me promise to find documents, which will tell me the identity of my true father." She let her arms drop to her sides and set her jaw. "Papa left enough money for me to journey back to Wind Briar to retrieve them. Twin Pines is now Jared's, although Jared seems to still believe Papa left the plantation to me. I don't want it." She couldn't meet his gaze. The wooden thump of rejection beat in her chest.

He didn't respond. Keelan's heart ripped and fresh tears burned the backs of her eyes. She swallowed the sob clawing its way up her throat.

A warm finger gently touched her chin, tilting her head up. "Keelan." The way he said her name was like a husky, velvet caress.

Hope nearly stopped her heart. Tremulously, she focused on his face. Glittering azure eyes, solid, shadowed chin, full, slightly open lips. Inky hair brushing his shoulders. Beautiful smile.

Wait—Landon was smiling. *Smiling*.

"I don't care," he said softly, then chuckled. "Now, *breathe*."

She inhaled, unaware she'd been holding her breath. "You don't?" Relief blew through her like a spring wind.

He shook his head. "I don't. That isn't important to me. *You* are. I said I wanted you with me. I meant it." His crystal eyes bore into hers. He took her hands in his. "Keelan Grey, for the first time in my life, I wished I was a titled lord or wealthy landowner instead of a merchant mariner, so I could court you and be deemed more worthy of your hand."

"If I cared about wealth and land, I would be married to that old goat, Pratt," she said flatly.

Landon's mouth twitched, and he kissed her fingers, one by one. Reaching up, he gently placed his palm on her cheek; his gaze held hers imprisoned, captured by those mesmerizing sapphire-hued eyes. Blue magnets.

"At the ball, you agreed to sail away with me," Landon said. "Will you still?"

Her heart gave an elated thump. He still wanted her! Regardless of her station, he still wanted her with him.

But...what about tomorrow?

Next week?

Next month?

Did it matter?

Unbidden, the image of Landon and Annette Camsby dancing at Doreen's ball surfaced in her mind.

How could she possibly trust her heart to him?

How could she possibly avoid *losing* it to him?

Landon pulled her closer, and she gasped at the hard heat of his body against her lightly clad chest. He lowered his head and ensnared her trembling lips with his. Her body thrilled at the unexpected kiss, but the soft plying of his lips calmed her. His tongue delved deep, soft, and warm in the cavity of her mouth. A heady sensation enveloped Keelan, almost as if Landon was a dark, sweet wine, and she had sipped too much of him. Her free hand involuntarily slipped up to his waist and clutched his shirt.

A soft moan rumbled in his chest. His lips moved from her mouth to her throat. His words, husky with emotion, stole her breath. "Speak a lie and tell me you do not want to be with me, Keelan."

"I cannot," she breathed. " I want to be with you. I want *you*." Not Garrison or anyone else. She closed her eyes and let her skin memorize the strong, protective circle of his arms. She focused on his scent, his touch, his warmth, and willed the memory to burn itself into her mind and soul.

Lifting her chin, he brushed his knuckles gently against her face, wiping away the new tears streaming down her cheeks. "You will still come away with me?"

A floorboard creaked loudly, and from the direction of the far doorway a voice rasped, "I'm afraid she has a previous obligation."

54

CHAPTER FIFTY-FOUR
CROSSING SWORDS

Keelan's breath hitched at the voice and with a startled growl, Landon immediately twisted her behind him. "Keelan, run!"

The small door in the far corner was open. Standing on the threshold was a tall man dressed in a black hat and cloak. In his hand, a saber, honed and lethal, glinted in the low flickering light.

That voice.

Fear crept up her throat as Landon pushed her into the dark shadows of the wall, toward the far door. "He sounds like one of the men who took me from my bedroom." Daniel had taught her how to defend herself with a dagger and a sword, but he hadn't been able to teach her how to defend herself against the terror freezing her limbs and numbing her mind.

Think. What would Daniel tell her to do? *Use what you have on you and near you. Defend and distract.*

"Seems I've lost my newly acquired warehouse full of goods," the strange man croaked.

"They weren't yours to begin with," Landon snarled, slipping a dagger from his waist with a leathery whisper. His sword was several feet away on the floor, where he'd dropped it earlier.

The man shifted his stance, and Keelan could now tell he had a dark cloth covering his face. His eyes glittered through jagged holes cut in the fabric.

The man tilted his head. "Regardless, I plan to take this small investment with me, as compensation of sorts for part of my losses." He flicked his saber at Keelan, a flash of dangerous metal. "You'll be coming with me, little chick."

"I'll send you to hell first." Landon eased a step forward. There was steel in his voice.

Keelan lifted her chin, grasped the end of the links dangling from her wrist, and tried to appear as if she wasn't terrified, but the shiver quaking through her body had nothing to do with the temperature in the room. She could do this. She would fight with everything she had.

Starting with the chain around her wrist.

The thin edge of the kidnapper's saber gleamed wickedly in the sallow glow of the lantern. He flicked it at the inert form on the floor. "Did you kill him?"

Landon's eyes hardened. "Not yet."

The man lifted the tip of his sword toward Landon. "Stand aside, man. Ye be at a fatal disadvantage."

Undaunted, Landon stepped forward and over Crowe's body, stopping inches short of the deadly saber's reach. His own sword now lay only a few feet to his right. He spread his arms wide and tossed his dagger from left hand to right hand. "Then we have different assessments of the situation," he responded, his steady, flat voice revealing nothing.

Keelan disagreed. A dagger against the long, sharp, deadly saber seemed to be quite a big disadvantage as far as she was concerned.

"Landon, be careful," she whispered in terror.

The man's head snapped up. "Landon? As in Landon Hart? Captain Landon Hart?"

Landon's shoulders tensed, like a panther ready to spring. "Yes, and *you* are?"

"My Christian name ain't well bandied about, but I'm Gampo to my men. And you owe me a ship." He lunged at Landon.

Landon beat the tip to the side and jumped back. "I owe you nothing!" he snarled. "Except a knife to your heart for killing my friend, Fynn Ahern."

Gampo straightened a little. "So it's true, then. Ahern's dead. A pity." He began to circle Landon. "My intention was to run that turncoat through with my saber at close range, so I could watch his life fade for what he did to my sister."

Keelan frantically scanned the room for anything else she could use as a weapon. A lantern hung from a spike in the wall; the shackles chinked with the movement as she eased it from the hook.

Never taking his eyes from Gampo, Landon flipped his dagger in the air and drew his hand back as if to throw it. Gampo ducked and jabbed his saber wildly at Landon's head.

Keelan screamed and swung the lantern. Momentarily distracted by the lamp, the man flung his arm up to deflect an attack. Taking advantage of Keelan's diversion, Landon dove toward his sword, tumbled neatly into a somersault, and finished upon his feet, sword in his right hand and knife in his left.

"Keelan, stay back!" Landon shouted. "Get out of here! Go!"

If Gampo was surprised at the new turn of events, he didn't show it. His only response was to grip the handle of his saber tighter, and coil like a snake, ready to strike. "Are ye aware how much a beautiful virgin is worth to a Persian trader?" the tall man sneered. "Fynn knew, I'd wager."

"Fynn wasn't a slave trader." Landon's eyes flashed, and he swung his sword.

Gampo parried and nodded toward Keelan. "Perhaps I'll find out how much the buzzards pay for this beautiful woman, soiled or not."

A low, dangerous growl from Landon breached the space between the two men. "Whatever amount it is, you'll be in no condition to collect it."

Gampo's harsh laugh cut through the thick air. He chanced a brief glance at Keelan. "Watch closely, little lamb, while I cut him into half penny pieces."

They circled each other again. Landon's gaze flicked uneasily to Keelan. To place his body in a position to regain his sword, Landon had to move away from her. Their tormentor soon placed himself between them.

Landon lunged, bellowing for her to run.

Run? She'd just got him back, and she wasn't about to leave him now. Not ever. Gampo blocked and parried. Their blades hissed and clashed repeatedly while they circled and lunged, their grunts and curses muffled within the closed room.

She was helpless at this distance. Every time she tried to sneak closer, Landon would yell at her to run.

Suddenly, to her horror, the large bulk of Crowe staggered upright directly in front of her. And worse, Landon appeared oblivious to the revival. A tangle of fear knotted in her chest, tightening as Crowe pulled a long ugly blade from his boot and began to creep silently toward Landon's back. There was no more time for contemplating her options. She had to act now.

The chain.

Keelan grabbed the end, lunged forward and flung a loop around Crowe's neck. Startled, the man dropped the knife and clawed at the chain. If she could just pull him off his feet, it would distract the pirate from Landon. Keelan hauled back with all her might. Her stomach flipped in panic when her bare feet slid out from beneath her. Crowe followed her descent and crashed to the floor. She did it! She stopped him.

Keelan rolled away, taking the chain with her, then crawled as fast as she could to Crowe's dagger. She grabbed it and drew her arm back, ready to defend herself. She could easily hit her mark at this distance, even from her knees.

Except Crowe wasn't moving.

She scrambled to her feet, her stomach lurching at the sight of his head, which was cocked at an odd angle from his body.

Gampo glanced over at Crowe, who was motionless on the floor.

"No!" he roared. He lunged toward her and swung his saber in fury and rage. Landon jumped in front of her and blocked the attack.

Gampo lunged at Landon again, his face a mask of fury and vengeance.

Instinctively, Landon brought his dirk down, but he could only partially deflect the blade, the saber slashing across the side of his ribcage. He twisted with a grunt and crashed the butt of his handle on Gampo's wrist, dislodging the saber. It skidded across the floorboards and disappeared into the shadows. Roaring, Gampo put his head down and plowed into Landon's wounded side. Both men crashed into the wall with a sickening thud.

Keelan's breath froze in her throat.

Disarm or distract.

She dashed to the saber, even as Gampo struggled to his feet and pulled a dagger from his belt. The saber's hilt was in her grasp before the pirate noticed she'd moved. Swinging the weapon up, she spun and lunged.

The clinking chains gave her away, and he yelped in surprise, slapping away her blade with his dagger. Fingers of pain clawed her back as she whirled again and sent the sword slicing toward his midsection. He stumbled backward, narrowly avoiding the sting of the blade once more.

Gampo's face twisted. "Think you're strong enough to scuttle me? My first mate was taken by surprise, but I'll not be," he sneered. "Let's see how ye fair against the bite of my sword, you daughter of a one-eyed whore!" He grabbed Landon's fallen blade and lunged.

Dear God, what had she done? Whatever Fynn's actions had been involving Gampo's sister had driven the pirate into a feud with him lasting for years. Would her fate be the same for killing the pirate's first mate?

She lifted her weapon, even as the agony from movement made little black dots drift across her vision. Her arms shook under the weight of both sword and heavy iron chain. She wouldn't last long under the strain.

"Landon!" He had to get up. She wouldn't be able to handle the pain and the weight much longer.

The next parry from her weapon was slow. She brought her sword up across Gampo's body, forcing him to jump back. The weight of the weapon threw her around, and she hissed at the burn of his blade against her shoulder as he spun past. His next blow jolted the saber from her grip, and it clattered to the floor.

She cried out, curling her throbbing hand into her chest.

He nodded toward the small door in the corner. "'Tis time for us to go. I hear footfalls in the hall and don't wish to engage in another skirmish," his voice was as cold as a London winter rain.

"You will not have me willing as long as I have the strength to resist," she snapped.

"I will have you, *claw-cat*, any way I deem fit."

Keelan chanced a quick glance at Landon. He stirred, thankfully. He was alive, but wounded. And unarmed.

Distract.

She glanced toward the rear door. Well, if Gampo wanted her, he'd have to work harder to get her. She took a deep breath, looped the chain around her arm and took off at a sprint. The pirate lunged for her and managed to grab the tail of Landon's coat, dropping his sword in the process. She stumbled against the doorframe.

So close! She squirmed, gasping for breath.

When the pirate tried to pull her to him and snake his arm around her neck, she ducked and plunged an elbow into his ribs. He grunted with pain, but still clamped his other hand over her mouth as he pulled her against him. Frustration and anger threaded through his voice.

"Be quiet, wench! If you scream again, devil take me to the fire, 'twill be the last sound you make! I still haven't reckoned whether I should kill ye now or later."

Keelan twisted her head, and his fingers slipped over her lips. She opened her mouth and bit down hard until she tasted blood.

Cursing, he jerked his hand away. She pivoted, giving her an opportunity to spin away, except she was nearly jerked off her feet.

"Oh no," he growled while holding her chain. "Ye can't go unaccompanied. Ain't safe fer a ewe white lamb like you."

She glared at the tall man holding her iron tether. "I will die before I allow you to sell me, you soulless bastard!"

He yanked hard and snarled, "Ye'll die if ye run, and ye can lay to that, says I."

Keelan's fingers silently groped in the jacket pocket for Crowe's knife. Instinct told her to lunge for the brigand's midsection; he yanked on the chain again and she stumbled. The knife bound for his belly sank into his thigh, instead.

His yelp pierced the still air of the cell. Dropping the chain, he clutched the hilt, and with a pained hiss, he jerked the blade free. Blood seeped through his trousers in a growing blotch.

A low scrabbling caught her attention and from the corner of her eye, she caught Landon crawling toward the saber, his shirt soaked with blood. Thank God, he was alive and moving.

Gampo shifted his attention to her and raised the bloodied knife. His lip curled back in a grimace of hot hatred and agony.

"You've run out of blades, dearie." He motioned to his wounded leg. "Do you really think this little nick will hinder me too much to collect ye?"

Probably not, but a lady could hope it would slow him down more than a little. Landon was almost upright, so she continued to draw Gampo further from him. It wasn't lost on her that for all his posturing and wicked threats, he hadn't dealt her a debilitating blow, even when he had the chance. Perhaps his plans were less nefarious. Unease slithered in her gut. Or perhaps he was simply keeping her in good enough condition to sell to one of those Persian princes he mentioned earlier.

Keelan backed through the far doorway, groping behind her for support. Chancing a furtive glance over her shoulder, she noted the rickety stairway leading down to a damp alley below. It wasn't the safest route, but it was certainly the most convenient. With one last prayer for Landon's safety, she turned and jumped down several steps to the landing, hitting hard enough to crumble to her knees. Rough wood scrapped the skin, and doing her best to ignore the sting, she scrambled to her feet.

Gampo roared for her to stop, as if she might actually heed his command. He clattered after her, limping down the brittle wooden stair. She'd done it! She'd drawn him away from Landon. Pausing long enough to gather up the iron links, she fled down the next flight to the street below. Several shadowed shapes poured out of a broken window and fled down the ally. Gampo's men? She hesitated. They appeared more concerned with running away than taking note of her presence, so she continued until her feet hit the dirt, then took off at a dead run.

His voice hailed her with hoarse fury, "You'll not escape me, Keelan Grey! I will find ye or may I be damned blood, eyes, and liver! Mark this—I *will* hunt ye down! You *and* that yellow-eyed bastard who bought ye! You'll pay dearly fer killing my first!"

A sickening shiver twisted in her stomach.

He knew her *name*.

She wasn't going to stay and find out what else he knew. Desperately hoping Landon had got himself to safety, she slowed enough to confirm Gampo still limped down the steps. He was almost to the alley, still bellowing like a madman.

55

CHAPTER FIFTY-FIVE
THE ESCAPE

Daniel. He'd know what to do.

Keelan hesitated. Talons of indecision clawed at her mind. If Daniel believed she ran away, then he would wait for her at The Whistling Pig.

Still, she couldn't go there dressed like this.

She groaned. The only place she could obtain clothing at this hour was Jared's townhouse. She almost laughed at the irony. With any luck, she'd be able to sneak in, dress and sneak out. Hopefully, Simon would aid her, so she didn't end up locked in her room again.

Gampo was hindered by a wounded leg, and she by several pounds of chain. She picked up her pace, praying her head start and speed would win out.

Zigzagging through the streets of Charleston, she was careful to stay in the shadows. Before long, her chest burned, and her legs screamed with fatigue. Tendrils of pain licked across the open wounds on her back. Cobblestones bruised her heels. Twice she slipped and fell.

She shifted the chain to her other arm. While Landon's black coat offered a small amount of camouflage in the dark night, it chafed painfully against her flayed back. She wanted badly to remove it, but her pale skin and white chemise would glow like a firefly at midnight. She gritted her teeth.

She was strong. And determined.

She would make it.

Except she wasn't sure exactly where she was.

Jared and Sarah had welcomed her and Papa to their Charleston house for the first month after they arrived. She'd visited the market by the waterfront quite a few times with her aunt. They had also shopped for supplies, such as copperas for disinfecting, and indigo, gypsum, sugar loaves for the kitchen, and dozens of other items, which led them to all corners of town. Surely, she'd notice something familiar soon.

Although it was difficult in the dark, she finally passed the apothecary where Aunt Sarah purchased needed herbs and remedies. She allowed herself a sigh of relief and a brief moment to catch her breath. Not much farther to go.

More confident now, she wove her way through the streets, backtracking only once until she found the house. A hastily roused house servant spoke through the door, "What you want at dis late hour?" he demanded, an irritated edge to his tone.

She struggled to regain her breath. "It's me... Keelan Grey. Please let me in."

The door flung open. The slave peered closer. "Miss Keelan? Dat really you?"

Simon! Thank goodness! Tears burned behind her eyes, her relief overwhelming. She wasn't sure what she'd have done if Uncle Jared had answered the door.

"Yes, Simon, it's really me," she panted. "Please... let me in."

He swung the door wide. "What's happened to you, Miss Keelan? Come in! Mr. Grey is here. Want me to hustle up to wake him, or should I fetch Ruth?"

"No!" Keelan answered quickly. Jared would lock her up again, and she'd be no better off than before. She hastily added. "I-I prefer Jared not see me."

The slave nodded in understanding. "Of course, Miss Keelan. I'll get Ruth to help you."

"Thank you, but I desperately need to get word to Daniel."

"He ain't in da house. Don' know what he done wrong dis time, but Mastah Grey locked him up in the barn."

Keelan frowned. Likely Jared's attempt to get Daniel to tell him her whereabouts. Information Daniel didn't have. Recalling the house slave's offer of assistance before, she decided to call in a favor. "Simon, I need your help."

"Yes, Miss Keelan, I can see dat. Stay here." The servant moved quickly down the hallway.

She waited a moment, not sure what Simon had in mind. Surely he wouldn't rouse Jared? Her stomach dropped, and her heart began to pound harder. She put her hand on the door handle and gave it a turn just as Simon reappeared.

"Here, Miss Keelan," he whispered. "Just leave it in the tack room door, and I'll put it back."

He pressed a key into her hand. A swell of relief softened her shoulders. She gave him a quick nod. "Thank you, Simon. I won't forget this."

"Stay safe, Miss Keelan." He reached around her and pulled the door open.

She slipped outside and darted to the darkened barn.

"DANIEL?" she whispered. "Daniel?"

"Mistress! Is that you?" he responded in a muffled whisper. The barn was dusty and dark. The night offered only the slightest sliver of moonlight.

"Where are you?" She peered into the shadows.

His voice became a little louder. "In the tack room."

She followed the sound of his voice. Keelan couldn't help glancing over her shoulder., expecting Gampo to emerge from every nook and every corner. "Why did he lock you in?" She worked the key in the door, but the lock didn't turn.

"Because you went missing. Jared got up and checked your room and found you gone. I've been so worried about you. Where have *you* been?"

Stubborn lock. Did Simon give her the wrong key? "I don't have time to explain," she answered. "We have to get away from here *now*. I'm being followed, I'm sure of it." The lock clicked, and she jerked open the door.

"Finally," she said.

"Who?" Daniel stepped out. "Who's following—Good Lord!" Catching sight of her standing in a tattered dressing gown and a man's overcoat, he paused and stared at Keelan in alarm. His eyes widened further when the links clinked against her leg.

She pinned him with a firm stare. This was not the time to revisit the past few hours. A shudder skittered down her spine. Those were memories she'd rather forget. "Daniel, we must go *now*!" How long would it be until Gampo and his men sought her out here?

Daniel whirled and ran to the rear of the barn. A moment later, he returned with a bulging feed sack slung over his shoulder. In his free hand, he clutched a new pair of boots and her waif's clothes.

"I purchased the boots for you after I delivered Slaney to her ship this morning," he said, handing them to her. Gesturing to the sack, he added, "I also hid some necessities in the barn in case we had to flee quickly. I wanted to be prepared in case any part of our plan went awry. Now I'm glad I took the precaution."

"Thank God you did," Keelan breathed. She couldn't be more grateful for the protection for her sorely abused feet. She quickly changed in the tack room, stuffed her torn clothes into Daniels sack, and together, they crept out to the street.

The night air remained still and thick. With the boots covering her feet, she was able to move more efficiently. By the time they reached the docks, Keelan had informed Daniel of the kidnapping, the suspicious involvement of Jared's warehouses, Gampo, and the rescue by Hart.

Daniel shook his head grimly. "I can't believe Jared would do such a thing,"

"Landon said much the same," Keelan whispered. "Yet, it seems too big a coincidence."

"Who was the tall man you spoke about?"

"He introduced himself as Gampo, the pirate with whom Captain Hart has been feuding. He kept his face covered and wore a long, dark cloak, and a large hat. For a moment, I thought it could be Everett, except this man was quick and skilled with a saber." Keelan recalled Everett's lack of grace in the ballroom. "He spoke only once, but after I struck his throat, he was only able to whisper."

Hopefully, the damage was permanent.

They heard the distant clop of hooves. The valet reversed direction and ushered her into a narrow alley, as a small cluster of men trotted past. The two fugitives pressed against the alley wall and held their breath.

Several more sets of footfalls approached from the opposite direction.

"Seen anything yet?" a low voice questioned.

"Nay, not a hair of either of 'em."

"We'll get the devil's pay if we don't find the lass fer the cap'n."

"Aye. I dinna want to be the one to tell 'im we couldn't find 'er."

"Best keep searchin'. He said she was probably headin' northeast, back to 'er Uncle's place off Queen Street. Remus, you head right there, and set up a look out for 'er. We'll work our way there."

"Aye."

The man who must have been Remus reined his horse around and took off at a gallop. After a few moments of discussion, the others decided to split up into three groups. Before long, they were on their way.

"You were right." Daniel glanced at her. "He's searching for you." He motioned for her to sit. "The Whistling Pig is nearby."

"Daniel, how will we pay..." She dropped to her knees, exhausted. What was left of her purse was back in Jared's town house.

The valet bent down and peered closely at her face. "I am not without coin, Mistress. Commodore Grey paid me well. And I made a vow to him that I would take you safely home, or wherever you wish to go." He nodded toward the harbor. "We *will* find our way." He knelt and took her hand, grimacing as the chains chinked in response.

"Miss Keelan. I love you as if you were my own daughter. I give you my oath, I will protect you until my death. You have always had my allegiance, and you always will. Never forget it."

She blinked away the tears setting fire to the backs of her eyes. She shook her head numbly. She didn't deserve such loyalty. "Daniel—"

He silenced her as he had done since she was a child, by holding his index finger in front of her nose.

"Please, Mistress, no more talk. You need rest and care."

Keelan leaned her head back against the bricks until the world stopped tilting. Her body throbbed with every beat of her heart. She became sharply aware of her burning legs and bruised feet and could no longer block out the flames of pain searing her shoulders and back. The muscles in her legs shook as she struggled to her feet. Sparks of fire fluttered across her shoulders. The sparks exploded in front of her eyes. Her vision narrowed until there was only one tiny little spark left.

And then even it went dark.

56

CHAPTER FIFTY-SIX
NEVER BETRAY A PIRATE

E verett's chest burned as if the fires of hell were already beginning to consume him.

His plan had failed. *Failed!*

Instead of slipping into the upper room of the warehouse and retrieving Keelan as he'd planned, he'd had to turn and bolt back to his office. Something had gone wrong, and the warehouse had been overtaken. Gampo lurched down the iron steps outside the warehouse and bellowed curses at Keelan as she ran the other way down the side alley.

His words echoed in his head....

"Mark this—I will hunt ye down! You and that yellow-eyed bastard who bought ye! You'll pay dearly fer killing my first!"

Something had gone wrong, and now the pirate was enraged with both Keelan *and* him. His hands shook as he pulled a key from his pocket and shoved it toward the keyhole. It clattered to the cobblestones at his feet. Cursing, he picked it up and tried again. After several long seconds, he managed to unlock the door, slip inside and swiftly lock it again.

He had to get out of Charleston. His mind churned with useless options. He didn't own a horse, so escape by land was unavailable to him at this hour. There were three ships at the docks. It didn't matter where they were going, he needed to get aboard one of them.

Lurching to his desk, he yanked the chair out of the way then dropped to his knees. Not daring to light a lamp, he skimmed his fingers in the dark over the rough planks for the slight gap in the floorboard. Once located, he pulled it up and reached beneath the floor for the leather pouch of gold coins he'd hidden there. They clinked softly as he brought them up and tucked them into the inside pocket of his waistcoat. It was all that was left.

A fist hit the front door, sounding like a shot from a pistol.

"Open up ye spawn of a split-tongued, spindle-shanked scug," a voice growled from the other side.

Gampo!

Everett's blood congealed in his veins. He spun in panic. The fist hit the door again. Catching sight of the back stair in the shadows, he darted up the first flight, not even sure of what he would do when he reached the top, legs burning with the effort. The sound of breaking glass echoed up the stairwell, and he practically flew up the second flight.

"Where are ye, ye scabrous jellyfish! I'll have yer heart for breakfast, I will!"

Everett glanced down the stairwell to check if a figure moved toward him in the darkness. The sound of a flint followed instead, and a dull glow seeped up the stair.

The pirate had found the lantern. "Thought ye'd just be able to buy her, did ye? Corrupted my first with yer gold coins and promises of an easy mark. Know ye the penalty of turning my crew against my orders? Of runnin' with the slave traders? 'Tis death. Death!"

The pirate's bellow thundered up the stairwell, pounded through Everetts chest, slamming his heart against his ribs in terror.

Death.

Everett jolted and spun toward the window. He'd only wanted Keelan. He'd offered payment to Gampo if he kidnapped her for him. The man had *refused*. A pirate refused easy coin. It had bewildered Everett. But Gampo's first mate had been more enterprising.

He wasn't a slave trader, only a buyer. A buyer! Keelan would have been put on the block in the secret back halls of the black market underground, but he had arranged it so that his bid would win her. He'd be her savior. She'd have to marry him then. She'd be in his debt. He'd save her when Hart could not. She'd see that Everett was the only man who could take care of her.

Gampo's enraged voice continued, "'The cargo is easy pickins', says he. 'No one will find it,' says he, the addle-brained bilge rat." The cracking of breaking wood and toppled bookshelves filtered up the stairwell.

Everett glanced around at his surroundings. Perhaps he could hide up here and wait until the pirate left, then he'd head over to the livery first thing in the morning and catch a coach north. Pirates didn't travel much to the north, did they? By land?

Highwaymen and Indian savages tormented travelers by land.

Everett's mind continued to churn. Gampo had remained in Charleston; perhaps his vessel was not yet seaworthy. An ocean passage might be both quicker and safer. He'd leave Charleston and go as far from the pirate as he could manage.

The light from the lantern began to grow and move. Was Gampo coming up the steps? The glow was still swelling, but its brightness was now muffled by a haze of smoke.

Fire!

Everett dashed to the staircase and glanced over the railing. Already the flames were beginning to lick at the bottom steps. He crept down and tried to peer through the smoke. Flames roared from his office. A surge of panic clutched his chest. His path out was blocked by the fire. Things were happening too fast. He couldn't keep his thoughts in order. What should he do?

Was there another way out? He gulped and took a deep breath. He was sweating. Knees shaking, he wrestled the window open, then leaned out and strained to make out details in the darkness. Another building stood across the narrow gap of the alley and it had a second-story balcony. Could he make the jump?

A shout echoed from the front of the building, sounding the alarm. Would Gampo be waiting in the shadows for him to flee the burning structure? If he was willing to burn down a building, the pirate would have no trouble waiting in an alley to sink a blade into his belly. Spurred by this new terrifying possibility, Everett placed a foot on the sill and heaved himself up until he was crouched in the window opening. Sweat dripped from his upper lip as he eyed the other balcony again.

More shouts rang out as nearby residents were awakened by the commotion and the smell of smoke. His breath was coming in quick, dry gasps.

Either jump or burn.

Jump or burn.

He jumped, then crashed into the wrought-iron railing before he managed to fling his arms over the top before his momentum changed from horizontal to vertical. He gripped two balusters and chanced a glance down. The ground appeared to be about ten feet or so away. His hands were sweating and even now his grip was beginning to fail. He had no choice. Letting go, he dropped to the ground, and bit back a cry at the stinging pain shooting through his ankle.

The alley was as unyielding as the railing and much filthier. It took him a moment to take account of his condition before he dared move. A sprained ankle and a bruised hip. He rolled over and pushed himself to his feet.

Move. Get away.

He limped away from the main road, through the back alleys and behind buildings until he came to the livery stable. The place was dark and vacant, except for a scraggly cat crouched in a corner perusing him with a wary gaze. Horses shuffled in their stalls, but otherwise, the place was quiet. Everett crept inside and climbed a ladder up to the loft. He collapsed on the hay and wept with both relief and terror.

Tomorrow he would take the first vessel out of the Charleston port. He didn't care where it was going.

57

CHAPTER FIFTY-SEVEN
CHASING GAMPO

"Ye shouldn't have fought me,"

The voice echoed grotesquely in Keelan's ears as a hot pain flickered across her shoulder. Dry, sweltering darkness swooped down and surrounded her body. She cried out and thrashed until her fist made contact with something hard and warm. A shoulder?

Then, a soft baritone murmured in her ear, and she surfaced, her throat raw and burning from screaming.

"'Tis all right, lass. You are safe now. Hush, Keelan, you're safe, my sweet."

The heat suddenly left, replaced by a strange coolness. She groped for it in the darkness. Long, gentle fingers grasped her hand. A soft kiss fluttered like a butterfly against her palm. Strong arms cradled her head and shoulders. Long fingers stroked her hair. She floated into the comforting arms of Morpheus and dreamed no more.

※

KEELAN STIRRED, moaning softly. She rested on her stomach. The first attempt to open her lids brought forth a blinding light, forcing her to squeeze her eyes shut again. She brought her hand up as a shield and tried to open them once more. A blurry figure rose and moved to the window to pull the shutters closed.

Much better. She tried to focus on the form. "Daniel?" she mumbled, unsure.

"Nay, Keelan, it's me."

The voice was familiar, but her brain was still too fuzzy to be reliable. She was on a straw pallet covered by thick fabric. A soft quilt was drawn up to her shoulders. The bloodstained boy's shirt was gone, and in its place was a long linen one.

The figure dragged a squat, wooden stool to her bedside, then sat. It creaked as he leaned closer.

Landon.

Landon!

He was alive! Thank God.

He reached over and brushed a strand of hair away from her face. "You're in a boarding room above a tavern called The Whistling Pig. How do you feel?"

Her brain behaved as if it were coated with mud. Brief flashes of memory flickered in and out, as she fought to remember the events which brought her here. She struggled to sit up straighter. Bright bolts of fire shot across her shoulders. She sucked in her breath and eased back down to the pallet. The sting forced her memory to return quicker.

"How did you find me?"

"I didn't," he said wryly. "Although I tried. My men searched the streets for you until daybreak. We even kept watch over your uncle's house but never caught sight of you. It was Daniel who came here and found *me*."

He clasped his hands in front of him. A chair sat near the door, Daniel's sack resting against the front legs.

"Where is he now?" she asked.

"I sent him down to get some supper. I thought you might be hungry when you awoke."

As if it heard, her belly let out a loud growl. She gently rolled to her side, facing him. The heat of a blush traveled up her neck and over her cheeks at the sight of his bare chest. Apparently it was a state he found himself in quite often, because his skin had become a dark bronze from the rays of the sun. Ebony hair curled loose around his shoulders and framed his head like a great black mane. A strip of linen was wrapped around his ribs. Dried blood stained a six-inch patch on his side. His stomach was flat and firm, and the tan breeches he wore seemed to fit his body like a second skin.

Keelan snapped her eyes shut. After a second, she glanced furtively at his face and he met her gaze with an amused stare.

The fire in her cheeks was almost more humiliating than getting caught staring. A dark blue waistcoat hung on a hook near the door.

"Are you too warm, Captain Hart? Or is it difficult for you to conform to accepted modes of dress after spending so many months at sea?" She stared at the wall beside his head. It was hard, but she found a small crack in the plaster and so she focused on it. Unfortunately, he was still very visible.

Drat. She should have found a crack further away.

He grinned wider. "I found a more suitable use for my shirt today, Miss Grey," he said, imitating her formal address.

"Oh?" She raised a disbelieving brow. "What could be more suitable than using it to cover yourself in a woman's presence?" Should Daniel return and find the two of them alone in the room with Landon half dressed... well, what would he think?

Landon shrugged, still grinning, "I found someone in greater need than I. That's all. However, if I am offending you, I shall eagerly request it be returned to me, post haste."

She sighed at the guilt his words conjured. He had given his shirt to another in need and she had berated him for it. Her cheeks flamed hotter at his mockery of her stilted admonishment.

She studied her hands and shook her head, ashamed. Her nails were still covered in grime from the warehouse. She pushed up her sleeve to inspect her sore wrists. A bit of bruising and chafing, a couple places where she'd rubbed the top layer of skin off, but no more damage than that.

In the silence, he waited for her response. She finally met his gaze. He was still grinning like a... Well, she didn't know what, but he seemed to find something quite amusing, like a joke he was still waiting for her to comprehend.

She struggled to remember his last question. Something to do with his shirt, yes?

"Nay. I'm sorry. I am just unaccustomed—" She stopped herself. He would think her a child if she admitted she'd never seen a shirtless man before. She reached up, grasped her cuff, and pulled it back down over her arm. It extended well beyond her hand. She stared at it more closely. It wasn't a shift or a nightdress. The realization brought with it another bout of heat across her cheeks and probably her neck as well. Blast it all.

She was wearing a man's shirt.

And if she were given a hundred chances to guess *which* man's shirt, it wouldn't matter. She'd only need one. She fingered the fabric and then instinctively brought the collar to her nose.

And if she'd placed a bet on the name, she'd be right. It was faint, the musky scent of him and the sea and the sun.

She cleared her throat. "I guess what I should say is, I'm unaccustomed to taking the shirt off a man's back."

His dimples deepened. "I insist you keep it. It's much happier on you than it has ever been on me."

That provoked a small smile from her. "How could a shirt possibly show emotion for a person? How does a happy shirt look?"

His expression warmed, and his eyes softened to a darker blue. "I can, for certain, tell this particular shirt loves you. See how it clings to your skin? Like a milk-sopped kitten? It's fallen hopelessly in love with you and yet has only known you a few short hours."

"If that's how you can tell, then most clothes must love their owners because most of them cling in some fashion or another." She tried not to look at his breeches again.

"Oh, not true, young maiden," Landon responded. "I can name several garments who are in extreme discord with their owners. Several of them belong to you, actually." He glanced left and right before whispering, "Renegades, all."

Keelan laughed. She couldn't help it. It was apparent Landon was diverting her attention from more serious matters by setting off on this verbal excursion into frivolity. She shouldn't encourage him, but she couldn't resist either.

"My wardrobe has always been extremely loyal, Captain Hart. Surely, I would know if there were rumors of such a discord."

He brought his hand to his chin, a finger resting across his mouth as if latching his lips shut. He sat up a bit straighter and spoke through his fingers. "Well, I for one have witnessed a few attempted escapes. Your green riding bonnet, for example, used those hideous peacock feathers sewn into the band to take flight from your head not once but twice. If you recall, I returned it to you the first time."

Her lips twitched, and she tried harder to restrain another laugh, because in all honesty, the picture was still vivid in her mind: Landon sitting on his horse, a leg thrown over the saddle horn, appearing as if he was perched on a woman's side saddle, with her bonnet sitting at a jaunty angle on his head. It made her giggle every time she thought of it. This time was no exception.

"And as *I* recall, when it was perched on your head it seemed quite at home."

"Of course it did. It knows a solid equestrian when it encounters one. I imagine it felt safer on my top than yours."

She narrowed her eyes in mock anger. "Then, good riddance to the treasonous article. To abandon a lady in her time of need—how lecherous. And deceitful."

Landon cocked his head as if searching his memory. "I do recall a jacket also left without bidding you a 'good day,' as well."

"I had tied it to my saddle. I thought quite securely," she said dryly.

"Ah, yet it departed, nonetheless. Along with a skirt, and a blouse..." His voice lowered a level. "And a shift, and a chemise, until there were... none."

The lighthearted banter they had been sharing shifted down a deeper, sultry path. The warmth of the day intruded into the room through an open window, and a thin film of perspiration covered her chest and arms.

He'd caught her bathing in a lake a few weeks ago and seemed unwilling to forget it, much to her embarrassment. It had been a foolish, impetuous decision on her part on a stiflingly hot, humid day. She'd had no idea he followed her.

"If I recall correctly, you intruded, *uninvited*, upon a lady bathing." Disrupting a perfectly tranquil moment at the lake where she had floated, peaceful and relaxed, leading to a brief second of shock, then to an intense surge of panic, which then lead to her to floundering for air, taking her deeper into the lake at which time she merely sunk.

And he'd taken his time helping her.

Dimples deepened, making her heart do that stupid flip. "It's a good thing, too. Had I not been there, the lake would have swallowed you whole," he said.

She tossed him a wry frown. "I was sinking, yet you took the time to remove your boots and stockings," she accused. "Although, I understand, taking off one's own boots can be a tedious task," she said. "And could take quite a long time, depending on the fit."

"Aye, but they are handsome boots. Made specifically for my foot by a talented Baracoan cobbler." Landon leaned back on the stool and propped his booted feet across the corner of her bed. The tall black boots were, of course, polished to an ebony shine. "The water would have ruined them."

"So you felt the need to save the boots before the maiden in distress," she countered, unable to still the twitch of her lips. "It makes me wonder where I might rank in the scheme of things in your life."

He took her hand and kissed her fingers. "The angels must tilt their head up to find your spot in my heart, sweet Keelan."

Warmth spread through her chest, down to swirl in her belly. He still wanted her. Did he love her? He'd never said so, but she desperately wished he did. Her heart, she feared, was already hopelessly lost to him, although she wasn't sure how, or if, she could yet admit it to him.

"Your side..." She gestured to the bloodied bandage, desperate to change the subject.

"It's not deep." He glanced at the wrap. "Mrs. Schoen dressed it for me."

The memory of all that blood streaming from his side made her shudder. "Thank you for helping me escape that awful place." A shiver clenched her spine, and she closed her eyes, took a deep breath and pushed away the terrible images from her dream. "You saved my life, of that I'm sure."

"And you saved mine at least once, if not twice," he countered softly. "I am forever in *your* debt, my sweet."

Seizing on the opportunity to take advantage of his silver-tongue, she arched a brow. "If I recall your teachings correctly, in some cultures, you would now owe me a life debt and would have to stay with me until a situation arose where you could save my life in return," she quipped.

A slow grin crept across his face. Azure eyes deepened to a molten navy, swirling with something heated and sensual. "Then I would make sure you were never in danger, so I'd have to stay with you forever."

Her breath hitched. She pressed her palms against her stomach, in a vain effort to keep the darn thing from hatching the thousand butterflies housed there. Why did the man have to be so incredibly handsome? She suddenly realized that she'd protect him with her life if the occasion ever surfaced again.

The vision of Crowe stalking toward Landon's back, blade raised high, invaded her mind. She shuddered.

"Crowe, is he—?"

"Dead? Yes." Landon sobered. Concern lingered in his gaze.

Keelan closed her eyes, sickened. She had killed Gampo's first mate. Her stomach lurched as the bile rose in her throat. A clean chamber pot seemed to appear from thin air as she heaved.

Several wretchedly embarrassing moments later, Landon eased her back to her pillow. From the stool beside her pallet, he studied her, without mockery or disgust. For that, she was grateful and a little less humiliated by losing what small bit had been in her stomach.

"It's understandable, Keelan," he consoled in a low stay voice. "You defended yourself, and me, for that matter. You cannot be blamed for what you did, under the circumstances. It is obvious you are not of the ilk to kill without cause."

"I have never killed a man," she whispered hoarsely. A new fear twisted inside her. "And he wasn't just any man, Landon. He was Gampo's first mate."

Landon's eyes widened for a brief second before they hardened. The muscles in his jaw clenched. "Gampo. He's never pursued us ashore before. He's always tried to intercept us along our trade routes. He's taken this animosity to an elevated level, although I don't understand the cause." Landon rubbed the heels of his hands over his closed eyes. For a moment, he appeared incredibly weary. He leaned his forearms on his knees.

Landon's reaction baffled her. Unless... "Have you seen Gampo before?" she asked.

He shook his head. Again, the vivid azure gaze locked on hers.

Fynn. What had Gampo said about Fynn? Something about a sister?

"It sounded as if Gampo had a personal vendetta against Fynn. What did Fynn do to his sister?"

Landon gave a shrug and shook his head again. "I don't know who his sister is, or was. I don't even know if she's alive or dead. Fynn never mentioned anything about Gampo, other than he was a pig-headed privateer who'd turned into an outright pirate over the years."

"But whatever it was, it's made Gampo your enemy, too." She stilled at the other thoughts pounding a warning inside her head. "Now, I'm his enemy as well."

Landon's eyes clouded as he nodded. "This development changes things. You aren't safe here. I must get you out of Charleston as soon as possible." There was something else hiding in the depths of those dark blue irises. A flicker of anger? Fear? Distrust?

Landon rubbed his forehead and closed his eyes. After a moment, he added, "Gampo overheard our conversation, Keelan. He's connected you to me now."

When she'd escaped down the warehouse steps, he'd called out to her.

"You will not escape me, Keelan Grey!"

Landon picked up her hand and rubbed little circles over her knuckles, sending little zips of lightning up her arms. "He will seek me out to find *you*."

Keelan's brow furrowed. "So what do we do?"

Landon took a deep breath, expelled it, and stared down at his hands. "We must separate. The sooner you are safely away from Charleston, the better. I'll arrange for you to travel with a friend of mine. Although he doesn't normally take passengers, he will take you and Daniel to safety. His ship is scheduled to depart tomorrow for Philadelphia. When you arrive, leave a message as to your location with the harbormaster, he's a friend. I'll find you."

A pang of disappointment pressed into her heart. She wanted to stay with him. Gampo would seek them out, but it didn't matter. Landon was her haven. She felt safer with him than without him. Besides, who would watch his back?

His voice still echoed earnest and warm in her ears: *"Sail away with me, Keelan. Let me show you the world..."*

His jaw clenched, and he paused before he captured her gaze again. "This war with Gampo has to end. I'm unwilling to put your life at risk or constantly worry about your safety. Once Conal and I hunt down Gampo and end this, I'll sail to Philadelphia. I have friends there who will take care of you until I return."

A painful stretching sensation gripped her heart. She didn't want to leave him. If the pirate fled Charleston, how far would Landon have to chase Gampo? To the Caribbean? South America? How long would she wait and worry in Philadelphia, not knowing if he was alive or dead?

This was no longer solely his battle. It was hers now, too.

"No," her voice was low but firm. "I won't run away and hide while you put your life in danger for me. I'm not a coward."

"Keelan, love—" he began.

"No." She cut him off before he could ply his honeyed words and infuriating logic. She wasn't going to give him a chance to try to change her mind. "I won't go anywhere except with you."

He sighed and tried again. "My ship hasn't been fully repaired and restored yet. You can't stay in Charleston. The longer you stay, the greater the chance Gampo's men will find you. I'm not able to accommodate you as efficiently. Besides, you'll be safer if you *aren't* with me. Gampo would be a fool to engage the *USS Glory*. You'll be protected."

She pressed her lips into a thin line.

Stubborn man.

Well, she could be just as determined. "You don't understand what

I'm saying, Landon. I don't want to be protected and safe unless I'm with you. Besides, I'm not helpless."

He rolled his eyes in exasperation. "While I admire your courage and skill with blades and swords, battles at sea are nothing like training exercises in a forest meadow with a man old enough to be your father."

Anger flared. "What are you saying? My skills aren't good enough to prevent me from being a burden rather than a self-sufficient member of your crew?" How dare he. She lifted her chin and lowered her brows.

He shifted on the stool and scratched the back of his head before answering, "I wouldn't have said it in those words, but, yes. You'd distract me. I'd worry I wouldn't be able to take care of you."

"I can take care of myself!" she snapped, indignant. Annoyed now. Why was he being so obstinate? "I have an idea," she continued hotly. "*You* travel on the *USS Glory* and *I'll* go after Gampo. I'll come fetch you when the battle is ended. You can stay with your friends and wait for me."

Landon flung his arms out wide. "That's preposterous!"

"How so?" she asked. "It's your plan."

"My plan is to keep you safe! I'd never leave you to battle Gampo alone," he snapped back.

"Exactly!"

"You—what? You agreed with me," he said warily.

He was so infuriating, she could scream. She jabbed her finger in his direction. "I can't let you leave me behind to battle Gampo alone. It's would be as hard for me as it would be for you, if we changed places."

He shook his head in bewilderment. "Keelan, it's completely different."

"It is *not*."

"It is *too*." His expression had darkened and when a knock sounded at the door, he barked, "Who's there?"

"Tis Mrs. Schoen, sir."

He rose from his seat, then scowling, pointed at her. "This discussion is not over."

"Damn right, it's not!" she retorted back.

He paused for a moment and stared at her with lowered brows, but she met his stare with a determined intensity. He reached the door and jerked it open.

A plump, cheery-faced woman waddled in, tray on her hip and a pitcher in her hand. "Och! Goot. Yur awake. I haf something for yu to eat, my dear." Her smile was wide and warm. She shifted her attention to Landon. "Herr Hart, der iss a man waiting for yu downstairs. He says it iss urgent." She nodded toward Keelan. "I vould like to tend to der young woman's wounds, if is ok?"

"Of course, Frau Schoen." He yanked his jacket from the hook, and Keelan caught the slight grimace as he shrugged it on. He bent down and spoke quietly in Mrs. Shoen's ear.

She nodded her head vigorously.

He inclined his head, *"Danke."*

Wait! Don't go!

Keelan bit her lower lip to keep herself from blurting out those words. Contrary to what Landon believed, she felt safer with him than she did without him. She'd worry less about him, certainly.

Landon paused and glanced back over his shoulder at her. "I will speak with Daniel regarding the details of your departure once I have secured them. God speed, Keelan."

He left.

Blast that stubborn man! If he thought she was going to sit idly by and do his will like a reticent little girl, then he was most surely mistaken.

CHAPTER FIFTY-EIGHT
A GIFT

By the next morning, the pain in Keelan's back and feet had eased a small amount. She sat up in bed enjoying an omelet flavored with small pieces of shallots and parsley, several mutton sausages, hot tea and bannocks made from Indian corn meal. She smoothed the front of Landon's long shirt she still wore. She really wanted the trunk and clothes she'd left at Jared's, although it was doubtful there was a safe way to get to them now.

A thump sounded outside her door. She heard a dull scraping sound as if something heavy was being pushed over the wooden plank floor. Following a light rap, the door opened a crack.

Mrs. Schoen poked her head in and grinned. "Goot morgen child. You are enjoying der food? I vill return to dress your wounds shortly, ya?"

Keelan smiled. "Thank you, Mrs. Schoen. Everything is delicious."

The woman grinned again. "Der is some ting here for you." She nudged the door wide and pushed a new standard trunk into the room.

Keelan eyed it curiously as she enjoyed her scone. Gesturing to the trunk, she said, "I am afraid you are mistaken, Mrs. Schoen. That's not mine."

The gleaming brass rivets and hinges contrasted starkly with the blunt walls, lumpy pallet, and rickety wooden chairs.

"It vas delivered this morgen. The man said to give you dis note." She handed over a small calling card.

It was Landon Hart's. He had written a message on the back, which she read quickly.

⊙⊱⊙

JARED AND EVERETT at all costs. Do not return or send for your property. There are men looking for you both in town and in the country. My friend Commodore Hall will take you to Philadelphia tomorrow aboard the USS Glory. *Daniel is in agreement and will accompany you. I've known the Schoen's a long time. You can trust them to keep your secrets. Any communications to me should be sent through them. I hope the contents of the trunk suit you well.*

Your Servant,

Landon

⊙⊱⊙

HA. Did he think Daniel's acquiescence to his arrangements would sway her mind? Although her anger and frustration had subsided since his departure, her convictions had not. Let him try to keep her from going with him.

Curious though, she climbed out of the bed and accepted the key from Mrs. Schoen and knelt to unlock the trunk. As she lifted the lid, she heard the Innkeeper's wife draw in a slow breath.

"Ooooh!" Mrs. Schoen said from over her shoulder. "Dat iss yust vat you need, ya? Iss goot."

She touched the soft silk chemise and stockings. "Oh, yes," she answered softly. "It's very, *very* good." Sliding several undergarments aside revealed two beautiful gowns. One was a soft gray, the other a deep green. A velvet cloak of the same dark green lay folded beneath the gowns. She also found two pair of slippers tucked neatly into the bottom, along with a bonnet identical to the one she lost during the stormwithout the feathers. She smiled.

"Would you please bring up some writing supplies? I must write a note of thanks to Captain Hart."

Mrs. Schoen nodded knowingly and grinned. "I will bring up to you."

In her note, she thanked Landon for the clothes. She also told him she appreciated his efforts to get her and Daniel safely to Philadelphia.

She didn't say, however, she would actually go.

⚜

THE NEXT DAY Keelan was able to move about the room with relative ease. Her back would be sore for days, but Mrs. Schoen's constant tending had kept infection at bay and sped the healing process. There were few places on her body that weren't sore or tender, and after spending the last two days prone, her joints were creaky and weak. To get her legs limber again, she limped about the room. She had donned the new chemise and stockings, but with a defined shudder had omitted the corset. Her attempt at putting on the gown was met with partial success as she stepped into the skirt and pulled the bodice up over her shoulders. The fit was amazingly accurate. Either Landon was fairly talented at estimating a lady's size or extremely lucky.

Eager to be on her way, she packed Landon's now clean and dry coat into the trunk he had sent yesterday, along with his shirt. Pausing, she ran her hand over the fabric. He'd provided a way to contact him through the Schoens, and it gave her a calmer sense of strength and faith. A knock on the door jarred her from her musings. "Come in," she beckoned.

Daniel stepped into the room. His concerned gaze searched her face beseechingly. "I have been so worried. Mrs. Schoen kept assuring me you were healing well, but I finally had to see for myself."

She smiled. "I'm glad you're here. I am much better, as you can see." She moved toward the open door. "I have a strong need for some air and a short walk. Would you stroll with me a bit?" she asked.

Daniel fidgeted. "I am afraid I have some bad news."

Her first thought was of Slaney. "Bad news?" The maid's ship had sailed a few days ago. "What is it?"

"At Captain Hart's suggestion, I have been spending the last two days down at the docks. He hopes to find out who had you kidnapped. He seems to think Gampo wouldn't have gone to this length, putting his crew in peril, unless he had an advantage of some sort. An informant or man in Charleston who could give him access to important information."

"That seems to be a lot to accomplish."

Daniel shrugged and added, "The captain believes they are connected and one man is responsible."

"Connected?" This was confusing. "I don't understand how I could be connected with the events surrounding Captain Hart's cargo theft."

Giving her a thoughtful look, he suggested, "Jared Grey owned *both* warehouses involved in the theft. The one originally storing the goods, and also the one used to hide them."

The connection was easy to identify. Keelan sucked in her breath. "Captain Hart mentioned that. I had forgotten. He thinks Jared might be involved?" She was convinced now Dr. Garrison was behind the series of tragic events surrounding her family and her, but she couldn't fathom why he'd involve Captain Hart.

"It's possible that he's a common link." Daniel acknowledged. "However, that doesn't mean that he's responsible. It could be someone who works for him, someone who would have access to the keys. There's no solid proof yet. The few pirates they captured the night he found you have refused to talk. Sheriff Pinkerton hopes their tongues will loosen when they are paraded past the gallows."

Everett could be involved, although the sudden transformation from a bumbling, yet well-meaning physician to a deranged kidnapper was hard to believe. A cold sensation skittered up her spine. It may not be that far a leap from a deranged jilted beau to a deranged kidnapper.

"What is your bad news then?" she asked.

"Mr. Schoen told me Gampo's men are searching for you."

"I know, Captain Hart mentioned it in his note."

"There is a reward for your capture, now." Daniel hesitated before continuing and eyed her carefully, "You are wanted for the murder of a man named Crowe."

Keelan gaped at Daniel. It was a moment before she could speak.

"Murder! But—he—I did not mean to—he was about to stab Captain Hart!" She inhaled deeply and drew herself taller. "Take me to the sheriff this moment. I am sure once he hears all the details—"

"No, Mistress." Daniel shook his head. "Captain Hart fears if your location is known, your life would be in danger. You must understand, Keelan, it is not the law who wants you. It's *Gampo*. Descriptions of you have been given to most of the dockworkers and any ship's crew still in port, along with the promise of quite a large reward for finding you."

A sudden frigid blade of dread sliced through her, as the meaning of Daniel's message sank in. Keelan's hand crept shakily to her throat, where she could feel the erratic pulse of her heart, and she sat down with an unladylike thump.

The manservant sighed heavily. "I'm sorry. You simply cannot be seen in this city as Keelan Grey, without risk of capture by thugs employed by Gampo, or those eager for his coin."

"No wonder Landon's note said to avoid sending for my property or going back to the town house." Keelan swallowed and met the valet's determined stare.

"There's more, Miss Keelan." He took a note from his pocket. "The harbormaster gave this to me. Commodore Hall received an urgent request to set sail to Philadelphia posthaste to fend off a British block-ade. They left yesterday at dawn."

"Oh. Well, good." She almost smiled. Landon's plan had failed of its own accord. He'd have no choice now but to let her go with him to find Gampo.

"Good?" Daniel looked at her curiously.

She glanced out the window, a bit embarrassed. "Captain Hart and I had a small disagreement with regard to the trip to Philadelphia on the *USS Glory*."

Daniels lips twitched. "Ah, then."

At her raised brows, he clarified, "It explains the state of irritation he was in when he and I spoke yesterday."

"He was being unreasonable," she mumbled.

Daniel cocked his head and grinned, unable to remain stoic any longer. "He said as much about you."

She might be stubborn, but she'd come out the victor this time. The walls of the small rustic room heaved in even closer. She wasn't sure she had the fortitude to hide out in the attic of The Whistling Pig for too much longer. Already, the heat and the cramped space made her long for fresh air and a brisk walk. "We should get word to Captain Hart straight away."

Daniel ran his bony fingers through his hair and shook his head. "I tried, but the *Desire* loaded her cargo yesterday evening and set sail down the coast early this morning, just prior to the *USS Glory*."

A small thunderstorm blossomed in Keelan's chest.

He left her behind! Landon weighed anchor to draw Gampo and his men away from Charleston and her. He was probably in the midst of a sea battle right now. Stubborn, unreasonable man!

How could he depart when he told her only yesterday the repairs weren't yet complete? Unless... unless he'd been *lying* yesterday.

An even more horrible thought floated to the top of her mind. Was he trying to get *rid* of her?

Putting her on Commodore Hall's frigate and also saying the *Desire* was not ready to sail was easier than telling her he'd changed his mind. He sailed *south*. In the opposite direction she was to go. Was he *fleeing* from her?

A loud rush of noise filled her ears, and the skin on her face prickled as if a thistle had been tossed at it. Maybe he didn't believe her when she'd told him Garrison's kiss was unwanted and undesired. He may have decided he couldn't trust her. Perhaps he'd come to the conclusion that having a woman in his life was simply too much trouble. Maybe seeing Garrison kiss her had brought back too many painful memories. A thousand thoughts and fears bombarded her head.

Slaney had warned her. Mother had warned her. She had warned herself.

A man of the sea always returns to the sea.

She recalled all her fears about falling in love with Landon Hart, all the reasons why she shouldn't have allowed herself to fall for his charms, all the warnings... But she had wanted to believe him, wanted to hope they could be happy together but those things had betrayed her, blinded her.

It had been foolish to ignore the warnings.

She would never be able to take the place of his first love, a life of adventure upon the sea.

A horrible empty chasm opened in her chest and sucked in every moment of happiness, every second of bliss, every shard of hope into darkness. leaving nothing but raw desolation in its wake.

He was gone.

Tears burned in her eyes. She'd hoped a fool's hope. So much had transpired over the past day. Landon's love for his ship and the prosperity of his business remained the most important parts of his life. A trip north would endanger him and his crew. Gampo's sole purpose now was finding and punishing *her*. Even worse, Landon and his fleet were not the targets of Gampo's revenge, *she* was. He could be simply taking advantage of the distraction she provided so he could flee unnoticed. But that was a coward's route and she may not have known Landon Hart very long, but she did know enough about him to understand that he was no coward.

She wanted so desperately to believe Landon cared about her and was trying to protect her. Still, she'd known him only a few weeks. Was he capable of such deceit and treachery? Was she so blinded by her attraction to him? It's possible his true nature hid behind his handsome features and charm, like Garrison's had hidden behind his gentle demeanor and kindness.

Daniel waited patiently for her to regain her attention. She'd known him her entire life and could tell he had more to divulge. She immediately read the expression on his face. "You already have a plan," she stated.

Daniel bit back a smile. "Yes, I do."

She took a breath and released it. "And I can tell I'm not going to like it much."

The corners of Daniels mouth twitched before he grinned. "No, Mistress, you are not going to like it at all."

✣ 59 ✣

CHAPTER FIFTY-NINE
THE DISGUISE

"I've managed to gain some interesting information," Daniel said, "Mr. and Mrs. Schoen seem to have a network of informants in the area. They might be able to help us." Daniel plucked his sack from the hook by the door and started looking through it. "I suspect the couple either harbors runaway slaves or provides information to assist them."

"I wondered about that," Keelan murmured. There'd been something about Landon's familiarity with the couple and a comment he'd made about gleaning information from them that had her curious, but there hadn't been an opportunity to ask for elaboration.

"Mrs. Schoen told me she'd heard Gampo wasn't the man in charge of Hart's cargo theft or the kidnapping," Daniel said. "Gampo has a silent employer, but no one seemed to know his name."

Keelan paced the floor. "As hard as it is to believe, I strongly suspect Dr. Garrison is involved somehow." His behavior these past few weeks changed. Drastically.

"He could have let the kidnappers into the house," Daniel mused, nodding.

She paused as her mind began to make other connections. "He had access to the warehouse keys." Daniel stopped rummaging and gave her his full attention.

The more she thought about it, the more sense it made. "It would have been easy for Garrison to borrow any of Jared's warehouse keys," she said. "Uncle Jared kept a spare set in his desk at Twin Pines." The full realization of what she was saying was overwhelming. She abruptly sat on the stool by her bed. Dread settled on her shoulders as a darker thought seeped into her mind. It was horrible. Ludicrous. Yet—made sense, somehow. "He's too smart to get personally involved, which could explain why no one captured at the warehouse knows the name of their employer.

"But why?" Daniel asked, shocked. "Why would he do such a thing?"

The doctor had been pleased that she was of no blood kin to the commodore. That fact had been important to him. "The passenger ship Papa accidentally destroyed," she thought aloud. "The assassin began targeting Papa's family shortly after the court martial." She clasped her hands together until her fingers ached, not wanting to accept what her mind was nudging her toward.

Daniel nodded. "Your mother's carriage accident was first. The commodore's brother's family was killed shortly after. Then the commodore became ill."

"Dr. Garrison mentioned something about losing loved ones at sea," she said, certain now that she was correct. Daniel's eyes widened, and he finished her thought for her. "This is all about revenge, isn't it?"

"If he had loved ones on the ship, he has reason to be angry."

Now she understood. *Rachel.*

More than once, he had called Keelan by that name. He carried a tattered letter from Rachel in his coat pocket, expressing her happy anticipation of their wedding day. Keelan's throat went dry.

Good Lord.

"It has to be Dr. Garrison," she breathed, glad she was seated.

"But what about the commodore's older brother?" Daniel asked. "Garrison was here when he was killed."

One didn't have to be present to be involved, did they? "He had Gampo's help here," she said. "He could have had another man's help in England."

"True." Daniel paced the small room. "When I spoke to Captain

Hart, he said he suspected his ship was being watched. The other piers had spies as well, along with Mr. Grey's house in Charleston." He paused and looked at her, concerned. "That means that *both* Gampo and Garrison are searching for you."

"I'll wear my sparring clothes and boots and disguise myself as a boy." She had fooled Landon Hart and Conal O'Brien the day she met them, hadn't she? And at close proximity.

Daniel's gaze lingered on her long auburn tresses. "You'll have to cut it, you know."

She sighed and waved her hand. "It's hair. It will grow back."

A quick knock broke into their conversation. Daniel stepped over to the door and opened it. Mrs. Schoen bustled in, bringing with her a strong odor of burned ham and carrying a bucket and several rags. She sat it on the small table. Straightening, she put her hands on her hips. "You haf' to leave. Der is no time to wait for anudder ship to come going north to Philadelphia. You must leave now. I vill help."

"What? Why?" The sudden turn of events was a surprise. She glanced at Daniel. The grim set of his mouth told her he wasn't as shocked as she.

"Gampo's men are downstairs," Mrs. Schoen said in a hushed voice. "They asked to inspect the rooms for rent and I suspect if we deny them, they will make tings difficult."

Keelan pressed a hand over her thundering heart. Would the pirates insist on searching the attic? Either way, she wasn't ready to find out.

Mrs. Schoen put the rags in the bucket and continued, "A ship leaves at sunrise in der morgen. My husband has arranged for yu employment. I vill work to hide you better, so you can leave here safely."

"I have a set of boy's clothes and boots," Keelan said, glancing at Daniel, hoping he was right and the Schoen's could be trusted.

Mrs. Schoen lifted a strand of Keelan's hair and shook her head. "Is not enough to change your clothing. Your hair is like a beacon. We must extinguish it or you vill be discovered."

"Extinguish it, how?" What solution was the woman about to offer? Cutting her hair was fine, but she wasn't about to shave her head.

"It's too risky for her to try to travel as a woman," Daniel said. "We could simply cut her hair and wrap it in a scarf or hide it under a hat."

"Und if der wind took der hat? Her hair got out of der scarf? She would be spotted immediately, and turned over to Gampo," Mrs. Schoen said. She pointed to the bucket. "I've made a dye. It vill stain your skin for several days. You vill not be noticed."

Keelan sat in silent surrender as Daniel trimmed her auburn mane up to her shoulders.

Mrs. Schoen merrily scooped up the fallen tresses. "Der local toy maker vill be so happy to have dis beautiful hair for his dolls."

She hoped he would pay Mrs. Schoen well for delivering the long red curls. It was the least she could do for the woman who had taken such good care of her and Daniel.

The next step was applying the dark brown stain to their skin. Made out of boiled black oak bark, black walnut hulls, a small amount of molasses and soot from a burned hog carcass, it was pungent but effective. Daniel left to pack his things, giving Keelan and Mrs. Schoen some privacy to apply the dye.

Several times, Mrs. Schoen soaked a rag in the mixture and rubbed it over Keelan's arms, legs, face and neck. She carefully dabbed the dye around the wounds on her shoulders and back, then for good measure ran it through her hair.

"A little less like a flame, eh?" she had asked, grinning.

A little more like a tiger.

She had to admit, it did mute the auburn tones quite a bit. She picked up the rag and rubbed it through the rest of her hair.

When it was all said and done, Keelan could pass for any one of several nationality types. And she smelled very much like a charred ham.

Mrs. Schoen bade her a cheerful farewell and left to deliver the bucket of dye to Daniel.

Keelan almost didn't recognize him when he returned. "Well?" he said as he turned before her.

"You look like a Spaniard I once met," she replied, grinning.

"We are Persian," he corrected. "I am Kahlil, a horse trainer, and you are my son, Mahdi."

Mrs. Schoen appeared at the door. "It is time to go. My husband has served Gampo's men a sample of his new bier." She grinned. "He is walking among them asking dem how dey like it. Dey are not noticing der back door now."

Keelan and Daniel moved as quietly as they could along the upstairs hallway, but it wasn't easy carrying her new trunk. She looked at the narrow stairwell warily. Not only was it narrow, the steps were steep. Unfortunately, not only was it the only passage to the first floor, it also ended at the back of the common room.

Mrs. Schoen went ahead of Daniel and waited at the bottom, holding open the kitchen door. Daniel heaved the end of the chest up and led the way, taking most of the weight. However, she, stooped over and panting from the strain, still struggled with the back end. Each step down was precarious and stretched the tender wounds on her back.

Daniel reached the lower landing and turned toward the kitchen door. They'd made it. She let out an audible sigh of relief when her foot touched the last step.

Except...it wasn't the last step.

Her miscalculation threw her off balance and slammed her into the wall, jarring the trunk from her grasp. It fell to the floor with a loud bang.

She froze. The room became deathly silent. Scowling and scarred faces turned their way. Her heart hit the walls of her chest; she was too terrified to breathe.

Mrs. Schoen's eyes widened.

Oh no. What had she done?

Mrs. Schoen recovered first and stomped her foot, releasing her hold on the door. "Vat are you doing?" She reached over and slapped the side of Keelan's head. "You clumsy boy! I told you to be careful! Now pick up dat trunk and pay attention or I'll take my husband's belt to yur hide!" She jerked open the door to the kitchen. "Git going! And have a care, dis time."

The men's attention shifted back to their drinks and conversation resumed. Daniel gave Keelan a relieved nod. She grasped the handle and followed him into the kitchen. Mrs. Schoen held open the far back door leading to the back alley. Once they made it outside, they lowered the trunk to the ground for a moment's rest.

Mrs. Schoen cast a furtive glance up and down the alley. "I tink you vill be goot from here." She gave Keelan an apologetic smile. "I hope I didn't swat your noggin too hard."

"I'm fine." She threw her arms around the woman's neck. "Thank you for helping us."

Mrs. Schoen patted the back of her head and kissed her cheek. "Yur velcome, child. God bless, and goot luck. Yu vill always be welcome here."

❧ 60 ❧

CHAPTER SIXTY
NEW HANDS

Keelan and Daniel could have been any light brown-skinned man and his son as they shuffled along the street. Both held tightly to opposite handles of the trunk. Daniel's soiled gray sack was perched on the lid and tied with a short piece of rope.

It was a bright, sunny spring afternoon in Charleston. King Street was a flurry of activity as hawkers scurried about setting up their carts with wares of every sort, vegetables, jams, wine, fruits, baskets, brightly colored yarns, meat pies, smoked hams, candles, livestock and a plethora of other necessities both big and small. Women tried to save the hems of their skirts by jumping over the slimy stream of malodorous run-off oozing along the curb, then stepping lightly across the slippery cobblestones, careful to avoid the piles of waste deposited by the various beasts of burden traveling the streets.

Daniel stopped at the base of a ramp leading up to a large ship. It had three tall masts and a variety of canoes and longboats attached to the sides.

"Must have been a whaling ship at one time." Daniel tilted his head up and examined vessel.

Keelan caught her breath as she read the name painted on the side.

The *Seeker*. Captain Conal O' Brien's ship, part of the same merchant fleet as Landon's ship, the *Desire*.

Captain O'Brien probably planned to follow the *Desire* south to Harbour Town, so their fleet of three could reunite and sail together. She'd almost balked when she learned they'd have to travel on the *Seeker*. If Landon didn't want her with him, why accept passage on a ship guaranteed to travel with him? He'd think she was chasing him like a loose duck, feeding his arrogance. Except, she *would* have chased him like a loose duck, anyway. She wasn't about to let him go south without her, or without telling her the truth about how he felt about her.

It didn't matter, the *Seeker* was not just their best choice, it was their only choice.

A stout, grizzled sailor sat on a small wooden crate near the ramp. He raised a shaggy brow as they lowered the trunk, and Daniel straightened to full height. He withdrew a tattered handkerchief from his sleeve to mop his face. He replaced the cloth and approached the sailor.

"I beg your pardon, sir. We have come at the suggestion of Mr. Schoen to inquire about employment. Does this vessel require additional hands?"

Keelan rounded her shoulders and did her best to look inconsequential?

The sailor scratched his chin thoughtfully as he eyed both of them.

Her fingers twitched nervously, and she studied the sailor's countenance. He was likely wondering if their claim to have been sent by Mr. Schoen was true. If he decided it was false, he'd reject them; they'd have to travel by land, which would be much more dangerous. They'd be mistaken for runaways, for sure.

She glanced at Daniel. They had dressed carefully. Their clothes were well-worn but clean. Both wore sturdy leather boots. Daniel's graying hair was pulled back and tied with a short yellow ribbon. Her now shoulder-length brown hair was secured in a similar manner. Mrs. Schoen had given her a worn straw hat. It flopped lazily on her head and she was glad for the protection from the sun, as well as from prying eyes.

"Aye, Schoen mentioned ye. We'll take ye." He held out his hand. "Name's Henry."

"I'm Khalil." Daniel shook it, then gave the sailor a brief bow. "This is my son, Mahdi."

"What skills bring ye to this ship?" Henry asked.

Daniel placed his hand on her shoulder. "This lad can cipher well. He can also cook and is knowledgeable in the use of healing herbs. I can also cipher and care for livestock. We can both handle arms of almost any kind." He drew himself up straight and raised his chin. "We are hard workers and have strong backs. While we have never worked aboard such a fine ship as this, we are quick learners."

Henry continued to study the two before him. Was Daniel's refined speech was confusing him?

"Are ye wanted for any crimes in the colonies or against the Crown?"

Daniel shook his head. "Nay, sir."

The sailor nodded, satisfied. "We lost our cook's helper a few weeks back, so the lad..." he nodded toward Keelan, "might be of use." He squinted at the older man. "How well do ye handle horses?"

"I ran a stable for my employer in England. Until his recent death, I also served as his personal servant."

The sailor nodded again. "That explains the way ye speak. The hold contains four horses, which are quite valuable. We needs a horse master with skills for care and healing. One of the mares thrashed about as we loaded her and has a nasty gash in her foreleg along with a couple of other scrapes."

Daniel felt that posing as Persians should help them avoid too much speculation from slave traders regarding their cultural orientation. Daniel had good instincts.

"Ship sails tomorrow. First light." Henry jerked his head in the direction of the ship. "Go on up and talk to Remus. Mention Schoen sent ye."

Daniel inclined his head in gratitude. "We thank you, sir."

Keelan reached down, grasped the handle, and helped Daniel heave the trunk up the plank. So far, Daniel's plan was working, thank the Lord.

The man named Remus sat on a barrel near the mainmast, a large leather-bound book perched on his knees. Mousy, brown hair hung straight down to his jaw. He was thick and muscled, making the book seem tiny in his hands. Daniel reiterated his conversation with Henry.

Remus tucked the front strands behind his ears neatly as he spoke. "Wages are one pound sixteen shillings a month total fer the two of ye. Ye'll start earning today, and at first landfall, ye can request half of what ye have earned be paid to ye. Ye'll git the rest of yer pay after the month. Ye should know we must first sail south to Harbour Town before we can deliver ye to Philadelphia."

Harbour Town. They were indeed following the *Desire* south instead of traveling north.

She stepped back. Why did Remus say "before we can deliver ye to Philadelphia" rather than saying "Before we can make sail for Philadelphia?" Did his assumption have anything to do with their association with the Schoens? Did Landon leave the Schoens with explicit instructions to get her north?

If Landon had changed his mind about wanting her with him, then the next best plan for her would be to travel back to England from Philadelphia. Her mind worked furiously. Yet, he had originally told her to stay there with his friends until he'd taken care of Gampo, hadn't he?

What if he hadn't changed his mind about wanting her and instead had lured Gampo away from her? She huffed a frustrated sigh. Too many questions. Not enough answers.

Go back to what I know.

Landon had made sure she couldn't defy his will, and put herself at risk by securing her passage via the *USS Glory*. If he didn't want her with him, then he'd not care where she went. Instead, he made sure everyone involved in her transport (including the Schoens) would take her north to Philadelphia. He'd expected her to be on the *USS Glory,* though, so the *Seeker* could set her course to trail Landon. If he left before the *Glory* departed, he'd have no way of knowing she'd been unable to board the warship.

While he went south to engage Gampo.

Was the captain of the *Seeker* aware Landon was taking on the pirate alone? She set her jaw. As soon as they were aboard, she'd seek out Captain O'Brien and inform him of her suspicions. Surely, he would know what was going on.

Daniel glanced at Keelan, oblivious to her thoughts. "It might put us behind Jared's letter to the London barristers, but we have no choice," he murmured for her ears only. "Hopefully, Slaney will get to the trunk before the estate auction takes place. Either way, we must leave Charleston now and get as far away from Gampo as possible."

As hot as the desire burned in her heart to find her sire, the trunk and its contents, it all meant nothing compared to Landon's life and safety.

She'd go south.

⚜

THE SAILOR NAMED Remus eyed Keelan and Daniel. "Any man who leaves the ship before the cargo is off, will forgo the second half his wages. They will be split into equal shares and given to those who stayed and finished the work. Do ye understand these terms?"

Both nodded vigorously.

"Then sign yer name or make yer mark here." He pointed to the column next to the one where he had printed their names and salary. Daniel stepped forward and dipped the ragged feather quill into the inkwell. He brushed the first drop on the rim, then signed his name and gave the quill to her.

She picked up the quill and dipped it into the ink, a slight tremor in her hand.

"First time at sea, lad?" Remus asked, a friendly tone to his voice.

For a moment, Keelan wasn't sure what to say. How should a boy named Mahdi speak? Henry didn't seem to think it odd when Daniel spoke in his clipped British accent. It would be easier if she didn't have to stray too far from her real self. It was hard enough to walk like a boy. She took a chance and simply lowered her voice a little. If Daniel could get away with speaking in his natural dialect, then so could she.

Daniel gently nudged her with his elbow, making her jump.

"Oh! Uhh. N—no. No, sir. I've been on a ship before, once—last year," she spoke so softly Remus had to lean closer to hear.

"Well, then. You should get along just fine." He reached over and clapped her on the shoulder, but almost fell off his barrel at the pained shriek he got in response.

"Don't!" she reacted on impulse, pulling away from the sailor and then stumbling to her knees, blinded by the pain. He'd inadvertently struck the deepest gash across her shoulder blade.

Remus froze, uncertain what to do or say next.

Daniel's face paled.

Her lips trembled as she spoke in a tortured whisper, "I'm sorry."

Remus scowled at her, obviously offended at her disrespectful manner. Daniel jumped forward to extend a hand. Grimacing, she grasped it and allowed herself to be pulled upright. Dear God, what had she done? She'd just ruined everything. Remus surely just realized she was a female by her screech of pain, unless he thought she was a young lad who's voice had not yet changed.

She prayed it was the latter.

Reaching up, she jammed the hat lower over her brow then slid behind Daniel, fists clenched at her sides as she tried to behave in a more humble manner. She could only breathe in ragged jerks. A sick dizziness threatened to pitch her to the deck. Tears burned in the back of her eyes and she fought hard to prevent them from spilling. How could she pass for a boy if she cried like a girl? Dread seeped through her veins. Had she ruined everything? She stared at the deck, awaiting the consequences of her actions.

Daniel attempted to regain his composure as he bent close to Remus's ear and whispered confidingly, "I left him for a few days with Mrs. Schoen while I sought work. I fear he's been a bit abused by one of the tavern patrons. Please do not take offense to the lad. I'm sure he won't be quite as sensitive to touch once the lashes on his back heal."

Remus' eyebrows shot up, then his features smoothed with under-standing. "Right then. Follow me and I'll show you the crew's quarters." With one last wary glance at her, he hopped off his barrel.

Keelan forced herself to steady her breathing. To distract her mind from the pain, she took note of the vessel they toured. The ship was long and broad with a lot of men moving about the deck getting the ship sea-ready. Barrels were lashed to the bases of two masts; the third had livestock fencing around it. Remus proceeded toward the main hatch, then down the steps to the lower deck.

So far, their plan was working, but neither one would let out a sigh of relief or let down their guard until they were free of Gampo, or on the grounds of WindBriar, whichever worked out for the best. She'd hear it from Landon's mouth before she made any more assumptions about whether or not he truly wanted her.

This plan had to work.

She clenched her teeth together in determination. Their plan *would* work; she'd make sure of it. Fingering the ring strung on the chain around her neck, her resolve grew.

They followed Remus down into the galley. He nodded to a slender, pale man pouring over a leather-bound book. "This is Marcel," he stated.

Marcel placed a short frayed ribbon on the page to mark his place, then slapped it shut.

"*Oui?* And who have we here?" he questioned in a thick accent.

Remus urged his charge forward. "This is Mahdi. He's your new cook's boy. He knows a bit about kitchens and healing herbs. He's taking young Billy's place," Remus said.

The Frenchman sighed and cast a skeptical perusal over Keelan. "And what would a boy like you know about working in zee galley?"

She squared her shoulders and took a deep breath, then lowered her voice as best she could, "I can make scones, bread and tea cakes. I can dress a chicken and smoke a ham. I can whip eggs and heavy cream fast enough, too."

Marcel cocked his head in surprise and then laughed. "We don't serve high tea to His Majesty here, but if you can make those things, you can learn to make hard tack. Come zen. We must first make a list for zee last of zee supplies we should buy at zee market and apothecary shop." He stopped and peered at the lad quizzically. "Can you write?"

She nodded. Finally, she offered something of value.

"*Bien*. Let us begin."

✥ 61 ✥

CHAPTER SIXTY-ONE
TO MARKET

It was not long before Keelan and Marcel were weaving their way through the crowded aisles of the large market near the waterfront. Marcel stopped at one of the stalls and began to negotiate intently with a short, wrinkled woman over the price of ropes of garlic and dried peppers.

Keelan's olfactory senses were bombarded with fresh and rotting fruit, livestock of all kinds, and the sharp tang of humanity in general. Thankfully, a slight breeze wafted in from the sea and helped to dissipate the odors a bit. It was still humid, and the bandages serving to both protect her wounds and bind her breasts were already damp with sweat. She was grateful for the large straw hat Mrs. Schoen had given her. It protected her head from the merciless rays of the sun and hid her face from inquiring eyes. While confident with her disguise, she was not willing to press her luck.

"You there, boy!"

Her shoulder was jostled lightly, and she jumped back, grabbing her hat before it flew with the breeze.

Keelan looked up and gasped.

Standing before her was Simon.

It was the first time she had ever seen the house slave from Twin

Pines appear irritated. In her presence, his face had always been a mask of somber servitude.

Simon frowned at her. "I asked you a question, boy. Don' you got the manners to answer?" He pulled out a faded green handkerchief and mopped his brow and cheeks as he huffed.

"Si—uh..." She caught herself quickly and gave him a slight bow, uncertain how she should act. "S-s-sorry, sir."

Simon put his handkerchief away. "I'm a looking for..." His expression froze. He leaned closer and peered at her face. "Miss Keelan? Dat *you?*"

She couldn't breathe. He'd recognized her! Now what would he do? The market was too crowded to flee. It was no use pretending. Best to just be honest.

She pulled her hat lower, totally deflated. "Yes, Simon, it's me."

The day the hurricane hit Twin Pines, she and Landon had been trapped in the cellar of an old cabin on the outskirts of the plantation. It contained a hidden passageway, and that day Simon had brought three runaways—a family—there to seek shelter.

The cabin served as a stopover refuge.

Simon used the cover of a violent storm to move the family. Later, she'd found out they were Pratt's runaways. The concept of slavery had never sat comfortably with her, nor had Pratt, for that matter. As a result, she and Landon had given the three escaped slaves what supplies they had and bade them a safe journey. She'd let them go and said nothing. Landon had kept the secret as well.

Simon lowered his voice. "What're you doin' dressed like *dat?* You all right? There's a bunch of strangers been by the house asking 'bout where you might be."

What should she say? She didn't want to tell him anything that would get either of them in trouble, but she needed to try to prevent him from telling anyone about her.

"Daniel and I are trying to avoid those people, Simon. They're pirates and mean us harm. Both Daniel and I are in disguise. We are preparing to flee Charleston. Please don't tell anyone you've seen me."

Simon's face softened a little as he sized her up and down. "You turned your head once for me, Miss Keelan. I can do the same fo' you, now."

She sighed in relief and whispered, "Thank you, Simon."

He bent down and murmured, "If'n you gets in a hard way, Mr. Schoen can help git you to a safer place. He at The Whistling Pig."

So, Daniel's intuition had been correct. The Schoens aided runaways. It all made sense to her now, after her experience in the tavern's attic.

Simon peered over her shoulder at the long row of stalls behind her and raised his voice a bit. "My Missus wants oranges and grapefruits, and our usual seller is all out. Did you pass any on dis row?"

"Yessir, we did, about halfway down." She pointed.

"Did you take a look at 'em?" Simon questioned. "It's a hot day, and I don't want to waste time and breath walking up and down the aisles if I ain't gotta."

"He was beginning to unpack a new crate," she answered, shifting her basket to the other arm.

"Ah, good. Thank you, boy. Good day to you." With a quick nod, Simon continued on his way without a backward glance.

Thank you, Simon.

She spied Marcel motioning to her from several stalls down and set off with her chin a little higher and a more confident step.

After a final stop at the apothecary, Marcel and Keelan made their way down a narrow alley as they headed back to the *Seeker*. Their baskets and leather satchels were filled with a wide variety of goods, as well as receipts for sacks of sugar, Indian meal, flour, and other heavier items, which would be delivered before dusk. It was a day well served, and now it was time to return to the ship, clean the galley, and make room for the supplies.

It had also been a long day, and she wasn't accustomed to the physical effort expected of someone in her new station. She wearily trekked behind Marcel through the streets of Charleston with her head down, watching her feet as she hopped around piles of dung and puddles of filth. They cut through a less crowded alley, offering a shortcut to the wharf.

Her mind drifted to Slaney, and she prayed the maid was safe and well. She should be nearing Philadelphia. How long would it take for her to find passage to England? Her thoughts were interrupted when she plowed into the cook's back. Her collision sent several packages from her basket tumbling to the street.

Mumbling a hasty apology, she squatted to retrieve the fallen parcels. A movement ahead of them drew her attention, and she peered around Marcel's legs and down the alley. Keelan's heart lurched as she caught sight of the gleaming metal of a long knife. The blade was clenched in the fist of a thick-chested man, who was standing a few feet in front of Marcel. A quick check behind her confirmed they were alone.

The man started to speak. "Ye'll hand over yer valuables, beginnin' with the purse on yer belt," he pointed his knife at the small bag of coins at Marcel's waist. "Leave yer goods on the street and keep yer hands where I can see 'em. Maggie will check yer pockets, in case ye forgot anythin'."

62

CHAPTER SIXTY-TWO
THIEVES IN THE ALLEY

A scrawny, middle-aged woman with long stringy hair stepped from behind the man. She pulled a small, thin dirk from the folds of her tattered skirts. The couple inched closer while Keelan and Marcel placed their things on the ground. Marcel untied his purse and dropped it next to his feet.

The woman laughed humorlessly. "Look, Errol, he wants me ter come git it. Maybe he thinks while I'm down there I'll do 'im a nicer service, eh?"

The man growled and shoved the woman toward the purse. "Kick the coins to me and go through his pockets."

"Hell, no, I ain't gittin' too close to 'im." She walked around Marcel and pointed her dirk at Keelan. "You, boy, pick up the purse and bring it here to me, *now!*"

Keelan swallowed and reached down for the purse. She glanced up at Marcel's face. He winked, then flicked his gaze toward Maggie with an almost imperceptible nod. Her heart began to pound, and she gave a quick nod back. Apparently, Marcel was not parting with his purse without a fight. Sparring with Daniel had trained her for this type of situation, but she never imagined she would ever be forced into one.

From her crouched position, she quickly dove to the right. As her palms hit the ground, she kicked her feet in a wide arc parallel to the alley floor. She clipped Maggie's feet neatly from beneath her skirts and brought the woman crashing to the ground. Keelan rolled away, and then scrambled to her feet in time to give her adversary a swift kick in the jaw, knocking her out cold. On instinct, she pulled from her bootleg the dirk Daniel had given her.

Marcel stepped over his purse and goods and began to circle Errol with his arms wide. She raised her blade and without hesitation, threw it. It sank into Errol's shoulder with a sharp plunge of quivering metal. He screamed and dropped his own blade to clutch the knife handle. He barely glanced at his partner, lying prone on the dank stones, before he spun and ran, the knife still in his shoulder.

It was several seconds before Keelan's breathing slowed and Marcel's jaw snapped shut. Even after he closed his mouth, he kept opening it again to speak, but seemed to be at a loss for words as he stared at her in amazement.

After a few moments, he said, "You are most useful in a fight, young Mahdi."

He then walked over to Maggie's still form and picked up her dirk from the ground. To Keelan's surprise, he handed it to her. "To replace the one Mr. Errol ran off with," he said, gruffly.

She bit back a smile and placed the knife into the leather strap around her boot. They picked up their things, and Errol's hastily discarded blade, then exited the alley to head once more for the ship. Every few moments, Marcel would glance down at Keelan, then shake his head and mumble to himself in French. They made a quick stop at the courthouse to report the incident, and provided the location of the unconscious women they'd left in the alley, and then returned to the ship.

Henry hailed them as they approached the ship's ramp.

"Hoy Marcel! Got the galley stocked full yet?"

"*Oui*! By zee end of zee day, it will be."

Henry nodded toward Keelan. "How'd the lad do fer ye?"

Marcel grunted and set his load down. Rubbing his stiff shoulders, he gestured for her to board. "Go on and put zee load in zee galley. There iz no reason for you to stay and listen to me talk about your heroics. Your ego will expand beyond your chest's capacity to hold it."

Keelan hurried past the men, eager to be out of their sight and away from their stares. She paused at the top and glanced back. Marcel gestured madly with both arms, while Henry stared at him with his mouth agape. These men had fought battles with pirates and still seemed to be surprised that she could throw a knife. How old did they think she was? Twelve?

A memory floated into her mind unbidden of Landon placing his dirk in her hand and saying; *"Cock your wrist like so..."* Would he have approved?

Landon Hart.

Handsome, charming, vibrant.

Stubborn.

Yes, she'd lost her heart to the man. But did she truly know him? Perhaps he was no more than a dandy who excelled at seducing women and avoiding attachments. She had suspected as much that first time they'd crossed paths. The truth will out when they next met, depending — would he be glad to see her again when the two vessels joined back together?

More than anything, she wanted to know if he still wanted to marry her. Sail with her. Be with her.

She rubbed her sore shoulders and sighed in frustration. For the thousandth time she wondered if Landon had changed his mind about marriage. What if he wanted her as his mistress, instead? Would she'd have the fortitude to defend herself against the onslaught of seduction and the heady charisma Captain Hart used as weapons? Shifting her shoulders back, she lifted her chin. Certainly, she'd become a spinster before she became any man's mistress.

She let her shoulders slump. Who was she fooling? So far, she'd lost the battle with that man's charm every time. She had no reason to believe her resolve had strengthened any in the past week.

She hadn't seen Daniel since earlier in the morning, so she quickly scanned the faces of the men on board as she made the trip to the galley. Several sailors paused what they were doing to watch her pass by. Her heart pounded nervously in her chest as she focused on hunching her shoulders and lengthening her stride in a more boyish fashion. It was one thing to simply look like a boy and quite another to act like one. It was even harder to remember to walk like one. Did she appear as nervous as she felt?

"Your actions and your gait are crucial to complete this illusion," Daniel had said. "You must carry yourself like a young man. And you cannot shriek at such things as bedbugs or rats."

Some sailors nodded or muttered a greeting. She did her best to respond in a like manner.

Sighing in relief, she dumped her things on the galley floor and sat down near them to catch her breath. It had already been a long day, and it was not yet noon. The ship creaked and groaned softly as it shifted in the quiet waters. She listened to the sounds of activity above as the crew went about their chores, readying the vessel for its voyage.

She was impressed by the cleanliness of the galley. She found several nearly empty bins, and it didn't take her long to unpack the supplies and put them away. Crocks of cane syrup and molasses fit neatly on a shelf in the pantry. Keelan took note of the tall lip on all the shelves, which obviously kept the contents from sliding against the cabinet doors when the seas became rough.

The sound of deliberate footsteps echoed down the steps. She straightened, expecting Marcel.

Instead, it was Daniel. "Good God, Miss Keelan! Are you all right?" he whispered in a concerned voice.

"I'm fine, really," she responded, glad to see him.

"Henry found me and told me what happened. He didn't want me to get a distorted version from the crew. Although he assured me my 'son' was unharmed, I had to see for myself."

Daniel's voice was as eager as a young boy's. "The news is all over the ship. According to Marcel, you single-handedly foiled two would-be robbers this morning!"

Keelan shrugged, trying to put Daniel at ease, but she couldn't hold back her grin. "It was almost like one of our training sessions."

Daniel reached out and squeezed her arm affectionately. "You did the right thing. I am proud of you." His next words brought a lump to her throat. "The commodore would have been *very* proud."

☙❧

KEELAN WENT about the rest of the day dodging elbows and questions. Sailors who had stared at her earlier with wary gazes now seemed more at ease with her presence. The men were a mix of old and young, brown and white. Most were scarred and missing teeth or fingers, all were shaded darkly by the sun.

Henry had warned them of her healing back, so they were careful to keep their distance. A couple of them forgot themselves and reached over to give her a hearty clap on the shoulder, but she was able to step quickly away, eliciting winks and chuckles.

"Marcel said ye were faster than a lightning strike, and I can say I agree," one had said laughing.

The good-natured ribbing continued during the evening meal as the crew lined up with their trenchers. She responded to the banter with small smiles or bashful shakes of her head, nimbly hopping and darting away from jutting shoulders and knees while plopping spoonfuls of rice and beans, Indian meal, bannocks and meat on their platters. According to Marcel, the captain always fed his crew a small feast the day before they set sail, since they'd be without such luxuries while at sea, making her wonder how bad meals would be while they traveled.

After everyone had their share, she and Marcel filled a plate and wandered up on deck to find a spot to sit and eat. Noisy gulls circled overhead, hoping to catch a stray morsel. Keelan found Daniel and sank down near him to eat her meal. She enjoyed the way the sailors wolfed down the bannocks she'd made. Marcel had been pleasantly surprised at her level of culinary skill and had allowed her to make them unassisted while he finished his inventory list for the captain.

"Zee Captain feeds his crew better zan most. We are in dangerous waters often enough, and he wants his crew strong and healthy to fight zee pirates."

Like Gampo? "Do you often run in to pirates?" she asked.

Marcel grunted and shrugged, "Often enough. We are all expected to assist in defending ze ship. And we do just zat."

After most had finished their meal, Henry stood up and gave a shrill whistle. The chatter stopped as he glanced around at the crew.

"I hope ye enjoyed yer last mainland meal. The captain should be ready to set the sails at daybreak tomorrow."

The crew cheered.

"Ye know the rules." Henry continued. "Ye bunk aboard the ship tonight. We need a sober and alert crew in the morning. If ye decide to leave the vessel, ye do so at yer own risk. The ship'll not wait for ye."

He shoved his hands into his pockets. "The captain will be taking on a few passengers this trip."

A slight groan arose as some men voiced their opinion to this last tidbit of news.

Henry held up his hand for silence. "Ye are not to speak to them unless they talk to ye first. Any argument requiring a judgment is to be brought to me quietly. Stay out of their way and be polite when tellin' them to git out of yers."

"Are there any petticoats?" a voice shouted.

"Ain't no business of yers who the captain takes aboard." He swept his gaze over the crew. "Now, git about yer tasks."

Keelan and Daniel rose and walked to the rail. A group of unruly seagulls squawked noisily overhead. "I wonder how many passengers the captain is taking," she murmured to Daniel.

"It can't be many because there are only two cabins still empty," Daniel replied. "The rest of the ship is stuffed with cargo."

She rubbed at her darkly stained skin, wondering how long the dye would last before she'd have to reapply it. Daniel had hidden a small bottle in his sack, hopefully it would last them as long as it was needed.

A soft breeze caressed her face, gentle as a butterfly's foot. She looked up and pointed her face in the direction of the wind.

"Aye, a good westerly is coming." Keelan and Daniel turned at Remus's voice. They'd not heard his approach.

He stopped near Daniel's shoulder. "Tomorrow's light will send us off under a good breeze, tho' the men will be wary until they catch sight of the passengers. We don't need no petticoats on this voyage."

"Why is that, Mr. Remus?" Daniel asked.

Remus leaned his bulk against the rail and picked his teeth with his fingernail. "Any salt who's been on the water will tell ye, havin' a woman aboard brings the bad luck." Nodding, he bade them good evening and swaggered away, whistling a nameless tune.

❧ 63 ❧

CHAPTER SIXTY-THREE
UNWANTED PASSENGERS

R emus was right. Dawn broke the next day, clear and fresh. The wind had picked up a little, and the ship pulled at its anchor like a filly testing her reins, eager to run. They all broke the fast with leftover bannocks and Indian meal porridge and then went about with their various duties, getting the ship ready to sail.

Marcel had dismissed Keelan to the upper deck. "Go fill your head with zee last sights of Charleston, boy," he said. "And while you are up zere, find out who our passengers are. I like to know who I cook for, eh?"

Keelan pulled her hat low to shield her face from the sun, as well as from inquiring eyes, ever conscious of hiding her feminine features. Spying a box tethered to the side of the foredeck, she perched herself on it as the men lashed down barrels and loaded the last of the ships' supplies.

A milking cow lowed morosely as she was pushed and pulled up the ship's ramp. Two spry nanny goats followed, bleating their bewilderment. Half a dozen pigs had been brought aboard earlier and grunted to each other from the small square pen near the mainmast. Several chickens darted hither and yon among the feet of the crew. She hoped she'd find their permanent roost. Without one, it would be a bit difficult to collect the eggs, since she would have to hunt for their laying spot first.

The remainder of the purchases Marcel had made yesterday arrived. Remus and Johnny carried the heavy sacks of rice, dried beans and Indian corn meal below.

She couldn't help but worry if she'd be recognized or found out. Uncertainty at her ability to play the part of a galley boy without giving away her fairer gender pulled at her stomach. Daniel had done his best to tutor her on her new position as a cook's boy and crew member.

"You'll be expected to help with the labors of the ship in addition to your culinary duties," he'd warned. "As slight as you are, I doubt too much will be put upon your shoulders. However, when told, you must attempt to finish the task as best you can. In the eyes of the captain and crew, you are a young male laborer, so you must act the part."

Throwing one of those heavy sacks on her unhealed shoulders was going to hurt, but there was no getting out of her duties, which was why she was surprised when the men waved away her offer to help with this task.

"Ye'll just be in the way, boy," Remus said gruffly.

"These sacks weigh more than you do, lad," Johnny teased.

"Go tell Marcel to unlock his pantry," Remus suggested.

She nodded and went to the galley. Whether they meant what they said, or were sparing her still-healing back and shoulders from the chafing and the weight of the sacks, she wasn't sure. Either way, she was grateful.

The sacks were stuffed into barrels and sealed in an attempt to keep out rats and other vermin. Additional barrels stowed hogsheads of rum, ale and whiskey. Brandy, wine and port were stored in a special pantry built off the galley. Marcel shut the tight-fitting door and then locked it.

Keelan returned to her perch and enjoyed observing the activities on the waterfront. A few of the crew found spots along the rail as well.

According to Remus, after the ship had been released from dry dock and her leaking hold sealed, small additional repairs had followed. Then, the cargo had been loaded and lashed down. The last of the supplies and rations had been purchased and stored.

They now awaited their captain.

Relief and apprehension battled inside her. The *Seeker's* captain was already an acquaintance, but what if he recognized her and refused to let her stay aboard? He'd already seen her sparring with Daniel in her waif's clothes, so her current disguise might not work with him at all. She made a fast decision to remain out of Conal O'Brien's sight as best as she could until the journey was well underway. Then she'd find out if he knew of Landon's plan to seek out Gampo.

Remus confided, "Word has it he had unfinished business of some sort."

A landau moved along the waterfront, its pace restrained but determined. It stopped at the pier where the ship was secured. The driver stepped down, opened the carriage door, and extended his hand. A slender glove grasped it and a woman gracefully alighted, like quicksilver from a glass bottle. Her dress was a deep gray and a feathered hat was secured at a smart angle on her head. From what Keelan could see, the woman's hair was as dark as a raven's.

A low groan sounded from Remus, "Well, look who's joining us for another sail," he muttered, spitting over the rail.

"Another?" Keelan inquired.

Henry strolled up behind Remus and rested his elbows on the railing. "Aye. She sailed this same leg two years ago. Except she was aboard the *Desire*. Surprised to see her on the *Seeker* tho', eh Remus?"

Remus nodded at Henry's earlier observation and frowned. "She's the other captain's—Hart's—bit o' fluff. She's a bad omen, mark me words. Last time she sailed with him, a fierce storm hit an' washed Stuckey overboard, remember?"

The other captain.

Hart. Keelan's stomach clenched into a knot.

"She chased him hard," Henry agreed, willingly filling her in on the gossip. "Cap'n Hart was pleased enough to have her attentions now and then, but after a couple years she wanted him to give up his ship, marry her and run her daddy's plantation." Henry laughed. "Devil may doubt it, but the captain had no desire for that life to be sure. He's a seaman, not a lubber, anyone who knows him knows *that*."

Keelan swallowed. The notion that the woman and Landon had

been lovers grated against her heart, even as she tried to steel herself against the sharp teeth of jealousy biting into her rational mind. She told herself it didn't matter. Hart was already sailing for Harbor Town on the *Desire*.

Remus added, "Cap'n sent her pretty little arse back home, in spite of it all. Ain't seen her again til today."

No new news there. Landon Hart had been gleefully unattached and unmarried when Keelan had met him at Twin Pines. Her mind took her back to Aunt Sarah's garden, the day he'd offered to free her tangled hair from a stubbornly rigid bush, in exchange for a kiss.

That kiss had been her undoing.

Or her awakening.

The memory led to a sensation of abandoned constraint and... longing. Landon Hart had kissed her, and from that moment forward she'd craved another kiss. Although she had done her best to resist the desire, when the opportunity had arrived she did not have the power or will to do so.

She was weak.

Henry nudged Remus in the ribs. "If Cap'n Hart rejects her, I wonder...what'll be her intentions whilst she's aboard?"

"Maybe she's set her bonnet on Cap'n O'Brien this time," Keelan replied with a half-hearted laugh.

Remus and Henry guffawed and slapped their knees at the suggestion. "Captain O'Brien likes him a skirt now and then, but he'd stay away from *that* skirt."

Keelan glanced down as the subject of their conversation stepped daintily to the base of the ramp from the pier. She gave a slight gasp when the lady lifted her head to inspect the ship.

The black widow, Annette Camsby, perused the faces at the rail.

Keelan's heart jerked in her chest. Annette and Landon.

Of course.

Now, she understood why they seemed to be so familiar with each other at Doreen's ball. Landon and Annette had been lovers.

Lovers.

Keelan scowled. That word, *lovers*, poked her throat like a stale biscuit. Were they still lovers? Would Landon have a difficult time resisting Annette's charms? Would Annette still want him?

She rolled her eyes and shook her head at the stupid questions. Of course Annette would want him. Why would she not? Landon probably rode straight to Annette's town house after witnessing that ridiculous kiss of Everett's on Uncle Jared's porch. A part of her heart crumbled. A dark, thick sensation oozed in and its weight pulled at her like a headstone.

So, this is how it felt to be jealous of another woman. This is what it felt like to have a broken heart.

So many questions and concerns flitted through her mind. How much of their journey did Landon's former mistress plan to make with them? What if Annette recognized her, as Simon had? Maybe she and Daniel should slip away unseen now, perhaps travel by land, if need be, to Philadelphia. It seemed possible. It would be infinitely better than sailing with the two of *them*.

She studied the pier and nearby boardwalk. People hawked wares, some strolled casually, stopping occasionally to inspect an item or two, everyone seemed to be in motion, except...

A figure leaned against a piling near the mouth of the pier. Her heart lurched. Orvis Pike had his gaze fixed on the carriage and the lady who had alighted from it. He was probably watching to see if it was Keelan. If Daniel hadn't discovered Gampo's reward for her capture, she might have arrived in the same manner as Annette Camsby.

Keelan's shoulders sagged. The boat was being too closely guarded by the pirates for her and Daniel to make a successful escape. Even in disguise.

"God's blood, there's *another* petticoat," Remus said darkly.

A second woman, holding a small bag, emerged from the carriage. She was dressed much simpler, perhaps a servant. Her head was covered, her features masked.

Mr. Henry barked to the men loitering closest to the ramp. "You there! Johnny! Remus! Haul up the rest of these ladies' things. The biggest trunk is to go into the hold, but put it in a handy spot, in case they should require it."

The men pushed away from the rail and shuffled down the ramp like men headed for the gallows. "Aye, Mr. Henry."

She scanned the pier for Orvis.

He was gone.

A cold sensation gripped her neck. *Where did he go?* She studied the pier and the boardwalk again, but there was no sign of the man.

Keelan pulled the brim of her hat lower so she could inconspicuously watch Landon's lover stroll along the deck. She gave a small internal sigh of longing as she admired the perfectly coiffed hair, the beautiful silk gown, and the petite gloved hands. She was exceedingly aware of her own state of dress: boots, baggy breeches, Landon's linen shirt. She reached up and rubbed the collar. Uninvited, the image of Annette Camsby dancing with Landon tugged at the raw strings of jealousy within her chest. They'd been beautiful together, two dark-haired figures waltzing around the room, talking, smiling...

Thinking of Landon also brought a lonely weight to her heart. At least if Orvis was still in Charleston, then so too, was Gampo, which meant Landon was safely sailing south on the *Desire,* either seeking the pirate or fleeing her. She gave a sarcastic snort.

If she'd listened to Slaney's advice and stayed away from the man, she wouldn't care if Annette Camsby was aboard. She pressed her lips together. The maid had been right about some things. Landon Hart was the kind of handsome rogue who could have a woman whenever and wherever he wished. He could easily make it a game to see how many maids he could woo, and leave swooning for his touch, longing for his kiss.

Unbidden, the hard warmth of his thighs against the back of her legs seeped in to her mind. His fingers on her wrist...

"Hold the blade like so..."

Warm breath against her cheek.

"Then cock your wrist and let it fly."

Hot moist kisses....his tongue probing her mouth with first tenderness, then desire.

Azure eyes pierced her mind.

Mocking.

Smiling.

Flashing in anger.

Clouded with concern.

Hooded in hurt.

Keelan's heart lurched. Now she ached with a kind of pain that pulled at her soul. For the past two-and-a-half years she had spurned countless suitors while making any number of excuses: too old, too arrogant, too uneducated, too poor, too melancholy, nose too big, belly too big.

Others had been refused by her parents because they were unworthy. She stifled a humorless laugh. Had a man born out of wedlock asked for her hand, he would have been laughed to the gate.

She pondered Landon Hart, the man who had once asked her to sail the world with him. He didn't seem like the type of man who cared much about what others thought.

Still...

Had he wanted me with him, she mused, *he would have taken me. Perhaps these circumstances are for the best. No matter how strong my affection, I will never stay with a man who does not love me, just as I would never want to be with a man I could not love.*

Yet...she *did* love. She loved Landon Hart whether she willed it or not.

The raw painful arrow of truth emerged through the bramble tangled around her heart like a crocus in spring. Much to the anguish of her flayed pride and common sense, she loved Landon Hart. When? How?

Oh, dear Lord, *why?*

She was being tormented by something she might never be destined to have. This was probably her punishment for being so cruelly selective with her previous suitors.

Her jaw tightened. It did no good to dwell on what could have or should have been. The past was the past. Her only hope was to focus on the future and the new path she must forge for herself and pray it would lead her home.

Perhaps without Landon.

A slow metallic ache spread through her chest.

She forced her mind back to her earlier reasoning. He'd left, so she had no choice but to follow his directions to sail north. Either he'd been striving to keep her safe because he cared for her, or he was trying to get rid of her.

So, he could be with his mistress.

Her gaze paused again on Annette Camsby, because apparently she liked torturing herself.

Remus had returned from his trip below and stood near Keelan. He shifted toward her conspiratorially, "Well, she is now the *Widow* Camsby. It seems her third husband died of the fever last winter. She asked to see the captain first thing. Poor Henry had to tell her he's not yet boarded." He chuckled. "Barely got the words out before he had to duck a flying chamber pot."

Keelan was hit with a sense of immanent foreboding, like a dark thunderhead on the horizon.

Remus gave her an odd look. "Yer a bit green, boy." He peered closer, then nudged her with his elbow. "Don't worry, ye'll git yer sea legs soon enough."

She nodded. Better to let him think she was getting seasick. Although thinking about Annette Camsby made her stomach lurch almost as badly.

Remus grinned at her. "Tell ye this, young Mahdi, we're going to have a rough few days. If Madam Camsby's in heat and is shunned again, she'll be wantin' another warm body to take to her bed. A young buck like you might just suit her fine." He reached over and feigned to cuff her ear. She quickly dodged his swing and mumbled, "It won't be me. I wouldn't want to catch anything."

Remus threw his head back and roared with laughter. "Smart lad, ye are, but there's not many a man on this ship with the same sense in his head or his britches. They'd as soon lay the lass now and worry about the other later." He hailed Daniel, "Mr. Khalil!"

Daniel walked up, nodded a greeting to Remus and Johnny, and leaned his forearms on the rail.

"How are the beasts?" Johnny asked.

Daniel rubbed his shoulder and grinned at Keelan. "The mare is a bit spirited. She slammed me into the boards as I was changing the dressing on her leg this morning. She's healing well, though. Has the captain arrived yet?"

"Nay. Not yet. He should be here shortly, " Remus responded.

"I was told to tell you and Johnny to report to the helmsman," Daniel said.

Remus nodded, and he and Johnny stepped away hastily to comply.

Keelan's gaze was drawn to another figure moving furtively toward the ramp. Even though he limped, there was something familiar about the man's gait. He carried a small trunk under one arm and a leather satchel under the other, similar to the medicine bag Dr. Garrison carried.

Dr. Garrison!

Keelan's heart pounded. *Dear God, please don't let him board this ship.*

God apparently had more pressing prayers to answer because Everett wasted no time lurching to the ramp like a startled stork.

Keelan gritted her teeth. She sensed Daniel stiffen beside her.

He bent his head and spoke into Keelan's ear. "We will have to make ready to leave this vessel as soon as we can slip away. It's not safe for you. I'll not have you on the same ship as Dr. Garrison."

Another surge of panic welled in her chest. A bounty on her head in Charleston, and Garrison on the same ship with her. How long would it take to find other transportation north? She glanced again to the spot where she'd seen Orvis earlier. Two different men had taken his place and appeared to be in casual conversation, but their eyes were fixed on the *Seeker*.

"Daniel," she whispered, "spies are watching the ship." She nodded toward the pirates. "It could be days or even weeks before another vessel is ready to journey north. And if war breaks between England and France, as Captain Hart and Uncle Jared predicted, it could delay our departure even longer. We must continue." She pleaded with the valet, "Please, Daniel. We can't risk the delay."

She couldn't leave now, she had too many questions. Why had her mother had a child with another man? Who was he? She clasped her hands together and stared at her stained fingers. What she really needed to know was if Landon had been serious when he'd asked her to join him, or if she was no more that a pleasant temporary distraction for him. Observing him and Annette together might give her the answer to that question. She couldn't leave until she knew for sure. Her mind told her to go, but her heart begged her to stay long enough to confront Landon and learn the truth from his own lips.

Really soft, really tantalizing lips.

Daniel closed his eyes and rubbed his forehead, as if his thoughts were causing him pain. "I promised the commodore I would take you to England and help you find your father. I will see my oath fulfilled and my duty done, Miss Keelan." He opened his eyes and his gaze sharpened. "But, not at the cost of your safety."

She supposed she'd feel the same way if their roles were reversed. "Henry said we'll sail from Harbour Town to Philadelphia. If you still think it is too dangerous, then we leave the *Seeker* and find a different ship northbound when we arrive in Harbour Town." She waited while Daniel contemplated their situation.

He gave her a reluctant nod. "It makes sense to stay aboard and then take stock in the next port."

A shout from Remus drew their attention to the dock below. "Hoy Captain! Yer late. Was she that good, or did she tie ye to her bed posts?" he called out jovially.

Conal O'Brien attempted a grin and nudged the shoulder of the man next to him. Keelan's breath froze in her throat as she gazed upon the stern and rather unmistakable face of Landon Hart, striding beside O'Brien.

Why wasn't Landon on the Desire?

Daniel grasped her arm. "What luck!" he whispered enthusiastically. "I'll have a word with Captain Hart as soon as I can meet with him privately."

They both observed Landon and Conal board the vessel amid additional shouts of greeting and raucous comments about activities ashore. The two simply waved them off, in good-natured fashion.

As Landon and Conal came closer, Keelan noted the weariness of their stride and the slump of their shoulders. The crewmen seemed to notice the stern set of their mouths and stifled any further ribald comments. Landon had dark circles beneath his eyes and a haggard look of worry blanketing his features. Keelan studied him. Relief and dread tangled together. In her heart, she was happy to see him again. Rather than wonder if he'd be happy to see her too, all she could think of was if he would seek comfort in Annette Camsby's arms again.

Annette Camsby.

Landon.

A thought hit Keelan like a slap to the face. His mistress was back aboard and had already asked for him. Annette had *known* Landon would be aboard the *Seeker*.

A loud rush of air filled her ears as the realization hit her. The trip to Harbour Town provided an excellent opportunity for the two lovers to rekindle their old relationship. How could Landon resist such beauty, especially if it radiated from a woman so willing to climb into his bed? Winning the argument with Daniel to stay aboard until they reached Harbour Town no longer had the same appeal it had a few moments ago. A darker question gripped her mind. After securing Keelan's passage aboard the *Glory*, had Landon sought out Annette to accompany him south?

Was that the reason he kept the *Seeker* waiting?

Keelan tried to swallow the rock forming in her throat at the thought of watching the two together.

Daniel nudged her. "I wonder what Hart's reaction will be when he sees Garrison aboard this ship." Daniel crossed his arms with a confidence she did not share. "My bet would be he's bound and turned over to the Charleston authorities."

She hoped not. "Daniel," she whispered, "if he's taken to jail and charged with kidnapping me, won't I have to bear witness to the charges?"

Daniel was silent as he pondered her words. "True enough," he responded. "'Tis better to keep our enemies close, where we can watch them. We have the advantage. He doesn't know we're aboard. Take care, Miss Keelan, to stay as inconspicuous as you can." He looked toward the main cabin. "I'll find a quiet moment to have a word with Captain Hart about our circumstances."

"Nay, Daniel, please don't!" The words fell from her lips before she could stop them.

He turned to her, surprise evident on his face. "In heaven's name, why not?"

Taking an unsteady breath, she stared at her clasped hands, not willing Daniel to witness her pain as she spoke. "I'd rather not burden the captain with my state of affairs at the moment. He might well feel obligated to take charge of my protection, and I will not be any more indebted to him than I am already. It's obvious to me much weighs on his mind at the moment, and I shall not add to his burden."

Daniel bent to peer at her. "It's my understanding the man cares about you deeply. Your protection would be less an obligation and more of a concern on his part."

Daniel had not seen Landon's interactions with Annette; he did not know their history.

She lowered her gaze and murmured. "I am uncertain of my standing with him at the moment, Daniel. It appears he has invited one of his previous mistresses to join him on his journey." She tilted her head in Annette's direction.

Daniel's features darkened briefly, then it softened in understanding. "We shall remain anonymous for a while then. At least until we can determine where everyone stands." He patted her hand affectionately. "It is unwise to make assumptions, Miss. Better to seek the facts of the matter."

As she pondered his words, her mind thrashed about in indecision. More than Landon's affection for her was at stake now. Her life was in jeopardy as well.

Daniel crossed his arms and nodded. "Let's bide our time for a few days and watch them. There will be plenty of opportunities to exit the ship in Harbour Town or even Philadelphia."

Keelan glumly nodded in agreement. She shifted her gaze back to the end of the pier and caught her breath.

Orvis was back at his post.

64

CHAPTER SIXTY-FOUR
WEIGH ANCHOR

Keelan had done her best both to help the sailors, and stay out of their way. Remus took her under his wing and gave her several specific tasks to perform. Unfortunately, she had to go to the starboard side to complete them, removing her chance to watch the pier.

When she went to back a couple hours later, she chanced a quick glance long enough to notice Orvis was no longer at his post. That should've given her some sense of relief, but instead, an uneasy shadow settled in her chest.

"Weigh anchor, lads!" Conal braced his legs, hands on his hips. "Hands to braces, set topsails, and let down the sheets!"

The anchor was raised, and the hoisted sails billowed full and urgent. The crew looked with satisfaction at the brisk gusts filling the canvas.

Landon stood near the helm, issuing additional instructions as sheets were adjusted and lashed. The sails snatched the wind, and the *Seeker* glided swiftly to open sea. Landon was as much a part of the ship as the mainmast. Standing with legs braced wide, the only disturbance in his countenance was the lingering look he gave to the Charleston harbor and the stoic expression on his face.

What was he thinking? Keelan glanced at the harbor and her heart suffered a brief pang of grief as she recalled standing by Papa's side the day their ship dropped anchor a couple years ago. She'd been grieving the loss of her mother.

Her life had been on a different path, then.

The wind gently moved them out from the waterfront and parallel to the shoreline. Charleston shrank quickly into the distance as the *Seeker* gained speed at the expert hands of her crew.

Landon stood straight and tall at the helm. So far, she had managed to stay out of his way, but eventually their paths would cross. A part of her yearned for it, as much as dreaded it. What would she say? *"Good day, Captain. I missed the ship I was supposed to board. Don't mind me, I'm just the cook's boy. Send my regards to your mistress."*

She swallowed, but couldn't squelch the prickly sense of foreboding that gripped her. How far would this charade take them? Would Landon recognize her before she was ready to doff her disguise? More importantly, how would he react? She clenched her teeth. Or would her presence ruin his plans with Annette Camsby (hopefully)?

After reaching deeper waters, the *Seeker* swung southward again, and the shore returned as a distant dark green line on the horizon. It seemed odd a ship should sail so far from the shore when it would soon make port again.

Henry had stepped up to the rail next to her, so she voiced her question to him.

He gestured toward the low line of land to the right. "There be a lot of sand bars and small islands along this coast, lad. Many a vessel has been run aground by less experienced captains. Easy pickin' fer the pirates then. Cap'n chooses to try to make them work a bit harder to catch us." He grinned.

Keelan gripped the rail nervously. "Do many pirates prey in these waters?" She thought of Gampo.

"Not as much as back when." Henry shrugged. "Blackbeard hisself raked these seas fer years. Why, Blackbeard's men stole ashore into Charleston one day and kidnapped a good number of prominent townsfolk quite a few years ago. He ransomed them fer medicine fer his crew." The man winked and then chuckled, "His men had the clap, ye see, and Captain Blackbeard knew they would not be able to keep their mind on their work if their cocks were itchin' like the devil."

The stain on her skin had better be masking the heat creeping up her cheeks. She ducked her head to hide her embarrassment and pretended to scan the shoreline. "Did he get the medicine?"

"Aye. He did. Put him out of business fer a while, still."

A flash of silver caught Keelan's eye, and the Widow Camsby floated by toward the steps leading to the helm. Landon' brow lowered at her approach, and he moved away from the wheel, permitting the helmsman to take over. He descended the steps and met her near the rail where Keelan and Henry stood.

Annette made no effort to lower her voice. "Good day, Captain Hart," she smiled sweetly over the frilly fan she fluttered before her face. "I sent word with your man before we set sail that I wished to speak with you privately, but alas, you never came. I am forced to seek you out instead." She pouted and angled partly away from him coyly and waved her fan at her chest. Keelan narrowed her eyes at the shameless flirtation.

Henry made a small choking noise. Landon shot a warning look over Annette's shoulder at the old sailor, even as a small smile tugged at the corners of his mouth. With an eyebrow arched, he then turned his attention to the young widow fluttering in front of him like a moth.

"Good day, Madame Camsby." He gave her a slight bow before gesturing at the activity around them. "As you can see, I have been a bit busy. Do you have a concern you wish to share with me?"

Keelan gulped and pulled the brim of her hat lower, while casting surreptitious glances at the pair.

Annette maintained her pout. "Well, yes, I do."

He waited, hands clasped behind his back.

"I had expected for you, as host, to see to the comforts of your passengers more appropriately," she chastised, in a hurt tone. "These voyages are extraordinarily boring. I need some companionship." She batted her long black lashes, then lowered her voice. "Join me in my cabin this evening. We'll sup together."

Landon's jaw ticked. He bowed graciously. "Forgive my poor

manners, Madame Camsby. I would be honored if you would join me for dinner this evening at eight."

It was as she'd feared. Landon and Annette seemed to be rekindling their relationship. It was time for her to move away. She'd heard all she needed to hear.

Annette lowered her lashes as a slow smile seeped across her face. She lowered her fan and swayed it in a slow sultry motion in front of her very ample bosom, which was straining against the bodice of her gown.

Keelan had seen enough. Clenching her fists until her nails bit into her palms, she turned away.

Landon continued, "Captain O'Brien and I have yet to meet the other passengers aboard. Tonight's dinner will give us all an opportunity to become better acquainted. I will then be able to introduce you to your fellow passengers, so you will have others to talk with to break the monotony."

His words made Keelan pause. He'd given her a very subtle rejection. She chanced a quick sideways glance at Annette from under the brim of her hat.

Annette's pleased expression faltered a little, but she nodded her head. "I look forward to this evening." She slapped her fan shut and made to leave, then paused before stepping closer to Landon. She placed her hand familiarly on his chest and murmured something to him. He shrugged in response, and she smiled wider as he offered his arm. They strolled away in the direction of the aft deck.

Keelan shoved her hands in her pockets and stepped away from the rail before she pushed Annette over it and into the churning sea below. Landon's reaction was more subdued than she'd expected. Not like a man happy to see his mistress. With those barbs tumbling around in her mind, she went below to check if Marcel was in need of her assistance. Pondering Landon's motivations and being near Annette's flirtations only gave her a headache.

KEELAN SPENT the next couple of hours helping the cook prepare supper for the captain, passengers, and crew, serving up rice and salted fish into various bowls and trenchers. She wasn't yet used to the bawdy comments and jokes the men tossed around, and her ears burned as she served helpings of Hopping John.

Marcel flew about the small galley like a fly in a jar, chopping sweet potatoes and stirring the pudding. He took a spoon, dipped it into the soup, and after blowing to cool it, took a sip. "Ah!" Marcel said, pleased. "Ze first meal at ze captain's table must be *perfect,*" he said with a flourish of hands. "All ze passengers will be dining wiz him and Captain Hart tonight." He cocked his head and peered at her more closely.

"You are most solemn, young Mahdi, is all well with you?"

Images of Landon and Annette together had been pestering her mind like a swarm of gnats flying around inside her head. She did her best to squelch them. It would not do for her to draw any extra attention from the cook. She had to keep her charade consistent and believable.

"Aye, sir. Just a bit off-balance. Remus said it might take a day or two before I got my sea legs."

"Ah," the cook nodded. "I have a remedy." He reached for a small tin and pulled out a dried piece of root. He sliced off a small bit and gave it to her. "Chew on this a while. It will help."

"What is it?" She eyed it curiously.

"Root of Ginger. Chew it."

She did as she was told and found the flavor unique and sharply pleasant.

Marcel pointed to the wooden box under the chopping block. "Pull out ze dishes and goblets from zat trunk over there."

Keelan opened the trunk and removed the woolen cover. Beneath it lay neatly stacked pewter plates, bowls, goblets and silver placed between layers of thick woolen squares.

The galley had two doors. One opened to a short hallway leading to the stairs and upper deck. She hadn't opened the second door. Marcel gestured to it now as he dunked a piece of bread into the sauce to sample.

"Set ze Captain's table. You will find ze linens in a cupboard in zere."

Keelan nodded and counted out the number of plates she would need. They clinked softly as she removed the cloth separating them and placed them in a neat stack. Nimbly stepping around the mumbling cook, she lifted the latch with her elbow and nudged the door open with her shoulder.

On the right was a desk strewn with papers and maps, as if someone had impatiently tossed them there. The desk was tightly affixed to the corner walls. Cupboards covered the rest. How many she would have to go through before she found the one housing the table linens? The opposite wall contained another door, perhaps a closet.

The table stood directly in front of her, its end bolted to the wall. The two long benches tucked neatly underneath were surrounded by a raised border of narrow planks, keeping them from sliding away.

She couldn't find the linens while holding the plates, so she moved back to the cluttered desk and gently shoved the papers and maps aside to put them down.

"I thought I was helping by clearing off the table."

She jumped, losing her grip on the plates. They tottered and began to slide toward the floor. The top two clattered on the wooden planks. A long bare arm reached over and steadied those that remained. Landon's handsome profile stirred a mixture of surprise, trepidation, and suppressed joy. He bent to retrieve the fallen items.

"I'm sorry if I startled you," he said. "You're the new galley boy, young Mr. Mahdi, correct?"

She hunched her shoulders, ducked her head and nodded, afraid to speak. She would have stepped further away if she could trust the rest of the dishes to stay put.

Landon collected the fallen plates and placed them on a bench. She glanced at his tanned back, and the muscles rippling beneath his skin with his movements. He straightened and pointed to the cupboard nearest the galley door.

"You'll find the linens in there," he said. "Please tell Marcel our guests have all accepted the invitation for dinner this evening."

She faced the cupboards, keeping her back to him, and listened as he walked away. It had never occurred to her his cabin could be accessed directly off the galley. She groaned. Now she would have to be ever vigilant to his comings and goings and not relax her charade even a little.

His voice startled her. "And, boy..."

She paused.

"The passengers are to be treated with the utmost respect, regardless of your personal feelings. Understood?"

Her stomach jumped as she shifted to peer at him from beneath the brim of her hat. Did he suspect anything?

Landon stood inside his cabin door, hand on the knob, and ran the other through the glossy black curls on his head. "While I have been told you are quite capable of taking care of yourself against thieves and ruffians, and it appears you have a keen ear for a yarn, I fear you might be lacking experience in the area of dueling with a woman's tongue and mood. Be warned that Mrs. Camsby tends to take out her anger on the nearest warm body." He glanced at her, a small pained smile played at his lips. "'Tis in your best interest to steer clear of her, as her mood on this trip may be quite dour."

Lips tightening, she nodded again.

"Good. Please tell Marcel to set out a bottle of Madeira. If I recall correctly, Mrs. Camsby has a liking for it."

She flinched and tried to ignore the sudden anger beginning to roil inside her. Of course he would stock his mistress's favorite wine! She clenched her jaw and nodding once more, didn't move or breathe until she heard him close the door. She yanked open a cupboard.

Steer clear of Widow Camsby, indeed!

She huffed at the notion that Landon Hart viewed her as a whipping boy. She'd like to see Annette *try* to strike her. Or was he warning her away from that gaudy piece of skirt like a prancing stag in rut?

"Sail away with him, huh!" She grabbed the tablecloth and shook it out with an angry jerk. "I am out of his sight for a fortnight and he is already strutting like a dandy to another. Lies, lies, lies."

His words were a farce, designed to steal a kiss simply for sport. With his lusts appeased, he would have left her for the next feminine form to catch his eye. Apparently, he preferred his beautiful mistress to accompany him on shorter trips.

She grabbed the plates from the desk and dumped them on the table with a loud clatter. She moved around it, slapping them down as she went.

"The arrogant lout. Conceited cad."

An amused voice sounded from the captain's doorway. "Have the trenchers insulted you, Mahdi? From the din you were making, I was sure you had been attacked by an angry stack of pewter platters."

She jumped. Landon's head poked out from behind his cabin door.

"Nay, sir," she said in a low voice, as she placed the last plate on the table. "I am sorry for disturbing you." She briskly escaped through the door into the galley.

When she entered, Marcel pointed to two steaming buckets near the door.

"Take zem to Captain Hart. Ze bath iz filled but for zee hot water."

Scowling, she opened her mouth to protest and then closed it again, as she could give no good reason to avoid her duty without arousing the cook's suspicion.

Fine. She'd simply knock, deposit the buckets inside the room, and let the captain add them to his own bath. Content with her plan, she hefted her burden, nudged the galley door open, and crossed the dining cabin to his door. Still fuming, she knocked smartly with her toe.

At Landon's beckoning, she entered. The water sloshed to and fro in the buckets as she pushed open the door. His furnishings were tasteful without being ostentatious. A mahogany tallboy stood against the far wall, while directly to the left stood a bed of the same, cloaked with a simple navy silk canopy. Next to the tallboy was a closed door which had to lead to the outside hallway.

Landon's voice resonated through the room. "Just pour in the water, Marcel."

She turned toward the voice and almost dropped the buckets. Landon was lowering himself in the tub, showing more of his natural state than Keelan wished to view. His hips were slim, his belly taut and flat. A thin line of black hair traveled downward—she squeezed her eyes shut, aghast at where her gaze traveled.

Thankfully, he did not look up, for if he did, he would have seen a heightened blush covering young Mahdi's face. Instead, he immediately reached for a slab of soap and rubbed it in his hands, then briskly rubbed the soapy suds over his face. He paused in his work and cocked his head to the side.

"The warm water, Marcel?"

Since there was no way to avoid her duties; it'd be best to take advantage of Landon's temporary blindness. Keeping her gaze carefully averted, she pitched the first bucket into his bath. In her haste to be done, she didn't think to divert the stream away from his body. The hot water hit him full force in the chest.

At his yelp of pain, Keelan froze, and it took her a fraction of a second before she jerked into action. She picked up a nearby pitcher and, to reverse the effect of the scalding deluge, flung the contents in the same general direction.

At the sudden blast of colder water on his lap, Landon's eyelids flew open. A bellow followed as soapy rivulets streamed in to his eyes. He hurriedly splashed his face to cease the merciless burning.

"*Damnation!*" he roared, rising from the water and reaching for a towel to mop his face. "Are you trying to maim me or geld me?"

Horrified at the sights he revealed, she stepped back as the sound of running feet approached from the hallway behind her. The cabin door flung open wide, hitting her full force on her backside and sending her flying headfirst onto Landon's chest. Momentum carried both man and waif back into the tall brass tub with a loud splash.

Conal's voice sounded concerned. "Landon, I heard—".

Her hips hinged over the lip and her feet flailed in the air as she made a desperate attempt to heave her upper body up and out. The smooth wet sides were slippery, and she couldn't push herself up. Her face plunged back in the water covering Landon's lap. She floundered madly to gain purchase and push herself upright. Landon finally grabbed her by the hair and pulled her face out of the water.

Sputtering and coughing, she braced a hand on his stomach and pushed herself upright. The realization of where her other hand rested put her into a mild panic. She fumbled to scramble from the tub, only to slip forward against his chest again. Fighting furiously to free herself from the proximity of his naked body, she shoved harder against him, this time eliciting a grunt of pain.

Landon growled, "In God's name, would you stop thrashing about before you succeed in making me completely useless to a woman ever more?" Frustration was evident in his tone, making Keelan cringe.

With measured patience, Landon stood up, grasped her around the waist, and made to deposit her out to the floor. However, both the boards and the tub sides were slippery. He lost his balance, causing his hands to slip up along her ribs.

She gasped and froze. His eyes widened, and his mouth dropped open at the soft curves beneath his hands. Their eyes locked and for a moment, neither seemed able to draw a breath. She jerked away from him, only to slip on the wet floor. There was no one capable of catching her this time. Her backside hit the wet wooden planks, causing her to expel a pained grunt.

Both Conal and Landon stood frozen with shock. Surprise and amazement give way to total disbelief as Landon's gaze slid over her body. The floppy hat had flown from her head when she fell in. Her hair had broken free of the tie, allowing it to hang in streams of wet, curly, ringlets. She chanced a quick glance down. In the struggle, her vest had come open. Beneath it, her soaked shirt clung to her like a second skin, leaving Landon a clear view of her chest. The silky white of her breasts contrasted sharply with the deep tan of her neck, face, and arms. Soft, pink peaks strained against the fabric bandages, leaving Keelan no secrets to withhold from his astonished gaze.

Likewise, Conal stood paralyzed in his tracks, jaw agape; hand still on the door latch. When he finally did find his voice, it came out as a lame croak.

"I'll... be... damned."

She scrambled away from Conal's surprised visage and backed against the far wall, snatching her vest closer about her.

Landon's voice was almost uncertain. *"Keelan?"*

❦ 65 ❦

CHAPTER SIXTY-FIVE
REVEALED

"Is it you, Keelan?"

Landon could hardly believe his eyes. Her skin was as dark as a native savage. Her hair had been cut and stained as well. If he hadn't felt the curve of her breast, he'd never have guessed the boy, Mahdi, was a woman. Although, if he'd looked closer, her eyes would have betrayed her. Those eyes haunted his dreams whether sleeping or awake, glittering emeralds with threads of gold in the center.

A weary air of defeat emanated from her like a sodden blanket. After a moment, she nodded mutely. Her shoulders dropped as she fixed her stare at the cabin floorboards.

"Conal," Landon strained to find his voice. "I must swear you to secrecy. Not a word of this to anyone, or Keelan's safety will be compromised. Please leave us."

"Aye, Landon." Conal's amusement was tightly contained behind the curt nod of his head. The corners of his mouth twitched. What the man found so bloody amusing was beyond Landon's comprehension at the moment. Keelan's presence on the *Seeker* muddled up his plan considerably. Annette Camsby's face filtered through his mind, and he mentally cringed at the added layer of discomfiture.

If both women had done what they'd been told, everything would have worked out.

The door closed; Conal's footfalls in the passageway died away. The air in the cabin seemed to sharpen and pierce his chest like a million needles in the rigid silence following the click of the latch.

Keelan continued to study the worn floor boards.

Did she have any inkling what she'd put him through the past couple of days? He couldn't find her. He'd slept little. He had feared she'd been retaken by Gampo, or worse, Garrison. He'd run out of places to search for her after she left the tavern. Schoen's maid had told him she'd gone with a dark man. The sun-bronzed skin of a seaman, of a pirate... of *Gampo*... had contaminated his thoughts, and he found he was unable to form a strategy. Conal dragged him back to the *Seeker* to settle for a bit and think things through. They had a route schedule to keep; lives depended upon it and to be late could be deadly. He'd wanted to track Gampo, the bilge rat.

Things made a little more sense now. The dark man the maid saw was likely Daniel, who would have stayed with his mistress.

The more Landon stewed, the angrier he became. Combined, the lack of sleep, worry, and frustration added to the relief at seeing her alive. It all churned into a roiling, turbulent swirl of emotion. Before he could stop himself, he grasped her shoulders, gave her a jolting shake, and brought his scowling face inches from her own. "What are you thinking, you little minx? Do you realize what you've done?" He shook her again. "You should *not* be on this ship!"

Her eyes widened, then narrowed. "Unhand me," she hissed furiously as she attempted to jerk free of his hold. "Your fingers bite into my wounds."

He immediately released her but did not move from his stance. Was all this a game to her? She remained frozen, rooted to her spot, her gaze on his face, eyes flashing green fire. Landon clenched his fists and shook his wet head in frustration. He snatched a towel and secured it about his waist, and then, in an attempt to cool his ire, paced the cabin.

"Conal and I have been searching for you. I received a message from Commodore Hall, belatedly, stating he was urgently summoned north. He feared he couldn't deliver you safely, so he chose to leave you behind. Schoen's had informed me of Gampo's offered reward, so I went back to The Whistling Pig, where we were informed you had left the day prior, although the maid knew not where. We rode to Jared Grey's town house, then to Twin Pines, to find it half burned to the ground, as was Garrison's residence and office here in town."

She gasped and her eyes widened. "Uncle Jared and Aunt Sarah, are they—"

"Unharmed," he said, quickly. "They were in Charleston at the time. Garrison's place burned down the night I found you at the warehouse. One of my men saw the doctor loitering about the livery and followed him here, to the *Seeker*. When he booked passage, we allowed it with the hope he might lead us to you." He continued to pace, expending the energy generated by hours of worry and fear. "Every place we searched and did not find you, tore at my peace of mind, nearly driving me mad," he said hoarsely.

Pausing in front of her, he gripped her upper arms again in torment. "My God, Keelan, I feared Gampo took you. I feared you *dead*!"

❦

KEELAN LIFTED HER CHIN. "Oh? You were *so* concerned for my welfare, you almost forgot about Annette Camsby's madeira!" Yes, she was acting stupid and jealous, but at the moment all rational thoughts seemed to have abandoned her, blast it. She peeled his fingers from her arms. "It would seem your anguish over my well-being took flight the moment she planted herself with such familiarity on your boat!"

"It's a ship, not a boat," he muttered, the edge of his mouth tight.

She poked his chest with her finger, wishing it were a dagger instead, so he'd feel the same sting. Dear Lord, just hearing his voice was painful for her. "You black-hearted snake! You wanted me on Commodore Hall's *ship*, because you had a liaison planned on *this* one with one of your mistresses. Your tender words and warm promises are worth less than the ocean water beneath this *boat*."

He actually looked chagrined. *Ha.* He'd been caught. At least he had the decency to be embarrassed. She'd wanted to hear the truth, and now she had. She'd been such an idiot. A naïve little fool.

No doubt he regretted the truth being outed more than his recent actions.

She propped her fists on her hips. "Sail away with me, Keelan. I want you with me, Keelan," she mimicked. Angry tears threatened, and she whirled away from him before he could see how deeply she had fallen for his ploy and how dupable she'd been. "I was nothing more than another conquest to you, a gullible maid, easy to fool. It's obvious you changed your mind and decided against taking me with you. Rather than being man enough to tell me yourself, you simply planned to toss me aside and flee." She strained to prevent her voice from breaking. "You put me on a ship heading north, while you intended to travel south with your mistress." She brought her fists up to her chest, and pressed them over her heart, but the pain and humiliation only sharpened when he didn't deny it.

Landon spoke in an even tone behind her; an edge of anger laced his words. "The *Desire* was too closely monitored, Keelan. Gampo heard us talking at the warehouse. He'd find you by following *me*. As a diversion, I sent my vessel south, thinking you'd be sailing the other direction with Hall. It was my hope Gampo would abandon seeking you out in Charleston, and think you'd left on the *Desire* and follow her to Harbour Town, which would have taken him even farther from you." A pause. "Dammit Keelan, I was trying to *protect* you! Choosing this scheme has only put you in more danger," he growled.

Strong fingers gripped her shoulders again, and he spun her to face him. She closed her eyes so he couldn't tell how badly she was hurting. He'd put himself and his ship in jeopardy by offering both as a decoy, which was admirable, if it were true. She wanted to believe him, yet feared the pain he'd inflict on her heart if she was wrong again. While his argument sounded logical, it could be a convenient lie. Annette Camsby was still aboard, probably preparing for dinner. Probably expecting to be served her favorite wine. Probably anticipating Landon inviting her into his bed.

It was too big a risk.

Keelan, gesturing to herself and the surrounding space, whispered angrily, "Daniel, and I had no choice but to choose this *scheme*." She pushed the dripping ringlets of russet and brown-streaked hair from her face. "We couldn't risk being discovered. Gampo's men seemed to be everywhere, watching every vessel. After the *Glory* departed, his men came to search the tavern, so we had to flee first and worry about the destination later. This was the first ship in the harbor set to sail."

Unbidden and unwanted, the image of Landon and Annette strolling about the deck earlier permeated her mind. Her throat constricted as if a stone were caught in the middle of it. She'd have to steel herself against seeing the two of them together during the voyage to Harbour Town, although she wasn't sure how. She'd sleep in the pantry, or in the hidden compartment with the runaways down in the hold.

The waves of power and anger resonating from Landon were beginning to become unbearable. She had to get out of this small space. Stepping back in the direction of the door, she drew a deep breath. It was time to push him out of her heart. It wouldn't be easy, but the first step would be keeping physical distance between them, starting now. "Please, just stay away from me. I'll depart when we reach Harbour Towne. I won't say anything to Mrs. Camsby, and I'll leave the two of you to yourselves."

He returned her gaze with one of hot, blue fire. In two strides he stood before her, his chest inches from her own.

She swallowed. This wasn't keeping with her plan to maintain distance between them.

Wide shoulders blocked the rest of the cabin from her view. Although she wanted to bolt like a frightened hare, she stood her ground.

Landon shook his head, a bewildered expression on his face. "Little fool," he muttered. Circling his arms about her, he brought her full against his hardened frame and her breath would have left her in a *whoosh* if she hadn't gasped in surprise first.

His lips captured hers, demanding, *insisting* she respond. This was madness. She had to be stronger than this! Keelan tried to pull away, but found herself paralyzed by his touch. His arms, like iron bands, held her immobile. His lips moved against hers in a way that made her forget where she was. His fiery kiss radiated a heat which spread through her body and warmed the core of her soul. His hands slid down her sides and slipped around to caress her buttocks, pressing her to him; the hardness of his passion pulled forth a yearning from deep within her belly. She wanted this, yes. She wanted *him*. Part of her wanted to shout with joy. He wanted *her*. But wanting wasn't enough, not for her. She needed him to want *only* her.

She desired him, yes, but not like this. Not with the possibility he wanted her, but didn't actually love her as she loved him. Especially not with his mistress here.

How was she supposed to defend herself against an assault like this? Landon's tongue played with hers in an exotic dance. The sweetness of his mouth tormented her self-control. Memories swirled in her mind like a tornado... The two of them, trapped in the small tattered cabin during the storm, his hands on her calves, his lips tracing fire on her thigh, the musky scent of him mixed with leather and rain, the beauty of his face, eyes like the sky. She was unable to hold on to one vision long enough to complete it before another took its place.

Except for one memory.

Landon and Annette standing close... her hand on his chest. Was he using Keelan for his own temporary satisfaction? Or Annette? Was he using *both* of them? Dear God, she was still unable to stop kissing him; her free will had vanished along with her common sense. Her affection for him was deeper than she wanted to admit, and although her mind told her to stay away from him, it was impossible to retreat when he was this close.

This warm. This passionate. This vibrant.

Still, she managed to bring her hand to his chest and weakly push against it. Curiously, instead of shoving him, her hand spread over hardened muscles rippling beneath her fingers. She gasped as his hand found her breast, then groaned as his fingers brushed away the fabric binding them, tracing a sensual circle around the taut rosy peak he had somehow freed from bondage.

His kisses traced a fiery trail down her throat, and she drew a ragged breath. As the air rushed into her lungs, her head sought to clear itself from the passion her heart and body so eagerly sought. She wanted more of this, but what if the end result was more pain? Would he be kissing Annette like this later tonight?

This time, she pushed harder against his chest.

"Landon," she breathed. "Stop!"

He stopped but didn't release her. His eyes bored into hers, a glowing, smoldering light visible in the deep blue depths.

"Don't you understand, sweet Keelan?" He traced the line of demarcation between the darkly stained skin of her chest and the creamy white of her breasts. "My allegiance is to you and you alone. Why would I seek another when my only desire is for you?"

Were these silky words simply a means to get her into his bed? How could she possibly believe him when he'd obviously planned on sending her to Philadelphia while sharing this leg of his journey with Annette? Landon danced with Annette Camsby at Doreen's ball, her hand on his chest, his arm on her waist. He seemed willing enough to endure her touch and affections then. What had changed? Anything? Nothing?

She couldn't afford to be enchanted by his charms and sensual kisses, but oh, how she wanted to be. She wanted to beg for it.

Although it took every bit of emotional and physical strength she could muster, she managed to push herself away from him.

"Keelan, don't—" he whispered hoarsely.

Disappointment and regret swirled into anger.

"You have succeeded only in convincing me you are no more than a rutting dog," she said woodenly, squeezing her eyes shut once again. "Now, unhand me at once! And please, don't do that again. Ever."

Distance. Distance. *Distance.*

His arms were slow to comply, but eventually he released her and she jerked away from his heat and penetrating gaze. She focused on repairing her appearance as best she could, given the condition of her sodden garments. The wet linen strips which served to both protect her wounds and bind her breasts were useless; they'd dropped around her waist in their soggy state. She groaned in frustration as the bindings ignored her fingers' demands.

"Perhaps I can lend some assistance," Landon quietly offered from behind her. Was that disappointment? His ruse didn't work, and she had discovered his scheme.

Keelan shook her head as she glanced over her shoulder and fought to keep her voice from trembling. "I doubt any assistance you offer will benefit me in any way."

He had donned his breeches and was rummaging through the lower drawer of the tallboy. "I might surprise you." He removed a long knife, a folded piece of soft doeskin, and a long leather lace. "Although I would prefer otherwise, under these circumstances I am forced to aid you in your quest to hide that soft feminine form of yours, which I have come to crave so deeply."

He placed the soft leather on the floor and then proceeded to carve several holes along the short sides of the rectangular hide. The muscles in his shoulders and back rippled with his movements, and she hated herself for admiring them.

"My original intent was to have this made into a pair of gloves. However, I believe it now must serve a greater calling." His sensual lips curved into the slightest smile. He moved to stand before her, holding the short sides of the doeskin in his fingers.

She eyed him warily. "A corset? I fail to understand how wearing *that* will benefit my disguise," she questioned, lifting a skeptical brow.

"It is not intended for that purpose, love," he replied, an amused glint in his eyes. "Remove your shirt."

"I will *not!*" she gasped, horrified. She was quite proud of herself for fighting off Landon Hart and his mesmerizing lure. Granted, it took her a few moments, but now that she'd managed to push him far enough away, she didn't dare jeopardize her position. She was weak, *too* weak to test her resolve so soon.

"This will cover you better over the bandage," he explained patiently but firmly. "Now, trust me and do as I say."

"I don't need your help. I can do it myself." The pitch of panic in her own voice made her clamp a hand over her own mouth.

"Keelan," a quiet note of exasperation permeated his tone. "I intend for this to be laced over your chest to disguise your—curves—better." He held up the leather and cord. "One of us must hold it together while the other threads the tie. Now, please, remove the shirt."

Realizing there was little she could do to dissuade him from his mission, she presented her back and shrugged out of the shirt which had once been his.

Despite the dark stain applied, Keelan was positive her skin still reddened at what she was about to do.

❧ 66 ❧
CHAPTER SIXTY-SIX
TRUCE

Landon's gut churned and his flayed pride smarted at Keelan's words. *A rutting dog?*

He'd bared his soul! He'd told her about the sacrifice he'd made by sending his ship ahead to Harbour Town instead of Philadelphia. Up north, he would have delivered the rice and indigo for a delicious profit. Harbour Town had no need for such cargo. They had their own rice plantations and indigo mills.

He'd even *told* her he desired only her, not Annette. She didn't *believe* him.

How could she not believe him? He'd never lied to her before, had he? Snatching his shirt from his chair, he clenched his teeth together to prevent any ill-timed words from falling out of the mouth that still ached to kiss her again. Her kiss had been tender and full of longing. He could sense it. The heat from her body ignited a fire within his. They'd experienced a rush of passion *together*. Somewhere deep in the delicate recesses of his soul, a sensation stirred in a withered hollow he'd believed had been destroyed long ago.

In his past, loving a woman had only brought on pain and humiliation. It had made him weak. He'd squelched it. Never again. At least that is what he promised himself.

But...he not only wanted Keelan, desired her; he *needed* her. He needed her by his side. She made him feel strong, confident and *whole*. A tiny thought wheedled its way into his mind, itching like a mosquito bite.

She didn't trust him.

At all.

Trust between them was crucial now, if they were going to be together. He had to be able to trust her to keep his secrets. If they were ever exposed, his life—along with many others—would be placed in jeopardy. How was he supposed to do that in confidence when she obviously didn't have faith in him?

Keelan took off the shirt, her movements jerky, like a wary doe. She'd put a barrier between them, more fragile than thin china. She feared he would shatter it.

He could. Easily.

But...what would that accomplish, other than give her a reason to call him a bully? What could he do to gain Keelan Grey's elusive trust? This was a new problem he'd never had to deal with before. His crew trusted him with their lives and their welfare. *Not once* had he ever been required to prove his worth or honor. To *anyone*. If anything, she should have to convince him *she* could be trusted.

The shirt dropped to the floor and his gut tightened as he stared at the angry slashes along her delicate back and shoulders. Fury welled in his chest. He'd spent days seeking an informant who'd reveal Keelan's kidnapper. He'd found nothing. Even the few men captured at the warehouse didn't know the true identity of Gampo's employer. The man was nothing more than a shadow. Landon would have liked justice to be done upon the bastard, but he couldn't find him, dammit. And Gampo escaped. Again.

Keelan adjusted the bandages, then crossed her arms over her breasts and peered timidly over her shoulder.

He placed the soft doeskin against her back, and then reached the ends around her chest, pausing as his knuckles gently grazed hers. She tensed and sucked in her breath.

Ah, then. She might not trust him, but she desired his touch, nonetheless. He could work with that.

"Would you care to hold the ends, my love?"

⚜

KEELAN SNATCHED the ends of the leather corset from his hands, and pulled them tightly against the center of her chest, determined to repel his charm. He peered around her shoulder. Smiling almost lewdly, he dangled the long lace before her eyes. "Would you have me apply the ties, or perhaps hold the leather, so you can string the laces?"

The cause for his amusement was quite clear. If he held the ends, she would have to trust him to keep them snug over her chest. She'd just as soon let a fox in to the chickens' roost. If she permitted him to string the lace, she'd have to endure the touch of his fingertips as he threaded it through the holes. As humiliating as the second choice was, it was definitely the lesser of the two evils. Hopefully.

"Proceed with the lace, Captain." She narrowed her eyes and added sternly, "But try to be a gentleman about it."

He gave her a gallant bow. "I am here to serve, my dearest."

"I ponder your comprehension of the term," she replied dryly.

Landon indeed took his leisure in threading the lace through the holes in the hide; one by one, despite the glowering looks she threw his way. He threaded each eyelet with extreme care and slow, deliberate movements. When the task was complete, she snatched the laces from his fingers and angrily tightened them.

"Scoundrel."

He gave her a lopsided grin as he allowed his gaze to roam at will. "I take pride in the fact I complete all my tasks with perfection."

"Bah!" She bent down to retrieve her shirt from the floor, missing the admiring attention he gave to her slender hips and backside.

"What am I to do with you, sweet?" Landon inquired softly.

She gave a sarcastic laugh as she buttoned the shirt. "Leave me alone. You have enough distractions as it is."

"Ahhh, but my love, that is impossible. It's imperative for you continue in your guise as 'young Mahdi' to keep you safe," he mused. He took in every detail of her appearance, from the snug fit of her breeches to the green fire of her eyes. "But, I cannot allow you to hang your hammock in the hold with the crew at night. Too risky. You'll have to sleep here."

She stared at him, aghast. *Was he mad?* "I will not!"

"You must," he stated firmly. "Keelan, you can't keep a hammock in the hold with the crew. You're bound to be discovered. It will only be a matter of time before one of the men joins you in the head, or surprises you at a most inopportune moment. At least here, you'll have privacy."

She bit her lip. In truth, her thoughts had traveled the same path earlier. Sharing sleeping quarters with Landon Hart, however, would be disastrous. "I will not play the doxy to your lusts," she said angrily. Best to get that point through his thick skull. "Instead, I shall leave that duty to Annette Camsby."

Landon stared at her a moment, the tiniest hint of a smile playing about his mouth. Then he shook his head. "I will harbor no arguments, Keelan." Landon said sternly. "With Garrison aboard, your safety depends on your identity remaining secret for a while longer."

He knew? She fixed an accusing glare on him. "You knew he was aboard this ship?"

Landon shrugged casually. "Had I known *you* were here, I would never have allowed it. This was an opportunity for me to watch him. I have my suspicions about Garrison, and I had intended to test them."

Doubt tugged at her mind. She wanted to believe him and trust him, but she was torn. He wanted her in his bed. He used concern as a ploy to weaken her guard. There had been no mention of marriage vows to accompany all the things he desired of her. By-blow or not, she wouldn't play the part of a mistress for him. Or anyone, but especially not him.

Ugh. Who did she think she was fooling? One touch from Landon Hart would melt whatever wall she managed to construct between them. She had to find a way to be stronger than that. Keelan clenched her jaw in firmer resolve. She would not allow his handsome features and beguiling charm to sap her resistance.

She would *not.*

Landon reached for his shirt and shrugged it on. "You'd best get back to the galley. Marcel will wonder what has become of you." He grinned. "No doubt, he'll think I saw fit to see to your bath, as well as my own." Landon's eyes sparkled with laughter. "He'll never realize how truthful that assumption would be."

That man! Keelan snatched up the buckets and stomped out. Landon Hart was not going to make this easy.

Well, he was about to find out she was stronger than she looked.

❧ 67 ❧

CHAPTER SIXTY-SEVEN
GAMPO'S SPIES

E verett studied the scribbled note.

I know where she is. Meet me in the aft hold. Now.

Something seemed off. Maybe it was the tattered piece of handbill upon which the message was written. Maybe it was because not many people knew he was aboard. He raised his voice as loudly as he dared, "Who gave this to you?"

The man shrugged. "Someone came up behind me and whispered into my ear. Told me not to turn around. Put the paper and a shilling in my hand and then told me to give it to the tallest man on deck. That be you." He moved on before Everett could ask another question.

Sweat beaded along his upper lip. Had one of his contacts found Keelen? Problem was, his fortunes had recently changed, and he was unable to pay the reward he'd promised. Perhaps the man would be desperate enough to negotiate. He pushed off from the rail near the aft deck and sauntered toward the hatch. He swept his gaze around the ship. Annette Camsby stood near the helm beside Captain O'Brien. The plainly dressed woman who'd accompanied her stood nearby. She glanced his way and gave him a slight smile, which he returned with a quick nod to indicate all was well.

֍

KEELAN APPROACHED the helm like a child tasked with cutting her own switch for her punishment. Annette was there chirping at Conal O'Brien like a spring bird. Time to tell Conal to return to his cabin so Landon could apprise him of "the situation."

The situation being her.

As she took the first step, a movement caught her attention, and she glanced over in time to catch sight of Dr. Garrison ducking below deck. It wouldn't have merited her consideration if the petite woman who'd accompanied Annette aboard hadn't dashed over to follow him.

There was something familiar about her.

Keelan stopped and peered more closely. The young lady paused to cast a furtive look about before she descended. For a brief second, her face was visible from beneath her bonnet.

Doreen!

Keelan had left a letter for Uncle Jared, telling him he could find his daughter with Mrs. Camsby. Did he read it? Was Doreen accompanying Annette or the doctor? She sucked in a breath. Both?

She started to follow her cousin, then remembered her prior task. She darted up the steps to the helm, found Captain O'Brien, and quickly delivered Landon's message. Annette's irritated expression at the interruption lifted her mood somewhat. At the captain's nod, she spun and headed below deck.

The lower hold was dark and reeked of old, wet rags. It was separated into three sections. The cargo was dispersed based on weight and destination. Sounds of a muffled conversation rose above the wooden beams, encompassing the hold like a giant ribcage. It took a moment to adjust her eyes; the light was thin, coming from a single lantern somewhere near the center of the space.

Keelan snaked her way between barrels, bales, and crates, following the low hum of murmured conversation. A high shriek, suddenly cut short, froze her in place. It was followed by a soft *thud*. Heart pounding and fearing for Doreen's welfare, Keelan crept forward, then paused at a familiar voice.

"So ye thinks ye can steal away without paying yer share to Gampo, eh?"

Orvis Hatch!

"I did no such th-th-thing," Garrison responded. "There were no shares. The plan failed. What do you want? Why are you aboard this vessel?" His voice rose to a treble pitch.

"Seein' as how Gampo couldn't find the wench what killed 'is first, I was instructed to take vengeance from yer hide instead, since ye be the one who paid us to bring 'er in." A pause. "Unless ye can tell me where to find 'er. Me bones tell me she's aboard here somewheres."

Keelan's entire body went rigid. Her intuition had been right; Everett Garrison had been responsible for the kidnapping. It made her wonder more about his claim that Doreen had misunderstood his instructions, and had given Papa too much medicine, killing him. Her mouth became dry. Somehow, she didn't think it was Doreen's mistake.

She peeked around a large crate and bit back a gasp. Doreen was slumped on the floor. Orvis had a knife at the doctor's throat and had him backed up against a wall of crates next to Doreen's motionless form. A trickle of blood darkened the floor beneath her cousin's nose.

She backed away to get help, then paused. If she left, she might return too late. Orvis looked eager to draw blood. She slipped the dagger from her boot and circled around to the other side of the large crate, hoping to stay out of sight a bit longer and get closer to insure a more accurate throw.

Dr. Garrison raised his hands, palms out. "I don't know where she went. After she ran from the warehouse, I couldn't find her either. I'm sorry."

Orvis drew his eyebrows low. "Gampo don't take lightly to them what's backed out on an accord. Them warehouse goods weren't no easy takin's like ye said they would be, and in the end, we didn't get no shares from our labors, neither."

The doctor's hands shook and his chin trembled. "Tell—tell Gampo I'll make it up to him. I—"

Hatch gave an incredulous snort of laughter. "Like I said, he wants it to come outta yer hide," he sneered, gripping Garrison's hair with his free hand. His blade flashed, and the doctor shrieked.

Keelan froze in terror. Orvis now held a bloody piece of the doctor's scalp, hair still attached in his hand. With a dark snarl, he raised his knife again. She jolted into action and moved from her hiding place to get a clearer shot. The ship pitched slightly and shifted her balance enough to cause her shoulder to bump the crate. Orvis sliced his head toward the noise.

He'd seen her. With no other choice, she drew back her dagger, and took the only option she had, which was to go on the attack or at least attempt to appear threatening. "Move away from them." Her voice sounded unnatural in her ears.

Instead of doing as she demanded, the pirate gave her a distorted grin that was more like a grimace, considering his face was still swollen and discolored from their earlier engagements. Everett stumbled to the side as Orvis drove the blade into his torso.

"No!" she screamed.

Orvis whirled, pulling a second blade from his belt, and strode toward her. "I'll have yer eyes fer fish bait, boy."

In a panic, she threw her dagger, but it went wide, slicing off a piece of Orvis's left ear. He flinched and howled. Behind him, Dr. Garrison struggled to pull out the blade buried between his ribs. Finally succeeding, he pushed himself away from the wall and staggered toward the pirate. Orvis grinned at her and raised his blade as he moved closer. Behind him, Everett lurched forward and with a desperate heave of effort, buried the dagger in Orvis's back.

The pirate fell face down and didn't move.

His strength expelled, Garrison began to collapse.

"Dr. Garrison!" She ran to help him, but his weight dragged both of them to the floor.

Doreen stirred and pushed herself to a sitting position. Her eyes were wide, and she numbly swept her gaze from side to side until she found Garrison crumpled in a heap on the floor. "Everett, my darling, what happened?" Doreen whimpered as she crawled toward them, oblivious to the blood dripping from her temple and nose.

The doctor had his hand pressed against his ribs; blood was still streaming between his fingers. Keelan ripped off her vest, wadded it into a ball, and gave it to him to press against his side.

He didn't look up from his task. "I need my medicine bag and some bandages." His words were choppy and pained. He glanced at Keelan. "It would help, boy, if you would press this wound firmly. I'm finding it hard to apply enough pressure on my own."

"Yes sir," Keelan replied and quickly replaced his hand with hers. For all he'd done to the people she'd held dear all her life, she couldn't ignore his injury. The doctor had just saved her from being attacked, and probably from being killed.

Doreen teetered to her feet. Keelan pressed harder to stop the blood from seeping and glanced at her cousin. "Make sure you have someone inform Captain Hart or Captain O'Brien what's happened."

Doreen's head snapped around in her direction. Keelan stilled. She'd forgotten to lower her voice.

Did Doreen recognize it? She quickly directed her gaze back to the doctor. The exchange between Orvis and Dr. Garrison had reaffirmed the decision to travel in disguise had been a good one. The pirates continued to seek her out. She couldn't risk another recognizing her like Simon had. Her heart pounded in her chest, and she felt Doreen's stare boring into her back.

Her cousin paused a long moment before she responded, "I will."

Dr. Garrison had pulled a handkerchief from his pocket and was pressing it against his wounded head. Keelan wiped the blood from his eyes with the corner of it. Two emotions warred in her chest. The first, anger at Garrison. The second was a grudging gratitude. She glanced at the still, face-down form of Orvis Pike lying a few feet away. If Dr. Garrison hadn't prevented Orvis from attacking her, she'd be dead. She'd panicked, and it had almost cost her life.

Everett grimaced as he readjusted the handkerchief. "Thank you. If you hadn't distracted him, I'd probably be dead, and so would Miss Grey." He glanced toward his side where her hand pressed. "Can you tell how deeply the blade went in?"

Keelan lifted her hand long enough to peek. "It went in at an upward angle under your ribs."

He closed his eyes. "Not too much damage then, only pain. I can instruct Doreen—Miss Grey, to dress it. I will need whiskey and bandages."

"I'll see you get them," she replied.

The sound of running feet interrupted their conversation, and Daniel's voice rang out in the dim light, "Mahdi, where are you?"

"Over here!" she called.

Conal, Landon and Daniel rounded the large crate and skidded to a stop.

"Are you hurt?" Landon's gaze swept over her body as she stood.

Keelan shook her head. "Dr. Garrison's been stabbed." She related the earlier conversation and events.

Landon's mouth thinned and his eyes glinted with something dangerous as she finished. "We'll lock the doctor in the rear hold until we reach Harbour Town." He gestured to Orvis and murmured to Conal, "It's doubtful he boarded the ship alone. Until we find his cohorts, tell Johnny, Remus and Henry to be extra vigilant around the newest hands we hired and report any suspicions to us."

Conal nodded grimly. "There's less than ten new hires, I'd figure. I'll have them move their hammocks together. Easier to keep track of them when they're off duty."

Doreen's voice warbled up and down as she scrambled around the crates. "I'm here! I'm back. I have the medicine bag," Her face was blood-stained and her hands shook as she brushed a handful of hair away from her eyes. She shouldered her way between the men, dropped to the other side of the doctor's prone form, and let out a shaky breath. "I've been assisting Dr. Garrison for the past several months. I know what to do."

Doreen removed a clean cloth and a whiskey bottle. She nodded to Keelan to remove her hand and when she did, Doreen doused the wound, causing the doctor to suck in his breath. A strong odor of spirits wafted in the closed air of the hold. Doreen immediately pressed the clean cloth over his wound. "Continue to put pressure on it," she instructed Keelan, without glancing at her. Keelan complied and Doreen rummaged through the bag again.

Garrison flicked his hand toward the bottle. "Whiskey. To dull the pain," he said hoarsely before squeezing his eyes shut.

Keelan reached for the bottle, but Doreen stopped her.

"Wait, I have something better," she mumbled, still rooting through the bag. "Ah, here it is." She pulled out a small, unlabeled brown bottle and scooted closer to Dr. Garrison's head, which she gently put on her lap, as if handling thin glass. "Everett, drink this." She put the bottle to his lips, he opened his mouth, and took a gulp. His eyelids flew open.

"That... wasn't whiskey! What did you give me?" The panicked pitch of his voice bounced off the wood hull.

Doreen's eyes shone with tears. "Don't fret, darling. It's the pain medication you purchased for Uncle George. The bottle you told me would take away the worst pain."

His face paled further. "No..."

Doreen stroked his forehead and reapplied the handkerchief to his head wound. Tears streamed down her cheeks and dripped from her jaw. "You said it was terribly expensive and only for severe pain, but I can't allow you to suffer like this. I care too much for you."

Everett Garrison's face contorted as he struggled to speak. "That's... not..."

He convulsed and Doreen let out a startled cry. "What's wrong? What's happening?"

Garrison arched and thrashed, jerking away from her. Keelan grabbed the bottle from Doreen's grasp and sniffed. It wasn't whiskey or vinegar. Her chest constricted as she put together all the pieces. Dr. Garrison hadn't just given Papa the wrong medication. He had instructed Doreen to administer poison to Papa the night he died.

The same realization stuttered across Doreen's face. "Dear Lord!" she cried. "Why? Why did you have me give this to my uncle?" Her eyes were wide with shock and terror.

"He killed my Rachel. My love," he choked. "She and my family... were on the ship he sank." He fumbled with the pocket of his coat and withdrew the tattered letter Rachel had written, accepting his marriage proposal. His hand trembled so badly, the letter almost fell apart. He pressed it over his heart. "My Rachel needed to be avenged." An odd gurgling sound emanated from his throat. He gasped and convulsed again, then his chest stilled.

"Oh dear God, please forgive me! Forgive me!" Doreen wailed, covering her face with her hands.

"It's not your fault," Keelan said softly, kneeling beside her. "You thought you were helping him. You didn't know." Doreen collapsed into her arms and Keelan held her even as tears welled in her own eyes. "You didn't know."

❦ 68 ❦

CHAPTER SIXTY-EIGHT
A SECRET REVEALED

Keelan scurried through the hatch as fast as her quaking limbs would take her. She jumped up the steps and on to the deck. She had a desperate need for fresh air to clear her head. Her mind screamed in torment from the brutal realizations pummeling her. She paused at the rail and gulped in several deep jagged breaths. She'd had her suspicions, but deep down she didn't want them to be true. Deep down, she had known.

Garrison. Murderer.

They had trusted him. Papa had helped and encouraged him to develop his practice. He'd preyed on them and their charity. *Garrison* killed Papa and hired pirates to kidnap her. Those actions had nothing to do with infatuation as she had errantly surmised. In the several months prior to arriving in Charleston, he'd played the part of an awkward physician with ease. She shuddered.

She had viewed him as a harmless, clumsy gawk of a man, who tried her level of tolerance as would a pesky fly. How wrong she had been.

She placed a hand over her heart and tried to will it to slow to a normal rate. How foolish of her to be so blind to his charade. She had been so concerned with her own problems, like avoiding a marriage to Pratt; she had missed what was happening beneath her nose. She clutched her hand against her chest. The locket and ring dug into her skin and reminded her of their presence.

Keelan pulled the ribbon, lifting the two items from the crevice between her breasts. She stared at the signet ring, a welcome distraction from the grisly scene below deck.

In the rosy, golden light of the setting sun, she gently traced her finger over the crest, wondering idly about the man who'd sired her. Was he a good father to his other children, her half brothers and sisters? She had always prayed for siblings. Would they accept her? Probably not, but she would still wish for it to be so. What other secrets awaited her in the darkness of George Grey's old trunk? Whose family's blood surged through her heart?

The man in the miniature stared back at her. What features did her true father's seed give her? The eyes? Her father's smiling green eyes sparkled at her as if they shared a secret. Her mother's eyes were gray, so perhaps, yes, the eyes. What of her warm russet tresses? Her mother's hair was a pale brown, her father's a shiny black. Whence came the red curls? Perhaps another relative, a grandparent, maybe?

She straightened. Pondering her heritage would not reveal her mother's secret any quicker. The probable presence of another pirate spy aboard made her quest more dangerous. Even so, she would see it through to the end. If her father's house did not welcome her, so be it, but the desire to meet her kin would drive her there, in time.

The ship's bell sang with a mellow tongue as it marked the end of the last dogwatch. Another shift of seamen would soon rouse from their hammocks for duty until the hourglass had been turned four times and the ship's bell rung eight.

A quiet voice rose above the creaking ship and the gentle splash of the sea against the sturdy hull. "You've had a rough time over these past few weeks. How do you fare?"

Keelan jumped, then managed a small smile as Conal O'Brien stepped forward and leaned his forearms against the rail next to her. His eyes were kind. She relaxed. "I'm alive. Considering the fate which has fallen on the rest of my family, I feel blessed, but I worry about the other pirates amongst us."

"As the captain is also the ship's master, I can see justice met for any offense aboard this craft. If we find them, I can have them put in irons and punished." He shifted his position. "Since they're likely wanted by the law, we'll deliver them when we make port in Harbour Town and let them meet their fate at the short end of a rope."

The shoreline had become a distant black line, and the sun began its inevitable descent. Wind snapped the sails, and the ship responded with a groan, ropes whining in the sheaves. "You have my sympathies on the death of your father," O'Brien said quietly.

Keelan swallowed. "Thank you. However, the man was not my father," she said hoarsely, fighting back the tears threatening to spill. If Landon hadn't already told him, he probably would soon. The two were fast friends. At least she'd be able to scrutinize Conal O'Brien's reaction to the news. She continued, "Not truly by blood, but he raised me as his own. I should have suspected Garrison was poisoning him. If I had paused to ponder the situation, I would have seen the entire puzzle laid out." Anger welled in her chest. Why hadn't she seen it?

"He fooled everyone." He put his hand on her shoulder and gave it a small comforting squeeze. "You can't blame yourself."

Her throat constricted. Keelan shrugged her silent thanks and wiped her nose on her sleeve.

He chuckled. "You're becoming used to playing the boy, Mahdi."

Realizing what she had just done was far from ladylike, Keelan gave the captain a chagrined smile. "So it would seem."

He rubbed the back of his neck, as if pondering a question before he finally spoke. "Ye said something that confused me. And I beg yer pardon if it offends ye in any way. Ye said Commodore Grey was *not* yer sire?" He left the question hanging.

A solitary tear broke free and began a lonely trail down her cheek. "On his deathbed, Papa told me he could not give my mother a child, so she went to another man... One who could... who could give her..." Her voice broke and she paused for a moment to gather herself. *Stop being silly. Crying about it won't change anything.* She should be happier. Now, she had the opportunity to choose her own path. That thought provided a bit more comfort.

After wiping her eyes, she showed him the locket, dangling on the ribbon with the ring. "My mother took a lover who sired me. And years ago, he looked like this."

O'Brien bent low and studied the miniature.

A young man. Dark hair. Green eyes.

His eyes widened with shock, then hardened with fury. "Where did you get this!" he demanded, snatching the locket from her fingers. He stared at it, then his gaze followed the red ribbon to the ring dangling at the end.

She stepped back at the unseemly reaction and eyed him warily. "Papa gave it to me. He said my mother cherished it." She studied him. His jaw was clenching and unclenching sporadically. "Why does it disturb you? Do you know him?"

He stepped close and looked hard at Keelan. "Yes, I know him," he said.

Her mouth dropped open. Could it really be this easy to find the identity of her sire?

O'Brien stared at the locket, then shoved it back to her. "And now, I think I understand the purpose of Uncle Fynn's meeting with Commodore Grey. He must have suspected."

"Suspected what?" Hart and O'Brien had visited Twin Pines to speak with Papa, but she knew not the topic. Her mind swirled with questions. "Who was your Uncle Fynn?"

His jaw tightened. "My mother's brother." He jabbed a finger at the miniature. "I have seen that portrait before, as well."

"You—you have actually seen this *same* portrait?" She stared at the miniature. "In God's name, where?"

"It hangs on the parlor wall in my parent's home, next to my mother's," he stated flatly. At her curious stare, Conal O'Brien inhaled sharply and then continued.

"That man is my father."

❦ 69 ❦

CHAPTER SIXTY-NINE
A SHIP ON THE HORIZON

Conal O'Brien braced his hands wide along the rail and leaned forward, letting his head drop. "Uncle Fynn must have suspected you were sired by my father. It was probably why he wanted to meet with Commodore Grey, to confirm it." He gave Keelan a sideways glance. "The Commodore told us he didn't know Fynn, but thinking back on it, neither Hart nor I felt he was being entirely forthright."

Keelan wasn't sure what to say. While she was euphoric because the search for her father's identity was completed so quickly, Conal had to deal with his obvious anger toward the man as well as his desire to protect his mother.

He shook his head. "If ye hadn't had the ring, I wouldna of believed ye. My da has always worshipped my mum. I canna believe he..." He looked away and stared at the sea flowing quickly past the hull. Bursts of spume sprayed in their wake.

It was easy to understand the turmoil of emotions swirling in Conal's gut. The same ones had assaulted her the night Papa died. Keelan untied the ribbon around her neck and removed the ring. She held it out to him. "This belongs to you, then. It is your family's signet ring, your crest, is it not?"

"Aye." He opened his hand, and she placed it on his palm. He held it up in the fading light and studied it a moment. "The four lions represent deathless courage in battle by four brothers. The wheat is a symbol of plenty. We are a clan descended of sea warriors." He gave her a small smile. "And more recently, sea merchants." He slipped the ring on his finger. "Thank you for returning it."

Her fingers curled over the locket half. "May I keep the miniature?" Papa said her mother treasured it because her father gifted it to her. It was the one thing she had which connected both her parents.

Conal nodded, his nostrils flaring. "My mother has one of her own, more recently painted." He dropped his head again. "I'm sorry. I shouldna have spoken to ye that way."

"Don't apologize." She wanted to comfort him, but wasn't sure he'd welcome her pity. She touched his shoulder with her fingertips. "I understand how you feel. It's been difficult for me to digest all this information as well. My life is suddenly not what I thought it was."

He swallowed and lifted his head to check the sails. "'Tis no fault of yours. It shouldn't be held against ye."

She looked out over the ocean at the sun, burning red near the horizon, uncertain how to ask the question burning equally hot on her tongue. There was no easy way to ask it. Perhaps she should simply blurt it out. "Why would your Uncle Fynn need to confirm my existence with Papa—Commodore Grey? I can't think of a reason why such information would be important to him."

Conal shrugged. "Fynn was never one to comply with popular opinion. He followed his own compass. There were many times I challenged his reasoning, but he always had a firm plan and in the end, it usually worked his way." He glanced at her through long, auburn lashes. "He and my father were tight as kin, although he was my mother's brother. I want to believe his interest in the commodore wouldn't cause my mum pain in any way." Conal pushed away from the rail. "There's no telling now. He took his reasoning to the grave with him." He bid her a good evening and excused himself.

The cow lowed forlornly from her pen. A nanny goat bleated a sympathetic response.

Keelan stood alone, still in shock.

The ocean waves broke against the ship's stern, the sails clapped and inhaled the breath of the wind. The sun had descended closer to the horizon, as if fleeing the thick clouds chasing it. Her mind swirled with the rush of recent events.

Everett. Murderer. *Monster*.

Conal. Captain. Friend. *Half brother?*

Her father—his father? What wicked, twisted trick of fate was this? How could the world be so small?

How could it be so cruel?

Her musings were interrupted by the dogwatch's cry. "Sail, ho'!"

Conal's voice boomed a short distance away. "Where away?"

"Near two points off the starboard bow, sir!" came the reply.

O'Brien strode across the deck. "Johnny, take the glass and go aloft. Try to make out what she is."

They all waited while Johnny scampered up. Impatience tinged O'Brien's voice, "What do you see, man?"

"Aye sir, 'tis a schooner with dark sails. She looks like the *Dragon*!"

Conal's voice barked through the evening mist. "Call all hands and make sail for her!"

A sudden flurry of motion arose from the deck.

"Mahdi!"

She jumped and shifted her gaze from the man clinging to the ropes at the top of the mainmast to the voice harkening her. Conal's piercing green gaze captured her own. Eyes like hers. Tussled, russet locks curled against his forehead, lifted by the wind. Russet locks like hers.

"Find Hart!"

She scampered below the deck. As Keelan neared the galley, low voices made her pause. Daniel and Landon. She couldn't make out what they were saying. As she was about to creep closer to listen, Landon strode past the door in the direction of his cabin and then paused at the sight of Keelan standing near the steps.

His face softened. "What is it?"

"A—a sh-ship," she stammered. "A ship has been sighted!"

His mouth tightened at the news, causing her stomach to twist. They were in trouble. Without a word, he flicked his hand, motioning her up to the deck before him. She wordlessly complied, fear pricking her skin.

Gampo had caught up with them.

⚜

LANDON ADMIRED Keelan's pleasantly curved backside as he followed her up the narrow steps. At this angle, he would have to be a fool or a blind man to not notice the womanly shape in front of him. He scowled and made a mental note to find her a longer jerkin to wear.

Landon's new concern was keeping Keelan's identity secret until Orvis Pike's cohort was revealed, removed from the ship and placed in the custody of Harbour Town's sheriff.

He mentally ran through the new faces he'd seen on the *Seeker's* decks. Orvis had done a good job staying out of sight; otherwise, Keelan would have recognized him long before the confrontation in the hold. Everyone must remain watchful.

He refocused his attention to the issue at hand and cursed. He'd hoped by sending the *Desire* southward early, Gampo would follow, taking him and his thirst for revenge further away from Keelan. A nervous twinge shot through Landon's stomach. Keelan was supposed to be journeying north, away from danger, not south toward it. The sighting of another ship made him anxious, but he'd wait until he had a chance to view it through the glass before he'd worry about Keelan's safety.

As long as it wasn't a schooner with dark sails, they'd be fine.

❧ 70 ❧

CHAPTER SEVENTY
DARK SAILS

"It's a schooner with darkened sails," Conal said. "Although they fly no flag, I'd bet my last pint of grog that it's the *Dragon*."

Keelan caught her breath and gripped the rail until her knuckles stretched thin and white. Gampo! Why did he come after the *Seeker*? Did Orvis or the other pirates find a way to signal them? Her heart stuttered. Or had Gampo known all along she'd been aboard?

"Aye, it looks to be her," Landon responded, his mouth set in a grim line. He snapped the glass shut. "We're heavy with cargo. However, they approach leeward, probably returning from following the *Desire* to Harbour Town. They must have discovered Keelan wasn't on her. We make the port in less than a day. I suggest we start with half the water barrels since we can replace them quickly and then lose the rations."

Conal stared at Landon a moment before he sent orders to the crew. "Lighten the load. Unlash and pitch over the water barrels."

"Aye, sir!" Several crew mates jumped to action.

"Clear the lashes and load!" Conal shouted. His order was repeated and echoed in relay. Additional orders were relayed as the cannons, called guns on a ship, were primed to fire. He flung a command at Keelan. "Take Johnny and Remus down to the galley and haul up the heaviest contents of Marcel's larder."

Sails were hauled high and guns loaded. Men carried up crates of smaller weapons, such as rifles, pistols and swords and lashed them to the masts. Conal and Landon continued to shout commands while Keelan hurried to locate the two crewmen.

She found Remus and Johnny and after relaying the captain's instructions, the three headed for the galley.

Marcel met them at the galley door. "What eez—" At the sight of the three of them, he shook his head and sliced the air with his hand. "Non! Take ze water first! I spend too much—"

"The water has been let go, Marcel," Remus shouldered his way into the pantry. "We'll start with the salted fish and rice."

They hauled large barrels and sacks of other staples up to the amidships deck. Marcel, Keelan noted with amusement, grudgingly pointed to the items he was more willing to part with and greedily protected those he was not.

"You will not take my citrons!" The red-faced cook grabbed the burlap sack half-filled with bright, yellow lemons and clutched them to his chest. "Throw the goat instead!"

"You can't throw the goat overboard!" The words were out of Keelan's mouth before she had time to think.

Marcel and Remus stopped arguing and stared at her oddly. She almost froze in panic. A galley boy probably wouldn't have said that. What would he have said? "Take the molasses," she suggested. "At least it will not kick you."

Remus grinned and nodded. "Aye. That makes better sense. 'Tis easier to toss, too." He took the crock and headed up the steps.

Marcel, however, continued to stare long and hard at Keelan. "Why would you care about a goat?"

Keelan swallowed. "It's not the goat I care about," she replied, fearing the frenzied beating of her heart was visible in the pulse of her neck. "The captain ordered water barrels overboard. We'll need the goat for the milk."

Marcel narrowed his eyes After a second he nodded and shrugged. "Makes sense."

With as much calm as she could muster, Keelan wiped her nose on her sleeve, grabbed a bag of onions, and swiftly followed Remus to the upper deck. She'd come dangerously close to giving herself away. After noting Marcel's reaction, she wasn't sure she was safe from discovery just yet.

Above deck, an active crew had readied the guns and unfurled additional sails. The pirate ship maneuvered to intercept them, tacking back and forth like a serpent.

"There's a second vessel!" The call came down from the watch. "Ahead on the larboard side!"

"A second?" Conal reached for the glass and put it up to his eye. "A cunning trap. I wonder if she's a prize crew or is part of Gampo's fleet."

"Prize crew?" Keelan had never heard the term.

"The former crew what's aboard a taken vessel," Remus answered. "It's what *we* don't want ter become."

Conal shifted his stance, lowering the glass. "Johnny, eyes on the larboard sloop!" Conal barked. "Call out if she changes course."

"Aye, Captain!"

The second boat was ahead of them and in-between the *Seeker* and the pirates. If they slowed and turned toward them and the *Dragon* swooped in behind, Conal's ship would be raked across the stern and aft, as well. The small portable guns the sailors set up fore and aft couldn't possibly defend them against two other vessels raking them with their broadside guns.

Conal focused on the pirates and their darkened sails, the ominous look on his face making Keelan catch her breath. Worry seeped into her limbs. He didn't have to tell her this was bad.

Landon's earlier observation had proven worthy. The *Seeker* sailed with the current and the winds. The pirate ship was approaching from the east and starboard side. By the time it was able to position itself along the same path, the *Seeker* had begun to gain speed.

⚶

A PUFF of smoke from the *Dragon* caught Keelan's attention. Immediately, a sailor gave a warning shout from the crosstrees before the report echoed over the water.

Conal whirled. "Helmsman! Hard to leeward!"

"Aye, sir!" The crewman spun the wheel to the left.

Landon barked another sharp order and a small sail was shifted. The ship changed its course, turning away from the dark sails.

To Keelan's relief, the cannonball landed well short, with a rather unimpressive splash. Elated, she whooped her cheer along with the crew.

Conal made an observation. "We're in range of their guns. We might not be able to lighten the load fast enough to outrun both of them," he said. He locked gazes with Landon, his gaze steady and predatory. "You know my take."

Landon crossed his arms. "The guns are ready." He held Conal's gaze a moment longer. "We have women aboard. We have to outrun them as best we can and pray we reach Harbour Town first."

Conal nodded. "I realize that." He glared at Gampo's ship. "I'd give my last drop of water to see that schooner sink to Davy Jones locker."

Landon merely nodded. They would not confront him today. Sails were trimmed, and the *Seeker* made another sweeping turn westward. The crew began wetting the canvas so it would hold more wind. Keelan carried buckets of seawater from the rail to Johnny, who handed them to another shipmate. Her shoulders burned under the strain. Although she tried to be careful, water sloshed to the deck, making the walk back and forth a slippery one until someone scattered sand over the boards.

"The little sloop has lowered her mainsail!" a sailor shouted.

Keelan's heart lurched against her chest in a mild panic. The *Seeker* bounded over the waves and would soon pass the smaller boat. Gampo's vessel still approached from farther west, and if it didn't alter its course, it would ram the smaller sloop broadside.

"What the devil is Gampo doing?" Landon leaned forward and focused on the other two boats. "Is he using the sloop as a shield?"

Conal scowled. "We won't attack the other boat, and he knows it. He'll come around then bolt out of her cover, ready to fire his port side guns."

Damage and destruction to the *Seeker* seemed inevitable. Keelan reached down and checked for the dagger strapped to her boot, hoping its presence would bolster her bravado.

It didn't.

"Keelan."

She jumped, startled at the sudden voice in her ear. She spun around and expelled a breath. "Landon, you almost frightened me out of my skin."

For a moment, concern left his face as he gave her a lopsided grin. "My apologies," he murmured softly. "I would never be able to forgive myself if I frightened you out of your skin." He paused while his gaze traveled from her eyes to her throat. A strange tightening in her belly moved with his perusal as it continued downward. "Not long ago," he continued, just audible, "while attempting to bathe, I found the feel of your skin most appealing."

"Captain," she could only breathe the words. "You have no scruples."

"Nay." He smiled devilishly. "I haven't a single one."

She wanted to walk into his arms and let his strength calm her fear. However, that would be counter productive to her current objective, which was *distance*. He stepped closer, and she caught herself breathing him in.

Stop it.

This was not being strong. This was being weak. This was definitely not keeping a safe distance. *Was* there a safe distance? Landon reached his arms around her and she almost jumped back, fearing he was about to embrace her in front of the crew. A stiff leather belt pressed against her hips as he buckled a pair of pistols to her waist.

His voice remained low, barely a whisper, while he focused on his task. "Keelan, we will not surrender this ship. If we have to engage, you are to lock yourself in my cabin. They'll have to make it past the crew and me to get to you." He placed his hands on her shoulders, his crystal gaze intense. "These pistols are only good at a short distance. Best at close range. Don't fire unless you have *no other choice*." He swallowed, his expression a swirl of emotion.

Concern. Fear. Despair.

Yet also...courage, ferocity, and determination. He would battle to the death for his crew.

For her.

She suddenly understood. If they were defeated, she would have a choice to make. She could let the pirates assign her fate, or she could determine her own. She stroked the cool, dark gray metal. Would she have the courage to use both of them? She couldn't find the words to speak, so she just nodded.

"My sweet—"

His voice barely reached her ears over the wind and the sounds of the ship flying over the water. She lifted her face and met his gaze. The pirates could only board the *Seeker* if they disabled her. They could only get to Keelan if Landon... The thought of him lying cold and motionless on the deck of the *Seeker* paralyzed her breath. A swirling gray cloud permeated her mind. Images of Landon cut through the fog, giving her a brief glimpse of each memory before it faded: Landon discovering her hiding spot in the garden... on his horse with her riding bonnet perched on his head and a leering grin on his face... fighting with ferocity sword to sword with Gampo in the warehouse... his eyes darkening to a deep blue just before kissing her...

The fog dissipated when he placed his hands on her shoulders and gave them a gentle squeeze. "Keelan, I love you."

Their eyes locked, and in that moment the wavering uncertainty skittering through the surrounding air calmed. Sounds became muffled; motion seemed to slow. In this single slice of time, she had an acute sense they were connected by a power stronger than fear, more resilient than the possibility of impending death. From the cadence of their breath to the rhythm of their heartbeats, they were bonded.

She raised her chin and took a deep breath. "I love you, too."

Whatever Fate had in store for them... let it come.

They would fight together.

CHAPTER SEVENTY-ONE
BATTLE AT SEA

Landon stood on the uppermost deck as the *Dragon* chewed away the sea separating the two vessels. Her hull was painted a blood red. Several sails were the same color; others were various shades of grey, blue, green, or white with numerous patches, making them appear more like a ragged quilt.

"It's him." Conal ground out the words as if they were pieces of gravel.

"Yes," Landon answered warily, his voice soft and even, as if he raised it but a little, the air around Conal would catch fire.

The sharply angled boat rushed to engage the *Seeker.* Landon stood at his friend's shoulder. "We're not murderers, Conal."

"I know that." Conal's jaw clenched hard. "However, I believe Lady Justice has earned her due." He stood still as a rock, except for the sea breeze lifting his hair from his broad shoulders. It was the first time Keelan had seen him without it neatly pulled back.

Landon leaned a hip against the rail, a figure of casual indolence, but Keelan knew better. Underneath he was tense and rigid, ready to spring into action if called upon. "True enough." He nodded. "But can you be sure the crew is willing? Can you be certain no innocents will be lost to satisfy the vengeance Gampo has earned? That second vessel might not belong to him." He pointed to the sloop. "Look, even now they seem to be trying to haul up her mainsail again, although I'm still at a loss why they dropped it in the first place. It wasn't something a seasoned crew would do."

Conal's gaze was fixed on the dark, two-masted vessel, which sliced through the waves toward them, but his shoulders dropped a little. "You're right," he finally answered.

Keelan noted the hard line of his jaw and the surrounding tightness of her half-brother's eyes. He was a man of honor; that realization made her happy and proud.

Landon nudged Conal's ribs. "We've outrun him before, we'll do it again."

Conal inhaled deeply through his nose and blinked. "Aye."

A distant boom made Keelan jump. She watched in horror as the small sloop's foremast shook, then broke in half. The top section folded down over itself and the sail fluttered crazily beside it.

"Perhaps it's not Gampo's prize ship after all," Landon mused.

"Well, she's about to become one, unless we can detain, or at the very least, distract the *Dragon*," Conal said.

❧

"Ho, Captain!" came a shout from the crosstrees. "The sloop's foremast has been crippled, but she's still hauling up her mainsail. The *Dragon* is almost clear of her."

Conal snapped to action. "Clear the braces! Man the port side guns! As soon as she passes the sloop, fire!"

Landon turned to Conal. "The second and third guns are filled with grape shot, one and four are armed with bar shot," he said, his voice confident and firm.

Conal nodded. "Send them a volley of grapeshot. Pepper the *Dragon's* mainsail and slow her down. Avoid sweeping the decks, if you can. Disable her sails. Aim high."

Landon strode across the poop deck. He'd strapped a saber to his hip and a gun belt around his waist. Long dark curls whipped behind his broad shoulders and her breath left her lungs.

He's magnificent.

And he loved her. *Her.*

Landon shouted to another man standing by the main deck hatch. "Two and three guns, at the ready! Aim high lads, aim high! We want to shred the canvas as best we can." The order was relayed below to the men manning the ship's guns. Keelan nervously tapped the handle of a pistol as she tried to follow the activity on the main deck below.

A puff of smoke from the *Dragon* warned the crew of an incoming shot. A cannonball ripped through the top railing of the *Seeker*, flew past Remus, bounced off the main deck, and then plopped into the sea. The entire ship seemed to pause for a breath while everyone checked to make sure all body parts were still intact.

Landon broke the silence. "Fire as you bear!"

"Aye, sir!"

A loud *boom* sounded, making the deck boards shake beneath her feet. She grasped the rail, and was enveloped by a cloud of acrid smoke, which made her cough. She pulled her shirt up over her nose. When it cleared, she scanned Gampo's boat for damage. Her eyes were watering so much, she couldn't tell if the sails had holes from the grapeshot. By the sight of men scrambling on deck and the sudden bobbing of the vessel, enough damage had been done to slow down their progress, somewhat.

Landon reached for the spy glass. "Looks like the small sloop has finally reset the mainsail." Conal placed it in his hand, and Landon peered through it for a few seconds. "Who the devil is commanding that boat, I wonder? They've released the jib the wrong—"

Another smoke cloud from the *Dragon* shot out from the broadside facing the small sloop, followed by a muffled boom.

"Looks like he's switched his sights from us to the boat," Conal braced his hands on his hips and rubbed the back of his neck. "I was wrong in thinking it was part of Gampo's fleet. She just happened to be in the wrong place. We canna help her now."

"If we fire the bar shot and take down one of the *Dragon's* masts, it might give her time to sail out of range," Landon said.

At Conal's nod, Landon raised his voice and gave the orders, "One and four guns, at the ready. Aim for the mainsail, boys! An extra pint of ale to the gunners who split it in two!"

As Landon's orders were relayed to the gun deck, the rest of the crew crowded around the rail to watch.

"Fire four gun!" Landon shouted.

Keelan was more prepared this time and covered her ears with her hands. At the shudder of the gun firing, she closed her eyes to the thick smoke. The breeze had picked up and soon whisked it away from the deck, and after a second, she dared open her eyes. The *Dragon* now had a drooping triangular sail near the front of the ship.

A shout rang out on deck, "A hit to the main gaff tops'l!"

Landon sent out another command to the gunners. "Fire one gun!"

Another shuddering boom jarred the deck. The wind drove the smoke ahead of the ship and she caught sight of the bar shot, just as it reached the schooner. Both fascinated and terrified at the same time, she watched it crash through the top of the forward lowest square sail and splinter the mainmast about midway way up. Then, the upper foremast slowly toppled and folded in half.

"Huzzah! Huzzah!" The sudden cheer arose on the decks of the *Seeker*, and the distance again grew between the two ships.

Landon's voice held a note of pride. "Good work, lads! A hit through the fore lower tops'l and foremast! Reload and stand ready. Load your guns and run them out!"

Keelan remained beside the helm as the crippled pirate ship forfeited the chase. Elation washed over her like a shower of sunshine, and she found herself laughing with glee. Landon grinned at her, and she couldn't help smiling back at him. Conal turned his attention to the wind in the sheets. "Helm a quarter point to starboard! Lay aloft and take in two reefs!"

"Aye, Captain!"

A flurry of other commands shot across the decks, and the crew moved with amazing agility to accomplish them. Sails were trimmed, and the *Seeker* shifted away from the *Dragon*. The smaller sloop limped toward the shore and crossed over their wake behind them.

"At least the smaller boat has an opportunity to flee," she said.

Conal peered through his glass at the sloop. "Small crew. I don't see any wounded sailors. It looks like there's damage to the foremast and sail. Unless they're lubbers or daft in the head, they should be able to make it to port using the mainsails before Gampo can ready his boat to give a chase."

Landon raised his brows and shook his head. "I'm not so sure of their skills, they should've never lowered the mainsail."

The *Seeker* continued to gain speed, and the wind snatched a wisp of hair from under Keelan's hat. If she hadn't fastened the chinstrap tightly, it would have probably flown away with the breeze. A loud clapping rent the air, and she followed Conal's sharp gaze to a loose mainsail, flapping faster than a sparrow's wing. A commotion soon followed near the main mast. A sailor scampered like a monkey along the topgallant spar. A second perched on the spar below and sawed at one of the sheets holding the main topsail.

Keelan held her breath. If they fell, it would surely be to their death. It almost appeared as if they were intentionally trying to cripple the *Seeker's* sail.

"Lash down that sail! Sheepshank the rigging best ye can, lads. Hop to it and with a will!" Conal turned, pulled his pistols from his belt, and fired a shot into the air. He aimed the other one at the two sailors aloft. "Either come down now or test the steadiness of my hand."

They froze for a moment and then reversed back to the ratlines to begin the climb down. Remus and Johnny, along with another dozen mates, were waiting and wrestled them to the deck. After a slight scuffle, the men were subdued.

"It appears we've flushed out the other spies," Landon observed. To Remus and Johnny he said, "Secure them in the hold. Keep them under close watch."

"Aye, sir," Remus responded. To the pirates he growled, "Move on, ye bilge rats. Ye'll git yer due soon enough. It's been a while since we got to see a good keel haulin'."

Both men paled and exchanged terrified looks before Remus and Johnny shoved them toward the hatch.

Conal glanced up at the crewmen, who worked fervently to repair the damaged rigging. "We're losing speed, dammit." His expression remained stoic, his mouth in a harsh line.

Landon clamped his hand on his friend's shoulder. "The *Dragon* is no longer in a position for a chase. We'll have our chance another day, my friend, when we have all three ships at hand." He jerked his head in the direction of the hold. "I'd like to have a conversation with our pirate guests below. Perhaps if we're persuasive enough, they'll share the location where Gampo roosts when he's not at sea. Then we could pay a personal call after our stop at Harbour Town."

Conal nodded in agreement. "Let's give them some time to contemplate their current situation. They might be more talkative after a time locked in the bilge with the ballast."

He issued orders to tack back and make a wide sweep, retracing their earlier path, but staying well outside the range of the wounded schooner's guns. Several members of the crew grabbed grappling hooks and stood at the rails. They made a sport of snagging items tossed overboard earlier, making wagers on who could recover their target first.

The *Seeker* continued its starboard arc until it was once again sailing south toward Harbour Town. Keelan breathed deeply, savoring their victory and giving thanks no one was hurt. The dark-sailed pirate boat bobbed on the water, and the little sloop still limped eastward toward the shoreline.

She hoped to never see them again, but she had a strange tingling along the back of her neck, and suddenly the distance from the two ships couldn't widen fast enough.

CHAPTER SEVENTY-TWO
A PROPOSAL

T he crew repacked and stowed the ammunitions and other weapons. The guns were once again tightly secured, powder and balls replenished and made ready for the next time they were needed. A light rain started, and was soon accompanied by a thin mist, which muted the usual sounds of activity aboard the *Seeker*. The vessel would soon arrive at Harbour Town, South Carolina. Everett and Orvis were both given a brief sea burial, during which Doreen had locked herself in Annette's cabin, tormented by guilt.

Keelan's heart filled with pity for her cousin. She'd talked with Doreen at length earlier, and as she suspected, her cousin had indeed recognized the sound of her voice while they were in the hold. Keelan told Doreen about Gampo and his desire for vengeance, and Doreen promised to keep her identity and location a secret. Her cousin had sobbed on Keelan's shoulder until her tears were spent.

"I'm so sorry, Keelan," Doreen repeated.

"Shhh... you can't keep the burden of this blame on your shoulders, Doreen," she'd replied. "Your intent was never to harm either Papa or Dr. Garrison. The fault belongs to Everett, and God will judge him now."

The daylight waned just as a fog drifted in. Within the hour it had thickened. It was not long before Conal ordered the anchor lowered. "Too many outer sandbars and shoals to navigate in the mist," he noted. "Tis better to wait 'til it lifts than risk running aground."

From her post near the mainmast, Keelan made out the vague outline of the ship's stern. Most of the crew went below deck to hang their hammocks and turn in, except for the few who sat around an overturned crate, and played cards by the dull yellow glow of the night watch's lantern.

The desire for some privacy to ponder her own thoughts, made her wander to the aft deck near the main cabin where she leaned against the rail to stare out into the gray curtain. The fog hid both ocean and horizon. She extended her hand, and the thick, wet mist swallowed it. Fog covered the ship in a translucent darkness, holding both Keelan and the *Seeker* captive and paralyzed. She shivered as its moist breath crept across her bare neck, unable to shake the trepidation skittering down her spine.

What of the hammock hanging in Landon's cabin? The strokes of his long, lean fingers on her skin, and the urgent demand of his kisses could easily bend her to his whim. If he but *touched* her, she would be powerless to resist him. Her heart pounded with need even as trepidation tingled in her stomach. She drew in a deep breath of calm, her path clear now.

He loved her. The knowledge made her light as a sparrow. He didn't ask her to marry him, though. A heavy fist of sadness settled in her heart next to her joy. Her intentions, while admirable and virtuous, had been no match for the intense and powerful lure of Landon Hart.

She loved him. He was cocky; so sure of himself that the fates acquiesced to his whims because it was too much trouble to argue. He loved adventure and changed directions with the tide and the wind, whether or not others could keep up. He was brave and strong and hungry for life. Yes, she loved him.

Falling in love with Landon was sure to lead to inevitable misery and heartbreak. Her will had not saved her; she had fallen anyway. A solitary tear broke free and crept down her cheek. She loved him and wanted to trust him with her heart, but she was afraid.

The promise of marriage seemed less likely now, and even less important. Another deep sigh of defeat swirled the air around her. He loved her *now*, but would he eventually break her heart? According to her mother, there was always another woman, another port city somewhere along the way to steal a mariner's attention and his heart. Whatever she and Landon had today, this hour, this minute was ethereal. Was it meant to last? She didn't know. He loved her today, and today would have to be enough.

Perhaps today should be enough. Who was she to demand more?

"Keelan."

The apparition of her thoughts walked toward her. The mist swirled around him as he strode through its vapor like a pirate ghost, unhindered by the same gray blanket holding her captive. The silver saber strapped to his waist stood out starkly against the black breeches and boots. The white linen shirt almost glowed against his darkly tanned skin. The top ties were unsecured, revealing his bare neck. Her pulse leapt as Landon stepped closer, and she desperately resisted the temptation to reach out and run her fingers over the broad expanse of his chest. Her gaze slid involuntarily up over his strongly boned jaw and paused on the small scar on his chin before lingering on his lips. Thinking back to the fiery kiss he had dealt her in his cabin earlier sent a flurry of awakening within her. Her breasts tingled from the memory of his touch and a strange ache began to pulse in her lower belly. She expelled her breath in a soft pant and finally found the courage to meet the scorching heat of his gaze.

Was he replaying the same memory?

Sapphire eyes flashed like blue steel with something combustible and a little unsettling. For a moment, she could not breathe. If he touched her, she'd surely melt.

⁂

LANDON'S HEART CLENCHED, and he reached up and tugged the strap holding Keelan's hair in a queue at the base of her neck, freeing her short auburn curls. He could not keep his fingers from delving into the soft tresses. Is this what it was like to be under a spell? His breath caught as her irises grew dark and limpid, like liquid emeralds. Her lashes fluttered then lowered to her cheeks, and she leaned her head into his fingers. He wanted her more than he had ever wanted any other woman. This desire was different; it was not only more powerful, but more possessive as well. Unlike past dalliances, he did not want his time to end with this woman—waif—sprite— imp.

Ever.

Keelan would always fight to forge her own path, with or without him. He could never ask her to compromise her morals or forsake her upbringing to be his mistress. She had already voiced her opinion on that matter, vehemently. Worse, she didn't trust him. What did he need to do to change that? He wanted her trust and devotion. He craved it. A wave of realization struck him like a storm surge from a gale.

He'd never be able to force her to trust him. He, of all people, should know that trust is earned, not demanded. If he wanted to keep her, he would have to do more. Be more. This line of thinking should have him running the other direction. Yet, for the first time in many years, it wasn't unpleasing. If anything, it drove him more strongly to her.

In Charleston, when he'd feared her lost, he'd been staggered by the emptiness surrounding him. Now that he had her, he wasn't about to be separated from her again.

Ever.

He needed her to stay with him. He needed her by his side. He needed *her*.

Tonight, this knowledge provided a calm sense of purpose rather than an intense desire to flee. But at the moment, he couldn't think of a single word to say to sway her favor to him. His grip on her hair involuntarily tightened, and his lips were on hers before he knew it. She was a fresh spring breeze kissed by the salty sea air. Her body leaned into him, and he wrapped his arm around her waist, pulled her closer and held her until their bodies blended together.

The thump of her heart against his, the whispers from her lips, the smell of the ocean in her hair, all combined into a heady spell which left him powerless and exposed.

And he didn't care.

KEELAN'S HEART pounded as Landon's arms wrapped possessively around her. She inhaled his scent as his hardened frame pressed against hers. Leather, salt air and musk drifted in her nostrils. His tongue teased her mouth open, tasting. Within the swirling the mist, their passions twirled and melted together. Nothing existed except his lips, his touch, his scent. Where there was Landon, there was warmth, comfort, strength.

Fire.

She pressed against him in an uncontrollable attempt to ease the sudden ache which began to spread, first within her belly... then lower. If he wanted her, she would give herself to him and allow herself to be loved for whatever span of time he willed it. Yes, it made her weak, but she didn't care. No man would ever match Landon's passion and power. She'd savor this small slice of paradise for as long as she could. The events of the day reminded her of her own mortality. Perhaps it was time to live for the moment.

His grip around her tightened, and his hand slid up to cup the firm roundness of her breast. She sighed as his mouth moved to her neck, leaving little molten impressions in its wake. It was impossible to complete a single thought. A low moan escaped from her throat, and her fingers instinctively buried themselves in his hair. She heard his voice in her ear, low and husky with emotion.

"Keelan, I need you with me. I cannot stay locked on land, yet neither can I bear to be separated from you." He cupped her face gently with his strong hands. Even in the near darkness his eyes glittered with something that made her want to dive headfirst into them. "I can't imagine living the rest of my life without you by my side." He rested his forehead against hers and his voice dropped, raspy and tortured. "However, I am a man of the sea, not the type to run plantations or city shops."

She swallowed, but the tangled mass of emotion in her throat stayed. It's not as if his words surprised her. In fact, hadn't she expected this? She'd been thinking the same thoughts seconds ago. "Yes, I know," she whispered, covering his hands with hers. "And I am not a woman who'd be content to stay home alone and await a man who is gone at sea. You know this as well."

Landon's voice lowered into an almost anguished whisper, as if he was both afraid to speak and afraid not to. "Yes, I know."

He'd asked her to sail with him once. Had he changed his mind? No matter. She would take tonight, and whatever amount of time they had until they dropped anchor in Harbour Town. She was a woman, and his crew believed a woman on a ship was bad luck. What more was there to say?

Landon grasped her hands and took a quick breath. "Keelan, I want you by my side, always. Will you sail *with* me, love? As my wife?"

✿ 73 ✿

CHAPTER SEVENTY-THREE
FREEDOM RUNNER

The shock of pure joy froze every muscle in her body. Did Landon Hart just request her hand in marriage? This man? This untamable sea captain? His words sunk in, reforming the foundation of her doubts, changing the framework of her soul. Keelan's jubilation was so powerful her heart seemed suddenly to pause in mid-beat, or maybe it simply exploded. Landon's hands framed her face, and she could only stare at the midnight eyes holding hers prisoner. Her vision of Landon, the handsome dandy of a sea captain, with a beautiful woman in every port city, dissipated before her eyes. In his place was this fearless, strong-willed man ready to love her, cherish her, and grow old with her.

Keelan responded the only way she could. Her slender fingers slid up and pulled his head down. This time, she captured his lips with hers, seeking the warmth and softness pressed against her mouth. His fingers traced the frame of her face, dancing over her skin, before cradling her jaw in his palms. He moved his lips from her mouth to her cheeks, kissing away the tears of joy, then moved up to her eyelids, brows and forehead. He slipped his arms around her and pulled her against his chest, and she nuzzled her face against his shoulder and hugged him back.

"There is something I must tell you first," Landon murmured.

Keelan stilled. She tilted her head back and looked at him. She already knew his past. What else was there? He'd been married once before. His wife had died giving birth to another man's child. "You already told me about your first marriage."

He shook his head. "It's not that." He paused as if to contemplate his next words. "I think I already know, but I want you to tell me how you feel about those who aid escaped slaves."

His question took her by surprise. Her mind went back to the Whistling Pig, and the suspicion she'd had about the Schoen's, Simon's warning, and advice to seek the couple out at the tavern if she needed help to flee Charleston.

There was also the runaway family trio who had escaped from Pratt's plantation and sought refuge in the cellar of an abandoned cabin where she and Landon had sheltered from a storm a few weeks ago. She had tended their wounds and Landon had left them the provisions he had in his saddle bags. Provisions that, truth be told, had been unnecessary to bring along for a short meeting with her Uncle at twin Pines.

Suddenly she understood.

"You help them escape, don't you?" she whispered.

He nodded, watching her every movement. "Fynn had started helping runaways years ago, after he himself had escaped his pirate captors. The Schoens, Simon, from Twin Pines, and the Ahern Merchant Fleet are all part of a small clandestine group of coastal residents and merchants who help slave families flee by transporting them north, to Philadelphia, then on to Canada."

He pulled away and took her hand, entwining his fingers with hers. "It's more dangerous aiding families than it is individual runaways. The three slaves we found in the cabin cellar a few weeks ago hid in the *Desire's* hold for several days. Because of repairs and stolen cargo, I was unable to leave on time for Philadelphia. Then, when Gampo put a price on your head, I had to send my ship to Harbour Town as a decoy. I must still take the *Desire* back up the coast to Philadelphia, where Fynn's family and friends will move them, and the others northward."

He stood silent and tense, waiting.

Keelan brought his fingers to her lips and kissed them. "I'm glad you help them."

A shadow floated away from Landon's face. The tense worry lines around his eyes softened. He pulled her into his arms and held her. No words were spoken. They stood together for a moment or two, and then he took her hand.

"Come with me," he whispered.

He led her to his cabin and opened the door. Conal and Daniel were already inside and turned toward them as the door clicked shut. She paused, confused. Before she could ask, Landon knelt before her. Keelan's heart stuttered at the intensity of his gaze and even more at the humility in his countenance. Where was the cocky grin? The seductive perusal?

He opened his mouth, closed it, and swallowed before taking a gulp of air. Heaven's breath, he was terrified. His eyes turned a deep shade of blue, like a midnight sea.

"Keelan Grey, I give my oath before the eyes of God and these witnesses to bind myself to you until death parts us. Before the eyes of God and these witnesses and upon my honor, I pledge my love, loyalty, and fidelity to thee for the rest of my living days. When we arrive in port, I pledge to seek out a priest to bless our marriage and confirm it is legally binding. If you will consent to have me as your husband for the rest of your life, place your hand in mine and join with me in a handfast, to bind you to me, and bind me to you."

Without breaking his gaze, he lifted his hand and offered it to her.

Kneeling at her feet, proud, guarded Landon Hart, now raw and exposed, offered his heart to her in the presence of her half-brother. Landon Hart, the man who'd said marriage didn't suit him. When had he decided to risk his heart again? It didn't matter. He trusted her to love him and love him she would. Landon's eyes shone with an indigo light that warmed her as only the truest love can.

Her legs trembled and wordlessly, she sank to her knees and placed her hand on his palm. His fingers closed over hers and he placed his other hand on top. Her eyes welled, and she fought to contain the tears. The emotion seeping into her chest made it almost impossible to utter a single word.

"Landon Hart," she said, her voice catching, raw with emotion. "I place my hand in yours before the eyes of God and these witnesses and bind myself to you as your wife. I pledge my love, loyalty, and fidelity to thee until death takes me from your side."

Landon's long, lean fingers gently uncovered her hand. He slipped a sapphire and diamond crusted ring on her finger. "My grandmother's."

She stared into those hypnotic, blue eyes, which glittered like the jewels on the ring and fell in love again. And again.

"My Keelan. My love. My wife." Landon brought her hand to his mouth and kissed her fingertips. Her heart skipped as he cupped her face in his hands.

"Congratulations, my friend!" Conal clapped Landon on the back, sending him tipping forward against Keelan. So, of course, he took the opportunity to kiss her.

Laughing, Conal hauled her to her feet, and then offered his hand to Landon and pulled him up as well.

"And, as ship's captain, I pronounce you wed! Best wishes, Mrs. Hart, for a lifetime of happiness." Her half brother grinned and kissed her hand.

"Thank you, Conal, for agreeing to bear witness," Landon replied, clapping Conal's shoulder.

Conal gave her a small bow before he turned to open a bottle of wine. Daniel took her hand and bowed over it. "I wish you a long and fruitful marriage, Mrs. Hart."

"Thank you, Daniel." Keelan looked up into her husband's sparkling blue eyes. He gave her a slow smile before his lips dipped to briefly capture hers.

"A toast!" Conal pressed glasses into everyone's hands. He raised his glass and the others followed. "May the seas of marriage be calm, the winds be swift, and the current amiable!"

Keelan laughed and raised her glass with Landon's in salute.

Conal pressed a hand to his chest. "And, on behalf of the O'Brien family, I welcome Landon as me brother by marriage, as well."

"It is an honor." Landon stepped forward, clasped Conal's outstretched hand and shook it.

"And, therefore, I give my consent," Conal continued with a grin, "for you to name your firstborn son after me."

They all laughed. Keelan threw her arms around Conal's neck and kissed him on the cheek, gaining a surprised smile from her half-brother. "It would be the very least we could do," she said.

"I believe," Daniel broke in, "our part in this grand affair is complete." He stepped to the door before giving Keelan a brief bow. "My lady, best wishes to you and Captain Hart."

"Aye to that!" Conal said, as he plucked the bottle of wine from the table. "Come, let us celebrate the day's events beneath the shelter of yonder mizzen mast with this bottle of fine wine and a deck of cards. By the way this bank of fog is acting, we won't be doing much else for at least a day or so."

Daniel opened the door and Conal stepped outside, giving the valet an exaggerated nod of thanks as he passed. The door closed.

They were alone.

Landon raised his glass, and she raised hers. Together they finished their wine. He plucked the stem from her fingers and placed it on the table before taking her into his arms.

The world floated away as his lips leisurely played upon hers. She joyfully returned the kiss, and he tightened his arms about her waist, pulling her closer. Their kiss deepened, fanning the fire kindled weeks ago in a garden in Charleston, on a fine spring morning in June. He broke the kiss and touched his forehead to hers.

"Since the day I gazed upon you floating on the lake, a beautiful, naked water nymph," Landon's voice sounded hoarse, "I have wanted to touch you in all the places my eyes admired. I'm like a man starved. I crave your touch, I crave your heart. I crave the energy from your presence."

They were drawn to each other, the two of them, like a bead of water seeks a dry edge of linen. "I'm yours forever," she finally whispered. "I can't imagine living another day without you."

Landon leisurely removed her shirt and breeches, taking his time to place kisses on her shoulders, her ankles, her knees, until she stood naked. Keelan's senses erupted as the warmth of his hand found the firm rounded swell of her breast, his thumb stroking until her nipple grew hard and aroused.

His other hand caressed her hip.

Keelan's heart had been pounding a staccato rhythm in her chest, but now it lurched erratically. Landon was about to make her his wife in body as well as spirit. It was expected. It was the nature of things, after all. It was what a husband and wife normally did on their wedding night. It was terrifying.

She longed for it and feared it at the same time.

"Keelan, my love, your image has haunted me, even in my daydreams, plucking at my thoughts, drawing my attention away from every task. For so long, I have wanted to have you near me, to hear my name fall from your lips, knowing I was forever in your heart."

"You've been in my heart longer than you realize, Captain." She could hardly take a breath as his hand pressed her hips against his. Her lips tried to form the words whirling through her head, but it was impossible. She could only breathe his name and curl her fingers into his hair, pulling, urging him closer.

Again, his lips descended upon hers, but this time they were soft and tender. Her pulse quickened, and a lovely warmth swirled inside her. His tongue beckoned hers to a dance in the moist warmth of her mouth.

"I taste honey and wine," he murmured.

After adjusting the light from the lantern until the cabin was bathed in a faint, orange glow, he lowered her to his bed. Her gaze followed his movements in timid admiration as he undressed. Broad shoulders gave way to a narrow, tapered waist. There was no doubt Landon was in excellent physical form. Crisp hair lightly covered his broad chest; his belly was flat. She caught her breath as her gaze skimmed lower. Landon's male reaction to her stare brought a sudden hotness to her cheeks. She quickly blinked and raised her gaze to his face. How would she possibly survive being impaled by that? She swallowed and for a moment, the panic swelled.

Sensing her unease, Landon gently brushed a wisp of hair from her cheek. "I'll be gentle, love. Trust me, soon you will hunger for this as much as I do." He traced her jaw line down her throat with light kisses. He made a slight detour to a soft, sensitive spot behind her ear and she almost forgot what year it was.

"Your skin is silky, like rose petals," he whispered.

His softly stroking fingers sent another shiver down her spine, eliciting a breathy sigh from her. This part was wonderful. Kneeling on the bed, he drew her up against him and captured her mouth in a soft, tender kiss. Keelan's heart pounded erratically as he stroked her skin with reverence, as if savoring every touch from her neck, down her arms, over to the small of her back, and down her backside.

A hot gasp escaped her mouth as he pressed her hips harder against his. His kiss deepened, and his inquisitive tongue distracted her from the unfamiliar hardness. His hand returned to her breast. Waves of heat swirled around her, then threatened to erupt when his thumb once again rubbed tight circles around the rosy peak. Her throat vibrated with a deep moan of pleasure.

"You like when I do this?"

She nodded, or at least she thought she nodded. He cupped her other breast and repeated the delicious caress, making her sway into him from the sheer pleasure of it. There was more, there had to be more. Something was building inside her, urging her to him, looking for more. The sensation pushed all rational thoughts from her mind, and she covered his hand with hers and pressed it more firmly and he responded by kneading her breast, making her knees weak. His lips moved to her neck, then on to touch the delicate tip of her ear. Keelan could breathe only in small fragments, and the air around her seemed to thicken as his caresses became bolder.

"If you like that, then surely you'll enjoy this even more."

He kissed his way down to her breast, then took her nipple in his mouth. The wonderful sensation had her fingers convulsing, and she delved them into the curls at the nape of his neck. Flames licked at her core as his hot, moist lips brought her near the brink of insanity. His hands wandered along her calves, moving behind her knees in a soft caress, up her thighs to the soft inner hollow near her womanhood.

Just when it seemed she would implode, he pressed her back to his bed and then began to leave a trail of molten kisses across her belly. "My God, you are so beautiful," Landon's voice was husky as he murmured against the pale skin of her stomach. "Like a goddess, bathed in gold and dipped in diamonds."

✣ 74 ✣

CHAPTER SEVENTY-FOUR
LOVE BOUND

Her skin tasted like wild cherries and sunshine. Landon inhaled the jasmine mingling with her womanly scent. When had he fallen in love with her? At the ball, when she had tried to fool him into thinking she was in love with Everett? Perhaps in the garden, when he had stolen a kiss under the guise of a payment for his silence, only because he could not resist the temptation of her sweet, full lips, which had fallen open in astonishment when he'd called her from her hiding place. Or was it in the early June morning, after dueling with Daniel, when she tore the blue scarf from her head and had given him a spry mocking salute before disappearing into the pines? Her look of brave determination when the *Dragon* had attacked?

Keelan.

His jewel. His love.

She was soft and strong, pliant as silk and strong as the tide. He wanted to hold her, love her, protect her and cherish her.

But more than anything, he wanted to devour her.

Her kisses drove him insane. It was all he could do to hold himself in check and not toss her on his bed and plunge himself into her just to ease his own long, smoldering hunger which had consumed him for weeks. He wanted to love her gently her first time. She arched against him and he sucked in his breath. If she'd let him.

The dew-kissed moistness of her mouth was sweeter than nectar. He brushed his fingers over shoulders, her skin like soft satin. She was everything he desired. The only one he desired. How could have she not seen it?

"Landon?"

Landon raised his head and lost his breath at the image before him. His gaze moved over his new bride's body. Fiery tresses teased by the sun fanned across the pillow beneath her head. Dark, auburn lashes touched her lightly flushed cheeks and her full, deep red lips parted in silent, passionate wonder. Firm, pink-tipped breasts curved gracefully to a creamy porcelain stomach. Lithe, shapely legs met at a tightly curled amber nest of wet heat. Her pupils had widened with desire, then went soft as his hand caressed her thigh and then slipped further to touch her warm moistness. His desire to have her was so powerful, he had to remind himself to keep his movements slow, his touch soft. He paused to kiss the other tender pink peak, and it pleased him to hear her swift intake of breath. Here was the most valuable treasure he'd ever seen, and she was his. All it had cost him was his heart. He smiled. It was a good trade, a good trade indeed.

❧

KEELAN'S WORLD was spinning through thick waves of pleasure. She ran her hands up along Landon's hardened ribs, across his shoulders, and pulled him to her. *Closer.* There was no control, now. Her body reacted without a thought to guide it. He needed to be closer so she could breathe him in, envelop him.

"I love you, Landon," she could only breathe the words.

His eyes became hooded, voice thick with emotion. "I love you, wife. I don't want to hurt you, but I've been told the first time..." He shifted gently and pressed himself against her opening and the tender shield of her maidenhead.

She stiffened and her eyes flew open. "*Landon...*"

His voice was low and calm in her ear. "Shhh... Keelan, my sweet love, relax. Let me love you. I promise that I will make you crave this." He caressed her breast then slide his palm down to cover the wet nest of curls joining her thighs; his fingers slid into her folds and she closed her eyes at the bliss she suffered from his fingertips. His caress deepened, and she moaned.

He spoke in a low, gravelly whisper. "You are so wet for me, Keelan. So warm, so soft."

His lips touched hers, and her hands slipped convulsively over the hardened muscles of his back. Her fingernails dug into his skin as the pleasure swirled and rushed through her like a mighty wave, curling then crashing into the core of her soul. Something needy and restless churned in her core. When the pleasure exploded within her, he pressed further and eased inside; the pressure mounted until the thin membrane broke. Pleasure and pain. And a sense of fullness. Inhaling swiftly, she buried her face into his neck. Her breath shuddered.

He stilled. The heat from Landon's body enveloped her; she kissed his shoulder then paused. The pain had subsided. Instead, she was filled with a warmth and a need she couldn't describe.

Landon's hoarse whisper brushed her ear. "Keelan, look at me, my love."

She leaned her head back and stared up into the deep pools of blue. His eyes were dark and sensual as midnight velvet, and she found herself falling into them like a petal into a glassy lake. His heartbeat was hammering against her chest. Or was it her heartbeat hammering against his? It was impossible to tell.

"I love you, Keelan Hart. You possess my heart, breath and soul."

A knot of emotion tangled around her heart. Her chest squeezed tight and warmth spiraled through it. "I love you back, Landon Hart."

His gaze imprisoned hers as he slowly, slowly started to move within her. There was little pain now, only movement, and her body took control, meeting his gentle, rhythmic thrusts. He filled her, fitting inside her as if his body was made for hers. They moved together in an even rolling motion, like the tide moves to and from the shore, with no beginning and no end. A deep hunger began to grow within Keelan's belly, and a soft moan escaped from her lips. Reaching up to Landon, she slid her hand behind his neck, and he responded by crushing her mouth to his. His thrusts quickened, and she rose to meet him. Landon's breathing became ragged, and he whispered her name. Urgent pulses of sensation flowed through her into Landon and from him into her until they were connected by something stronger than sinew and flesh. Their souls entwined and melded together in a golden flare of light. Little explosions detonated deep inside her and they both cried out with pleasure as he spilled himself deeply within her.

Fate brought them together.

Love bound them for life.

⚅⚄⚅

THE CRADLE-SOFT ARMS of Morpheus seemed to have just rocked Keelan to sleep, when a harsh, brutal pounding sounded upon the cabin door.

"Captain Hart!" An urgent voice penetrated the early morning quiet. "Sorry to intrude, sir, but you're needed on main deck straight away."

Keelan did not recognize the voice heralding her new husband from her side this morning, but she was immediately resentful. She wasn't ready to relinquish her husband, her companion, her source of warmth, comfort and strength, so soon.

Landon acknowledged the intrusion with a growl, "What is it, man?"

There was a slight pause. "The prisoners locked in the hold have escaped, sir. They have stolen one of the canoes. Cap'n O'Brien's fumin' mad and means to give chase."

CHAPTER SEVENTY-FIVE
ESCAPE

Landon tensed at the news of the pirates' escape. Keelan's chest tightened. If the escaped spies reached Gampo and revealed the location of the *Seeker*, even the dense fog wouldn't keep them safe. Gampo had made it clear he meant to avenge Crowe's death personally. Since he blamed her for it, he'd come after the *Seeker*, putting people she loved and cared about in danger.

She still wasn't sure if Gampo had pursued them from Charleston because he'd found out she was aboard, or followed simply because the *Seeker* was part of Fynn Ahern's fleet, Gampo's long-time rival. She snuggled closer and Landon reached his arm around her shoulder.

"What started this feud between Fynn and Gampo?" she asked.

Landon took a deep breath, scrubbed his face with his other hand and gave a baffled laugh. "Those two salts had been at odds for the past twenty-five years, although no one seems to remember why. Fynn always remained tightlipped about it. His only plan of action was to do as much damage as possible to Gampo's ship without killing anyone." He shrugged. "Gampo seemed to have the same intent. Both did their best to hinder the other's business and disrupt each other's trade, like a couple of old, toothless dogs."

"Have many people died?" she asked. A light shadow of whiskers covered his jaws. Curious, she traced her fingers along his chin.

"No lives were lost in all those years. Brendan, Fynn's son, said Fynn died because he was hit by falling debris from a splintered mast. In truth, Gampo's shot had been high. He didn't rake the deck with grape shot, which tells me he had no intent to kill."

She moved her hand to his chest and marveled at the ripple of muscle beneath her fingers as he shifted to turn toward her a bit more. She raised an eyebrow. "Now, you've lost Fynn and Gampo's lost his first mate and his sister. It's become a blood feud, hasn't it? Gampo is still pursuing the fleet, so it doesn't seem like he's ready to call a halt to it." She was a part of this now. It wasn't because she married Landon, it was because he had married her.

Landon stared into her eyes for a moment, contemplating. "Conal and Brendan are determined to see him hang for causing Fynn's death."

"Where's Brendan now?"

"He's waiting for us in the harbor with Fynn's ship, the *Reward*."

There was something else bothering her. In fact, it had been lingering on the fringes of her mind for the past few days. "When we were in the warehouse, Gampo mentioned something about his sister. He seemed to believe Fynn had somehow wronged her. He mentioned Fynn would know how much a Persian would pay for me," she said. Although she felt safe in Landon's arms, she couldn't suppress the shiver that skittered across her shoulders.

He hugged her closer. "Fynn has never engaged in the slave trade, rather, he's done much to foil it. His group of Freedom Runners is proof."

"Gampo seems to be convinced Fynn sold his sister," she said.

"Gampo is mistaken." Landon smoothed a stray strand of hair away from her face and kissed her forehead.

"How did you come to be on Fynn's ship?"

"My parents died when I was twelve. Then Fynn took me in. I was lucky."

WHEN HE WAS YOUNG, it had taken wits and strength *and* luck. Landon twirled his finger in a lock of Keelan's hair. "Fynn had recently lost his brother to the same fever which killed my parents on the journey to America from Ireland. Although Fynn and Risa had children of their own to care for, they took me in and raised me as their own." He stroked his fingertips along the soft skin of her arm. "That old salt told the best yarns."

Fynn's stories invoked images of daring rescues, duels, and true love. He moved his fingers in small circles up to the silky skin of his wife's shoulder.

"When Fynn's wife, Risa, was a young maid, she was taken prisoner from a prize ship and sold by the pirates who'd captured it. Gampo gave the pirate captain a small fortune prior to the sale to buy her before she was placed up on the block."

"It seems odd that Gampo is outraged that Fynn might have bought and sold his sister when it appears he has his fingers in the slave trade as well."

Landon leaned close to her ear and breathed in deeply before he continued. Jasmine. Keelan always smelled like jasmine blossoms. She moved her hand from his chest up to her shoulder where his hand rested and wove her fingers with his. Her breasts brushed against his arm, and he fought to remember what he wanted to say next.

Ah yes, Uncle Fynn's new bride.

"Fynn had been enslaved by the same pirate ship. By the time it made port, he'd fallen in love with Risa. Before Gampo arrived to collect his prize, Fynn sneaked in and helped her escape from the pirate's gaol."

Keelan's eyes widened. "She was in a cell? Was she in love with Fynn, too? How did he release her?"

He smiled a bit roguishly. "No. She was most definitely not in love with Fynn. She was a Spanish aristocrat's daughter. He was a young seaman. He freed her by outwitting her guards. However, *that* is a story for another day."

Keelan looked down at their threaded fingers and hesitated. What was on her mind? She was contemplating something important. He waited.

After a moment, she raised her gaze back to his, and he was almost rendered powerless by the intensity of her dark green stare. A ring of gold rimmed her pupils and then flared out into the emerald irises like an exploding star.

"Did she eventually fall in love with him? Did they travel together? Did they love each other? Were they happy?" she asked.

"So many questions." He pictured Keelan as a young girl, small and thin, strong and impetuous, desiring the love and compassion of a mother and a father, yet left bereft. In his mind's eye, he could see her holding a babe in her arms, smiling. He wanted her to have a family because when he looked at her, it was all he could see.

Family.

Keelan desired to know her sire, and by damned, he and Conal would make sure she met him. Even better, she'd become part of a family the two of them would create together.

Bound by love, forged in their hearts and unbreakable. When he looked at her, he saw his future, his life... *happiness*.

Landon brought their hands to the small space between their bodies and brushed the pink buds of her nipples with his knuckles, and marveled at how her pupils widened and her breath shortened.

He continued, "Yes, and they were happy. Fynn and Risa sailed together. It was unconventional, even cursed by other sailors, but the two did it, anyway. They loved each other and nothing kept them from spending their lives together." He locked his gaze with hers. "Just like you and me."

Keelan smiled. "Yes, just like you and me." She kissed his knuckles. "Tell me, did they marry?"

"Yes," Landon admitted. "And when he sailed, Risa stood firm by Fynn's side. They had two sons, Brendan and Ronan, and both grew up on the ship. When Fynn sought horses from Persia to trade, Risa rode with him over the desert." Landon took a long, pensive breath. "It was Risa who offered shelter to two runaways and then wrote to a friend to help deliver them to safety. Fynn then organized an alliance. To this day, we still do our best to aid families seeking to escape to their freedom."

"Fynn must have loved Risa very much," she said softly.

Landon kissed her shoulder. "Fynn said Risa was the fairest gem he'd ever met and that he'd never encountered another woman like her, nor would he ever expect to find another again. She was his light. His star. Just like you are mine."

⚜

ANOTHER LIGHT RAP on the cabin door reminded them of the business at hand. "Sir—Captain Hart. Sir?"

"I'll be right there," Landon finally answered. He pressed his lips against the hollow of her throat, then trailed kisses up her neck before whispering in her ear. "As much as I would wish otherwise, it appears we must dress and take care of the issue at hand." He smoothed his hand over her side and down to her thigh, sending shivers through her lower belly. His palm moved between their bodies, tracing a fiery path upward. Gently probing fingers caressed the moist curls before slipping past her folds and making intense circles around the little island of pleasure nestled there. "Although, I would rather dally longer here, as my husbandly duty demands."

This man. The things he could do with his fingers made her forget her own name. She pressed her hips against his hand and trailed her fingers over his lips, down his neck, and across the taut muscles of his chest, struggling to speak. "Then... when time... permits, I shall expect you to fulfill your duties as... demanded," she breathed, happy she could at least form the words. Her breath came and went in soft pants, his strokes against her sending swirling eddies of delight through her lower belly.

He caught his breath as her hand moved lower. "Indeed."

⚜

KEELAN KNOTTED the scarf behind her head and gave a small sigh. "Although this disguise is easy to move in and comfortable, there are times I wish I could wear a gown again and enjoy the more feminine life I used to live." As she had earlier suspected, he was indeed a scoundrel when it came to keeping the ends close enough to tie together.

Landon chuckled and finished securing the leather corset. "I distinctly recall you garbed in something very similar to this when we first met."

She could only shrug. He had a point.

He gave her a wink. "I must admit, I'm enjoying the respite from the need to defend you from love-struck sailors. 'Tis hard enough to disguise your more womanly curves as it is." He tweaked her bottom.

She gave him a mock scowl before she shrugged into one of his old shirts, then pulled up and fastened her trousers.

He traced the line of demarcation, stretching across her chest. "Hopefully, it won't be for much longer." He plopped a worn, floppy straw hat on her head and gave it a secure pat. "Your bonnet, my lady." He chucked her under the chin before planting a lingering kiss on her lips. "We can't take the risk of Gampo confirming you are aboard. For now, you must remain Mahdi, the emerald-eyed, cook's boy and son of a Persian horse trader. Next to Lin, Jorge, Renaldo, Hugo and Sakura, you should blend right in." He winked. "You'd be the only one with all your fingers and toes still attached. I hope no one notices."

Landon strode across the deck toward the small group of crewmen gathered by the main mast. The fog still hung about the ship like a sodden, gray blanket, muffling the sighs of the sea and the voices of the crew. The fog had kept them from moving the ship closer to Harbour Town's docks. Conal still felt it was too risky to navigate.

It helped to have the scarf; it restrained her curly cropped hair. The moisture in the air would have made it even more unruly. The sailors tied scarves around their heads much like Ruth, the plantation cook, had done at Twin Pines. Depending on the head, it either kept hair out of the way, or scalps from burning under the early summer sun. She'd had done her best to imitate the style. However, as comfortable as her clothes were, she still longed to enjoy other womanly pursuits.

Needlepoint, she could be content without, but a fragrant bath...

"Three of Gampo's men easily managed to gain access to the *Seeker* as deck hands; it's unnerving," Landon muttered.

"It would have been worse had they been successful in sabotaging the sails," Keelan answered as they came upon a cluster of men gathered in a circle near the main mast.

"How in the hell did they escape?" Landon ran his fingers through his hair in frustration.

At the sound of Landon's voice, the crewmen parted to reveal Conal squatting near Henry, who was groggily trying to sit upright.

"Near as I can make out," Conal answered, "a few minutes after the change of the watch, Miss Grey came around with a jug of wine she'd stolen from the galley. Somehow, she managed to persuade Marcel to unlock the pantry. She told the men on watch she was grateful to them for saving her from the pirates, and she wanted to reward their bravery."

Landon's eyebrows rose. "Are you telling me a single jug of wine inebriated the entire watch?"

"It weren't no ordinary wine, Captain Hart." Johnny stepped forward from the group. "The wench only offered us a wee bit. Barely two fingers worth in a tiny cup." He shoved his hands into his pockets. "Next thing I knew, Remus was tryin' to shake the teeth outta me mouth."

"Well, ye was quiet as a stone, man!" Remus retorted. "For a minute, I thought ye was dead!" He scratched his head and muttered, "Johnny's never missed waking me to take my turn. When I woke up on me own and the rest of me watch still in their hammocks, I knew somthin' wasn't right."

Johnny rubbed his temples. "Still feels like I was hit in the head with a rock hammer."

Conal gave Landon a humorless smile. "It seems Henry asked for two shares before he was to climb up to the crow's nest. We found him tangled in the rigging about halfway up. He's still fairly out of sorts."

"Remus and Johnny, take Henry to his hammock," Landon said, a hardened edge to his voice. "Where's Miss Grey now?"

"We found her tied and gagged in the hold below," Conal answered.

"But, why would she help them?" Keelan asked. She was both outraged and bewildered. Doreen's current actions seemed out of place. She'd changed on this voyage, and for the better. Something wasn't right.

Conal took an angry breath. "She was threatened. One had freed himself during the night. She'd been on her way to the deck to empty the chamber pot when he attacked her. He told her if she didn't help them escape, they'd kill her and sabotage the ship, so Gampo could take it. Miss Grey said she made the decision she believed would save lives rather than place them in danger. She felt it was her only choice."

"So she drugged the watch to keep the pirates from killing them?" Keelan asked.

"Yes." Conal said.

Poor Doreen. That thought stopped her. There was something she never thought she'd think about her cousin. "I believe she has an aunt here in Harbour Town," she said.

"I'll offer to provide an escort there for her," Conal said. "She's with Mrs. Camsby at the moment. She was quite shaken. I'm hoping Mrs. Camsby can comfort her and help her regain her composure somewhat."

Johnny and Remus returned, and the Conal directed his next order to Remus. "Prepare a longboat," he ordered. "Johnny's men can go ashore first, along with Marcel, who needs to replenish some of our galley supplies. I'll prepare a missive regarding the two renegades, which we can deliver to the authorities."

Remus spoke up. "T'would seem the bilge rats might be only an hour ahead of us. We could catch 'em!"

Landon nodded. "Aye, they have only two men rowing, and one is wounded."

"There is another piece of good news," Conal added. "According to Miss Grey, one of Gampo's men mentioned that once they were back aboard his ship, Gampo would head for his home on an island off the coast of Jamaica."

Landon caught Conal's gaze and his eyes gleamed like a cat ready to pounce. "He's holing up. We can catch him when he makes landfall."

"I'd like nothing better than to watch him swing." Conal spun on his heel and tossed over his shoulder, "Remus, tell Madam Camsby we shall take her and Miss Grey ashore within the hour. Johnny, get the men ready to depart before the next bell, only the next watch stays aboard. I want to find those men." To Landon, he said, "Let's meet with Brendan to discuss setting a course for Jamaica. Together, we have a score to settle with Gampo."

⚜

AT LANDON'S BECKONING, Keelan slipped through his cabin door, and placed on the table a small breakfast tray of bannocks, jam, and tea she'd assembled in the galley. The activities they shared last night left her famished.

Her husband stepped forward, closed the door, and took her in his arms. Husband. A soft sensation hugged her heart. She slid her hands around his neck. "I brought us some breakfast."

"The nourishment I seek is not on that tray." Landon's eyes glowed warmly as he gave her a slow seductive grin. "In truth, the sustenance I crave only *you* possess." His head dipped and his lips found the pulse now pounding erratically in her throat. The food could wait.

Keelan caught her breath and murmured hoarsely in his ear, "But, all I possess, I have already given to you."

"Then I want more of the same."

He moved to her mouth and kissed her deeply. Keelan's fingers dug into the firm muscles of Landon's shoulders while his hands traveled freely down her sides and around her waist, before slipping in the back of her breeches.

He trailed kisses along her jaw to that sensitive spot behind her ear. "I will forever demand one more kiss, one more caress, one more night of enchantment," he murmured in her ear.

"Good. I shall be happy to provide it." She smiled.

Keelan's own hunger grew deep within her belly, and she arched against the hardness pressed against her. A low growl rumbled in Landon's chest, and he skimmed his palms against her naked backside before pulling her hips against his.

"Well, I guess I should have knocked!"

Keelan jumped at the sound of Annette Camsby's voice and attempted to disengage herself from Landon's embrace. His arms only tightened around her and he whispered into her ear. "Stay put, Madam, unless you wish to show her the effect your proximity has had on me."

Keelan ceased her struggles immediately. However, their display witnessed by another caused a hot blush to suffuse her cheeks, and mild panic to well in her chest. Would Annette blurt out what she'd seen to the crew?

"Yes, a knock would have been appropriate, Mrs. Camsby," Landon responded coolly. He slid his hands from her breeches and then casually caressed Keelan's back. She half turned to face Annette.

Annette's eyes flashed at the formal address given by Landon. She swept her hand toward Keelan. "So this is why you have refused to visit my bed?" she asked flatly.

Keelan caught Landon's gaze. Calm. Warm. Ornery.

"You've ignored me because, you have turned your lust to young *boys*?" Annette's voice dripped with disgust. "You're sick in the head."

Keelan bit back a sudden snort of laughter.

Amusement warmed Landon's eyes as he grinned down at her. "Not necessarily," he said.

Annette sauntered forward, hands on her hips. "Tell me, *Captain*, what does the crew think of this? Or do they not yet know? Because I assure you, your dirty little secret will be out within the hour unless you and I can come to a mutual agreement." She pointed commandingly to Keelan. "You may go. Landon and I are going to have a private meeting."

Although Landon managed to remain calm under Annette Camsby's attack, Keelan bristled at the woman's obvious threat against her husband. She whirled and faced the widow. "Whatever 'dirty little secret' you're prepared to tell the crew would be a complete lie."

"Really!" Annette exclaimed in mock surprise. "Let me see if I understand your argument. Or have you already forgotten I have just seen you in his arms, kissing him like a *lover*!"

Landon chuckled and leaned forward to whisper in Keelan's ear, "Well, she's right about the last."

Try as she might, Keelan could not hold back a giggle.

Annette became more incensed. "You dare mock me!"

"Madam Camsby." Landon intervened. "I believe it is time for the appropriate introductions to be made. Allow me to introduce to you, my wife: Keelan Grey Hart."

Annette's jaw dropped. "Wha—what did you say?"

Landon stepped from behind Keelan and bowed formally. "This is my wife, Keelan Hart."

"*Wife!*" Annette sputtered. "This is preposterous! You're not married! I have *met* the woman, and I assure you, sir, this is not she!"

Landon continued smoothly, unaffected by Annette's outburst. "Keelan, please allow me to introduce Madam Annette Camsby, late widow of Mr. Edward Camsby of Charleston."

Keelan pulled away the scarf hiding her hair. She closed half the distance between Landon and the stunned woman and spoke softly but with a cool firmness, "Although we both attended my cousin Doreen's cotillion ball, I assure you, we have never been formally introduced." She took great pleasure watching Landon's former mistress' mouth freeze open and gape in ill-concealed shock.

Landon moved to Keelan's side, grasped her hand, and then raised it to his lips.

"Tell us, Mrs. Camsby," Keelan asked, sinking into a formal curtsy, "exactly what do you intend to tell the crew?"

� 76 ✥

CHAPTER SEVENTY-SIX
THE REWARD

After demanding her trunks be loaded immediately on the longboat, Annette Camsby soon beat an irritated retreat to the main deck to wait its departure.

Landon placed a kiss upon Keelan's smooth brow. He was much comforted and proud of the strength and confidence radiating from his wife's gaze. "While Conal and I meet with the authorities, you and Daniel can accompany Doreen safely to her aunt's home."

Keelan gave a small sigh of pleasure. "I must admit, I cannot wait until I can and enjoy a nice, warm, relaxing bath with lavender oil and fragrant soap and—"

Landon chuckled and squeezed her tighter. "Let's stay the night in town. I'll find a room at the Harbour Town Hotel and we shall bathe *together* this evening. We'll dine with Conal and Brendan. When we board the *Desire*, I intend to introduce you to the crew as my wife."

The delighted sparkle in her emerald eyes warmed his heart. She pulled his head down and her lips beckoned his. She kissed him with the sweetness of Jamaican sugar cane. His hands moved over her buttocks and up to capture her breasts. The heat grew inside of him as her nipples hardened against his touch and her breath turned into a gentle breath of desire. Lifting her into his arms, he strode across the cabin and lowered her to his bed.

"I believe I have an obligation to fulfill," he said, a hint of a smile tugging at his mouth.

"You certainly do," Keelan said, grinning impishly, "and the delay will cost you extra."

❦

THEY FOUND the stolen canoe tied to a piling near a dock. The fog was still a thick grey wall, although it seemed to be thinning somewhat. The *Seeker* was nothing but a faint shadow in the distant mist. Anchored just offshore, Landon could vaguely make out the shadow of his ship, the *Desire*.

Conal followed his gaze. "The fog should burn off by evening. Let's plan to shove off at high tide on the morrow."

Landon nodded as he gestured to one of the men to haul up Keelan's new trunk. He wanted to surprise her. He brought the trunk containing the dress he'd purchased for her in Charleston up from the hold and smuggled it aboard without her noticing. She might not be able to dress as Keelan Grey Hart in public, but he'd make sure she would be married in a gown worthy of a bride on her wedding day.

Conal jostled the shoulder of one of the men tying off the long-boat. "Make sure the men are ready to re-board as soon as the *Seeker* is anchored at dockside and flying the Blue Peter."

"Aye, sir."

Landon was certain Keelan was already anticipating her warm, scented bath. He smiled. He had another surprise planned for his new wife.

After sending Keelan and Daniel to deliver Doreen to her aunt's house, Landon and Conal spoke with the local constable. They reported both Gampo's attack and the assault and attempted sabotage by the three men who'd stowed aboard the *Seeker*.

Next, the two men stopped at the church on Baker Street and made the necessary arrangements for Landon and Keelan to be married. The priest kindly offered to marry them the same evening. The hefty purse Landon had left with the little man might have provided additional impetus to get the deed done, along with the knowledge Landon and Keelan had taken the ancient vow of a handfast and thus had already consummated their marriage. A low vibration resonated within Landon's chest and it took a moment before he realized he was humming.

Humming.

He ignored Conal's quizzical brow and curious look and strode forward to the docks. Locating the third ship in their fleet, the *Reward,* anchored dockside, he hailed her captain Brendan Ahern, who bade them to come aboard.

A tall three-masted barquentine, the *Reward* was the largest vessel in the Ahern Merchant Company fleet. A newly replaced mizzen mast stood shiny and bright against the scarred hull and ship's deck. The scent of freshly applied pitch lingered with the salty air of the sea. Muffled sounds of low waves, slapping the ship, mingled with the blunted voices of men aboard and other translucent activity in the early morning fog.

Fynn's eldest son shook Landon's hand warmly. Fynn's untimely death had been hard on them, but Brendan had taken it the hardest, of course. He'd seen the mast explode when the bar shot hit it, and although he said he had bellowed a warning, he'd been unable to reach his father in time to save him from the deadly shards which had rained down.

"The new mizzen is in place, I see," Conal observed, shaking his cousin's hand.

"Aye, and has been for nearly a fortnight," Brendan responded. "Anxious I am, to get her underway. I feel helpless as a spring lamb anchored dockside for so long." His jaw clenched as he flung his arm in the direction of the open sea. "While that rat, Gampo, is out there somewhere, probably seeking a hole in which to hide his cowardly arse."

Landon and Conal exchanged hooded looks. Brendan hated being bored, which occasionally led him to act before thinking, since to him, action was always better than stillness. Like Conal, Brendan believed in an eye for an eye and was obviously biting at the bit to get his hands on Gampo.

Would Brendan find peace if he avenged his father's death? Although it was quite possible, he simply seized the challenge because it demanded a call to action. When Landon had lost his parents, he had been too young, too stunned, to understand how grief paralyzed the limbs and the mind...suspended one like a hawk on an updraft. Thankfully, before he'd been dashed on the ragged shoals of death and loss and loneliness, Fynn had saved him.

"Yer like a shark, you are," Conal said to Brendan as they followed to his cabin. "Always on the move, ye can't stand to be still a single second." He clapped Brendan on the back. "It's a good thing we've arrived then, eh?"

Brendan gestured them inside and strode over to his desk, moved aside a tattered leather-bound book and pulled a bottle of whiskey from a drawer. "Aye to that. What kept you? I'd been just about to set sail for Charleston to seek you out when the *Desire* arrived and I received Landon's letter. I waited as instructed, but the information provided was bloody thin."

Conal picked up the old book from Brendan's desk. "What's this?"

"It's one of my father's journals," Brendan answered. "Odd though, it wasn't with the others." He pulled open a desk drawer and gestured to the gap in the back. "It was hidden in here. I haven't had a chance to read through it yet." He pushed the drawer shut. "Tell me what happened in Charleston."

Conal put the journal down. "We went to Twin Pines to meet with Commodore Grey, as Fynn had planned. However, Grey was unable to tell us why Fynn had arranged the meeting." Conal accepted a whiskey from Brendan. "Although Landon and I both suspect he wasn't being entirely truthful."

Brendan sat, picked up his glass and took a sip. "So you visited Grey. That couldn't have caused such a long delay in returning here." He cocked a questioning brow.

Landon leaned against the doorjamb and frowned. "We ran into Gampo in Charleston. He followed us and managed to make off with some of our goods. It took time to reclaim it." He tossed down the drink and scowled at the empty glass. "I almost had him, Brendan. He took Keelan. He'd bought her, just like he did your mother. I almost had him."

Brendan splashed a bit more whiskey in their cups. Conal added, "The hurricane interfered with the delivery of the additional cargo our friends from Philadelphia commissioned us to acquire."

Brendan rolled his shoulders, leaned his head back, and took a deep breath. "And the additional cargo is where?"

Landon pressed his lips into a thin line. "Part's in the hold of the *Desire*, the rest is still in Charleston." Transporting runaway slaves north to freedom was always a big risk, but to Fynn, it was more of an obligation. His merchant business might have been a little less profitable than it could have been, but Fynn didn't care, claiming it made him a wealthy man in mind, body and spirit.

Conal observed Brendan carefully. "It's not what you'd hoped to do, but we have to go back to Charleston, and retrieve it, and then transport it to Philadelphia straight away, before it's discovered. We're risking all our necks as it is."

"Blast. I really wanted to set sail for Jamaica." Brendan paused with his glass halfway to his lips. "Who's Keelan?"

CHAPTER SEVENTY-SEVEN
MYSTERY TO LIGHT

T he sun was up in the sky somewhere, shining its noonday rays. The fog seemed to be conceding its grip on the harbor somewhat.

Landon touched the small of Keelan's back to signal they were leaving. Normally, he'd offer her an arm, but it would cause quite a few heads to turn, since Keelan was still dressed as Mahdi.

He glanced at his bride. The glimmer in her eyes when they talked about sailing to South America or Asia made his heart swell. She was as excited as he to begin their journey together.

In less than a day, they'd be legally married. Conal had agreed to stand as a witness. Brendan promised to attend as well.

His stomach rumbled. The breakfast tray Keelan had brought to their cabin earlier had gone untouched after Annette's intrusion. The feel of his wife's bare bottom had lingered near the forefront of his mind after Mrs. Camsby departed. He'd whispered the need to revisit the encounter, much to Keelan's amusement, then eager agreement.

The trio stopped at the tavern across the street from the hotel and ordered a small feast. A short time later, warm bread, cheese, and various cold chunks of meat arrived, along with tankards of ale. Keelan took a sip of her mug, wrinkled her nose and pushed it toward Conal, who accepted it joyfully. Laughing, Landon signaled for the tavern maid and ordered a glass of spiced wine for her instead.

He wanted to reach over and grasp Keelan's hands and inwardly cursed the circumstances which forced her into disguise. He wanted to tell her about the wedding ceremony he had arranged. He wanted her eyes to light up that he'd kept his word. She had doubted him, but he had kept his word.

When he had pledged his heart to her, he'd meant it. With the simple handfast promise, he could have lived the rest of his life, content. Yet, something more drove him to seek the legal documentation; it was one last bridge of trust they had to cross together. She had to fearlessly join her life with his, with absolute conviction, and believe with her entire heart he was a man of his word.

The tavern door opened, and he glanced up. Brendan paused and scanned the room; his gaze found Conal, and he weaved his way around a few tables until he reached them. He clutched a ragged tome as if it were a wounded bird. It was the old journal of Fynn's he'd had found hidden in the desk.

Landon nodded toward the door. "Brendan has decided to join us, I wonder what—"

"Conal!" The catch in Brendan's voice made Landon stop in mid-sentence.

Conal raised his mug. "Hoy, Brendan! Pull up a chair and join us. There's someone I'd like you to meet." He glanced at Keelan and grinned.

Brendan seemed not to hear as he grabbed a chair. "Conal, you have to read this."

Landon leaned forward and grabbed Brendan's forearm, then nodded toward Keelan. "Brendan, this is—"

But Brendan was already talking to his cousin. Landon sat forward and placed his chin in his hands. Apparently, this was important enough to cause his friend to forget his good manners.

Brendan continued, "I started to read bits and parts of my father's journal." His eyes were focused on Conal. "It's about the stolen child Da used to talk about, remember?" He looked at Landon, then grabbed his shoulder and shook it roughly. "Remember, Landon?"

"Yes, we remember." Conal responded first, even as Landon was nodding his head. "Kidnapped from the crib while my family was visiting my aunt in London. I know that much, I was a wee lad at the time."

"Yes, but there's more," Brendan's eyes gleamed, and he squirmed in his chair like a young boy in church. "A few years ago Da overheard a conversation in a pub. A bo'sun was talking about the coin he'd made stealing a babe from the lady who jilted his disgraced commander, and how he was feeling guilty about the deed."

Conal gave Brendan an exasperated look. "Ye can't possibly think—"

"Just wait a moment, Conal, let me finish," Brendan began flipping through the pages. "Listen to what my Da wrote." He pressed open the journal and began to read.

Curious, I offered to buy the man a drink to hear his tale. Since he was already half in his cups, he spilled his story quite liberally. According to the man, he was instructed to enter the residence of a home at the same cross street as my brother-in-law's in England.

The child he took was approximately a year in age with curly auburn hair and an energetic temperament, (the same as young Cailyn's). It would be too great a coincidence that my niece Cailyn and another child, baring the same age, hair and character would be stolen from the same cross street. I'm convinced I've found the man who has taken my sister's child from her cradle.

I did not let on I was in any way involved in the matter, as I didn't want to scare the man away. So, I inquired about his commander.

When I asked his commander's name, the gentleman became quite agitated, saying his commander had been a good commodore and lead an effective crew. He wouldn't divulge the name. However, I later found out the man was none other than Commodore George Grey.

Several years ago, Grey had doggedly pursued my sister's hand and took the matter quite badly when she refused him. He eventually married and purchased a small country house and a shop in Chatham. He wrongly ordered an attack upon a civilian passenger ship a thrice of years ago. Unfortunately, Grey disappeared shortly after his court martial. The bo'sun mentioned the name of a titled gentleman who'd been good friends with the commodore. I shall research this further, but my first assumption is that Grey had Cailyn kidnapped as a means to punish my sister for refusing his hand in marriage years before.

Upon hearing the name *Commodore George Grey*, Landon glanced at Keelan. Her face had paled beneath the fading dye and her gaze flew to his and widened. With a shaking hand, she fumbled for her wine and knocked the glass over, interrupting Brendan's narrative. Landon tossed his napkin over the spilled wine and gestured for another glass while keeping a watchful eye on his wife.

Brendan shoved the book across the table to Conal and jabbed the next page. "Read this."

Conal began reading, then turned the page. He paused, flipped the page back, and reread it, then looked at Keelan and swallowed. It was a long still moment before he spoke, gesturing to the book. "Uncle Fynn believed the bo'sun expected there would be a ransom. He took a gold ring and a locket as proof of the child's identity and gave them to Grey when he handed over the child."

He turned the page and continued reading.

"The bo'sun described the locket as a miniature portrait of a beautiful woman with hair like a sunset on one side and a dark-haired gentlemen on the other. He broke the locket in two, leaving one half in the empty cradle and wrapping the other half in the blanket with the child.

Conal removed the ring from his finger and put it on the table. *"Along with a ring which had four lions carved on the crest."*

Keelan reached inside her shirt and tugged the red ribbon holding the locket miniature and pulled it over her head. She placed it next to the ring, causing the table to go silent. Brendan looked from the ring to the locket to Keelan, and a sudden dawning of realization rippled across his face.

Landon leaned forward and put his hand on Brendan's shoulder. "Brendan Ahern, please allow me to introduce you to my wife, Keelan Grey Hart, of Chatham, England, raised as the daughter of the late Commodore George Grey of the Royal Navy *and* I believe, your cousin."

CHAPTER SEVENTY-EIGHT
FAMILY

"C'mon, Landon." Brendan said irately, taking in Keelan's clothing and darkened skin. "I'm being serious."

"As am I," Landon said.

"He's telling the truth," Conal said, staring at Keelan. "I witnessed the vows. She's in a disguise to protect her from Gampo's assassins."

"Well, I'll be..." Brendan leaned back in his chair, cocked his head and studied Keelan for a moment, then studied Conal, who hadn't taken his eyes off Keelan since he placed his ring on the table.

"We'd all given up," Conal said hoarsely, shaking his head in disbelief. "But Fynn hadn't. He promised my ma he'd never stop searching. He finally found you. He found our sister." Conal's eyes glistened with tears.

Keelan's throat constricted at his words, and her lungs felt twice their normal size.

Sister.

She was a *sister*! Her ears started to ring. Conal had said *our sister*. She had more than a father. She had a mother and Conal, and Brendan, her cousin.

She had a *family*.

A large tear fell unchecked to the table, followed by another. Conal wiped the third away from his chin before it could fall, his eyes still wide. "You're not my father's illegitimate daughter. You're my baby sister, Cailyn. The one who was stolen from her bed when I was a tiny lad." His face broke into a wide smile. He slapped his hands on the table, then jumped to his feet.

Conal lifted Keelan off her chair and enveloped her in a tremendous hug. They were both laughing and crying at the same time. Conal pulled Landon up, hugged him, clapped Brendan on the back, then grabbed Keelan again and kissed both her cheeks. She laughed and her heart swelled with both glee and love for her husband and her brother and the family she had yet to meet. Never had she dreamed her life would turn out this way. She was with the man she loved. She was part of a family. She was finally *home*.

"Now, dear one," Conal was saying, pulling her hand, "sit ye down again and let me tell ye about your younger kin. You got yer lovely red curly locks from our mother. In fact, I'm a bigger idiot, fer not seeing the resemblance, except for your eyes and chin. Those come from our da. Now, about your younger, twin sisters. Ciera, she's married with a wee one of her own. Carina is... well... she's an adventuresome sort." He shifted in his seat as if he'd just sat upon a burr. "She's not home much, and it'd probably be best if ye learned about her later. Then there's Aislyn, she's almost sixteen. Lastly, there's our brother Ian, who ought to be thirteen by now."

Brendan cleared his throat and Conal quickly added, "And there's Brendan, of course, and his brother, Ronan, your cousins. I'll not go into the rest of your cousins just yet, it'll only confuse you."

She had so many questions! Where to start? "Where do they live in Ireland?"

"Most of our family lives in Philadelphia now," Conal said, eyes brightening. "As soon as this fog lifts, our fleet is heading north. You'll meet them soon. I canna wait to see their faces when they see you."

Keelan couldn't stop smiling. It was like a dream. Better. Reaching over, she gripped Landon's arm, and he nudged her with his knee under the table in response.

Conal and Brendan talked to Keelan for almost an hour about her kin. Landon added a story here and there where he could before he finally stood and gestured to Keelan.

"I made a promise to my bride that I would arrange a wedding and provide legal documentation of our marriage." He took Keelan's hand, not caring who noticed. "And I have done so."

Her heart nearly stopped. A wedding?

Conal nodded. "Good, then. I knew ye'd make good on yer promise to me, sis."

A moment ago, she didn't think she could feel happier, yet she did.

"We are to be married at Christ Church at dusk." He nodded at the two other men at the table. "I'd be honored if the two of you would join us as witnesses."

"Of course!" Conal picked up his mug in salute. "I'll be havin' to give away the bride, of course."

Keelan grinned at her brother. "Then, I beg your leave, to prepare for the ceremony."

Brendan and Conal stood. Brendan grinned and stuck out his hand to Landon. "Congratulations, my friend, I wish for you and my cousin a long and happy life."

Conal wasn't looking as happy as Brendan. He took in his own stained breeches and scarred boots. "This won't do. I have a much finer coat and breeches in my locker on the *Seeker*." He glanced at Landon. "If I take the canoe, I can get to the ship quickly and retrieve my best." He chanced a sideways glance at Keelan. "Our ma would expect it," he added in a chagrined tone.

Brendan was staring at Conal's boots. "Do you have *any* boots with a shine on them, Conal? If not, I can lend you a pair of mine."

Conal frowned. "Of course I do, you lame-brained dolt. I bought them the same time as you bought yours." He froze, then gave Keelan a sideways grimace. "Yer pardon for me language, Keelan."

He looked like a guilty child, and Keelan couldn't hold back her laughter. "We shall await your return," she said. Keelan caught Landon's gaze before she continued, "I'm sure Landon will demand a longer soak, since his last bath was disrupted most tragically."

Conal chuckled while Brendan sat back, looking from one to the other in confusion.

"Aye to that," Conal responded, laughing. "Aye to that."

❧ 79 ❧

CHAPTER SEVENTY-NINE
NEVER TURN YOUR BACK ON A PIRATE

Landon was true to his word, and Keelan enjoyed a long, leisurely soak at the hotel. At least, it was leisurely until he joined her in the tub. It was some time later before they emerged, quite flushed and well-pruned. To Keelan's delight, the additional time in the bath had soaked off several shades of the dye, leaving her skin the color of clover honey, and her wet hair a deep amber.

Thanks to Landon's nimble fingers and patience, she stood before the mirror at last, in the grey satin gown her husband had purchased for her in Charleston. The natural tint of her hair was beginning to show, and the result was agreeable, much better than the tiger stripes.

Landon wore black breeches, shined boots, a new white linen shirt, and a deep navy waistcoat. He'd contained his dark satin locks with a black ribbon. For a second, Keelan forgot to breathe as she studied her husband. He was so handsome, she could hardly believe he was hers. Her love for him, which pulsed with every beat of her heart, seemed to be the only source of balance in her body. She closed her eyes and took a deep breath.

"Keelan." Landon's deep baritone broke into her reverie and she lifted her lids. The apparition standing near her could have been a

Persian prince with crystalline blue eyes. "You're so beautiful," he said. Taking her hand, he spun her to him. The warmth of his lips on her fingertips made her stomach quiver. "This isn't a traditional path to the altar." He gave her that boyish grin which used to infuriate her. "However, you and I haven't had a traditional type of courtship, have we?"

She smiled, shaking her head, then reached up and touched his cheek. "No, we haven't and I'm glad."

"Well, our vows will be more traditional when we speak them before the priest," he said, tucking her hand under his elbow. "It's only a short walk to the church from here. Conal and Brendan will meet us downstairs and then we'll walk to there together."

When they descended the stairs, Brendan was already sitting at a table in a corner and sipping a mug of ale. Upon catching sight of Landon and Keelan, he rose to his feet and gestured for them to join him. He had on tan breeches and tall chestnut-toned boots. A light grey waistcoat and darker jacket outlined his broad shoulders and tapered waist. She made a mental note to ask Conal about family stature. How could she be so petite when her brother and cousin were as big as trees?

Landon reached out and shook his hand. "So you really *do* know how to dress for an occasion. I must admit, I was skeptical."

Brendan laughed. "You'll find I have a few polite characteristics, as well." He gave Keelan a deep bow. "Greetings, Mrs. Hart. May I say you look radiant today?"

Keelan curtsied and bestowed a brilliant smile upon him in return. "Thank you, sir. You are quite dashing yourself."

"Very smart boots," Landon added.

Brendan grinned. "I expected you'd be jealous. It's the reason I purchased them. Wait until you see Conal's. You'll turn greener than a field in May."

Landon pulled out a chair for Keelan, then ordered a couple glasses of wine and another ale for Brendan. Raising his glass, Brendan said, "A toast to the happy couple on this special day."

Keelan raised her glass. A shadow fell across the table.

It was Henry. He was disheveled, as if he'd just been roughly awakened. Were the effects of the drugged wine still taking its toll on the poor man? She paused mid-sip. Hadn't they left him aboard the *Seeker* to rest and rehabilitate?

"Captain Hart, Captain Ahern," Henry nodded to each man then snatched his hat off his head as he faced her. He stepped forward and squinted his eyes, as if she wasn't quite in focus. After a second, he blinked and gave her a slight bow. "Uh... Hello, Miss."

Landon cocked his head. "What is it, Henry? You look a bit rough. Is something wrong?"

Henry dragged his gaze from Keelan and nodded vigorously. "Yes, sir! A band of pirates have taken the *Seeker*, sir. They put most of us on longboats and set us adrift, pitching the oars over the starboard side of the ship. It took us quite a while to fetch 'em then row ashore."

This information sobered both Landon and Brendan, and they sat forward in their chairs. "*Most* of the crew? Where's O'Brien?" Landon asked quickly, setting down his glass.

"Still aboard the ship," Henry said, shoulders slumped. "He was caught unawares when they came aboard. They trussed him up along with Remus and his watch."

Oh no, Conal! Keelan's hand crept to her throat.

Brendan was already on his feet. "I'll prepare the *Reward* to give chase immediately." He paused, concern creased his face. "The cargo bound for Philadelphia..."

Landon took a deep breath, then took Keelan's hand. She wanted to go after her brother. But Landon had an obligation to deliver the runaways; they were depending on him and had placed their lives in his hands. She gave him a slight nod. He had a duty to perform. She wouldn't interfere.

"I'll see it delivered, then join you in your search." To Henry, Landon asked, "Did you happen to note the bearing?"

Henry rocked from one foot to the other, wringing his hat in his hands. "Didn't need to. They made it no secret they were heading to Jamaica and needed the cargo in the belly of the *Seeker* to use as a tribute to the Pirate King."

Brendan stiffened. A flash of panic crossed his face before he nudged Landon. The two of them walked a few steps away and spoke for quite a long time. She couldn't hear what they were saying, but by the expression on Landon's face, it was grave.

Landon reached for Keelan, and she stepped into the shelter of his arms. He hugged her tightly before he spoke, "I'm sorry, love, we won't be able to exchange wedding vows this evening. We'll be hard-pressed to get Brendan's ship underway fast enough to catch sight of the *Seeker*." He tried to give her a small reassuring smile. His eyes, however, were flooded with concern.

"Don't apologize," she said. "Our wedding is secondary to the issues at hand."

He nodded. "Brendan will be able to set sail immediately, since the *Reward* is ready to depart. We'll sail the *Desire* back to Charleston and arrange for our cargo to get to Philadelphia using another Freedom Runner. Then, I'll be free to follow Brendan to Jamaica, and join in the search for Conal." He kissed her fingertips. "I wish I could join the chase right away. However, with other lives on my shoulders, I must fulfill my prior obligations and promises. We'll only be a few days behind."

"I understand," she said. Turning to Brendan, she placed a hand on his forearm. "Find my brother."

Brendan covered her hand with his and squeezed. "I will." He turned his attention to Landon. "I'll leave word for you with the harbormaster in Baracoa. There are a couple of crew mates still there, I'll put their location in the note for the harbormaster. I dropped them off to recover from their wounds after the last attack with Gampo. If they're healthy and healed, I'd like you to bring them along." He tossed some coins on the table and left.

"Baracoa?" She'd never heard of Baracoa.

"It's a Cuban coastal town we use as a stopover port on the way to Jamaica," Landon explained. A strange light flickered in his eyes and he smiled. "I think Brendan has been keeping secrets, but we won't know for sure until we drop anchor at port."

Offering an arm to Keelan, he took her back to the hotel. Within the hour, they had changed, retrieved their things and joined Henry and his men in the longboat. Keelan was once again dressed as Mahdi. Although it was unlikely the pirates returned to Charleston, the reward offered for Keelan was likely to be still active. She'd have to remain disguised until they were well away.

She'd have to reapply that dreaded dye. In fact, she'd probably need a really good reason to eat ham ever again.

A slight breeze had kicked up, and the fog appeared more translucent than it had earlier. The *Desire,* as well as other ships in the harbor, seemed more clearly defined. While the men rowed, Keelan glanced over to where the *Seeker* had been. The empty space looked wrong and uneven, as if the vessel had tried to leave a sign that she was unwillingly dragged away. Even the gulls seemed disconcerted, their cries sparse and muffled.

As soon as they boarded the *Desire*, the crew hoisted the blue flag and rang the ship's bell, alerting the crew the ship would soon depart. Landon took Keelan on a tour and introduced her to several of his men as Mahdi. He sent Henry to interview the newer crew mates.

"If Gampo has spies on this ship, I'd like to flush them out before we're underway," Landon told her. "Henry has a way of asking questions that can make an innocent man feel guilty. If a man shifts his eyes at the wrong time, Henry will pounce on him like a hungry cat." He headed toward the hold. "Follow me. It will be a short while yet before we can be away. I have something to show you."

Below, he lit a lantern and took her hand, leading her toward the aft section of the hold. Freshly cut wood, livestock, and hay wafted through the air. Of course. Landon had purchased a horse, Orion, from her uncle. A loud snort confirmed her suspicion. There were two new timber stalls in the center of the hold. Landon paused at the first one, and Orion immediately poked his nose between two slats in the side. Landon laughed and walked around the corner and opened the top half of the stall door.

"How was your first sea voyage, my friend?" Landon stroked the stallion's neck.

Orion gave another snort and nuzzled Landon's pocket. He winked. "I think he's more interested in meeting his neighbor."

"His neighbor?" She glanced at the other stall. "Did you buy another horse?"

Landon nodded. At the sound of Keelan's voice, a set of hooves rustled the straw next door, followed by a low whicker. Her heart leapt. "That sounds like..." Keelan reached over, opened the second stall door, and peeked inside. "Juliet!" She reached in and rubbed the mare's nose, then laughed with glee. In the shadows wobbled her dark-eyed, young foal, peeking at Keelan from behind his dame's hind legs.

Landon moved behind her and slid his arms around her waist. "This is my wedding gift to you, my love." He kissed the top of her head and then let out a frustrated huff. "And I promise you, there *will* be a wedding, soon."

"Oh, Landon, thank you for buying Juliet from Uncle Jared. I feared I'd never see her again." She turned in his arms and put both palms on either side of his face and kissed him. He tightened his hold around her waist and pressed her body against his. His hands traced a path up her side to her breasts and gently stroked her until her nipples tingled and her lower belly ached.

"My gift makes you happy?" He leaned his forehead against hers and she found she liked this little show of his affection.

"*You* make me happy," she replied, kissing him again.

He reached for her hands. Entwining his fingers with hers, he said, "And you make me happy, sweet Keelan. Wait—*Cailyn*."

She laughed. "They are so much alike, it doesn't matter." She sobered. It seemed wrong to feel so happy when her brother was in the hands of pirates. "I fear for Conal."

He pulled away enough to look into her eyes. "You don't know Brendan well, but I do. I sailed with him and his father from the time I was twelve years old. Brendan—" Landon paused, looking up as if he'd find inspiration for his word choice written on the bones of the hold. "Brendan is like a dog with an old stocking. He won't let go until he has complete possession." He squeezed her shoulders. "He'll find the *Seeker,* and we'll free Conal. I promise you as soon as our business is complete we will join him. We'll find both your brother and your cousin."

She wanted to believe him, she truly did; her mind wouldn't let go of visions of Conal being tortured by Gampo and his crew. "But, Gampo is a cruel man. What if he—"

Landon pulled her into the circle of his arms and gave her a comforting squeeze before releasing her slightly. She was startled to realize he was chuckling. How could he take such a situation so lightly?

"Why do you laugh? I'm concerned and terribly fearful for Conal, and Brendan as well," she said, both bewildered and annoyed. "How can you be so light-hearted?"

Landon bent down and kissed her cheek, then trailed his lips down her neck, raising the gooseflesh on her throat, shoulders, and arms. "Because, I've been around both Conal and Brendan long enough to tell you that I almost feel sorry for Gampo for raising their ire." He pulled away and traced his finger along her jawline. "I promise you, Keelan, we will find them."

A tight warmth radiated from her heart throughout her chest, and her eyes watered. Rather than try to express what she was feeling, she drew his head down and kissed him. He pulled her hips to him, his hardness urgent and hot against her belly. This time, it was her hands traveling down his ribs and over his muscular buttocks, and sliding into the back of his breeches.

"I'm slightly disappointed in your boat," she murmured.

He pulled away from her and lowered his brows in a mocking scowl. "The *Desire* is a *ship*, not a boat," he said sternly. "A *boat* has only two masts. A ship has three. The *Desire*, as you can well attest, has three masts. Therefore, she is a *ship*, not a boat." He tugged playfully at her hair before sweeping his arm around the hold. "And why are you disappointed? She's almost as big as the *Seeker*, although just a little shorter stem to stern."

"I have yet to be invited to the captain's cabin," she said, fighting hard to appear disappointed. "So, I must come to the conclusion that there is none, and I shall have to lash up my hammock with the rest of my mess mates."

"It will be my distinct pleasure," he said, eyes warm and knowing, "to give you a personal introduction to the captain's cabin." He lowered his head for another kiss.

Landon's aura would always consist of leather and the sea, of the wind and the earth, and he belonged to her and she to him. Wherever in the world Landon would go, she would be at his side.

He was her home.

He grasped her hand and then led her toward the hatch. Before leaving the quiet darkness of the hold, he paused and enveloped her in the warmth and love of his embrace. "I love you, wife."

She smiled. "And I love you back, husband."

PRAISE FOR CHLOE FLOWERS

Complete the trilogy with
If You Give a Hellion Your Heart

An accident robs Landon of his memory and turns his new wife Keelan into a stranger.

Worse, a series of catastrophic events has Landon accusing Keelan of conspiracy and betrayal.

Each explanation sounds more and more outlandish, and her hope for Landon to remember her love becomes more and more futile.

Can she persuade him to trust her before the bounty hunters close in?

Keelan's fight for Landon's love soon turns into a fight for his life.

If you love romance swirled with adventure and intrigue, you'll love reading about Landon and Keelan's road to their happily ever-after!

☙❧

EXCERPT from
If You Give a Hellion Your Heart:

A long, lithe, orange cat darted past Keelan as she walked down the narrow passageway to the galley. She poked her head around the corner. Marcel wrestled a barrel toward a closet along with Yanda, a young brown-skinned girl. Now that they were safely away from port, the family of runaways had come out of hiding to help the crew.

"Mahdi! Where have you been, boy?" Marcel drove his hip in to the barrel, but it only moved an inch. "Come, help us prepare for the gale."

"Captain Hart had me hauling the ropes. What can I do here?"

The little girl paused to clutch her stomach. Marcel harrumphed and glared at her while he rocked the barrel forward in small steps, "Dozens of men to help with ze sails and no one helps old Marcel."

"Where is Elle?" Keelan asked Marcel. Yanda's mother, Elle, had been a cook for her last master, so it seemed practical to place her in the galley.

"She iz checking the cabinets in zee next room, making sure they are latched." He glanced up at Keelan and muttered, "Useless lubbers, both of zem."

When Elle stumbled in from the next cabin, arms pressed tightly against her belly, Keelan understood and took pity. The woman glistened with sweat. Her eyes were red and her face ashen.

Seasickness. It's hard to want to do anything but die when hit with that kind of nausea.

Marcel gestured to the other side of the barrel. "It iz heavy, but we must lock it in zere. You push, I pull, eh?"

She nodded and together they managed to wiggle the cask into the narrow pantry closet while Marcel spat a string of French curses at the stubbornness of the barrel, at Elle's lack of strength and Yanda, who vomited on the floor. After it was secured, he pointed to a bucket of sea water and a mop and the girl nodded with a mumbled, "Sorry, Monsieur."

They secured the pantry shelves to prevent items from pitching to the floor in rough seas. Marcel placed a tin of dried meat, biscuits and a couple rounds of cheese handy before he shut the door. He nonchalantly pressed a broken biscuit into Yanda's palm on his way out and popped the other half into his mouth.

From there they moved elsewhere on the orlop deck, tying down loose items or stowing them. Port holes were closed and locked, although seawater had already surged in. They trudged through an inch of water on the lower decks. The ship pitched and groaned. Keelan caught her breath and listened to the *Desire's* inhalations and exhalations. Would it stay together through the storm or break into pieces? She studied the beams. Like huge fingers clutching a vase, they held the squirming ship in their grasp. The vessel squealed and moaned her pain and distress.

Marcel, sensing Keelan's trepidation, pointed to the water which had seeped in. "Iz from the hause bucklers."

At her confused expression, he tried again. "Zee pressing of zee ship against the water when swells come, push water through zee house bucklers. The *Desire*, she iz strong and brave. And nimble as a cat. No reason to worry. We have sailed through worse."

As they finished, a large group of crewmen came down below and collapsed wearily at the tables propped between the guns on the gun deck. Marcel jerked his head toward the galley and they went to prepare the meal, which would be nothing more than a piece or two of dried beef, hard biscuits, grog and a chunk of cheese.

The lurch and groans of the ship had Keelan gripping edges of the tables as she staggered past. She'd been getting used to being on the water, and actually enjoyed it before today. She still moved like a land-lubber and was anxious to develop her "sea legs." Lanterns swung in unison, casting quick shadows followed by fans of light. The *Desire* pitched sharply and Keelan stumbled. A burly arm shot out and grabbed her collar.

"Careful, boy," Gus said. "Best ye find a spot and stay there."

"How do you keep your footing when the ship bucks and tilts?" She was breathless from her effort to stay upright.

Gus sat back and scratched his salt and pepper beard, then gripped his tankard before it flew to the floor. "Seein' how yer father is a horse-master, I'll put it this way..." He finished his grog. "When the horse jumps a hedge, do ye try to keep yer seat straight and still on the saddle?"

At last. Here was something with which Keelan was familiar, although she hadn't jumped a horse since she was twelve. She shook her head. "You'd fall off if you tried to keep your seat on the saddle. You have to stand in the stirrups and keep your legs soft to absorb the impact of the landing."

Gus cocked his head. "Ye Persians sure do use peculiar language, but, aye. So, ye does the same thing on the water. Mount the *Desire* as ye would a proud filly. Ye'll never tame her, so don't try. All ye can do is melt into her rhythm. Keep yer knees soft and let her rise up to ye. When she sighs and falls away, don't fight her and try to follow. Let her go. She'll come back to ye in her own time. Keep yer guts even with the horizon and ye won't gets seasick."

Keelan let go of the table and heeded his advice. Sure enough, it was similar to jumping her pony. She'd have to mention this method to poor Elle and Yanda. She grinned her thanks to Gus, then asked, "Where's the captain?"

"He has first watch," Gus replied, dipping his tankard into a bucket hanging from a rope secured to the ceiling. "Best fer ye to stay below, outta the way, though."

After serving the men their rations for the evening, she helped Marcel secure the galley before she went back to the cabin. The room tilted and shifted, causing her feet to slide and her stomach to slam into her ribs.

Keep my guts even with the horizon. Keep my guts even with the horizon.

Relaxing her legs, she allowed the *Desire* to take the lead in this rolling dance. A powerful wave hit the ship, and she was pleasantly surprised and happy with the way she rode it. Now that Gus had revealed the secret to handling the motion, it was much easier to move about. Although it would probably be even easier if she could see the horizon.

She slipped a couple biscuits in her pocket for Landon and left the galley to make her way to the ladder and up to the main deck. Was he alone at the helm? She'd forgotten to ask Gus. If so, perhaps he might like some company.

When she raised the hatch, a lash of stinging sea spray hit her full in the face. The main deck forward sloshed with water, and the entire ship rose and fell in a furious coupling with the sea. The waves crashed against the ship's sides and exploded into the air, spraying the decks.

For a second, she hesitated. Her old self might retreat below to stay dry, but the boy, Mahdi, would be more courageous, wouldn't he? She looked toward the helm. Her husband's form was blurry figure amidst the torrent. If Landon could brave the gale, so could she. Had she not once raced a horse through similar weather, trying to beat a terrible storm? This couldn't be any worse than that.

Keelan climbed out and took a step. The deck jolted, as if trying to fling her away from the safety of the hold. Everything was shiny and slick with seawater. Her feet flew away from her and the tilt of the ship sent her crashing to the boards. Gasping, wet and bruised, she pulled herself to her feet by grasping the lines attached to a belaying pin.

Terror pulsed through her limbs. This was a mistake. She shouldn't have come up on deck. She'd underestimated the power of the ship and the winds and the storm. Landon was only a hundred feet away, but he might as well have been in China. Through sheer will and self-preservation, she managed to gain her footing in time for the *Desire* to send her tumbling toward midships, her shriek of alarm flung into the sea by the wind.

Panic ripped through her chest. Unless she found some sort of solid purchase, she'd soon be flung like a piece of cloth into the furious ocean. Rolling across the glistening boards that locked together to form the bones, the sinew, and the skin of the *Desire,* she splayed her hands and legs in hopes of catching something, *anything*, as the brave vessel heaved against the rage of the ocean.

She tumbled against the side of the ship. Thank goodness there was a plethora of ropes secured to belaying pins, providing something to grasp while she struggled to her feet. The ship fell into another swell and just as she gained her footing, her feet flew away from her again, and she hit the deck hard, her breath knocked from her chest. Before she had time to inhale, the *Desire* saw fit to pour her into a space between two of the petite guns on the deck, instead of tossing her into the sea. She curled her cold, wet fingers around the thick ropes securing the gun and held on for all she was worth.

If she'd had the time, she might have screamed or sobbed in fear, but the tempest didn't permit a pause for such frivolous displays. It only continued to pound the ocean like a giant child throwing a tantrum, plunging the left fist into the water, then the right, then the left again.

Keelan peered through the rain back to the hatch leading into the hold, then the distance to the helm, and then to Landon. Retracing her steps back below was more treacherous than continuing her fight to the helm at this point. It took every ounce of strength and courage to release her grip from the ropes and drive forward, where two other sailors were clinging on to the wheel with Landon, straining to keep the ship from broaching into the sea.

The thrumming, creaking and whistling of the ropes, lines and spars cracked and whined in her ears. The wind and rain pelted her skin. She'd no idea the storm had become so viscous while she'd been below. In her defense, she'd no idea what to expect of it, but then again, she'd never been one to take heed of a storm warning, had she?

To say that the journey toward the helm was arduous would have been grossly understating the event. If she'd been any less stubborn, she'd never have made it. The bowsprit reared up skyward as if to impale the turbulent clouds, making Keelan's legs as heavy as stone. Then it swooped down to crash into the waves in a violent explosion of white, which had her teetering on her toes, light as a mouse. She finally made it past the main mast encircled with the barrels she and Daniel had secured earlier. Only a few paces to go, thank God.

Several smaller sails were still in service, their sheets flat and rigid in the wind. Shielding her eyes against the salt spray, she sought Landon. His feet were braced wide, and he was heaving his broad chest into the wheel. His dark wet curls whipped around his face, his jaw set. She pulled herself toward the companion ladder that led up to where he stood. Almost there.

"Keelan!"

His shout stopped her. There was a note of panic in his voice that made her pause. He waved his arm. "Move leeward! Starboard!"

Confused, she froze.

"To your right!"

A loud crack followed by a low rumble sounded behind her and she turned as the barrels around the main mast came loose. They began to roll away, toward the front of the ship. One hit the foremast and split open, spilling sand across the deck. The bowsprit once again crashed down into the waves.

A jolt of horror shook her limbs. Next, the front of the ship would rear back up and when it did, the barrels would reverse direction and roll toward the stern.

Toward her.

Dear God, help me.

She turned and ran. The pitch of the ship had her running up a steep, slippery slope. A half dozen strides away from her goal, the plume of water hit and shook the front part of the ship. For a second the rumble ceased.

But only for a second.

Panic nearly paralyzed her limbs. The barrels began to roll and bounce toward her. She turned toward Landon. He had leapt down the companion ladder toward her.

"Take to my arm!" He reached out to her as his boots hit the main deck. "Hold on!"

With that, he grabbed her and flung her toward the shelter between two canons secured on the right side of the ship as a barrel clipped the farthest gun, and launched into the air, whirling fiercely. Twisting his body, Landon put himself between Keelan and the flying barrel.

It hit them with the force of a raging bull, then crashed to the deck and broke into pieces.

Keelan gasped in pain and tried to take a breath. A heavy weight prevented any movement. She was face down on the deck. She craned her neck enough to see Landon's body covering hers. And he wasn't moving.

"Landon!" she cried his name. No movement, no sound. Nothing.

Another voice pierced the gale. She strained to raise her head until finally, Landon was lifted away from her. A sailor dashed up the companion ladder to take the helm along with two others. Gus tossed Landon over his shoulder and Ronan, Brendan's brother and her cousin, grabbed Keelan's wrist and pulled her to her feet.

Together, they battled the pitch and roll of the ship to the captain's cabin. Gus dropped Landon on his bed then turned to her, his eyes flashing. "What the blazes did ye think ye were doin' out on that deck? Yer a *lubber*. Ye ain't got any sailin' know-how. Ye just 'bout killed yerself and yer captain, ye witless scamp!"

Gus's fists were clenched, and he advanced upon Keelan like a raging ox. If she hadn't been braced against the cabin wall, she'd have collapsed right there in her boots. As it was, she was trembling so violently, her teeth clattered against each other.

Ronan stepped between Gus and Keelan. "Twas a greenie mistake, sir." His eyes shifted between the two. Gus hadn't been told that Keelan was Landon's wife. They'd decided to wait until after they left Charleston.

In Gus's eyes, she was a young boy, a novice and a liability. Gus was as furious as the tempest outside. "Well, if it wasn't fer this gale, he'd get five lashes from the cat," he spat, shaking his fist.

Ronan cleared his throat and shifted on his feet. "Mahdi has some knowledge of healing. He can help the ship's sawbones treat the captain. It'll keep him outta the way."

Gus scowled, then shrugged before stomping out. "Go git the surgeon then, Ronnie. I'm on watch," he snapped before slamming the door.

Keelan leaned against the cabin wall and squeezed her eyes shut. What had she done? A choked sob escaped her throat, and she fell away from Ronan's grip and staggered to her husband's bedside. "Landon!"

His shirt was soaked and stuck to his chest like skin. She placed her ear over his heart and closed her eyes, listening.

Dear God, please let him be alive.

Was that a soft, distant heartbeat?

It was!

She examined him, checking for bruises, blood and feeling for broken bones. A small trickle of blood flowed from his ear.

"Let's pull him out of these wet clothes, Miss Keelan," Ronan whispered, touching her shoulder. "The doc will want to see all of him."

❂

A day later, steady rain still pummeled the ship, but the wind and rough seas had abated, somewhat. The sun tried to shove its way through the grey blanket, but the clouds refused it.

The ship's surgeon examined Landon's head, touching a large lump on his temple. "It hasn't changed since last night. A good sign. We'll just have to wait it out," he said, packing up the wooden carrier holding his surgeon's supplies. "That large bruise on his upper back and shoulder may be hiding a broken bone or rib, but it's the hit on the head to worry about."

"How long until he wakes?" Keelan asked, dreading the answer.

"Don't know." He shook his head, turning toward the door. "He may not."

Two days later, Landon still hadn't moved nor made another sound since he'd been placed on his bed; not when they'd removed his clothes, nor when Keelan poured whiskey on the small cut on his temple. Landon didn't even flinch. Putting her head on his chest, she checked yet again for his heartbeat.

Again, she folded her hands and made her appeal to God for Landon to gain consciousness soon. Her chest flooded with regret. If only she hadn't tried to traverse the deck in the storm. If only she'd stayed below and out of the way, Landon might not have been injured. Why hadn't she simply turned back?

For the thousandth time, she whispered, "Please Landon, my love, wake up." She pressed another kiss on his forehead.

This time, as if he'd heard her, Landon's eyelids twitched and he let out a low moan.

"Landon?" Keelan tried to keep her voice level and calm, but she couldn't contain the intertwined notes of relief and concern.

His eyes finally opened, and he slowly moved his startling blue gaze to her face. His expression changed from wariness to confusion. He lifted his head and winced.

She pressed his shoulders back down. "Go slowly, you're hurt."

"Where am I?" He rubbed his forehead.

"You're in your cabin aboard the *Desire*. You were hit on the head and have been unconscious for two days," she explained.

He attempted to sit up, then grimaced and sunk back to a reclining position. "What happened?"

Keelan bit her lip, then answered, "It was my fault. I shouldn't have come up on deck. We were hit by a rogue barrel during the gale. I didn't tie it down correctly. You were struck on the side of the head and back by one of them. Do you remember that?"

"There was a storm?" His hand was over his eyes, as if the light pained him.

He didn't remember the storm? She spoke in a low tone, "Yes. It's blown us quite a way off course, but Gus said we should arrive in Charleston in a day or two, depending on the wind and the current."

Landon glanced at her from under his hand. "What about Captain O'Brien and Captain Ahern? Did they weather the storm fairly? Have their ships been sighted?"

For a moment, Keelan wasn't sure how to answer. It was impossible for either to be sighted. Both ships were currently bound for Jamaica. Perhaps now wasn't the time to tell her husband his memory was off. She put her hand on his chest. "You're a bit disoriented. You were hit hard."

He stared at her hand, then brushed it away impatiently. Hurt by this, she sat back and regarded him. He was acting... differently.

Something was wrong.

His cool, aloof stare had her heart pounding in her chest and her stomach flipping in trepidation.

"Who are *you*?" he finally asked.

Continue the adventure with the next book:
If You Give a Hellion Your Heart!

MORE BOOKS BY CHLOE FLOWERS

WANT SWEET ROMANCE INSTEAD?

Read Chloe Flowers' *The Hearts of Adventure Sweet Romance* Series!

PIRATES & PETTICOATS NOVELS

If You Give a Hellion Your Heart
Not 'til Death Will She Part
Pirates & Petticoats Book 3

Remember me...
His memory of her is gone.
Bounty hunters are closing in.
Her fight for his love soon turns
into a fight for his life.

*NOTE: This is the *sexy version* of the novel *The Heart of a Bride*, (Book 3 of The Hearts of Adventure Sweet Romance Series By Chloe Flowers).

An accident throws him back five years into his past turning his new wife into a complete stranger.

Worse, a series of catastrophic events has Landon accusing Keelan of conspiracy and betrayal. When each explanation sounds more and more outlandish, her hope for Landon to remember their love becomes more and more futile. Bounty hunters are closing in and a nefarious landowner has discovered Landon's secret identity. More than ever Keelan needs Landon on her side if she's going to save both their lives.

Can she persuade him to trust her? Will he remember his love for her before it's too late?

If You Give a Smuggler a Secret, If You Give a Rake a Reason and *If You Give a Hellion Your Heart* is a trilogy that follows Keelan Grey and Landon Hart on their adventure of discovery and a love of a lifetime. Two hearts have never battled harder to be together...

If you love romance swirled with adventure and intrigue, you'll love reading about Landon and Keelan's road to their happily ever after, because true love always finds a way.

If You Give a Pirate a Treasure
She'll Steal your Heart for Good Measure
Pirates & Petticoats Book 4

Her twin siblings have been kidnapped.
The ransom is a ship called The Seeker.
She's not a real pirate.

But their lives depend on
her playing the part.

*NOTE: This is the stand-alone, *sexy version* of the novel *The Heart of a Pirate*, (Book 4 of The Hearts of Adventure Sweet Romance Series By Chloe Flowers).

Captain Conal O'Brien's ship is overrun by the most unlikely band of pirates to sail the seas. When he discovers their true objective, he develops a scheme of his own. But these nutty brigands aren't who they seem to be, and if Conal's not careful, he's going to lose his heart as well as his ship to a lady pirate determined to possess both.

Stevie Sauvage is on a quest to find a hidden family treasure. When her eight-year-old twin siblings are kidnapped by the pirate, Captain Gampo, and the ransom demand is a merchant ship, she must find the courage to conquer her fears and fight for those she loves before time runs out for the twins.

If You Give a Pirate a Treasure is a high seas, historical, pirate romance filled with action and adventure, mystery and intrigue, and a quest for hidden treasure (with a few laughs along the way).

What readers have to say:

> *This storyline itself was well thought out and engaging. I have read a fair few "pirate romances," and I have to say that (this book) is up there with the best. FANTASTIC READ!!*
> *I thoroughly enjoyed (the book), and I look forward to reading more books from this author. Well done, Chloe Flowers!*
> *I Highly Recommend.*
> *- Amazon Review*

If You Give a Spy a Scheme

He'll Fight to be Redeemed
Pirates & Petticoats Book 5

He steals for the French crown.
She heals for the Catholic church.
He will heal her heart.
She will steal his.

*NOTE: This is the stand-alone, *sexy version* of the novel *The Heart of a Spy*, (Book 5 of The Hearts of Adventure Sweet Romance Series By Chloe Flowers).

"Dramatic, engrossing, suspenseful, exciting."

French Privateer and former pirate, Captain Drago Gamponetti is given one final mission from his employer, the king of France: reclaim religious relics from a New Orleans cathedral. Trouble begins when he's forced by a mysterious, veiled, novitiate nun to swear on the Bible to protect the very items he was instructed to steal.

Church healer, Eva Trudeau hides more than her face behind the veil. The convent has been her safe haven since she crawled, beaten and bloody, to its door nine years ago. When an old enemy re-surfaces and threatens to drag her back into the dark underworld from where she'd escaped, both she and her dark pirate captain stand to lose everything they've fought so hard to protect...including each other.

What readers have to say:

Set against the backdrop of the famous Battle of New Orleans, This story will have you turning pages into the wee hours of the night. If you love pirates, history, humor and a bit of romance you will love this newly released book by Chloe Flowers. The author has a way with historical fiction that enthralls and entertains.

ABOUT CHLOE

Chloe supports the National Breast Cancer Foundation.

Chloe Flowers constantly looking for the next adventure. Her pets have always been named after her favorite characters or action heroes: Indiana, Luke, Gimli, Thelma, Rocket, Forrest, Al Giordino, Severus, Mushu, Mérida, Gibbs, Jack...Dead Pool (he's a goldfish).

Chloe is an award-winning author and the recipient of the University of Akron, Wayne College *2018 Writer of the Year* Award. She writes small town contemporary women's fiction, and historical women's action and adventure romance novels about scoundrels, pirates, and spunky, independent heroines.

Chloe's biggest fault is the apparent inability to say "no" whether it's in response to a call for aid or a double-dog-dare to hike home through 30 acres of a snow-covered forest at midnight...during a full moon. It was early morning during said adventure when she came upon a group of sheriff's deputies searching for a lost girl. So, of course she offered to help (turns out, they were searching for her).

She is a member of the Romance Writers of America, Northeast Ohio Romance Writers where she served as president in 2020, and RWA Contemporary Romance Writers, The Beau Monde Romance Writers group, where she served as secretary 2017-2019.

She has given workshops and presentations on creating a critique group, how to provide effective critiques, story structure, marketing and self-publishing lessons to writers groups, library patrons and school children.

In 2014, she started her own small publishing company, Flowers & Fullerton. Currently, she's the publisher of record for authors Sheridan Jeane, Heather Knight, H.O. Knight as well as herself.

Chloe has a weakness for good red wine, Calvin & Hobbes comics, pie, dark chocolate and brown-eyed guys with beards, which is probably why she digs pirates, men in uniform and treasure hunters and writes about action and adventure and of course romance, which is the greatest adventure of all.

RUTH'S RECIPES

The recipes Ruth used to create her scones, bannocks, brandied fruit and Indian corn mush are inspired by dishes mentioned an *An Antebellum Household Journal Including the South Carolina Receipts and Remedies of Emily Warton Sinkler,* by Anne Sinkler Whaley LeClercq. I purchased it in Charleston when touring a plantation home.

If you'd like to try the recipes, you can find some versions of them here:

www.chloeflowers.com/recipes

They are fun to try (however, I have also included a more modern version).

Enjoy!

SCONES

COMBINE:

3 cups of Flour
4 T. Sugar
1 T. Baking Powder
1/2 tsp Salt
Cut in 3/4 cup of Butter with 2 knives used scissor-fashion until you have coarse crumbs

Separate 1 large egg, and put the yolk into 1 cup of milk and then stir it into the crumbs until just mixed.

Separate dough in half and put one half on each end of a baking sheet. Using your hands pat each into a circle about 7 inches round.

With a floured knife, cut each circle into 6 wedges, but do not separate them.

Beat the egg white with a fork and brush the tops of the dough rounds.

Options: gently press raisins, dried cranberries, raw pumpkin seeds, or chocolate chunks onto the tops and bake 25 minutes at 400 degrees.

❧

Here's a recipe for Ruth's Corn Mush; it rocks when it's drizzled with maple syrup! It's neat to know that it hasn't changed much over the years. It's exactly like my grandmother's recipe.

Corn Mush (gluten free, I might add)

Best to start this the night before so it can cool in the fridge.

Bring 3 cups of water to a boil.

Mix 1 cup of corn meal, 1 tsp salt and 1 cup of milk together.

(*NOTE: Keep in mind, just like anything, the quality of the corn meal influences the flavor of the dish. I've had SUPERBLY flavored mush and stuff I wouldn't fed a cow.)

Using a whisk to defend against lumps, slowly pour the corn meal mixture into the boiling water.

Stir until it comes to a boil BUT FOR THE LOVE OF PETE, DON'T QUIT COOKING IT! Put it on low and allow the moisture to cook out of it for about 20 minutes, depending on the corn meal and the heat level. CONTINUE to stir it every minute or so while you're reading the paper or watching the Hallmark Channel.

Here's how you know it's done: you can part it with a spoon like Moses parted the Red Sea; the spoon you're using to stir it will stand by itself when stuck into the middle of the mush; if you pull a spoonful out of the pot and turn it upside down, it will defy gravity and stick to the spoon.

Pour into a loaf pan, or casserole dish, whatever. After it cools (easier if you refrigerate it overnight, but if you cook it long enough to where it's sliceable when it cools, you're golden) slice it about a fourth of an inch thick, and fry it in a pan filled with a fourth an inch of oil. (Hey-no one said this was low cal, just delicious).

It takes a while to fry mush. You want it golden brown around the edges. The color will change from a pale yellow to a sunflower yellow.

Drain it on a thousand paper towels. (Yeah, I squish it to get most of the oil out).

Serve warm. I love it plain or slathered with syrup. Your choice. Enjoy.

Oh...umm... Sorry about the pot. To make it an easier clean up, add a couple of cups of water along with a teaspoon of baking soda. Bring it to a boil. Plop the lid on it and turn off the heat. Let it sit there until it's someone else's turn to do the dishes. In our family, we call those 24 hour soaking pots.

Good luck.

Shirred Eggs

12 strips bacon

    2 tablespoons diced bell pepper

    2 tablespoons diced onion

    6 medium-size eggs,

    6 teaspoons heavy cream, divided

    4 teaspoons grated Parmesan cheese, divided

    Freshly ground black pepper, to taste

    Garnish: fresh herbs or 2 sprigs fresh chive, or grated Parmesan and a pinch kosher or sea salt

Instructions:

Preheat your oven to 400° and set a rack to the middle position. Arrange the bacon strips on a parchment-lined rimmed baking sheet or a wire rack placed inside a rimmed sheet pan and cook until lightly browned but not crisped, 12 minutes. Remove from the oven and reduce the temperature to 325°.

Lightly grease 6 muffin cups (or 6 7-ounce ramekins), and line the sides and bottom of each with 2 bacon strips. Combine the diced pepper and onion in a small bowl, and spoon 1 heaping teaspoon of the mixture into the bottom of each cup, followed by 1 cracked egg. Add 1 teaspoon of cream, ½ teaspoon of Parmesan, and black pepper to taste.

Bake until the egg whites are opaque, 12 to 15 minutes.

Serve in their ramekins, or use a spoon to transfer them to a small serving dish. Garnish with herbs or chive, or a bit of grated Parmesan and a pinch of salt, and serve warm.

OPTIONS: use shredded hash browns instead of bacon (brown them first before adding the egg).

Use any kind of cheese or vegetables you prefer.

Top with salsa, avocado slices or toast points.

BANNOCKS

(Originally a Scottish bread) evolved to this recipe in the low country where corn meal was more plentiful than oats:

> Boil 1 pint of milk and whisk in 1 pint of Indian Corn Meal.
> (Yep-use the same container to measure)
> Beat well the yolks of 4 eggs with 1 pint of cold milk.
> Add the 4 egg whites.
> Add 1 tsp baking soda.
> Add 1/2 tsp salt
>
> Bake.

Yup. That's the recipe. I did some experimenting, and found that if you make 1/2 inch thick, round, scone-like patties, about the size of a dessert plate, and place on a cookie sheet and bake at 350 degrees for about 12 minutes they turned out fine. Traditionally, you would grease a cast iron skillet and cook on the stovetop. 15 minutes for the first side, about 10-12 on the other side.

* If you want a more *traditional* Scottish Bannock, then you need a recipe that calls for oat flour or barley flour. I found a terrific one developed by chef Theresa Carle-Sanders. On her blog "Outlander's Kitchen," she presents historical and character-inspired recipes from the fictional world created by Diana Gabaldon, author of *The Outlander* series. It's *brilliant*. I found one similar to it on another recipe site and tweaked it a bit until I came up with the one below. I have made flaky southern biscuits for years, but I have to say, the oat flour keeps the bannock moist without falling apart. I like it better that a regular biscuit, plus they are good even when they're cold!

TRADITIONAL SCOTTISH BANNOCKS

Yield: 12-18

Preheat oven to 400° F.

2 Cups All-Purpose Flour

1 Cup Oat flour (or you can use old-fashioned or quick oats-just pulse them in a food processor or blender until fine)

2 Tsp Baking Powder

1 Tsp Baking Soda

1 tablespoon Sugar

½ tsp. Salt

½ cup of cold Butter, cut into small pieces

¾ Cup Cold Milk

½ Cup Greek Yogurt

Combine all dry ingredients in a large bowl and mix well. Cut cold butter pieces into dry ingredients and mix well. I like to use a pastry cutter.

Stir together milk and yogurt. Add to dry ingredients and stir with wooden spoon to make a sticky dough.

Turn onto a floured counter and sprinkle with more flour. Knead dough lightly 5 or 6 times, working in additional flour, so that dough is no longer sticky

Roll about ½" thick. Use a biscuit or a 2" square cutter. You can also use a floured butcher knife and cut squares with it. Don't forget to keep dusting it with flour before you cut. Depending on the size of the square, you should get at least 12-18.

I usually use parchment paper instead of greasing a cookie sheet, but either works. Bake until just golden around the corners, about 15 minutes. Cool on a wire rack for a few minutes before serving.

Serve warm with butter, honey, or jam. For a more savory version, add 1/2 cup of shredded cheddar cheese in with the dry ingredients and serve with meats or soups.

MARCEL'S RECIPES

A note from Marcel: Preparing Salted Fish

"Add a glass of vinegar to ze water in which you soak your salted fish, it will fetch out most of ze salt."

The dishes Marcel served were inspired by recipes from the day. Keelan's recipes for Bannocks and Scones were inspired by an *An Antebellum Household Journal Including the South Carolina Receipts and Remedies of Emily Warton Sinkler*, by Anne Sinkler Whaley LeClercq. I purchased it in Charleston when touring a plantation home; it's filled with wonderful information about life in the Lowcountry.

HARD TACK

- 3 Cups of White Flour
  - 2 teaspoons of Salt
  - 1 Cup of Water
  - A cookie sheet
  - A mixing bowl
  - A knife
  - A clean common nail

1. Preheat your oven to 375°.

2. Mix the flour and salt in a bowl.

3. Gradually mix in the water until you form a dough that doesn't stick to your hands.

4. Use a rolling pin to flatten the dough into a square. Make sure it's no more than half an inch thick.

5. Cut the dough into 9 squares.

6. Using the nail, make a 4×4 grid of holes in each piece.

7. Put the pieces on an un-greased cookie sheet and bake for 30 minutes.

8. Turn the squares over and bake for another 30 minutes.

9. Remove from the oven and allow to cool.

Eating it dry can certainly crack a tooth!

(Recipe courtesy of http://urbansurvivalsite.com)

Author's comment: So...hard tack is rather bland for our palates but adding garlic salt or onion powder helps a bit...

Keep in mind these biscuits were usually served with something else, like gravy, soup, coffee or grog, so soaking it does make it easier to chew.

As an aside...The Amish make a similar biscuit that they give to teething babies. I made them for my crumb snatchers and they loved them. They never finished a single one, though. Those things were so hard and solid that the best they could do was make them gummy for a little while. Eventually, the dog ended up with them. I think he buried them in the shrubbery.

Hard tack is a lot like a teething biscuit...

TEETHING BISCUITS

Break 2 eggs into a bowl. Stir in one direction until creamy. (I don't know why, maybe it's an Amish superstition, just do it).

Add 1 cup of sugar.

Continue stirring in the same direction. (Again, just go with it unless you're a rebel, then rock on).

Gradually, add 2 to 2 1/2 cups of flour and continue stirring until mixture is stiff (I'm still assuming we stir in the same direction, just doing as I'm told like a little lemming).

Roll out to a thickness of 3/4 inch. That's honkin' thick, but we want to make sure pieces won't easily break off, right?

Here's the fun part: the Amish recipe says to cut out donut shaped cookies, which makes sense for little hands to grip. I used a dog bone shape (c'mon...the dog ended up with them anyway) that was easy to grip, but had an end that wouldn't fit entirely into the baby's mouth (otherwise we have a gagging issue, blech). Feeling sentimental one day, I used hearts. Donuts are probably your best bet. If you don't have that shape, use a drinking glass and make the donut hole with a shot glass. (Yeah, well, we all make do, don't we?)

HOPPIN' JOHN

1 1/2 Cups Dried Black-eyed Peas
   2 Smoked Ham Hocks
   1 Chopped Onion
   1/2 tsp. Crushed Red Pepper Flakes
   Salt and Pepper to taste
   4 Cups of Water

Put everything above into a pot, cover and bring to a boil. Reduce heat to medium-low and cook for 1 1/2 hours

Remove ham hocks from pot, and take meat off the bones and cut into pieces and return to the pot.

Add 1 1/2 cups of rice to the pot, cover and cook until rice is tender, about 25 minutes.

Do yourself a favor, use fresh, good quality rice, it really does make a difference.

Top with shredded cheese, if you'd like, or hot sauce. I'm a bit of a dare devil, so I add both.

www.ingramcontent.com/pod-product-compliance
Lightning Source LLC
Chambersburg PA
CBHW032255020726
47495CB00001B/122